A HOLLY JOLLY EVER AFTER

Also by Julie Murphy and Sierra Simone

A Merry Little Meet Cute
Snow Place Like LA (A Christmas Notch in July novella)

A HOLLY JOLLY EVER AFTER

A CHRISTMAS NOTCH NOVEL

JULIE MURPHY and SIERRA SIMONE

AVON

An Imprint of HarperCollinsPublishers

Homewrecker definition on page 114 powered by Oxford Languages.

HarperCollins books may be purchased for educational, business, or sales promotional use. For information, please email the Special Markets Department at SPsales@harpercollins.com.

FIRST EDITION

Designed by Diahann Sturge
Map by Diahann Sturge
Illustrations and art throughout © Amanita Silvicora; ninfea; Macrovector; clip art; ibom; bomg; fourSage; GN.Studio; EVA105; Nikitina Olga; Ninya Pavlova; Aleutie; marrishuanna; Bonezboyz; Inspiring; YoPixArt; Egudinka; robuart; Nemanja Cosovic; pixelliebe; MG Drachal; Vecotrpocket; FOS_ICON; Rinat Khairitdinov; aliaksei kruhlenia; olhahladiy; ProStock Studio / Shutterstock

Library of Congress Cataloging-in-Publication Data has been applied for.

ISBN 978-0-06-322264-9 (hardcover)
ISBN 978-0-06-335929-1 (international edition)

23 24 25 26 27 LBC 5 4 3 2 1

To our Ashleys (Lindemann and Meredith) for
being the Addisons to our Winnies.
(And to Joey Fatone for being the Joey to our Fatone.)

Yes, I am Daddy.

—Graham Simpkins, *The Holiday*

Be a good girl and tell Santa what you need.
This Christmas, Santa aims to please.

—INK, "All BeClaus of You," *Merry INKmas*
(Bootcamp Records)

Teddy Ray Fletcher

When Teddy Ray Fletcher's children were little, his fridge was covered in finger paintings, macaroni art, and paper mosaics framed with Popsicle sticks. He kept their masterpieces in his office and hung them in the hallways of his house; he made mouse pads and coffee mugs with their pictures and proudly showed them off to his friends, his performers, and complete strangers alike.

That said, Teddy rarely knew what those early pictures were supposed to *be*—occasionally one might be able to identify a flower or a cat, but for the most part, Teddy tried to see the pictures the same way his then-wife talked about the abstract art at the galleries she was always dragging him to: as a display of movement and color.

Or something like that. Teddy hated abstract art.

But he didn't hate his *kids'* art, and so as a father, he promised himself he would never be handed an adorable mess and say, *Um, what is it supposed to be?* He just praised them for being perfect little geniuses, telling them that they were just as good as Picasso or Monet. Or the people who drew *The Wild Thornberrys* cartoons.

And so today, when his twenty-something daughter bounced into his office and plonked a shiny rectangle onto his desk—a rectangle with a cylinder attached by a still-twist-tied cord—Teddy didn't ask what it was supposed to be. He said, "Astrid, this is so great! Did you make it yourself?"

Sunlight winked off the medusa piercing right above her upper lip as she rolled her dark brown eyes. Her eyes, curls, and warm sepia skin were her mother's. (Her lactose intolerance and penchant for semi-regrettable body modifications were all Teddy's.) "It's a prototype, Dad. Obviously."

He lifted it up, giving his best all-knowing-dad expression as he did. "It's a great prototype, sweetie. It's very proto."

"Do you even know what it is?"

Teddy looked down at the thing in his hands—hands still sunburned from an outdoor MILF shoot near Big Bear. Astrid's contraption looked like a Walkman with a tiny microphone attached, except that everything was made of a matte plastic he suspected had something to do with being phthalate-free. "Is it for"—he mentally cast around, trying to think of where he'd seen tiny microphones before—"TikTok? Are you going to be a TikTok star?"

"*Dad.* It's for Venus!"

Venus was Astrid's eco-friendly sex toy startup, and one of the reasons Teddy had expanded his operation last year to produce wholesome holiday movies along with regular non-wholesome pornography. (The other reason was his son's art school tuition, which Teddy tried not to think about without a glass of Jim Beam in his hand.)

"Ah," Teddy said. He still had no idea what it was for.

Astrid beamed. "It's a solar-powered vibrator!"

"I thought you were doing the nipple clamps first," Teddy said, setting the prototype down and looking up at his smiling daughter. He was a terrible investor—not because he didn't believe in Astrid's climate-conscious vision, but because once she started talking about polyvinyl and thermoplastics, his attention started wandering to things like the new doughnut place in Westwood or if maybe he should text a certain pant-suited talent manager he couldn't stop thinking about.

"I'm still trying to source a carbon-neutral steel supplier for the clamps." Astrid sighed. "But I've been thinking about maybe doing more of a tassel-type thing with vegan leather instead— Oh, hi, Sunny!"

Teddy's eyelid twitched as Sunny Palmer bounded into his office. Her cat, Mr. Tumnus, had eaten some vital cord coming from the back of her computer last month, and ever since then, she'd been using Uncle Ray-Ray's equipment to edit her solo videos. Which Teddy didn't mind per se, but having Sunny here was like having a tiny kitten in the office. She got into every-thing, squawked at inanimate objects, and sometimes fell asleep in sunbeams before bouncing awake and coming to pester him while he was trying to squint his way through the latest edition of union bylaws for his performers. She was a lot. And Teddy preferred *a lot* when he didn't already have his hands full of Christmas movie bullshit, like he did today.

"Ooh, your proto-vibe came in!" Sunny squealed, reaching toward Teddy's desk and snatching it off the top like a tattooed Swiper the Fox. "This looks amazing! Will it charge on cloudy days? Do you think it would charge in space? Also, Teddy, there's someone here for you. She's finishing a call and then she'll be in."

"If she's making a delivery, tell her she can just leave it inside the front door," Teddy said automatically, turning back to his laptop. It woke up with an obnoxious *I'm an ancient computer please let me die* whirr.

"No, no," Sunny said absently, her attention on the solar-powered sex toy in her hand. "It's what's-her-name from Christmas Notch. The mean sexy woman. Steph something."

Time slowed down; Teddy's pulse sped up. It was thundering in his ears, and it matched the pounding in his chest.

Steph.

Steph was here.

Steph was here and he still had toasted BLT crumbs on his shirt.

Panicked, he tried to brush his shirt clean—along with his mustache—while also simultaneously straightening his desk and making shooing noises at his daughter and his performer to leave . . . which they characteristically ignored.

And then it happened.

Steph D'Arezzo, talent manager and the most perfect woman in the world, walked through his office door like she did it every day.

He hadn't seen her since they'd slept together seven months ago at a Fourth of July barbeque, but it didn't matter. His body remembered the press of hers like it was yesterday. And the impeccably tailored pantsuit she wore—cherry red with a black top underneath—would have reminded him if he hadn't remembered. It showed off those soft hips, those even softer breasts, and those long legs, which ended in black heels sharp enough to cut the five-tier wedding cake that appeared in his sappiest, most private daydreams. A single string of pearls hugged the base of her long, pale neck; her hair was down in dark waves.

She wore lipstick the same color as her pantsuit, and it made Teddy shift in his seat.

Say hi, he coached himself. *Say hi and then tell her you missed her. Maybe she's here for barbeque sex part two. Say hi. Say hi.* He managed to open his mouth.

Except then Sunny, who'd sidled up to Steph and was gazing up at the manager with a look somewhere between awed and horny, spoke first. "Are you my mommy?"

Steph seemed accustomed to the half-feral Uncle Ray-Ray's family after being on the set for *Duke the Halls*, because she ignored Sunny and walked right to the front of Teddy's desk and braced her hands on the top. Like he was a naughty student and she was a teacher, the prettiest teacher in the world.

His heart jumped right into his throat.

"Word on the street is that you have a script," Steph said.

Oh.

She wasn't here for barbeque sex part two. Teddy's heart burrowed mopefully down into his stomach.

"It was just finished last night," he managed to respond.

Teddy's company was producing the first-ever Hope After Dark movie this year—a film that would combine the unironic joy of the Hope Channel's usual fare with the soft-core raunch that he'd grown up watching on Skinemax. Even better, the movie was still a Christmas movie! *Santa, Baby* was about a soon-to-be Santa Claus sowing his wild Santa oats before he took over the proverbial reins to the sleigh. The young Santa would be played by none other than Steph's client Kallum Lieberman, former pop star (and present-day leaked-sex-tape star).

"Kallum should get it in the next week or so, if he's worried about having enough time—"

"I'm not worried about that," Steph interrupted. "I'm here because you still don't have a Mrs. Claus, do you?"

"Ah." Teddy squirmed. The truth was that despite the viral success of *Duke the Halls* and its meta-fusion of wholesome holiday fun and sex-drenched lead actors, he and his new casting director still hadn't found someone to star opposite Kallum for *Santa, Baby*. Or more so, they hadn't found someone that their director, Gretchen Young, *also* liked. "We're working on that."

"Gretchen hasn't found the right fit," Astrid said, coming to his defense. "It's not because he hasn't been trying."

"I believe you," Steph said. "And that's exactly why I'm here. Because I have an idea for who our Mrs. Claus should be."

"I'm all ears," Teddy said, and then added, "Not really. I'm only two ears."

Everyone in the room groaned.

"I appreciate the sentiment," Steph said, with a sharklike gleam in her eye, "because this idea is a little unconventional . . ."

Part One

CHAPTER ONE

Winnie

My name is Winnie Elizabeth Baker, and except for the one time I let a friend pierce my belly button, I have done everything right.

When my parents wanted me to spend every weekend auditioning for local commercials, I did exactly as they asked.

When they wanted me to upend my life at age ten and move to Los Angeles to star in a wholesome family sitcom, I did that too.

I hid my narcolepsy from the industry so well the tabloids still have no idea.

I married my childhood sweetheart when I was eighteen years old, and I didn't even kiss him until the day of our wedding.

I was a model daughter, a model wife: sweet, friendly, well-behaved. An icon for young women with purity rings everywhere.

So then why was I sitting in a therapist's office, holding up my phone, and gesturing at what was on the screen like I was the glummest Vanna White of all time?

"And then Dominic Diamond dredges up this old picture, and now all anyone can talk about—again—is how Winnie Baker lives to make a scandal out of herself." I dropped my phone in my lap, not wanting to look at the picture anymore, even to prove a point. I'd already seen it thousands of times anyway: a seventeen-year-old me, passed out in a car in front of the Chateau Marmont after that year's Teen Choice Awards. My head was lolled back on the headrest, my normally fair cheeks were flushed red, and my mouth was hanging open.

Picture-me looked drunk, and even worse, picture-me looked *sloppy*. Promiscuous, even, according to my parents. In many ways, the picture had been when everything changed for me; it had been the beginning of the end.

"Dominic Diamond is a gutter-dwelling sociopath," Renata said calmly. As a therapist to actors, models, and—if the rumors could be believed—a certain California-dwelling prince, Renata was more than familiar with Dominic Diamond. He was a gossip blogger turned gossip influencer who spared no one in his nasty content updates, and I'd believe in a heartbeat that he was the subject of many sessions here in Renata's office. "He's not allowed to change how you see yourself."

"But this is bigger than Dominic," I said, swiping my screen to show the next image on the post. It was a screenshot of a headline from a major news site. "Former Child Star Hospitalized After Drug-Fueled Music Festival in Texas, Says Anonymous Source." And then another screenshot, this time from an article published yesterday: "Troubled Actress Once Famed for Promoting Family Values Now Officially Divorced." "Everyone thinks I'm off the rails now. That I just randomly got a divorce for no reason. Like a hypocrite. Like a—like a crazy person."

"I don't like that word," Renata put in mildly.

"People on social media like it," I mumbled. My ex-husband liked it too, even if *lazy* was his preferred insult of choice. *If you weren't so lazy, you'd have better work than Hope Channel movies. If you weren't so lazy, you'd be healthier, and if you were healthier, you'd be pregnant by now.* And so forth. *Lazy* was a word that cut twice: once, because I considered myself to be disciplined, diligent, in control at all times, and twice, because my narcolepsy meant there were times that discipline and control were beyond me no matter how hard I tried.

"I did everything right," I said finally, telling her what had been running through my mind all day. "I thought I was a good daughter, a good wife, a good actor. But it didn't matter, did it? Michael cheated on me anyway. My parents still sided with him. And the *one* time I did do something for myself, something that was supposed to be fun, I ended up puking my guts out in a Texas desert, two hundred miles from a real airport. I missed the shoot for my next project, and the Hope Channel recast me, and now the entire world thinks I'm irresponsible. And I don't have a job and I can't repay the Hope Channel the money I owe them and everything is gone and I blew it all up myself—and it wasn't even a regular music festival! It was UnFestival, which is an exclusive desert experience and so much more than a regular festival could ever be!"

I sucked in a breath after that surprise monologue, blinking back the burn behind my eyelids. I wanted to cry. But I'd been raised better than that; I'd learned better after fourteen years of marriage. Being out of control wasn't welcome in my life, and had never been.

"You can cry if you'd like," Renata said, almost as if she knew what I was thinking, but before I could respond, a tiny alarm beeped from her watch.

Our session was up.

She sighed at her wrist as she silenced the alarm. "Next time, I'm going to remind you earlier that there's no need to hide your feelings here. But for now, I want you to remember what you told me during our second session, after I'd asked you to come up with a goal for our time together. Can you think of it?"

"Yes," I said, eager to be a good therapy student. "My entire life, everyone else has defined Winnie Baker for me, but now, I want to define Winnie Baker for myself. I want to be a new ·Winnie."

Renata nodded. "Maybe think about what that means in conjunction with what people are saying online right now, hmm? And what we can and can't control?"

"Okay," I said. With great confidence, because a new Winnie was not going to care about what people said online. Just like how a new Winnie was never, ever going to make the old Winnie's mistakes.

And Old Winnie had made quite a few, indeed.

COMING OUT OF Renata's building always felt like coming out of a womb, and I had to blink in the bright California sunshine for a few minutes until I could see again. And that was *with* my sunglasses on. In January.

"Finally," a sharp voice said next to me, and I nearly jumped out of my skin.

But when I turned to issue a panicked "no comment," it wasn't a paparazzo at all, but a tall woman wearing a knotted trench coat and a smile that was somehow bossy and reassuring at the same time.

"I've been waiting here for five minutes," the woman said, making *five minutes* sound like *twelve hours*. She stuck out a manicured hand, which I took. She had a quick, hard handshake. Michael would have hated it.

It made me like her immediately.

"Steph D'Arezzo, talent manager," she said briskly. "Nice to meet you."

Steph. Steph. The name swam hazily to the surface of my memories. "You're Nolan Shaw's manager," I said. Before I got sick at UnFestival and had to be recast, the former bad boy of pop Nolan Shaw was going to be my costar in *Duke the Halls*. I'd been nervous about working with him when I'd signed on—even after his years out of the spotlight, I couldn't picture him as anything other than the beanie-wearing boy-Jezebel I'd known as a teenager—but my distrust had been misplaced. He'd been fiercely supportive of his girlfriend, Bee Hobbes, when she'd been exposed as an adult content creator, and he'd also been nothing but a consummate professional since then, even helming a reboot of the reality show that had once made his career, *Band Camp*.

"That's right," Steph said. "Do you know how I made my name in this business, Winnie?"

I shook my head. Family and faith-based content was a whole other entertainment world, and where all of my career had taken place. I only had the faintest handle on the goings-on of the industry at large.

"I spin straw into gold. I take washed-up, scandal-ridden frogs and I turn them back into princes. Et cetera. Do you see where I'm going with this?"

"You rehabilitate celebrity reputations," I guessed.

"That's right. I do fixer-uppers exclusively, but if that fixer can't be uppered, I move on, because sometimes teamwork does *not* make the dream work, especially if half the team is a god-damn mess." Steph reached for her purse, stopped. Huffed at herself. I got the distinct vibe she was a former smoker. "But it turns out," she continued, "that sometimes a little scandal is good for business. I thought Nolan Shaw falling in love with Bianca von Honey was the end of his comeback, but it turbo-charged his career instead. If I'd had a hundred years and even more assistants grabbing me cold brews, I still couldn't have masterminded the boost he got from living his cute, messy life the way he did last year. You see what I'm saying?"

I didn't see. All I'd gotten for my brushes with scandal were broken contracts and estranged parents. And Dominic Diamond posts.

Steph seemed to know what I was thinking, because she crossed her arms and regarded me with an arched eyebrow. "They screwed you over pretty good, huh?"

"I—"

"Let me guess," she went on. "That Michael guy cheated on you, and you wanted to keep it private, and then he rewarded you by spinning the story to make it sound like you were the bad one. I'm guessing he was behind the leak last year about your hospital stay being for drugs instead of exhaustion?"

I flushed. That was exactly what had happened.

"'Winnie Baker's Fall from Grace,'" Steph said as if quoting a headline only she could see. "It's a good story. Because saints love to hate sinners, and sinners love knowing that the saints are all secretly sinning too. Everyone clicks that headline. Everyone."

"You don't have to tell me that," I said as politely as I could.

Steph nodded. "You're right. I don't." She leaned forward, a glint coming into her eye. "Doesn't it piss you off that he got to keep everything? The good reputation, the gigs, the moral high ground?"

"Of course it does," I said. Breathed. "All I wanted was to move on. But he wouldn't let me."

"Because he's a chode and chodes think small, Winnie." Steph reached into her purse and pulled out a card. Her business card.

I took it, not sure what was happening.

"Have you heard of Hope After Dark?" she asked, snapping her purse shut.

"Um, yes," I said. Everyone had—the announcement that the Hope Channel was veering into racy content had been a bomb-shell no one had missed.

"The lead actor is my client. Kallum Lieberman, one of Nolan Shaw's former bandmates. I believe you two have met before?"

Met. Memories of that fateful Teen Choice Awards flashed through my mind: Blue eyes, a surfboard falling onto my foot. Hobbling around the after-party with my toes throbbing inside my kitten heel, narcolepsy clawing at my brain. Escaping the party at the Chateau Marmont to hide in the car, where I'd curled up on the seat and let drowsiness take me under.

And then the picture. The infamous picture. Taken by none other than Kallum Lieberman and posted to his MySpace that very night.

"Yes, we've met," I finally answered.

A nod. "Well, I think you'd do great opposite him in the first Hope After Dark movie."

For a moment, I thought I didn't hear her correctly. That I was mistaken. Then she gave my confusion a sharp smile. "Think about it. You have a Hope Channel contract you've never fulfilled, right? One in the process of being canceled because you broke their morality clause while you were at UnFestival?"

Ugh. "Yes."

"What if you didn't have to pay back the money you'd gotten from signing the contract? What if you could still satisfy that contract with a different Hope property?"

"I've already tried," I said. "Before my agent dumped me. They said with my reputation, they couldn't cast me in anyth—"

Steph interrupted me. "That was then, Winnie. This is now. After *Duke the Halls* and the way its stars have blown up after the Bianca von Honey scandal, Hope is seeing things in a brand-new light. And who better to head up their spicy new start than their fallen angel?"

"It would never work," I said, still utterly bewildered. "I can barely believe they're doing Hope After Dark as it is, but to work with *me* again? They'd never go for it."

"Oh, they already have," Steph said smugly. "And they loved the idea so much they begged me to get you to sign on, pronto. Which means the role is yours if you want it. A salvaged contract, a salvaged bank account, and who knows? Maybe a whole new direction for you."

"I can't be in a sexy movie," I murmured as I looked back down at her business card. The idea was ludicrous. I'd never even seen a raunchy movie. I didn't own a single sex toy, I'd never even . . . done things to myself, and I was pretty sure the only time I'd ever had an orgasm was while I was asleep and dreaming raunchy dreams that never seemed to star Michael. On the night my divorce was finalized, I'd drunk half a bottle of wine and Googled the word *pornography* for the first time in my entire life . . . and then I was so embarrassed by myself that I'd slammed my laptop shut and binged TikToks about spooky lakes instead.

And the thing was that I *wanted* to get rid of these walls in my mind; I wanted to watch porn and sexy movies and be the kind of person who could make dirty jokes. The kind of actor who could star in a Hope After Dark movie. But I wasn't. I was Winnie Baker and I was something much worse than a prude: I was a former prude who had no idea how to un-prude herself.

"Just think about it," Steph said. She patted my shoulder and strode off, trench coat flapping just above her high heels as she walked. I was still holding her card like it was a live grenade, half tempted to lay it on the curving cobblestone path that led to Renata's tucked-away building and walk away. Forget this conversation ever happened.

But I didn't do any of that. I put the card in my pocket, squared my shoulders, and went home.

HOME WAS NOT the house I'd lived in for over a decade, nor was it my parents' house. The former was Michael's—bought for him as a wedding present by his mom and dad, who ran a faith-based media empire and had more money than every megachurch in Texas twice over—and the latter I was tacitly no longer welcome in. So I was currently bunking in an old friend's pool house. She also happened to be the only friend I had left.

I stopped by her back door on my way back to the pool house and saw her sitting at the kitchen island with her chef-made meal and a glass of something clear, which I knew wouldn't be water. Sure enough, when I slid open the door and stepped inside her minimalist kitchen, I saw a half-empty bottle of Grey Goose on the counter.

"Winnie!" Addison exclaimed, spinning on her stool and padding over to me in her bare feet. They were pale—she was due for a spray tan soon. "I had the chef make dinner for you too tonight."

"Thanks, Addy," I said, giving her a big hug. Actor, singer, and self-identified girl boss Addison Hayes had been on another show—a semiserious drama about a widowed pastor and his family—when we were both teenagers, and we'd been put together as manufactured best friends by our management teams. We had matching careers, matching blond hair, matching purity rings. I even did guest vocals on her first album, which had been the launching pad for her wildly successful crossover music career.

We'd drifted apart after the Chateau Marmont incident—all my time and energy was sucked into repairing my image after that—but had reconnected a few years ago, when we'd starred in a Hope Channel movie as long-lost sisters who fell in love with a pair of long-lost brothers. She'd been the only one to stay in touch through the divorce, much less to offer any help, and while we kept it hidden that I was living here so she wouldn't be tainted by association, she'd still welcomed me with open arms and even more open vodka bottles. I'd be grateful for that welcome until the day I died.

"How was the shrink?" Addison asked, sitting back down and picking up her fork to eat her tiny square of white fish.

I found a plate tented with foil on the counter and got myself a fork. "Fine. I complained about Dominic Diamond."

"He's a fuckface," Addison said. "Do you wanna vodka about it?"

Addison's willingness to (1) curse, (2) drink, and (3) talk about sex like we didn't grow up having accountability partners to make sure we weren't thinking about genitals *ever at all* had been really strange at first. And then it had become incredibly freeing, because I realized all the things I used to worry would make me a bad person . . . wouldn't? Or wouldn't necessarily? Because Addison was a lot of things, but she was also kind and loyal and a good listener, and she opened her home to me when I had no other place to go . . . and maybe when it came down to it, being a kind person was more important than having an empty swear jar.

"I might vodka about it later," I said. "But something else interesting did happen, actually . . ."

After I finished telling her about Steph and the Hope After Dark offer, Addison was staring at me, her perfectly contoured face gone ashen, like I'd just told her I'd picked up a hitch-hiker off the road and that he was going to live in her backyard sauna now.

"And you immediately told her no, right?" asked Addison. "I mean, what the fuck? *The* Winnie Baker in a TV-MA movie? You have a brand!"

"Addy," I said, gently, tiredly, because I had to keep explaining this to people. "The brand is dead. There is no more *the* Winnie Baker. There is only Winnie Baker who got strung out at UnFestival."

Addison sniffed in my defense. "Anyone should be so lucky. That's an exclusive desert experience."

"This is what I keep trying to tell people!"

"But baby girl," my old friend said, suddenly serious. "No brand is dead while you're still alive and pretty. You know what our circle loves more than anything? A good redemption story. And you have all your cards left to play when it comes to one. Make a big deal about how you've stopped backsliding and about how you're trying to work things out with Michael, because your heart has been changed. And then the jobs will come back, the money will come back. Hell, maybe even Michael will come back."

"But I don't *want* Michael back," I protested.

"Duh," Addison said, flipping her shining, camera-ready waves over her shoulder. She'd been on QVC every day this week selling leggings for her lifestyle brand, Wishes of Addison, and she hadn't messy-bun-ified her TV hair yet today. "But think of the optics, Winnie! Couple reunited! Love conquers all! You'll feed the narrative with a *People* story and joint public appearances at our church, and everyone will eat it up."

I made a face, and she gave me a look like I was being deliberately childish.

"I'm not saying *love* him again. Shit, I'm not even saying *only be with him*. Just get back together for publicity's sake and then secretly see other people. Famous couples do it all the time."

"You don't do that," I pointed out. Addison was a rare single woman in our sphere.

"That's because I have some mileage left on the whole 'living my calling' angle," she said, picking up her fork and gesturing with it like there was an invisible PowerPoint presentation she was teaching from. "I predict that in two years, Wishes of Addison will be anchored enough that I can transition into the 'I've just found the love of my life' phase of my career, and then by thirty-six, I'll start the baby phase. After that, Wishes of Addison will launch its new arm, Baby Wishes, and I'll sell the company and take a job as the chief creative officer. And then? Hotels." She nodded at her fork and then started digging at her fish again.

"You want to own hotels one day?"

"Fuck yes," Addison said through a bite of swordfish. "Do you know how much good I could do for the world as a hotel owner? First item of business: every hotel room bathroom has a proper, working fan. Every single one. And a bidet! Second item of business—"

"Is this really my only option?" I cut in, looking down at my own plate of fish. I still hadn't sat down yet. "Get back together with Michael unless I want to secretly live in your pool house forever?"

"Girl, no," Addison said. Now the fork was pointed at me. "I'm not telling you to be Michael's doormat. I'm just saying that you should *pretend* to be in public. And then do whatever you want in private. Play the game, but still have fun."

"Is that what you do, Addy?" I asked. For all the time we spent together, I didn't actually know what her romantic life was like. Given how open she was with me about everything else, it was a little strange that I didn't know anything more than that she sometimes slipped away at night.

The fork sank down a little, and Addison's gaze dropped with it. "I do my best," she said, but for the first time since I'd walked into her kitchen, she sounded a little uncertain.

And it struck me how ridiculous it all was. Here we were, thirty-two years old, household names, and still feeling like our entire lives had to be played by a set of rules that was handed to us when we were too young to choose for ourselves. And I was abruptly sick of it.

Not just *tired* of it and not just *sad* about it. But sick of it. Fevered, flushed, shaking. My body readying its defenses to fight off the past that corralled me, the bleak future that beckoned.

I want to define Winnie Baker for myself. That's what I'd told Renata today. Either I meant that or I didn't. And if I was going to mean it, then I needed to *mean* it.

I set down my fork. "Fuck it," I said and pulled Steph's card out of my pocket.

Addison's eyes went as round as Wishes of Addison tealights (only $12.99 at Target and on wishesofaddison.com) as she watched me reach for my phone.

"What are you doing?" she whispered.

"What has playing the game gotten me, Addy? A cheating husband, a public divorce, and therapy bills that I can barely pay. If the world thinks I'm a fallen angel," I said, dialing Steph's number, "then at the very least I want to choose my own wings."

CHAPTER TWO

Kallum

Kallum?" Payton asked from beneath me, her legs spread like an invitation as the last letter of my name slipped into a moan. "I . . . This feels good. Like, so supergood . . . But I can't miss the bouquet toss . . . so maybe we could speed things up here . . ."

"Oh right. Yeah." I flipped my tie over my shoulder and began to thrust deeper and harder. I always liked to take my time, and I did aim to please, but just like the Slice, Slice, Baby motto said: *Speedy delivery guaranteed or your next pie's on the house!*

She buried her chin into her shoulder and let out a low groan through her teeth, like if there were a pillow to bite down on, she would. "Wait, wait, wait! Can you do the thing?" she asked breathlessly.

"The thing?" At this pace, I couldn't last much longer. Payton was one of my sister's oldest friends, and one of the first girls I'd ever seen without a bra under their clothes. (Unless you counted my mom or Tamara, and I definitely did not.) Bras were dumb. So, so dumb. I loved the swoop of a woman's breast without one—a preference I discovered at a young age thanks to Payton. Fucking Payton now, though, in her best friend Natalie's bridal suite, was the kind of teenage fantasy too good to be true.

She ground back into me. Was this love? It could be love. It might be love.

"You know, the dough thing," she said as she slid off my dick and waited for me to make my move.

I inhaled deeply, ready to put her right back where she was. God, I said I wouldn't do this. I said the last time was the last time . . . but this really was the last time. I couldn't say no to Payton. I'd never be able to live with myself.

She pouted and her nipples pressed through the silk of her bridesmaid's dress, begging me to run my mouth over the fabric. But then I'd break the most important rule of fucking at weddings: do not, under any circumstances, ruin the dress. Sex with clothes on was A+++. Five pepperonis out of five. But having to be gentle and careful with those silly dresses no one ever wore again after that one night always made me feel like a bumbling giant at a tea party.

But one day I would fall in love and I'd treat my dream girl to a new dress every day just so I could tear it to shreds every night . . . with her permission, of course. And maybe one day was today, who knew?

From the other side of the event hall, the DJ's voice echoed through the thin walls of the former nunnery turned hipster venue. "Ladies, ten-minute warning before that bouquet toss. Let's get ready to ruuuuuuuumble!"

Wedding DJs were the worst . . . but Nolan always said I only thought that because I saw myself in them. To that I said, *Don't you put that evil on me, Nolan Shaw*. But maybe I *was* just like a wedding DJ. You couldn't tell me those guys dreamed of playing weddings when they were young and dumb and still foolish enough to dream. Back in my INK glory days, I thought I'd be living it up thanks to a long-lasting solo career after me, Nolan, and Isaac would eventually go our own ways. At the very least I'd be producing music, but here I was instead, the owner of a regional pizza chain, fucking his way through half the weddings in the greater Kansas City area.

There was the sex tape, though. That had been a surprisingly not-awful thing—well, unless you asked my sister and my mother. (Or myself, if my head had too much space to think as I was falling asleep at night.)

Speaking of Nolan though, he was supposed to be here. All Natalie had wanted as a wedding gift was for me and Nolan to sing "A Love Like That" from our sophomore album for her first dance, but he backed out at the last minute, and when Natalie found out I was the only crooner left standing, she not-so-gently told me that they'd just have the DJ play the original recording.

Yeah, that one bruised my ego.

But to be fair, we did hook up a year and a half ago at Chad and Chad's wedding—yes, they were both named Chad. The next day, Natalie went on to catch the bouquet and then meet her newly acquired husband at the post-wedding brunch—and she turned out to be the latest in a long line of bridesmaids to find the love of her life soon after shagging me. It wouldn't have been so bad if word hadn't spread across the whole group of people Nolan and I had grown up with. These days, I'm the most sought-after party favor at any wedding, luckier than catching a bouquet.

At first, it was fine. But after the sex tape and the rash of weddings over the last year, I was starting to feel like the pizza you left in the fridge the night before leaving for vacation.

But Payton . . . I couldn't say no to my former crush, now, could I?

"Ten minutes," she said. "Let's try to wrap this up in two. I gotta check on Natalie before the toss. Your sister did her bustle, and no offense, but her fingers are about as nimble as a pack of Hebrew National Hotdogs."

Right. I nodded. The grand finale. I had to make this good. Payton was the kind of woman who left detailed ratings on Google. If I didn't give her a mind-blowing orgasm, she'd make sure everyone we grew up with knew about it. "Let's do this," I said, "but maybe try not to drop my sister's name while we're boning."

She gave me a small salute and immediately squealed as I hauled her up by her soft, round hips and flipped her over. She rucked her dress up around her waist and leaned over the arm of the velvet settee. Okay, I could turn off my stupid, mopey brain long enough to enjoy this teenage fantasy come to life.

She readjusted her nude mesh underwear and pulled it to the side, an act of politeness and filth all at the same time.

Midwesterners are nothing if not considerate.

And yeah, she was right . . . I could do a lot in two minutes.

Without warning, I thrust forward and Payton threw her head back in response, her soft black tendrils turning messy as they cascaded against her back. She bit into her own palm to silence herself, and that right there was enough to make me come.

Even though I knew I shouldn't (if rule number one was the dress, rule number two was definitely the hair), I wrapped her locks in my fist and gently tugged.

"Oh God, Kallum, say it! Please. Say it!"

And that was it. That was enough to kill the mood. At least in my head it was. But my head didn't bother to deliver that message to my stupid dick, which was basically on the verge of spilling.

"Say it," Payton begged.

I took a deep breath and let her hair fall back over her shoulder before I slapped her ass and plowed into her just like I had with another bridesmaid in my now-infamous sex tape. "And that's what I call tossing the dough," I said with as much enthusiasm as I could muster as she pushed back against me, our rhythm sending her over the edge . . . and well . . . me too.

Consider this dough tossed.

"WHAT'D I MISS?" I asked as I sat back down at our family table between Dad and Tamara.

"Not a goddamn thing," Dad said, like the most hopeless man in the world. My father (God bless him) had sat through more bat mitzvahs, bar mitzvahs, funerals, weddings, birthdays, showers, and anniversary parties than any human person should have to in their lifetime—especially my dad, who communicated in grunts and nods and still referred to INK as my little high school band. (He was proud though, in his own way. I once found a stash of INK clippings tucked away in the bottom drawer of his impeccably organized rolling Craftsman toolbox.) All the social events Jacob Lieberman suffered through were in the name of love, however, because being married to Josephine Lieberman required more schmoozing than the fucking mayor.

Mom reached into her purse and handed me a Styrofoam container. "You missed the cake, but don't you worry, Mommy had one packed up for you."

"Aw, thanks, Ma," I said as I opened the container and scooped a bite of Chantilly cake into my mouth.

"Where the hell have you been?" my sister said as she flopped down beside me in the same color dress as Payton wore but in a different style.

I turned to her and made the mistake of making eye contact. That's all it ever took with Tamara. She was tall and sturdy, with the same strong eyebrows and pale olive complexion we both shared, and she could see right through my charm like no one else could. And she was also the owner of a T-shirt-printing empire on Etsy, which turned out to require more cutthroat instincts than you'd think.

She slapped me with her beaded clutch. "You piece of shit!"

"What?" I asked as innocently as I could with my mouth still full of cake.

Beside me, Dad's head began to droop as he dozed to Cardi B's "WAP" playing on the dance floor.

"Tamara, don't hit your brother," Mom said in her shushing voice, which had a particularly triggering effect on my sister.

Still, I couldn't help but parrot our mother. "Yeah, Tammy Cakes. Don't hit your brother."

"Well, maybe I wouldn't hit my brother if he didn't fuck Payton!" she said as Toby, one of the triplets, flung himself into her lap, practically knocking her chair over. (I swore, those six-year-old meatheads didn't know their own strength.)

"Is it over yet?" he moaned.

Dad shook his head awake, like an old cartoon character. "Not soon enough, kiddo."

"Kallum would never do that," Mom said, still talking to Tamara. "Come here, Toby. Come see Bubbie Jo."

"Mom, you've got to be kidding me," Tamara said as Toby fled for his grandmother's welcoming arms. "You have to stop pretending Kallum's some kind of angel. At the very least, you could treat him like an adult man. Let's not forget the sex tape that humiliated the whole family."

Mom willfully ignored her and held Toby in her lap, whispering soft words in his ear. Watching her with him was like a flashback to my own childhood. I could practically smell the butterscotch on her breath. It had taken Mom a while to get over the sex tape, but once she had, it was as if it never happened . . . which was why the news I had to break to my family tonight might just destroy her.

"Kallum, baby," Mom said, "did you ever call that sweet girl from the health department?"

"Ma, I can't date my health inspector. That's a conflict of interest," I explained.

She rolled her eyes. "So politically correct these days. That girl might be the love of your life—the mother to my grand-children."

"The second mother to your grandchildren," my sister inserted.

Mom didn't take the bait. "You should call her. I think April Kowalczk"—that was Nolan's mom—"might even know her mother from Jazzercise."

Toby threw his head back before burrowing even deeper into her, which was enough of a distraction for her to drop the conversation.

I turned to Tamara and whispered, "How'd you know it was Payton?"

She swatted me again, and this time much harder. "I knew it! You only go after the bridesmaids, and there's only two brides-maids tonight, you buttface. Me and Payton. And it certainly wasn't me."

A chill of disgust rolled down my spine.

"The feeling is mutual," she confirmed.

Tucker, my brother-in-law, sauntered across the dance floor and then sat down next to Tamara with his arm draped over the back of her chair.

"Where are the other two?" she asked, referring to the other two triplets, Tristan and Theo. With a total of five kids, my sister was doing a constant headcount.

He pointed across the room with his chin. "Over with your auntie Fran. She's giving them fifty cents for every plate they help clear."

"She knows there's a catering staff whose job that actually is, right?" Tamara asked.

Tucker shrugged. "What can I say, babe? We've got some little entrepreneurs on our hands."

She leaned over and kissed his cheek before whispering, "I think I'd rather them be doctors like their daddy."

I couldn't help but roll my eyes a little. Tucker's face was plastered across billboards and bus benches all across the city. He was a urologist and the self-proclaimed "Vasectomy King of Kansas City," though I personally referred to him as Dr. Dick— something my father found hilarious.

Despite Tucker being a little bit of a tool, he was good to my sister, and after all she'd been through, she deserved it.

"All right, party people," the DJ said, "it's time for that bouquet toss."

This was the perfect time. Mom would be in a good mood from all her favorite romantic wedding traditions and Tamara was just a little bit drunk. Dad was practically asleep. And Tucker . . . well, I didn't really care what Tucker thought.

"I have news," I blurted.

"Us first," Tamara said.

"What?" I asked. "Is it another baby?"

Tucker snorted and threw back the rest of his Scotch. "God, I hope not."

In addition to the triplets, Tamara had an older child from when she was seventeen and then her youngest, Talia, who was conceived just a few days before Tucker went under the knife for his own vasectomy. Needless to say, a sixth kid was not part of the plan.

"Is now the best time to talk about this?" Mom asked Tamara.

"The best time for what?" I asked, the panic in my chest tightening. "Ma, are you okay? Is something wrong with you or Pop?"

"No, no, no," she said, enjoying my concern just a bit.

"They're fine," Tamara told me.

"I don't get what the big deal is," Tucker said before turning to me. "We're going on a cruise for Hanukkah this year. There. Now he knows."

My heart sank. "A cruise?" I asked. "But I get seasick. You guys remember the last time." Soon after INK split and I moved back home to Kansas City with what money I had managed to save, Cruising with the Stars reached out to me about filling a spot on one of their cruises to the Bahamas after Kelly Clarkson had to drop out at the last minute. I'd get a nice paycheck, and the suite they offered me was big enough for my parents, Tamara, and her oldest kid (and my favorite nephew), Topher, who'd been thirteen at the time. I'd only made it through one performance before getting so violently seasick they had to fly me home from Nassau. But hey, the family got to swim with dolphins.

"We know," Tamara said diplomatically. "Which is why we wanted to let you know now . . ."

"So that—what? I could train my nausea-stamina or something? I'm going to be puking my guts out over the railing the whole time." This didn't make any sense. Lieberman family Hanukkahs, particularly the first and last nights, were more cherished than any other holiday. Hell, even when I was on tour, I was sure to be home. I even brought Isaac and Nolan back with me on more than one occasion.

Mom gave Tamara a panicked look, and even Dad was awake now.

"Kallum, you're not going," Tamara finally says. "I mean, you could if you wanted to, but no one's going to want to be your nursemaid the whole time."

"But why Hanukkah?" I asked. "You could all go any other time, but—"

"Mom has always wanted to go on the Cruise of Lights, and well, Tucker and I are taking Mom, Dad, and the whole family for their fortieth anniversary."

It was hard to argue with that. Mom had ordered catalogs for the Cruise of Lights every year since we were kids. A cruise chock-full of Jewish entertainment, all-kosher dining, and even trivia nights. Even though our family didn't keep kosher and there wasn't a shortage of trivia nights on the family social calendar, the cruise was still the woman's dream come true.

"You never know," Mom said as Toby fell asleep in her lap, "you just might find a nice girl before then who you'd like to share the holiday with."

Tamara studied her half-eaten cake. Before she met Tucker, Mom had spent every waking moment looking for a suitable bachelor who would consider courting a single mother. I'd never really been marriage material, and my sister and I butt heads on lots of things, but at least she had my back on that.

"Your turn," Tamara said, softer than usual. "What's your big news, little brother?"

"You all know how Nolan did that movie, *Duke the Halls*, and it really took off?" I asked. "And he even met his girlfriend, Bee?"

"His mother is just so proud of him," Mom said. "And I watched it twice!"

Tucker nodded. "Gentiles really know a thing or two about holiday movies."

Pop scoffed. "Everyone knows the best Christmas movies are made by members of the tribe. After all, didn't Irving Berlin write *White Christmas*?"

Mom beamed at him.

"Well, the execs at the Hope Channel were so psyched about how well Nolan's film went that they asked me to star in one too."

For a very rare moment, my entire family was silent, and even the smooth R&B song playing in the background seemed to melt away.

And then they burst into sidesplitting laughter.

I could have just waited until the movie came out. Ya know, forgiveness after the fact? But if I did that, Mom might never get over it. Better to warn her of things to come. I learned that lesson after failing to mention the sex tape to her before it was all over the internet.

"Want to hear something even funnier?" I asked. "They've got me playing a young Santa."

Pop's eyes went wide before he began to laugh even harder. "Put that tummy you got going to good use!"

I gave him a half-hearted grin. Well, fuck. Here goes nothing. "It's actually part of a new initiative of, uh, *scintillating* holiday movies called Hope after Dark."

Everyone continued on laughing until Tucker tilted his head to the side. "Bro. Like . . . a Christmas porno?"

Mom was the first to stop laughing, and then Tamara, and then Dad.

"What does this mean?" Mom asked, her voice now full of alarm and suspicion. "Hope After Dark?"

"You didn't actually say yes to this, did you, Kal?" Tamara asked. "Not after everything that industry has put you through. Everything it's put all of us through."

"Of course he didn't," Mom said.

I looked at her then, and I could see the disappointment already forming in her soft hazel eyes. Of course I said yes. The moment Steph called me with the offer from Teddy, I was in. It was foolish. I had everything I needed. A thriving business. Family who loved me. But after spending my teen years being every girl's last choice for a fake boyfriend at slumber parties, seeing T-shirts with my face hitting clearance racks nationwide, and being the only member of INK to not receive an offer for a solo album, there was nothing else for me to say but yes.

Not only had the sex tape made me relevant again, but for the first time, *I* was the hot one. I was the sexy one with the dad bod and the sexual enthusiasm of a tattooed line chef.

And just maybe there was a life for me outside of Slice, Slice, Baby and being the most okay-est uncle ever. (It wasn't my fault that baby Talia cried every time I made eye contact with her.)

"The contract is signed," I said. "I leave for LA in two days and then I'll go to Vermont for three weeks of filming."

"What about the restaurants?" Dad asked, suddenly concerned for my pizza empire.

"Topher is in charge while I'm gone," I explained. "And he's cat-sitting Bread too."

My sister's jaw dropped. "You mean to tell me that my twenty-year-old son is in charge of your entire restaurant chain for nearly a month and you didn't even speak to me about it first?" Tamara asked. "He's still in school!"

I nodded. "The staff is solid, and Toph can troubleshoot. I'm just a phone call away."

Mom stood, hoisting Toby up with her. "I'm ready to leave. Tammy, we'll take the boys home and relieve Talia's babysitter."

"But, Ma, you'll miss the send-off for the bride and the groom. There're supposed to be sparklers," I tell her. "Your favorite."

"I'm not feeling very well," she said in the same curt tone she used the day she found out I'd agreed to change the spelling of my name from Callum to Kallum for the sake of INK. (You couldn't spell *ink* without a *K*, ya know?)

"Good night," I said with a nod. "I love you."

My father came around the side of the table and gave me a firm grip on my shoulder. "Night, son."

Beside me, Tamara shook her head before gulping down the rest of her wine.

Just beyond our table, I watched Payton reach above her head, a laughing grin on her face as she caught Natalie's bouquet.

The tradition lived on.

CHAPTER THREE

Winnie

The Hope Channel office was a glass and granite nightmare in Studio City, lined with boxy bushes and with absolutely no visitor parking.

Addison pulled her G-Wagon up to the curb, put it in park, and then chirped, "Home sweet reliable paycheck home!"

I looked down at my trembling hands, wondering if it was my narcolepsy medication making me jittery. With my type of narcolepsy, I didn't have to worry about sudden losses of muscle tone, only extreme sleepiness during the day and screwed-up sleep at night. The medicine helped a lot, but it wasn't perfect, and sometimes it made me feel a little fried during the day, like a long-haul trucker on his seventh cup of coffee white-knuckling the steering wheel.

Then again, this might just be good, old-fashioned about-to-make-a-sexy-Santa-movie nerves. It had been two weeks since I told Steph I'd take the role, and for every hour of those two weeks, I'd doubted my decision, because:

1. I wasn't sure if I even knew how to be sultry on-screen, given that I wasn't even sure if I'd ever been sultry in *real life*. Michael certainly claimed I'd never been—one of the reasons for his infidelity, he said.

2. After the divorce, I'd finally stopped living on the edge of starvation in order to maintain the "right" image, and my body had changed. My tummy was softer, my hips were rounder. My thighs were not runway-model thighs. And that was all going to be on camera. (And then on Hopeflix, where viewers could easily grab as many unflattering screenshots as they liked.)

3. Kallum Lieberman was my costar. The same Kallum Lieberman who took the infamous Chateau Marmont picture . . . the catalyst for my life being turned upside down.

4. Could Santa even be sexy? What about smelly reindeer and a velvet capsule wardrobe could possibly be sexy???

Addison faced me and took a long slurp from her iced beet juice. "It's just an intimacy coordination meeting," she said. "Everything will be supersafe and slow today, I promise."

"Have you even done one before?"

"Well, no, but I watched an *SNL* skit about them once. So chillax, sweetie, it's going to be great."

"Is it obvious I'm nervous?"

"Girl, you're turning that heated seat into a vibrating seat with how much you're shaking. Take a deep breath—and maybe an edible—and then go show the world what I already know: that you're a sexy narcoleptic flower just waiting to blossom."

"I don't have any edibles," I pointed out, but I did take a deep breath.

"I have some in my purse, *obvi*," Addison said, but I was already waving her off and unbuckling my seat belt.

"Thank you for dropping me off," I said, sliding out of the car.

"No worries! I'll be nearby in a Wishes meeting, so just call when you're done. And, Winnie?"

I shut the car door and looked back at my friend through the rolled-down window, knowing she was about to say something kind and empowering, and that it would fill me with confidence and courage, and that I would use her words to draw strength from for the rest of the *Santa, Baby* production schedule. "Yes, Addy?"

"Let me know if Kallum's actually packing or if those were just good camera angles in his video, okay? I have a bet with my spray tan girl."

And then she sucked down another two inches of beet juice and took off, tires screeching on the asphalt.

". . . AND YOU'RE GOING to love coming back to Christmas Notch," Don was saying to me. "Hopeflix is sparing no money bringing Hope After Dark to life, and we're even building custom sets. Just wait until you see the sleigh where Santa first seduces your character! No spoilers, but the gold carriage the British monarchy trots out for parades has nothing on this. Except for the actual gold, maybe."

Don Dilly was a Hope Channel producer—one I'd worked with several times before—and I got the distinct impression from his bright chatter and constant gesturing that he'd been told to hype up the project and hype *me* up as well, probably to reassure me that I was firmly back in the Hope Channel's embrace. Unfortunately for him, no number of monarchy-topping sleighs was going to settle the metallic panic currently roiling in my chest. And it didn't help that the hallway we were walking down was lined with framed Hope Channel movie posters— several of which had *me* on them. Me smiling or me with a face full of Christmas wonder or me looking beatifically up at a bland man in a sweater.

Seeing all these past Winnies—happy, slender, blank—was beyond disorienting.

I wasn't *her* anymore.

So why was I *here*?

"Now the intimacy coordinator is a hoot, a real hoot," Don was saying, and for the first time, I detected some nervousness under his otherwise chipper tone. "Quite the character, very different from people we usually have on set—well, *Duke the Halls* being the exception. Anyway, Hope After Dark is a really exciting direction for Hope Media at large, and we think some out of the box thinking is warranted in who we partner with, but that being said, he is a little—"

The door at the end of the hallway crashed open, revealing a white man about my age with blond hair, a beach-ready suntan, and the face of a Ken doll. One hand held a phone in front of his face, and the other hand held the ugliest dog I'd ever seen in my entire life.

"I don't care how good he is with animals, I don't want him around Miss Crumpets when she's visiting you!" he was yelling into the phone. "And you owe it to me after you stole my lube dispenser from my bedside table, and don't lie and say you didn't, because my sister *saw* you, and you know it's emotionally mine after spending the last two years cleaning lube off the floor because you didn't know how to use it right, and that stuff *stains*, Levi!"

"—out there," Don finished heavily. "He's a little out there."

For the first time, the intimacy coordinator seemed to notice that he wasn't alone in the hallway, his blue-green eyes narrowing at us. From the end of his phone, someone was yelling back at him, but he ignored them and used his ugly dog's paw to point at me. "You. Winnie Baker. I'll be back for you and Kallum when I'm done with this." And then he was pushing past us to the door outside, the dog wriggling in excitement the whole way.

Don cleared his throat in the ensuing silence. "Should I show you to the meeting room?"

He didn't need to show me—I'd shivered through enough AC-blasted meetings in these offices that I could have probably drawn the building's vent schematics from memory—but I still let him take my elbow and lead me into the room, which was empty save for us, the furniture, and a pink plastic box on the meeting room table.

No Kallum. Not yet. I took in a sudden breath and realized I'd been holding it all this time.

Okay. Okay, I could do this. I'd white-knuckled my way through narcoleptic episodes, through diets so brutal that gallons of coffee were the only way to stop my stomach from chewing itself apart, through long dinners with Michael where he never tore his eyes away from his phone to talk to me. If I'd made myself uncomfortable for him, for my parents, for my old agent, then why couldn't I make myself uncomfortable for *myself*? For something that I wanted to do?

The new Winnie Baker had herself under *control*. The new Winnie Baker had her shit *together*. And she was going to make a sexy Santa movie and show the world that she was here on her own terms, dang it.

A small *ding* chimed next to me, and Don glanced at his smartwatch. His face paled as he read the message. "Oh crapping heck," he mumbled.

"Everything okay?"

"A snowstorm just hit a set in Georgia, and now a ten-thousand-dollar-a-day machine for making fake snow is stuck in the real snow. Excuse me, I'll be back as soon as I can." Don ducked out, already pulling his phone free, and then it was just me in the room. Just me and the vents keeping the room at the approximate temperature of a meat locker.

I didn't sit, still needing to force myself back into Winnie Baker Has Her Shit Together mode. Instead, I paced around the table and dragged my fingers over the surface, stopping when I got to the pink plastic box, which was none other than a vintage Barbie-branded Caboodle.

An *unlatched* vintage Barbie-branded Caboodle, and even though I knew it wasn't polite to snoop, I lifted the lid anyway and then stared at the contents inside, unable to piece together why they were all in the same place. Body tape, thin pieces of foam that reminded me of the shells stuffed inside bra cups, kneepads, baby oil. I picked up a flesh-colored piece of fabric that was sewn into the shape of a pouch and then stared at it for a moment.

"That would be my pickle pouch," came a deep, cheerful voice from behind me, and I startled, dropping the pouch as the lid to the Caboodle lightly clunked back down. I turned around to see Kallum Lieberman standing only a few feet away—and then had to tilt my head back in order to keep seeing him, because oh my God, had he always been that tall?

Tall and *big*. Like big enough to be throwing logs at one of those Scottish competitions made up entirely of burly men in kilts. His head practically scraped the ceiling, and his shoulders were broad enough to cast a shadow over me. The graphic T-shirt he wore under his denim jacket clung to the outward curve of his stomach, and his big, sturdy thighs pushed against his jeans.

And his hands! They were massive! Surely they couldn't have been that big when we were younger? Because I'd never seen hands like that, hands the size of dinner plates, and they looked so impossibly strong, like he could wrap his fingers around my arms and lift me bodily off the ground without so much as a grunt.

Somehow, totally unbidden, the image of those hands on my waist floated to the surface of my mind. Stroking my hips.

Pressing into my skin. Searching out my navel and the little dents at the small of my back.

With a flush, I realized that I'd been staring at his hands. His hands, which were down by his thighs, and it must have looked like I was staring at his—

"Making sure the pouch will fit?" Kallum asked with a giant grin. Through the dark blond of his beard, a dimple pulled, and then something in my stomach felt like it was falling all the way down to the floor.

"Because I already told Jack he'll need to find something larger," Kallum added. "Like a sock hat. Or a sleeping bag."

He laughed, and it was deep and happy, like he didn't have a care in the world. And maybe he didn't. Maybe he walked around oblivious to everything, leaving a trail of dropped surfboards and sleeping Winnie Baker pictures behind him.

I stuck out my hand and pasted on the biggest smile I could. "Winnie Baker," I said. "It's lovely to meet you in person."

His smile faded a little, the dimple disappearing under the beard. "You don't remember meeting me before?" he asked. "At the Teen Choice Awards? I'm Surfboard Guy, remember?"

"I thought it was more polite not to mention it," I said delicately, and then the dimple reappeared.

"You don't ever have to be polite with me," he said, finally taking my hand, and my stomach did the falling thing again as his hand practically swallowed mine in the handshake. It was shockingly warm in the cold room, and maybe the rest of him was that warm too. Maybe if he hugged me, it would feel like slipping into a hot bath. "I'm the kind of guy you can be yourself with."

It could have been a sound bite, like something that would have been printed under a giant, glossy picture of his face in *Tiger Beat* magazine, but it didn't sound fake or rehearsed at all. It sounded like he meant it.

"And I'm sorry for the surfboard thing," he added, his thick brows pulling together. "I get clumsy when I'm nervous. Well, unless I'm dancing. Which doesn't make sense, because I've been plenty nervous performing before, but if I'm dancing, it never seems to matter."

I thought I knew what he was saying. "It makes sense to me. All the moves are choreographed ahead of time. You don't have to think or make decisions or wonder if you're doing the right thing or if people will be upset with you. All you have to do is follow the plan."

"Yeah," he said, although the line between his brows didn't disappear. "Something like that."

"And it's totally okay about the Teen Choice Awards," I said. "It's all surfboards under the bridge."

That did ease the serious expression on his face, and I was almost sorry when he released my hand back into the cold air of the room.

"Ah, I see the Clauses are getting acquainted," someone said, coming through the door and closing it. It was the man from the hallway—plus the ugly dog, which was now tucked securely against his side like a football. A pink tongue was drooping from the side of its mouth and it was looking around the room with cataract-shiny eyes.

Too late, I realized the pouch was still out on the table in front of me, making me look like a total creeper, but when the intimacy coordinator's eyes landed on it, his face split into a delighted smile. "You're already digging in, I see. Excellent."

"No, I—" *Come on, Winnie! Be the unruffled composure you want to see in the world!* But before I could answer about the penis-holding pouch in a very unruffled, very composed way, Kallum was stepping in for me.

"I was showing her your sex Caboodle," Kallum said smoothly. "So she could know all the tools of the trade and stuff."

I shot Kallum a grateful look and he winked at me.

"What a good Caboodle Yoda you are," the coordinator said, setting his dog down on the table. It took two steps and then laid on its belly with its head raised and its eyes staring straight ahead, like a very small sphinx. The coordinator sat at the seat next to the Caboodle and opened it up to tuck the pouch neatly back inside.

One of Kallum's massive hands curled around the back of a chair and pulled it out for me. "Milady," he said gallantly, gesturing to the seat.

I sat, wondering if I'd judged him unfairly all those years ago. Between the surfboard and the picture, I'd assumed he was an inconsiderate wang. But today he'd apologized for the Teen Choice Awards *and* he'd helped me through the awkward pouch moment. Could I have been wrong about costarring with Kallum?

Maybe . . . it wouldn't be so bad?

Maybe this whole *Santa, Baby* thing wouldn't be so bad?

"So," the coordinator said as his dog started gently—wetly—snoring, "about me. I'm your intimacy coordinator for this shoot, and my name is Jack Hart."

"I knew I recognized you from somewhere!" exclaimed Kallum, and Jack gave a little bow.

"I assume you are familiar with my body of work, which is of course as groundbreaking as it is extensive." Seeing my blank look, Jack added, "Porn, Winnie Baker. I mean porn."

"You make p-pornography?" My voice caught on the word, and then I flushed. And then flushed about the flushing. I hated sounding like such a fuddy-duddy (and I hated getting embarrassed about it even more).

"Darling, I *am* pornography," Jack declared, not seeming bothered by my reaction in the least. "I've been redefining the medium since I was twenty, erasing boundaries and inspiring ode-like Pornhub comments for years. My oeuvre defies categories and transgresses expectations; I've been called 'bold,' 'fearless,' and 'eerily limber.' My bisexual Hoover Dam orgy has been viewed over a million times, and I've had not one, but two! Two toys! That were molded from my anatomy—both of which come with discreet yet stylish travel cases, by the way."

My mouth was open. I had so many questions. There were toys made to look like real people's bodies? Was the orgy inside the Hoover Dam or on top of it? And what on earth was this eerily limber person doing at the Hope Channel of all places?

He seemed to sense my confusion, because he said, in a slightly less declarative voice, "But then I got divorced, and my ex-husband ruined my career, and despite *all I've done* for pornography as an art form, I'm forced to seek gainful employment elsewhere." He sniffed. "Unfortunately for me, but fortunately for the world, the only thing I'm good at is making sex look amazing on camera. Since I can no longer find people willing to brave my ex-husband's ire to perform with me, I had to pivot, and now I'm officially certified to make other people's sex look good on camera. Or their fake sex at least."

I was still trying to process that I was sitting next to an actual porn star, to someone who'd had sex for money. My entire life, pornography had been held up as an example of how far our modern world had fallen into sin, as the single seediest vice a person could have.

And yet the man sitting next to me didn't seem seedy at all. He seemed like any other LA-dweller: great hair, perfect teeth, elevator pitch at the ready. High-need dog with an obvious backstory.

I mentally shook myself. I'd managed to slough off so much of what I'd grown up thinking, and so I had no idea why my stereotypes about pornography had stuck around. And I was done with thinking that way. After all, my replacement for *Duke the Halls*, Bee Hobbes, was also a porn star and seemed to be awesome. And heck, I was making a sexy movie myself now!

Also your costar is no stranger to adult entertainment himself . . .

I looked across the table at Kallum, who'd sat down at some point during Jack's introduction. I knew Addison had watched his sex tape after he'd officially licensed it and rereleased it, and she'd said it was the dirtiest thing she'd ever seen. (She'd said it like a compliment. Also a compliment: "The man-fur on that guy!")

My eyes dropped to Kallum's hands as Jack kept talking. There was a faint sprinkle of hair on the backs of his hands, gold like the hair on his head.

"So the main thing I need to stress before we get started is that sex will fuck with your head sometimes. Even fake sex. Even fake sex with lots of crew members nearby holding heavy equipment. On paper, we're all grown-ups with rational brains that recognize we're doing a job, but in reality, lots of us are horny meatbags with easily confused limbic systems. So while much of what we do will be sneaky angles and pretending—and while we'll have some barriers in place for when we're not pretending—there will be times when you need to remind yourself that it's just biology. Got it? Just. Biology."

"Just biology," I echoed.

Kallum was nodding, looking totally at ease, like he didn't need this reminder at all. And he probably didn't; a man with a sex tape probably wasn't a man with an easily confused limbic system.

"Thank you for coming to my TED Talk," Jack said and then tapped the screen on his phone to wake it up. The background was a picture of his dog sitting in front of a crumpet with a birthday candle stuck in it. "Now," Jack continued, tapping his email icon and then opening an attachment, "we'll be in Christmas Notch next week, which means we need to get your first love scene mapped out before we go, since it's being filmed on day two. We're going to review the scene together, and then I'll chat with you both separately about your thoughts. And then we'll reconvene for the . . . choreography."

Okay.

Okay.

This was the way I thought things would go. Boundaries, limits, ideas. Choreography. And choreography would be easy, right? Like I'd told Kallum earlier, there was something re-assuring about knowing the dance moves ahead of time.

And it would be extra reassuring for someone who didn't know very many, *ahem*, dance moves at all.

We went over the scene—a newly minted Santa would take my character, Holly, for a ride in his sleigh, which would lead to fingering, which was mostly unexplored territory for me in real life—and then Kallum and I took turns stepping out of the room so Jack could privately go over boundaries and limits with us.

When it was my turn, I told him—honestly—that I had none.

The ex–porn star looked at me skeptically. His dog, Miss Crumpets, startled herself awake, barked at an empty chair, and then laid her head back down. "Are you sure?" asked Jack Hart.

"I'm sure," I said confidently. The new Winnie was excited for this. The new Winnie was *ready*.

Jack twisted his pretty mouth but then he shrugged. "I also basically have no limits, so I get it. That said, if we get to something that doesn't work for you, let me know."

Not going to happen. So what if I was still nervous about all of this and still unsure of my costar? I was an actor, a professional, and I Had This.

Except, as Jack arranged two chairs side by side to make a pretend sleigh bench, as Kallum sat next to me and then draped one of those Scottish log-throwing arms over the back of my chair, the low-simmering panic I'd felt all morning flamed into something much, much hotter. He was so easy in his skin, so confident and casual about bringing our bodies close together, and I . . . was not. I wanted to be, was *determined* to be, and yet I couldn't get my muscles to unclench, couldn't get my spine to soften.

"Okay," Jack said, sitting on the table in front of us. "So we've said all the flirty words, et cetera et cetera, now we get to the good stuff. Kallum, this is when you say, 'Spread your legs for Santa, baby,' and Winnie, I imagine this is one of the shots Gretchen will want to show either dead-on or from the top. The more hotness points we can rack up before the actual touching starts, the more we can get away with hiding later. So go ahead."

My brain was blank. "What?"

"He means go ahead and spread your legs," Kallum said, and something in my chest flipped over.

I didn't think I'd ever noticed how deep his voice was before now, but Kallum had been the bass singer in INK, hadn't he? He'd been the powerful, thrumming voice below Isaac's crooning, and now that same deep voice had just told me to spread my legs.

Swallowing hard, I did as Kallum said. I was wearing jeans today, and so it wasn't like anything was being exposed, but I suddenly knew what Jack meant about the easily confused limbic systems, because I'd never done anything like this, ever, not as an actress—and not even as a wife. Because when Michael and

I'd had sex, words had never been involved, and neither had any kind of sexy preliminaries.

I obediently parted my legs, and Kallum cleared his throat.

"Now, I'm pretty sure you'll be wearing a skirt for this, Winnie, so I think a nice lingering shot of Kallum's hand moving up your thigh would work here."

I managed a professional-sounding *I agree*, and then Kallum's hand was on my thigh sweeping up to the middle seam of my jeans. Even though his palm was on the top of my thigh, his hand was big enough that his fingers were brushing along the inside of my leg. Just like they would be if he really were pushing his way up to feel under a skirt.

Sparks followed his touch, and my breath hitched once, twice, and then his hand settled to a stop. A polite two inches away from my vagina.

"Good breath work, Winnie," Jack said appreciatively, and hot blood rushed to my cheeks, because I, uh, hadn't been doing the breath work on purpose.

"Now, we'll probably sell most of this scene with close-ups on your faces, cut in with a few shots of Kallum's hand under the skirt. But I was thinking Kallum could be kissing your neck while your character comes?"

"Good idea," I said, Kallum's hand still burning a hole through my jeans.

"I like it," Kallum said cheerfully, and then Jack made a circling gesture at me, as if to say *continue* . . . and I realized with a slow horror that I needed to pretend to have an orgasm. Or at least move my body in the same way that I would when I was pretending later, and oh God, how do people have orgasms on-screen? Did they thrash around like Meg Ryan in *When Harry Met Sally*? Did they smack their hand against a car window and then drag it back down like Rose in *Titanic*?

It didn't matter. I was going to do this, I was going to figure this out, and so I did my best fake orgasm, tossing my head back and letting my mouth hang open, as if I were mid-moan. But then Kallum didn't pretend to kiss my neck like he was supposed to. In fact, he didn't move at all, and when I lifted my head to look at him and Jack, Jack looked genuinely confused. And Kallum looked ready to laugh.

I straightened up in my chair, embarrassment torching my skin.

"Well, that's not great," said Jack at the same time Kallum said fondly, "You looked just like that picture I took of you at the Chateau Marmont!"

And now I was one giant bonfire of humiliation. I thought of the picture in question, of my mouth hanging open, my ungraceful slump, and yeah.

There wasn't anything less sexy in the world.

CHAPTER FOUR

Kallum

Winnie's cheeks flushed as she bit down on her lip, her eyes darting from the floor to me to Jack to Miss Crumpets and then to the floor again.

Her. Lip.

Between her teeth.

I couldn't look away. Yes, she was gorgeous all over, with that innocent girl-next-door look, with those high, rounded cheeks, gently curved brows, and long, thick lashes. Throw in an adorable nose and eyes in a hypnotizing shade between blue and green, and you had a certified knockout. But when she caught that soft lower lip between her teeth . . . when she released it oh-so-slowly and left her pink lips parted in something that looked so much like a pant or a gasp or a bitten-off whimper—

Jack's phone erupted into the chorus of Christina Aguilera's "Genie in a Bottle," startling me, Winnie, and Miss Crumpets, who popped to her feet in a surprisingly spry move, and started barking in tune with the song.

"Fucking shitwaffle," Jack hissed, looking at his screen. "We'll pick this up again when we're in Vermont. I have to deal with my ex and the fact that he's foisting a stepfather onto Miss Crumpets before she's emotionally ready. Class dismissed."

He scooped up his tiny rat dog and marched out the door like Julia Roberts in *Erin Brockovich*.

I turned to Winnie to say—I don't know, whatever you say to the American sweetheart whom you dropped a Teen Choice Awards surfboard on, but she bolted from her chair, pushing her way out the door before I could even comprehend that she was gone. And suddenly I was sitting in a Hope Channel conference room with Jack's fake-sex first aid kit.

Looking from the door to Winnie's empty chair, I forced my brain to rewind to the last, pre–Christina Aguilera moment that caused Winnie to bolt.

Her big O—no. We made her feel silly. *Fuck.*

I made her feel silly.

The hardest part of performing is when everyone else isn't playing along with you, and Jack and I just stared at Winnie like a couple of goons.

Well, at least I did.

But I couldn't help it. When I got the call that Winnie had signed on to play the lead opposite me, I was convinced I was going to walk out of my house and get hit by a bus—or that the engine was going to fall out of the ass of my plane to LAX. My mom always told me and Tammy that people were most likely to have near-death experiences after really, really good news. It was the universe's way of putting you back in your place. So since that call from Teddy, I'd been waiting for the other foot to drop . . . and maybe my misfortune to counterbalance the scales was that Winnie was bound to be miserable working with me.

I couldn't let that happen, though. I had to nip this in the very cute bud before things got any worse.

Just as I stood, my phone vibrated.

> **Topher:** All's good here at Slice, Slice, Baby. Where do we keep the extra bank deposit bags at the flagship location? Does Winnie Baker smell as good as she looks?

I shoot off a quick reply.

> **Me:** Bottom filing cabinet. Don't be a fucking creep, kid.

And before thinking better, I typed, But yes. Better.

Down the hallway, I found the restrooms with one of those fancy water fountains for reusable bottles between the men's room and the women's room.

I didn't know that Winnie was actually in there, but my Spidey little brother's intuition was tingling, and after years of Tammy Cakes holing up in the Jack-and-Jill bathroom dividing our childhood bedrooms, I felt pretty confident. So I posted up against the wall with my arms crossed and waited.

Just when I was about to give up and see if she'd fled the country altogether, the door swung open.

Winnie nearly jumped out of her skin at the sight of me.

"Hey," I said in the softest voice I could manage.

"Um, hi," she said, the apples of her cheeks glowing and her eyes slightly puffy.

"You left kind of fast," I said, my brows beginning to furrow just like Dad's always did when he sat at the kitchen table every Monday night to balance his checkbook. "I wanted to make sure you were okay."

"I'm fine," she said a little too quickly.

I stepped forward. "Are you sure?"

Her lip trembled for a brief moment, before she shook her head like she was getting into character and doing her best to shed all evidence of Winnie Baker. She looked left, then right at the hallway lined with Hope Channel movie posters—many of them starring her.

She leaned toward me, slowly filling the gap between us.

My dick twitched. This little crush was going to get me in trouble. How was I supposed to keep my downstairs flaccid when we were pretending to have sex if her just leaning close enough for me to smell her citrus-scented shampoo was enough to make me feel like a teenage boy?

"I'm worried I can't do it," she whispered, and then clapped her hand over her mouth, like she'd take it back if she could.

I forced my inner horndog to shut up. "Can't do the scene?" I asked. "Or the whole movie?" I was so excited to be working with Winnie that I hadn't even taken a moment to realize how off-brand this all was for her. But I just thought maybe she was branching out after her divorce or that this was the Hope Channel's way of keeping their die-hard fans happy.

"I just don't know if I can be, uh, sensual. On camera."

Down, boy, I reminded myself. "Oh, there's nothing to it," I assured her. "A fake orgasm isn't all that different from a real orgasm. At least, that's what I've been told," I added. "My knowledge about fake orgasms is limited, given that my only foray into adult content was one-hundred-percent real pleasure— hers included." I gave her a wink—and oh my God, was that smarmy? That felt smarmy.

"But I've never had an orgasm," she blurted.

My whole body froze, except for my dick. Because of course it didn't. *Whaaaa?* I mouthed. Winnie Baker had never had an orgasm?

Winnie Baker had never had an orgasm.

I pursed my lips together to stop myself from smiling. *Winnie Baker had never had an orgasm.*

And that sucked. But holy fuck. What I wouldn't give to show her what it meant to truly give herself over to feeling good . . .

Okay, dick twitching again. *Be cool, Kallum. This is a job. This is a professional setting. Winnie is my* coworker. *This is watercooler talk or whatever!*

Her hands flew up, fingers bracing against her temples. "Oh my . . . I'm so sorry," she said as she began to step back so that she was flush with the bathroom door. "That was really inappropriate, I shouldn't have—"

"No, no," I said, holding up my hands. *Say something, man.* But not a stupid thing. But what if this was my moment to put myself out there? I wanted so badly to take Winnie's hand and march her right out of here to the brand-new and pointlessly modern hotel the Hope Channel had put me up in. What would it feel like to drag my nose past her collarbone and between her breasts, just drinking her in?

But no. Winnie had confided in me. I couldn't just throw myself at her. That's what Wedding Hookup Kallum would do. And I was done with that.

"This is important stuff," I said, as I realized she was holding her breath, just waiting for me to speak, and all I wanted was to comfort her in any way I could and to let her know that she was okay and normal, and if she had this problem, other people did too. But instead I talked out of my ass with absolute confidence. "And I'm glad you told me, because I have the perfect solution."

"You do?" she asked, full of hope.

I nodded solemnly.

Don't say Sit on my face. *Don't say* Sit on my face. *Don't say* Sit on my face.

"I do," I said. "*Research.*"

"Research?"

"Actors are always talking about research in their interviews, right?" I asked, the words spilling out of my mouth faster than I could think of them. "Well, in this case, your research will be the best research in the world—orgasms. Having them, watching them, having some more. Until you have a few good ways in mind that you can fake them for the camera."

"Research," she repeated faintly.

I gave her a big grin and had to literally stop from patting myself on the back. "That's all acting is, right? Taking what we know from real life and turning it into make-believe? We've got almost a week before we're in Christmas Notch, and I bet that's more than enough time to get your PhD in poon-monsoons, Winnie Baker. Hell, Jack Hart himself is basically a living textbook. You should search for some of his videos this week. Maybe not the Hoover Dam one though." I'd seen that one and it was definitely an upper-level course.

"I—ah. Okay," she nodded astutely. "Research. I'll do my research."

"Okay, let's see what we're working with here," Luca, the head of the costuming department, said as he knelt in front of the tailoring pedestal. "You sure you don't want me to leave the room while you try it on?"

"Should you buy me dinner first? Maybe even just a food truck snack, or something," I said. "Uh, but no. I'm fine."

Luca smirked. He had light beige skin, highly coiffed black hair, and today was wearing an oversize black sweater and black leather pants. Even back home in KC in the midst of a late spring snowstorm, I'd be sweating my ass off in his outfit. Forget the greater LA area, where air-conditioning was about as strong as someone gently blowing on your neck.

"That depends. On the dinner," he clarified. "I'm vegan, pizza boy. Well, I guess technically I'm currently vegan-curious. At least while I'm Stateside, and away from real gelato. And this isn't a date, or even a hookup. This is a fitting." He held his hand out to reveal a diamond-studded band on his left hand. "Besides, I'm engaged."

I nodded as I stepped onto the pedestal and began to un-buckle my belt. "Right. Sorry. That was a bad joke. Not that this is a sexual thing . . . I mean, it's *for* a sexual thing. But not a real sexual thing. Sorry. Nerves. Congratulations, by the way."

"Surely you're not nervous about this?" he asked, swinging his measuring tape around like he might hypnotize me. "You didn't seem so shy during your latest . . . motion picture."

I cleared my throat with a grunt before undoing my pants and fully dropping trou. "That?" I asked with a chuckle. "Nah, I'm not nervous about your little pouch. About leaving my twenty-year-old nephew in charge of my business for a month so I can run away to film a soft-core Christmas movie when I could just be living a mostly quiet life with my family back home? Yeah, I'm nervous about that. Did I mention I'm Jewish?"

"I'd probably be Wiccan if I weren't so lazy. So much work. And do you know what a bundle of sage costs in LA County these days?" Luca sized me up from the waist down, taking in what he'd be working with. "So I guess it wasn't just the angle then," he said.

I grinned. "Nolan warned me about you," I told him, "but you're not nearly as vicious as he said you'd be."

Luca scoffed as he handed me a pouch to try on while he turned his back. "Vicious? I'd be lying if I said I was anything other than flattered."

I scooped my junk into the little pocket of fabric, but it became immediately clear that this one wouldn't do the job. "Do these things come in sizes?" I asked.

"Mind if I take a peek?" Luca asked.

"Go for it."

He spun around and nodded thoughtfully. "We're going to need a bigger boat."

After digging through his magic box of dick pouches, he came up with a few more options and also matched my skin tone to some color swatches.

As I put my pants back on, Luca sucked in a breath before saying, "You were my favorite."

"What?" I asked. Not because I didn't hear him, but because I didn't often hear those words.

"God, this is so unprofessional of me," Luca said as he dug into his Gucci backpack that was either real or a really good fake. He held out a black T-shirt and a silver fabric marker. "Could you maybe sign this for me?"

I held up the shirt and recognized it immediately. "Whoa," I said. "Talk about an artifact. I'd be honored." I took the marker and spread the shirt out on the table. I couldn't remember the last time I'd been asked for my autograph. (Technically, I was asked to sign the shipping manifest when a new pizza oven was delivered to my flagship location three weeks ago, but that didn't count—even if I did at first think I was being asked to sign for INK-related reasons.)

This specific shirt though was from the merch run from our second stadium tour. Across the top in a neon-green font were the words: KALLUM NATION. Beneath that, I stood with my arms crossed and my legs spread in a wide stance. Despite the tough pose, there was a smirk on my face. It was definitely you-can-trust-me-because-I'm-the-fat-funny-one energy. Anytime we had individual merch for INK, like T-shirts with our faces on them, my print run was always lower than Nolan's and Isaac's. But I didn't let it get to me. How could I? I was on top of the world with my two best friends.

After scribbling my signature with the silver marker, I handed it back over. "Nice to know that someone actually bought those," I said.

Luca blushed. "I've got a whole trunk full of Kallum Lieberman merch, I'll have you know. You, former ice-skating princess Emily Albright, and Martha Stewart. My holy celeb trinity."

"Well, bring the whole collection next time," I told him, my chest puffing with a little bit of pride.

Luca's gaze narrowed. "Don't say it unless you mean it."

I chuckled. This guy was intense, but I liked it. "I mean it. See you in Vermont?"

"With bells on," Luca sang.

As I WALKED out of the main offices, I stopped to take a quick picture with the Hope Channel sign. Steph had been on my ass about developing a social media presence beyond pizza. This would make her happy. I whipped up a quick caption about just finishing my first fitting for *Santa, Baby* and hit Share. Since the video leaked, I'd had an influx of followers, and even though I felt like a dinosaur on the internet, I was willing to do whatever Steph said to give this career rebound a real shot. If I was going to piss off my family, I'd better make it worth it.

The Hope Channel sent a car service to take me back to my hotel. When the driver asked if I'd like any music, I told him to turn on whatever he wanted to listen to, so as the Lakers game blared through the speakers—the sound of shoes squeaking on the basketball floor and announcers talking too fast—we sat in the kind of traffic that made me homesick for the much-less-traffic-afflicted KC.

As the sun dipped below the smoggy horizon, the day began to slowly sink in.

Winnie Baker—the same Winnie Baker who made me feel like a fucking animal when I was a teenager—had just admitted to me that she'd never experienced an orgasm. To top it off, I just got fitted for a dick pouch to wear during the steamy Christmas movie we were about to start filming. My business was on the line. My mom and sister were pissed at me. And all I could think about was the shape Winnie's lower lip would make as she shuddered with pleasure—preferably given by me.

Why was I doing this to myself? Even if something somehow happened with Winnie over the next few weeks, it wouldn't last. As much as I hated it, I couldn't deny my romantic history: I wasn't the kind of guy that girls stuck around for. And screwing my way through weddings looking for The One couldn't last forever, but it was a good enough time. Eventually some of those girls would get divorced, and maybe one of them would settle down with me. I'd make an okay second-round pick one day. Babies hated me anyway—especially my niece. If I so much as accidentally looked at her, she'd erupt in bloodcurdling screams, but I could be a stepdad to an awkward tween or something. Twelve-year-olds liked free pizza, right?

When I finally made it back to the hotel, it was dark, and I was on the first flight in the morning back to KC to wrap up just a few more things before disappearing for the better half of a month.

I was exhausted. I needed to sleep.

But all I could think of was Winnie, standing in that hallway, leaning into me. Sitting beside me on our fake sleigh as my hand wrapped around her delicious thigh.

Reaching for my phone, I opened YouTube and typed in a phrase so familiar that my phone autofilled it after the first two letters.

Winnie Baker lip biting compilation.

Yeah, I was fucked.

CHAPTER FIVE

Winnie

*C*hristmas music was playing from the TV as I cuddled a bottle of wine to my chest like a teddy bear and screwed up my courage to move my index finger. I was inside my usual room at the Edelweiss Inn, the plaid-wallpapered establishment that had hosted me for every Hope Channel movie I'd ever made here in Vermont. Hosting that came complete with a welcome basket of my favorite Vermont treats: maple sugar candy, flannel pajamas, and Darn Tough socks. It wasn't something the Hope Channel arranged, just the owner of the Edelweiss Inn, and it was a nice touch, even if the maple sugar candy was mostly already gone.

Filming was set to begin *tomorrow*.

Tomorrow, and I still hadn't done any research yet!

With a sigh, I looked out the window to the flurry-bitten darkness outside. Even though I couldn't see a thing, I already knew what I'd see once the sun came up tomorrow. A clump of forested mountains kissing the sky with a cluster of chimney-topped houses and gas streetlamps nestled below. I used to love coming to Christmas Notch to work; I loved the unfiltered, shameless happiness of a place where it was Christmas all year long. But maybe that hadn't been the only thing I'd loved about it, because I'd always known exactly who I needed to be in Christmas Notch, precisely the role I needed to play. Like I'd told Kallum back in LA, there was something comforting about all the moves being choreographed ahead of time, and Old Winnie's life was nothing if not completely choreographed.

But now the new dance moves were just Be the New Winnie, and I was failing at it, because I didn't know how. It was one thing to sit in my therapist's office and say confidently that purity culture was bad, but it was another thing entirely to be in a sexy movie, publicly (and forever-on-streaming-ly) putting my money where my mouth was.

Or I supposed in this case . . . the other way around?

I looked back to where my finger hovered over the clickpad of my laptop, and then with a strangled groan, I slammed it shut and jumped to my feet and started pacing. I was still cuddling my bottle of wine.

The idea of getting aroused on purpose, of *touching myself*, was so embarrassing, even after a week of thinking about it. But even more embarrassing was faking an orgasm in front of Jack and Kallum and realizing I looked like I'd had a narcoleptic sleep attack right there in the office. We hadn't even really started this movie, and I was already a giant, ridiculous failure, and maybe that meant this new post-Michael, post-people-pleasing version of myself was a failure too—

Ugh. No.

No, I wasn't going to go there. I deserved better than that kind of talk about myself, even if it was from myself, and I was too old to pretend I didn't know the difference between pushing myself and punishing myself.

But I was also too old to pretend I didn't know the difference between giving myself some grace and also maintaining a status quo that had stopped working for me years ago.

That status quo was about to end now, dammit.

I set my shoulders and marched back to the knotty pine desk in the corner of my very plaid, very green-carpeted room. With a determined *plonk*, I set the wine bottle down, dropped into my chair, and woke up my laptop screen.

There, in softly side-lit glory, was Kallum. A single screenshot of Kallum from two years ago, a bowtie hanging loosely around his neck as he stood in front of what was clearly a hotel bed. His hands were at the fly of his tuxedo pants, and his eyes were directly on the camera. I knew that he was looking at the person holding the camera, but it felt like he was looking at me . . . like those dark eyes and parted lips were for me and me alone.

Maybe that was why this tape had blown up when it first leaked. Not because Kallum was postered all over teenage walls a decade ago—but because he made the people watching the video feel like they were in the room with him, shoved backward onto a bed and given his full, avid attention.

Heat curled in my chest and tied itself into a knot. I knew it would be smarter to watch some other video, I knew there was an entire internet of pornography out there that I could choose instead. But I told myself that this would be *double* research, because surely knowing how Kallum had sex would help us during our takes? Surely it would be good for me to know how he acted in bed, what sorts of little touches and sounds he might make when we were filming a love scene?

I mean, really, this was the smartest way to go about this whole sexifying project, and anyone who knew all the facts would agree with me, and it obviously had nothing to do with his big, strong-looking hands or his Scottish log-throwing body. It had nothing to do with the fact I kept wondering what that body would feel like on top of me, his stomach and heavy thighs pressing me into the mattress while he——

Nope. Nothing to do with that. Of course I wasn't having those thoughts about the person who once accidentally ruined my entire life with a single picture!

And so with a deep, determined, and very professional breath, I clicked once, twice, and then a final time.

I was officially the owner of Kallum Lieberman's now-fully-authorized sex tape.

THE FIRST DAY of real work was surprisingly familiar. Yes, we were about to make a movie about Santa getting it on. And yes, the director and screenwriter were new to me—along with a very dramatic costume designer named Luca—but so much else felt the same. Same adorable town, with its snowy town square and twinkling lights, same harried production assistant

Cammy trying to keep an entire movie on schedule. Same routine of wake up, makeup, shiver in the snow while you drink coffee through a straw so you don't mess up your movie-ready lips.

In fact, maybe it was too much the same, even down to staying in the same room. It was screwing with my head, doing something so familiar, and then flipping down to tomorrow's pages and seeing the words *sleigh* and *fingering* on the same line.

After filming two scenes at a small petting zoo outside of Christmas Notch (my character, Holly, was a reindeer conservationist), the late February sun was sinking, and I hadn't seen Kallum around once. I didn't care, of course; he wasn't set to shoot anything today, and it wasn't like I needed his input on scenes where I discussed the benefits of reindeer milk, but it still felt a little lonely to be kicking off this wild, weird movie by myself. Like I was the only one who showed up to a game with my uniform on or something.

Gretchen Young, the director, and Pearl Purkiss, the screenwriter, were dreams to work with, however, and by the time I finished with the day's shoot, I was almost hopeful that I could do this. I could be Holly Jollee, reindeer-saving sexpot and the future Mrs. Claus. All I needed now was to learn what it felt like when I had an orgasm so I could mimic it on-screen.

And I'd been *so close* last night. I mean, if we defined *so close* as actually having bought a pornographic video before deciding it was far too late to watch it and going to bed instead. But I could get closer tonight.

In fact, tonight I was going to go all the way (with myself), and I knew exactly how to make it happen.

After the crew van dropped me off at the Edelweiss Inn, I marched straight to the front desk, where Stella, the simultaneously harried-looking and slow-moving proprietor, stood folding hand towels with bells sewn to the corners.

"Hi, Stella," I said over the jingling of towel bells. "May I change rooms, please?"

Stella paused wrist-deep in faded terry cloth. "Something wrong with yours?" she asked.

Nearly ten years of visiting Christmas Notch had taught me to be careful when it came to Stella, because she was one of those people who loved her business and yet also hated doing her job, so there was a fifty-fifty chance that any request could be met with either uncomfortably intense assistance or outright hostility.

"Nothing's wrong!" I chirped. I could hardly tell her that I was having a mental block trying to masturbate in my room, so I said instead, "I'm just hoping for a change of scenery."

Suddenly, Stella leaned forward, making the towel stack jingle. "Say no more, sweetheart," she said with the air of a confidante. "After my divorce, I couldn't even stay in the same town as my ex. Moved all the way from Winooski. You deserved better than him, I don't care what they said on Facebook about you."

"Thank you?"

She was already turning to the pegboard with the keys on it. I wasn't sure what she was looking for, since the keys had been out of numerical order for at least a decade, but she seized on a key with the flourish of a sommelier selecting the perfect wine and then handed it over.

"Take your time moving things over," she said, going back to her towels now. *Jingle, jingle* went their belled corners as she moved a stack to the side and began on a new one. "We're empty except for Hope Channel staff until spring break next month, so I don't need your room anytime soon."

"Thank you," I said, meaning it this time, and then strode toward the stairs, hoping I didn't have *I'm going to masturbate tonight* written all over my face. Seriously, how did other people do this? Weren't they worried that people could . . . well . . . tell?

Maybe not. Maybe nobody could tell. It wasn't like I believed masturbation was going to poison my ability to love or enjoy sex—a little hard to believe that when I'd never masturbated and had still had a miserable sex life with Michael—but the gulf between *not believing* and *just doing it already* felt so big.

If Addison were here, she'd give me a shot of vodka and tell me to stop pussyfooting around—literally. And I was ready to. Right now.

I went to my old room and gathered my laptop, a bottle of wine, and the Romantic Wishes candle I'd brought from home (strawberry and chocolate scented, $38 on QVC and at wishesof addison.com). And then I left my old room, walked down the end of the hall to the Yule Log suite, and let myself inside.

New room, new me!

Except the minute the door swung all the way open, I was greeted not by a fresh array of cherry-red duvets and candy cane–shaped pillows, but by billows of steam. I stepped forward, my brain still not digesting why my new room was a sauna, and then a very tall shape moved out of the clouds.

I screamed.

The shape screamed too, jumping toward me and turning as if he'd thought I'd screamed because there was someone behind *him*, and then I had the slow, breath-crushing sensation of becoming aware that the shape was Kallum Lieberman, and that Kallum Lieberman was completely, utterly *naked*.

"Oh thank God, there's no one there," Kallum breathed, as if totally unaware of the *actual* terrifying moment going on, which was that he! Was! Naked! "You scared me there, Winnie Baker."

I couldn't seem to speak, couldn't seem to ask why he was here in my new room or ask if all his bath towels had been stolen by a towel gremlin. All I could do was stare.

And stare.

And stare.

Kallum Lieberman looked cute in everyday jeans and a T-shirt. Kallum Lieberman looked sharply handsome in a rumpled tux in his sex tape. But naked?

Naked, Kallum Lieberman looked like he was in the business of hauling people over his shoulder and dragging them off to the nearest bed. Naked, Kallum Lieberman looked like some kind of Viking—and not a Skarsgård-esque Viking, mind you, but like a *real* Viking, that would have plundered a misty shore and then made merry with plenty of meat and mead after. His chest was so broad and his arms were so big, and the rounded curve of his stomach was dusted in dark blond hair, and so were those thighs, and oh my God, there was his—his—

My eyes snapped up to his face, and luckily, he was looking behind me at the open door, as if trying to piece together what was going on, so he didn't notice that I'd just been staring at his junk. That I'd just confirmed for myself that he'd been very, very right about needing a bigger pickle pouch from Luca.

He swiveled his head back to me. There were water droplets clinging to his short beard, dripping down a strong throat to his collarbone.

I swallowed.

"I, um. They were going to move my room." I held up the key, hoping it shored up how weak my voice sounded. "Stella must have mixed up which rooms were empty."

Kallum didn't seem stressed at all that he was naked . . . or that I'd just walked in on him while he was naked, and he grinned. "Bet you got a surprise, huh?"

I rolled my lips inward and looked up at the ceiling. This room was so dang, *dang* hot. From the steam, probably. "Yep. I—um—I guess this one is yours?"

"It is," Kallum confirmed, finally turning back to the bathroom and reaching for a towel. I was staring at those wide shoulders like I was about to be tossed over one, and the thought made me strangely restless. I moved my eyes away from those sea-raider shoulders, and they landed on his backside as he was bending over to get a towel. His butt was rounded, plump, and I hadn't ever thought about a man's backside before, but maybe that was because I hadn't seen Kallum's?

It was squeezable, *bitable*, and I . . . I wanted it. I didn't know what I'd do with it once I had it, but my entire body itched with the need to step forward and—I didn't even know. Lay claim to it, maybe. Grab it and say *Mine, mine, mine*.

Holy heck, one look at Kallum naked and all of a sudden, *I* was the Viking. I wanted to grab him and feel him and make him help me with this new ache deep in my belly, and oh my God, I needed to get back to my room right now. *This* was the feeling I'd been needing to get started; this was what I'd been looking for!

Kallum emerged from his bathroom with his towel around his waist, but I was already going back through the door. "I'm so sorry for walking in on you!" I apologized over my shoulder. "I really am!"

"No worries, Winnie Baker," he said comfortably. "Come back anytime."

I BARELY MADE it back to my old room before I was tearing off my shoes and ponte pants and then crawling onto my bed with my laptop. No time for the wine or the candle right now; I needed to strike while the iron was hot.

I had Kallum's video pulled up faster than I'd ever done anything on a computer before and once I pressed Play, I turned the volume up just enough to hear his voice come over the speakers.

"Are you sure?" Sex Tape Kallum asked the woman filming him from the bed.

They were the first three words of the sex tape, and even though they comprised a question, they didn't sound hesitant or uncertain. Not when his jaw was that tight. Not when his fingers were that deft as he unknotted his bow tie. Instead, the question sounded *hot*. Like it mattered to him that his partner was all in, because he was about to give them the full Kallum treatment.

Sex Tape Kallum left his tuxedo shirt on, but rolled up the sleeves and unbuttoned the top two buttons, and then bent down to make out with the woman on the bed. She was in a bridesmaid's dress, and as they kissed, she turned the phone so the viewers could see Kallum's hands disappearing under the skirt of her dress. So they could see the cords of his forearms flexing as he did something under her skirt to make her whimper.

Breathing hard, I paused the video and reached a hand under the blankets of my bed, thinking of those flexing forearms. I pushed my fingers inside my panties and immediately encountered . . . wetness. Like, so much wetness. Too much? I couldn't remember ever being slick like this. Not that I touched myself very often in the past; only when I'd needed to check my cervical mucus to see if I was ovulating or not.

But it didn't feel bad. It felt good, actually, like my body was telling my brain that it agreed Kallum had great forearms too, and a great butt, and that he'd feel so good on top of me, holding me down, and that the hair on his thighs would feel so good on my skin as his body moved against mine.

With a deep breath, I pushed a finger inside myself.

And then stopped, impaled on my own hand, not sure what to do next.

Should I move it in and out, to mimic intercourse? Should I add more fingers? Surely, this couldn't be that hard. People must like masturbating because it feels like intercourse, and intercourse was a mechanical process I was very familiar with. In and out, in and out, harder and faster was better, et cetera et cetera.

I tried a few different things—I even tried flipping over onto my stomach and grinding against the bed like I sometimes woke up doing—but slowly, the heat in my stomach evaporated and the urgency to *do something* about the churning throb between my legs faded away.

I sat up, shook my hair out of my eyes, and thought for a minute. How could something that teenagers figured out with zero help be beyond a lady in her thirties? Growing up, pastors had made self-pleasure sound like something anyone was at risk of doing at any moment, but I'd just tried valiantly for fifteen minutes to follow in Onan's footsteps and couldn't make a single thing happen.

I flopped back against the pillow, defeat crawling up my spine, with its cousin embarrassment slithering just behind it. Maybe I was broken. Maybe there was a reason my body couldn't do this. Even as a married woman, I'd never crossed the finish line with Michael, and he was objectively hot and with enviable stamina. Even when I'd been eager to get into bed with him, convinced that *this* was the time I'd have great sex and finally reach those promised shores of godly married pleasure, I could never seem to translate that eagerness into, well, satisfaction.

Addison would still be on the QVC set on the West Coast, so I couldn't call her to beg for her help, and even if I could, I had no idea what I'd say.

Help, I don't know how to have sex with myself?

Help, I saw my coworker's forearms in a video, but now I can't get off thinking about them even though I really, really want to?

She'd just tell me to vodka about it anyway. Vodka and—

Inspired, I pulled the laptop back over, and with my left hand, tapped out a question in the search bar. *Google is your fri-e-end* was Addison's singsong rebuke whenever someone asked a stupid question. Well, tonight, Google was going to be more than a friend. It was going to.be my accomplice.

I typed in: *How to masturbate with a vagina?*

The results were more serious and clinical than I would have thought. Articles from well-known magazines interviewing sex therapists, videos from people talking about how to masturbate after illness or surgery, sites that sold sex toys and sex aides.

But I was a simple girl, so after skimming the first page of results, I went back to the first link and clicked it.

It was a wikiHow article, and it had illustrations, and wow, wow, *wow*, there were so many ways a person could get the job done. A rolled-up towel between the legs.

Nipple pinching. Even . . . cucumbers?

But one illustration caught my eye, and after studying it for a moment, I looked past the laptop to the heart-shaped Jacuzzi tub at the far end of the room.

Yeah, I wasn't about to look a Jacuzzi horse in the mouth. Because everything else sounded more like PhD level diddling, but I needed a remedial class. And the idea of sitting in front of something mechanical and letting it do all the work sounded like just the ticket.

I schlepped my laptop and candle over to the table by the tub, lit the candle, and started filling the thing with water. While I waited, I undressed and watched another few minutes of Kallum's video, feeling my body kick back into *do me* zone after watching him kiss his way up the bridesmaid's thigh to where her lace thong met the crease of her thigh.

"Your beard tickles," she whispered as Kallum kissed around the edges of the lace.

"Just wait till you're riding it," he replied and then tucked her thong to the side and kissed her bare flesh until she moaned.

All riled up again, I stepped into the tub, lowered myself into the warm water, and turned on the jets. I eagerly sidled up to one, positioned it right in front of my groin like the wikiHow diagram showed, and waited for the promised orgasm.

Except it was like planting my camel toe in front of one of the big sprayers at the car wash, or maybe one of those things they used to clean old area rugs on TikTok, and I had to curl my hands over the edge of the tub to keep myself from being blown backward by Poseidon's own Jacuzzi jet.

I stayed planted there for several minutes, unsure if it felt great or if I was being hosed off like a bar patio, but the orgasm never . . . came. Although I did feel very clean now.

Maybe it was just *that* jet? Old hurty-squirty over there? Because surely this wouldn't be on wikiHow if it wasn't widely accepted knowledge, and so I should hop back in the Jacuzzi saddle and try again with a different jet?

So I tried another, and then another, and then another, and in all sorts of contorted positions, until I finally gave up and sat back in the water, confused.

This time, however, my lust didn't die off. It stayed burning in my gut, thrumming through my intimate places. It felt almost like having a fever, this need, with shivers and goose bumps and delirium, and even though I was frustrated and disappointed with myself, I was also happy that I could feel this.

Excited that I'd been brave enough to try.

Tonight, I'd done something I never thought I would do, and yes, it didn't work out this time, but maybe I'd nab that elusive orgasm prize tomorrow night. Or the night after. Or the night after that, because I did know this: I wanted to keep trying. And not just for *Santa, Baby*, but for myself too.

CHAPTER SIX

Kallum

"O h, wait, wait," said Nolan in my earbud. "This one is my favorite." He cleared his throat. "'I wish he'd rip me apart like a lobster.' Oh, this one is nice and direct: 'Rail me, Kallum.'"

"It's literally just a photo of me cheesing in front of the Hope Channel sign," I said as I sat waiting in my makeup chair for the PA to walk me to the set. "And I only took it because Steph wanted me to make more content for social media."

"'Murder me, Daddy,'" he reads off. "Whoa. There's lots of daddy kink in these comments. 'Break me like a glowstick, Daddy.'"

"Comes with the dad bod territory," I explained. "I guess #PizzaDaddy has turned into a whole hashtag."

He snorted. "Lots of eggplant emojis. 'Be sure to call your doctor if you've had a Kallum-related boner for longer than four hours.' Or 'I want to use his face as a bicycle seat.' Huh," he said. "Your sister left a comment too."

"Awww, Tammy Cakes. What does it say?"

"'You have shit in your teeth,'" he read.

"Man, did I really?" I open up the Instagram app on my phone and zoom in on the picture. "I had pepper in my teeth that whole time with Winnie? Jack didn't even say anything to me!"

"I've only met Jack Hart once," Nolan said, "but he definitely struck me as the type of guy who would gladly tell you if you had something in your teeth."

I used the reverse camera on my phone to check my teeth now, because I couldn't expect Winnie to be fake turned on by my hipster Santa character if I had continental breakfast remnants in my teeth. "Jack was pretty upset about his ex and a doggy stepdad or something. I don't know. I just really hope he and his ex put Miss Crumpets's well-being first and foremost."

Nolan was silent for a minute, and I could almost see him giving me one of his curious looks. "Yeah, bud," he finally said. "Me too. So, I guess Tamara is still pissed you took the job?"

I let out a heavy sigh. "Yeah, she sent me a long text this morning saying it's not too late to back out. Did I tell you the whole family is going on a Hanukkah cruise this year?"

"Without you?" he asked. "They know you get seasick."

"Exactly!" I said.

"Kallum?" a voice called from the other side of the door. "They're ready for you."

"Gotta run, broski," I told Nolan.

"Get your sexy Santa on," he said. "Tell Winnie I said hi, and that I'm still sorry about the time I accidentally puked in her clutch at the Grammys."

"You're still trying to pretend like that was an accident?" I asked. "How do you accidentally puke in a clutch?"

"Well, it being her clutch was an accident. Not that it would be better if it had been someone—you know what? You have a fucking sexy Santa movie to film, and I have a stack of Bee's pancakes to inhale, so—"

"Bee's pancakes? Is that like a sexual thing or—"

He grunted out a laugh. "Just regular old pancakes . . . this time."

"Kallum?" the voice called again.

"Coming!" I yelled back.

I hung up the phone and stuffed my AirPods back in their case before walking out to meet the production assistant, a short girl not much older than Topher with light bronze skin and freckles.

"Hey, I'm Kallum," I said.

"I'm Cammy."

I held out my fist for her to bump.

She looked at my hand for a minute before knocking knuckles.

"Let's make a fucking movie, Cammy."

FOR MY VERY first day on set, we shot in a red-painted barn, which served as our fake sleigh parking garage. My character, who went by Nick when outside of the North Pole, was sowing his wild oats in an effort to find his very own Mrs. Claus so he could follow in his father's footsteps—or bootprints.

"Kallum!" Gretchen called as she jogged over to meet me. Her long box braids bounced as she came, and she had flurries slowly melting on her long eyelashes and her medium brown cheeks. A nose piercing winked in the light beaming from the tungsten lamps. "I'm so sorry we haven't formally met yet."

"Gretchen," I said. "Come on now. We've met."

She covered her face. "Me licking your face on a dare at some premiere afterparty hardly counts. I was really hoping you'd forgotten about that."

"Are you kidding?" I asked. "I didn't wash my face for days." I thought about that for a minute. "Actually, to be honest, my skin care game didn't really kick it up a notch until we got that Neutrogena deal the next year. I wash my face a lot more now."

"Well, whatever you're doing these days, keep it up."

I held a hand to my cheek. "This is what I call pizza oven heat therapy . . . and big beard energy."

"Which is closely related to his big dick energy," Jack said with a whistle as he breezed past us.

"I don't think that sort of language coming from our intimacy coordinator creates a safe work environment," Gretchen called after him in her best I'm-trying-to-be-chill-but-you-make-me-feel-not-chill voice.

"Morning," Winnie said as she stepped up beside me, her shoulder briefly brushing against my arm.

"Good morning, Winnie Baker," I said, before motioning to my costume. "I wore clothes for you this time."

Winnie's cheeks flushed. "Good job with the clothes. You look great in clothes. Not that you didn't out of—"

"I'm just going to go ahead and stop that sentence before it gets any worse," Gretchen said with a sympathetic smile.

Winnie held a thumb up. "Thank you."

I forced back a laugh. God, I loved watching Winnie squirm. I bit down on my knuckle as that thought blossomed into something much, much more.

"Okay, follow me," Gretchen said. And as we approached the video village where a cluster of director chairs and monitors were set up for producers, a few crew members, and our screenwriter, she added, "This is Pearl, my girlfriend, and the woman behind our script."

Pearl, a pale, willowy woman with lavender hair, stood up from where she'd just finished placing a grid of crystals around her chair. She held her hands to her chest and closed her eyes, like someone told her we were playing charades and her word was *gratitude*. After a moment of silent gratitude, Pearl opened her eyes and approached me, her hands reaching up to brace my biceps. "You're more jolly than I even dreamed you would be."

"Uh, ho, ho, ho?"

Gretchen laughed, and then Pearl. I looked at Winnie, who shrugged as she joined in, so I chuckled along with them.

"The script is great," I said as we all quieted down.

Pearl held her chin. "Is it? I've been toying with the last page . . ."

Gretchen took a half step behind Pearl and opened her eyes as wide as they would go as she slid her hand across her neck and then made a heart with her hands.

"No!" I shouted, slowly putting the pieces together.

Pearl jumped with a delighted, yet alarmed squeal, like she loved for the universe to surprise her.

Gretchen wound her hand in a quick circle, encouraging me to continue.

"I love the last page," Winnie blurted.

"Yes," I said firmly, looking at Winnie as I nodded along with her. "We both do. We were just talking about it last night, how the last page is the best part. It's the shining beacon of the whole script! It's your magnum opus."

Gretchen held a hand up to let me know I could slow my roll a bit.

"Oh," Pearl said, her voice just a little smug. "Well, if you insist."

"Are we making some fake sex or what?" Jack called from the other side of the barn where my glossy red sleigh was parked.

I turned to Winnie as we walked to the admittedly amazing sleigh. "Did you do your research, Baker?"

She bit down on that plump bottom lip of hers. "I guess I can't use the dog ate my homework excuse for this one, huh?"

I wanted to ask more questions—like a lot more—but we were already at the gilded steps leading up into the sleigh and Winnie was being helped in by Jack.

Once we were both seated, Jack stood on one side of us and Gretchen on the other.

"All right, you two," Jack said, "this shoot is a three-week quickie, and we've got lots of ground to cover, but if either of you feel like you need a time-out, we will slow this whole machine to a grinding halt."

Gretchen cleared her throat. "'It's no trouble' is what I think Jack meant. So yes, we have a chaotic schedule and time is money, but not at the expense of your comfort with the more intimate scenes."

"Right, right, right," Jack said. "So we're going to take it from the top. You two just met up at the Tipsy Antler after finding each other on the hookup app Jingle Bells. Kallum, you swiped on Winnie after having a sweet little love-at-first-sight moment in the town square. Winnie, you've exhausted all your options in this tiny little town and even your rescued reindeer are getting their own happily ever afters. Plus you're both, like, horny as fuck." He turns to Gretchen. "Did I miss anything?"

She nodded once. "'Horny as fuck' just about covers it."

"Horny AF," Winnie whispered. "Got it."

"We'll be talking you through it as we go," Gretchen reassured Winnie. "The sexy bits will have music going over it, so we'll be able to coach you out loud."

Gretchen and Jack then retreated to their posts and it was just me and Winnie. The intimate scenes had a pretty bare-bones crew, so it was a little too easy for my brain to think that it really was only the two of us.

"Quiet on set!" someone called.

A short guy with a ponytail stepped out in front of the camera with the clapboard.

"Whenever you're ready," Gretchen called as the guy moved back behind the camera.

Winnie inhaled deeply and then let it all out as she sat up and pushed her chest out, transforming into the perky and earnest reindeer conservationist she was meant to play. "You're not from around here," she said.

I stretched my arm out behind her like we'd rehearsed. "Do I stand out that much in Cypress Valley?"

Winnie giggled. "You'd stand out anywhere." She turned to me and our lips were close enough to touch.

"I've spent my whole life on the nice list," I tell her. "But you make me want to do very naughty things."

"Show me," she said in a breathy voice. "I'm a visual learner."

That was my cue! Operation Horny AF was a go. I curved the arm I'd slung over her shoulders so that my hand could cradle the back of her head as we pressed our mouths together. It took every ounce of brain power to remind my body that this was a job and that we were just two posable dolls breathing into each other's mouths. Without tongue. Definitely without tongue.

This part seemed to come easily to Winnie; she'd done plenty of stage kisses before.

I rested my hand on her bare thigh without letting my full weight bear down on her. She was soft and warm, and I wanted so badly to let my fingers really get a grip. My cock pressed against the zipper of my jeans, and I was so, so thankful we were sitting.

She let out a dramatic moan, and even though I knew it was fake, blood began to pulse in my ears.

"Good," Jack said, his voice not even tearing me away for a moment as Winnie and I drew back from one another and I smoldered harder than I've ever smoldered before.

"Nice, Kallum," Gretchen said. "Winnie, a little less sleepy and more doe-eyed."

At Gretchen's note, Winnie opened her eyes so wide that it looked like she'd just seen a dead reindeer.

Um. Okay.

No one said anything else, so I let my hand travel up her thigh and into her short little skirt where my fingers kept a safe enough distance while my arm made pumping motions.

Winnie's head rolled back and she made a guttural noise like she'd been possessed.

No one told me to stop, so I continued on through Winnie's exorcism. She was supposed to do her research, but I guessed getting in touch with your own sexuality was a lot to bite off in just one week.

Still, I couldn't help but be absolutely enamored with her possessed orgasm, which was perhaps one of the cutest things I'd ever seen. It was the kind of funny thing that made me feel like we were two teenagers in a basement goofing off.

After a few minutes, she threw an arm against her forehead and slumped against the sled like she'd just powerlifted double her weight.

"Cut!" Gretchen called.

"The power of Christ compels you!" some tall, old dude at the props table said with a chuckle.

Gretchen whirled around on him. "Off my set! Now."

Winnie's brow furrowed as she looked up to me. "Am I supposed to know what that means?"

"It's from *The Exorcist*," Pearl said in an airy voice as she joined us.

"Personally, my favorite line is 'Your mother sucks cocks in hell,'" Jack said as he approached the sled.

Winnie's chest began to rise and fall in quick succession. "I—I looked like I was possessed?"

Seeing her upset like this set my whole body on edge, and I'd do just about anything to make her feel better. Truly, I would have ripped a phonebook in half and then torn through a mansion's worth of drywall for this girl.

"By lust," Gretchen quickly added. "Possessed by lust. And it's so important that we get your version of these scenes at all different levels, so that was good. Really good. We started off big, so now we can take it down a notch."

"It was great," I told her. "Very believable. That guy was just some old fart. He didn't mean anything by it."

She looked from me to Jack to Gretchen, her eyes brimming with tears. "I think I need a minute," she said as she stepped over me and out of the sleigh. And then ran out of the barn.

I stood up immediately to go after her, but Pearl held up a hand. "Let me handle this one."

With a nod, I sunk back down. I didn't have any more right to go talk to her than Pearl did. And maybe she'd feel less awkward with another woman.

Still, she was upset and I wanted to fix it.

Gretchen patted my shoulder. "Pearl is good with, uh, feelings."

"Can't fake an orgasm if you've never had one," Jack said beneath his breath.

"Do you really . . . ?" Gretchen paused. "Actually, if I were sentenced to sleep with Michael Bacher for the rest of my life, I don't think I'd be able to finish either."

Pearl nodded astutely and mumbled something about "yoni powers" as she followed after Winnie.

Jack reached over and pinched my cheek. "Such a teddy bear," he said before walking off.

"Maybe we can circle back to this scene later this week," Gretchen said mostly to herself. "The Hope Channel owns the barn, so we can pop in and out thankfully."

I sat there in the sled, waiting for my next instructions as the crew members began to reset the scene should Winnie reappear.

I felt bad for Winnie. I wanted to fix it. I wanted to make it better. I wanted to make her laugh.

But I was also really fucking angry at Michael Bacher. What kind of guy has the honor of marrying Winnie Baker and doesn't even take the time to learn how to pleasure her? If I ever had someone like Winnie, I'd memorize their body from head to toe. I'd learn every little thing that made them gasp and plead.

Fuck. If Winnie Baker were mine, I'd have a goddamn PhD in making her come.

Paging Dr. Lieberman.

CHAPTER SEVEN

Winnie

An hour later, I was standing next to Pearl Purkiss inside a cramped building off the state highway called the Toy Shop 2. Above a display of dusty condom boxes, an equally dusty TV played a video of a lady demonstrating the stretchiness of a silicone penis ring. The painted cinderblock walls were lined with see-through clothes and shelves of sun-faded boxes; a magazine rack against the wall nearest to the door was a study in glossy overstimulation: a flesh-toned collage that reminded me of cold cuts at a grocery store.

Heart pounding, I kept moving into the sex shop, trying to act cool, so cool, like this was stuff I saw every day, like *Tentacle-shaped butt plugs, no big deal, am I right?*

Pearl, on the other hand, squealed at every other thing she came across.

"Oh, a *dragon* dildo, Winnie! Do you think they make dragon penis sleeves too?" Another squeal. "And look, look, look, it's *an actual Vajankle.* I thought those were a myth!"

She pulled me in front of the Vajankle, which was not a myth—and was exactly what the name made it sound like—and then the realization hit me like va-sledgehammer.

I was in way over my head. Like *waaay* over.

I thought watching a sex tape was hard-core? I'd had no idea how deep the well of human sexuality ran! And I wasn't a well at all, I was just a puddle . . . a half dried–up puddle with a slick of gasoline shimmering over the top, that's how not a well I was.

"He-e-ey," Pearl said, coming to stand in front of me, her already large eyes getting even larger. "Your aura has just gone really murky."

"It has?"

Pearl nodded at me, like a wise and concerned aura doctor, and gently touched my face. "And I don't have any obsidian or selenite with me, so I need you to push through this, sweet Winnie."

Push through this? Push through being a living punch line after years of being a living headline?

"I don't think I can, Pearl," I confessed. "I mean, not the aura thing, I guess. But pushing through my, um, intimacy problems." I pressed my hands to my face, trying not to think of everyone's reactions to my god-awful performance today. "I'm so embarrassed."

"Wait. Wait." Pearl's hands came around my wrists, frigid but soothing. "Why are you embarrassed?"

"Because I—" I stopped. Swallowed. Looked around the store for any employees and didn't see any. "Because it's embarrassing to be thirty-two and not know what my body does when I have an orgasm, you know? It's embarrassing to feel like I'm the only one who's behind, who's not in on some secret that I really, really want to be in on, but I just don't know how to be. Ugh, it's even embarrassing to be embarrassed!"

"You stop it right now," Pearl said, with more firmness than I would have thought her capable of. "Everyone—and I mean *everyone*—who likes having sex is still learning new things about how they like to have sex. For example, I was today years old when I learned I wanted a dragon dildo, even if it's made of"—she made a face—"silicone."

"Is silicone bad?"

"Glass is best. Rose quartz too. I have this quartz egg—" She stopped herself. "My point is, there's no age when people stop learning about their bodies. Maybe you got a later start than some, but you're still in the same wonderful race."

"That's really kind of you to say," I said politely as I cast my eyes down. My view of the red-and-white linoleum floor was framed by her arms and her torso; she wore a clear raincoat over two layers of sweaters. "But this is more than a late start. This might be *too late*."

"Uh-uh," Pearl said, voice still firm. "There's no such thing as too late for something you want. And I'm guessing there is a reason you don't know as much as you want to know, right?"

A *reason*? Singular? I could almost laugh if I weren't so embarrassed. I could tell her about my teenage bookshelf full of books like *I Kissed Dating Goodbye* and *And the Bride Wore White* (if the memory of that bookshelf alone didn't make me smash my face against the Toy Shop 2's linoleum first). I could tell her about my accountability journal, about my purity ring engraved with the words *True Love Waits*. About the uncountable times I'd heard the phrase *stumbling block*, as in: *Don't be a stumbling block to your brothers.*

As in: *You don't want your brothers to sin because of you, right?*

"Like your ex-husband," Pearl went on, bringing me back to the here and now, standing in front of a Vajankle. "How long were you with him?"

"Fifteen years," I replied automatically. We'd met filming a movie called *Treasures in Heaven* when I was seventeen and had gotten married on my eighteenth birthday. "Fourteen of them married," I added.

Pearl dropped her hands from my face and did a wide-eyed nod, like she was asking me to connect the dots.

Which I did.

"I know, I know," I groaned—quietly, still conscious that an employee must have been milling around somewhere. "I guess it's no surprise he wound up cheating on me."

Cheating with a limber twenty-something named Olivia who—according to her social media bios—was a "seeker looking for her next adventure."

A next adventure she'd apparently found inside Michael's designer briefs.

"That is not your fault, so don't allow that negativity inside your headspace. *He* sounds like he vibrates at a very low frequency," Pearl added disapprovingly. And then her face brightened. And brightened some more. She reminded me of a lavender-haired Grinch whose heart was currently growing three sizes. "That's it, Winnie! I can't believe I didn't think of it before!"

"Think of what?" I asked, confused.

"*Vibrating,*" she said with the tones of a sex shop prophet, and then grabbed my arm and dragged me to a set of shelves framed with tinsel and wound with Christmas lights. Every single product on the display was holiday-themed, from the white fur handcuffs to the butt plug with a bell on the end. Pearl grabbed a box with the triumph of someone grabbing the last dress at a sample sale and then pushed it into my hands.

The Peppermint Stick, the box read. It showed a cylinder that looked like a big candy cane, with a tapered end and a sticker that said the charging cord was included.

"And this just in case," Pearl added, placing a small bottle of peppermint-flavored lube next to the box.

The vibrator looked so small, compared to a Jacuzzi at least. "Do you think this will help?" I asked, wanting to hope but also remembering how wikiHow had betrayed me last night.

Pearl did a shuffle thing with her feet, and I realized she was dancing. "*Help?* You'll be riding that Peppermint Stick into the sunset! Until the battery is dead, at least. One time, I composed an entire series of erotic villanelles while straddling a vibrator," she confided, now looping her arm through mine and shuffling me toward the cash register, where a pierced college student had appeared out of nowhere. "It won me my first-ever poetry grant. Vibration is good for the arts."

I HAVE TO PEE.

I was lying on my new bed in the Edelweiss Inn—I'd finally moved into a different (and non-Kallum-occupied) room earlier today—with the Peppermint Stick buzzing between my legs. I'd let the vibrator charge while I showered, changed, and had a check-in call with Gretchen where I assured her I'd be back in the proverbial sleigh tomorrow. And then I'd cracked open my laptop and watched more of Kallum expertly working this bridesmaid into a frenzy. Big hands on her breasts. Long fingers working into the slick opening of her sex.

I had a crush on the man's hands.

Like a hand perv.

It was the image of his fingers pushing into the unnamed bridesmaid that led me to finally reach for my mostly charged vibrator, turning it on the lowest possible setting and carefully touching the tip to my left flap. Like I was expecting it to shock me like a car battery when it made contact.

When it didn't, I gradually moved it to my vagina and slowly inserted it inside. I was already slippery from watching Kallum on my laptop screen, and the toy wasn't very thick, certainly not as thick as two of Kallum's fingers would be together . . .

I had to stop it with the hand thing. It was bad enough watching a coworker's sex tape, even if he'd officially licensed it, but I felt confident I could mentally compartmentalize the sex tape from real life. After all, it's not like I was going to see him in a rumpled tuxedo going down on a bridesmaid while we were together in Vermont.

But I would see his hands literally all the time. I would *feel* them, during takes, during intimacy coordination meetings, and every time I thought about it, his hands on me, my heart kicked in my chest, like it was jumping to send more blood *everywhere*.

Funnily enough, moving the vibrator in and out didn't do much for me, but when I held the toy inside and pressed it against my front walls, pleasure ran through me like a train, making my toes curl. I did it again and turned up the speed of the vibrator—accidentally turning it up fast enough to make me squeak—until I found a speed that felt good. Like really good. Really, really good.

Except . . .

Except it was kind of hovering at *Really Good* and not jumping to, say, *Holy Shit*. Or *Oh My God, I'm Going to Scream*.

In fact, it also sort of felt like I needed to pee. Was that a normal feeling? Should I just push through it like it was a long road trip and I wanted to make it a few more exits before I stopped at a gas station Subway? Should I take five and then circle back with a fresh outlook and an empty bladder?

Rap, rap.

A knock at the door made me freeze where I was, bathrobe gaping open and legs bent like a frog's. The *bzzzz* between my legs suddenly seemed unnaturally loud, and oh my God, what if the person on the other side of the door could hear it? What if they knew???

I tried to turn the toy off—succeeded only in hitting a jet engine speed that made my teeth chatter—and then finally pulled it out and managed to fumble with the button enough that it stopped humming.

Rap. "Hey, uh, Winnie?" came a deep Grammy-nominated voice. "It's me, Kallum."

I was on my feet before I even knew what I was doing, striding toward the door as I tugged my robe back around my body and belted it. Just before I flipped open the security lock, I became aware of the Peppermint Stick still in my hand.

Oh God, oh God, oh God—

I hurriedly wiped the toy on the hem of my robe and then dropped it in my pocket. I flung open the door and tried to look cool and collected.

Kallum blinked, probably not expecting me to be in a bathrobe with mussed hair at six in the evening. Did I look like I'd just been masturbating? Could he guess?

"Hi," I said in my most normal voice. I was an actress! I could do this! "What's up?"

I must not have sounded as casually non-horny as I thought I did, because Kallum swallowed. In a *way*. A way that made me aware of how wet between the legs I was.

"I wanted to make sure you were doing okay after today," he said. He flicked his eyes down to my robe. "But I didn't mean to intrude, I just wanted to . . ."

He trailed off, his gaze still trained on my robe. No, on the *pocket* of my robe; the not-deep-enough pocket where half a candy cane–striped vibrator was clearly visible. And then his eyes slid past me to the bed, where there was a Winnie-size dent in the duvet. Where my laptop rested, currently paused on a frame of Kallum three fingers deep in a bridesmaid.

I couldn't breathe. My thoughts were nothing but thought-flurries—tiny, fluttering, elusive. Disappearing before I could catch them, look at them.

Kallum's hands flexed by his sides, and then curled, his fingers rubbing restlessly against his palms before they flexed again.

And then he met my eyes, and his were such a bright and burning blue that I felt like I was standing inside the heart of a flame, and his jaw was so tense, and his chest was heaving, and I had an absurd idea, a horrible idea, an idea that I should never, ever speak aloud.

"Will you help me?" I blurted.

The door was still open behind him, and he checked the hallway before looking back to me. His Slice, Slice, Baby staff T-shirt clung even tighter to those massive shoulders as he did.

"What are you asking me, Winnie Baker?" he asked in a low voice. A low voice that I recognized from the sex tape. Under my robe, my breasts were heavy-feeling, full. I had goose bumps everywhere.

"I want you to help me have an orgasm," I said, trying to sound confident and unconcerned, like this was all just everyday stuff for me, like this was just work. Same thing as needing help running my lines, right? Totally the same.

"Research not going well?" asked Kallum. There wasn't any judgment in his tone, only a little bit of ruefulness, like he was rueful *for* me. Like he wanted it to be going well for me.

"It's not," I said sadly. "And I tried a Jacuzzi jet and everything."

"I . . . What?"

"And you're supposed to be good at making people orgasm, and that's all I want, just one orgasm, just so I can know what it feels like once in my life, you know? Yes, that's your video over there, and I know it's maybe weird that I'm watching it, but I didn't even know where to start with regular porn, and I *know* you, and it felt safe to me, and the way you make her feel so good—"

The door slammed shut and Kallum was striding forward, making me walk backward to the swivel chair in front of the knotty pine desk. His hands, warm even through my thick robe, curled around my shoulders and he pushed me down onto the seat.

He stayed standing, and more than ever, I understood the word *loom.* He was looming over me, but it was incredible, thrilling, to have all that height and strength and intensity bent on me.

"Show me," he said. His voice was still low, but it was rough now too, like the words were being dragged from his chest. "Show me."

This was a terrible plan, a reckless thing, and yet I could not care when Kallum sounded like that, when his big hands and broad shoulders were right here, when his eyes were no longer fire-bright but glowing like stars.

Slowly, I reached for the vibrator in my pocket and pulled it free. It didn't feel like a silly novelty toy now, not with the way Kallum was watching it, not with the way he worked his jaw to the side as I clicked it on.

A *bzzz* filled the room and I spread my thighs in the chair, knowing he'd be able to see the center of me, wet and swollen and wanting.

His voice was rougher than ever when he spoke. "Open your robe."

My free hand trembled a little as I plucked at the terry cloth knot—because I needed it, I needed to undress, and I couldn't remember ever feeling that way, not even in my marriage. Like anything between my skin and a person's stare was too much, and I would die if this person couldn't see my body right this instant.

Seeing my struggle, Kallum knelt with a finessed ease that reminded me that he had been an incredible dancer once upon a time, and lifted his hands.

"Okay?" he asked. His hands were poised in the air, ready for permission.

"Okay," I whispered, and he easily unknotted the belt for me. "You can touch me," I added, in case my request for help earlier was being misunderstood. "I want you . . . I want you to touch me anywhere you think will help. Everywhere."

He met my gaze. "If I do something you don't like, tell me."

"Okay," I agreed, caught in his stare. "I'll tell you."

His hands moved from the belt to the edges of the robe, which he parted—not cautiously, but deliberately. Like he wanted to remember every single second of his uncovering me. Like unwrapping me as a present was just as fun as playing with me later. The robe fell all the way open and hung from my shoulders, revealing my naked breasts, my soft stomach, the private place between my legs.

Kallum did that swallowing thing again, the ball of his Adam's apple moving up and then back down.

"Now," he said. "Show me."

I took the gently buzzing vibrator and positioned the tip of it at my seam, pressing in until I found my opening and then sliding the toy inside. I had to sit on the edge of the chair to do it, but Kallum didn't seem to mind. His eyes were on where I slowly penetrated myself with the vibrator, over and over again, his hands braced on his thighs. His fingertips were digging into the denim there, but otherwise he didn't move, didn't react to what I was doing.

"This is what I was trying," I explained. "And it feels good, but I can't seem to get past it feeling good to something better."

Kallum lifted a hand, and I instinctively arched a little, thinking he might touch me between the legs, that he might touch my breasts or stomach. But instead he ghosted his fingers over the top of my thigh.

"You're a little tense," he murmured. "Good tense or bad tense?"

I didn't know. Maybe mostly good tense, but also . . .

"You're the only one who's seen me naked aside from Michael," I explained. "I guess that feels strange." And my body had changed since I was married too, although I sensed Kallum wouldn't care about that.

Kallum straightened, and before I could ask him what he was doing, he was reaching behind his head and yanking off his shirt. He threw it casually to the side, an act that was weirdly sexy in its unconscious arrogance, and then turned back to face me.

"Now you're not the only one half undressed," he teased, but I couldn't laugh, not when the sight of him without a shirt was like finding myself suddenly in midair, with nothing underneath me. Because yes, I'd seen him last night without a shirt, but now he was *so close*, and now I could look at him without feeling like I needed to tear my eyes away, and I could see the bunched points of his nipples, the way the hair on his stomach thickened in a line under his navel. It felt so primal for him to have hair on his stomach, and I never would have thought I'd be into that after being with hyper-groomed Michael for so many years, but I wanted to run my fingers through it, I wanted to feel it pressed against my belly.

"Back to this pretty pussy," he said, and his words made me squirm. He talked like that in his sex tape too, words like *pussy* and *dick* and *fuck*, and I loved the way they sounded when he said them. Not rude or tawdry, but thrilling. Fun.

His hand found mine, and he pulled, guiding the vibrator out. I tried to let go, thinking he was going to hold the toy for me, and he shook his head. "You're going to play a game," he said. "The game is Find Where This Feels Good, and the only rule is that you can't put the toy anywhere inside your body. Only on the outside."

That seemed awfully limiting, but I was too hypnotized by the fingers curled around my hand to argue. "And what will you be doing?" I asked.

He used his free hand to tuck my hair behind my ear. Heat crackled through me.

"I'll be playing my own game," he answered. His smile was wicked. And then slowly, with plenty of time for me to tell him I didn't like it, he pushed his thumb toward my center. My *pussy*. And then it breached me, sliding in as far as he could push it.

I leaned back in the chair, breathing hard, and moved my hips a little, needing something. Needing more.

"Winnie Baker," he said seriously. "You have to play your game too."

Oh right. Vibrator. Places on the outside of my body.

Unsure where to start, I moved the vibrator up my stomach to the underside of my breast, and then circled the areola there, quivering when the tip of the still-wet toy brushed over my nipple. Kallum made a strangled noise as I moved the vibrator away and there was a smear of my own arousal left behind, and then he moved forward. Again, slowly enough for me to stop him.

He licked my nipple, as if to lick the taste of me off my skin. He groaned again and pulled the tip of my breast into his mouth, sucking hard. It was wet and hot and soft and ticklish, and I was moaning, because that along with his touch inside me was *amazing*.

He pulled away with a sharp breath, like a starving man flinging himself away from a banquet. "Keep playing your game," he rasped. He removed his thumb and sucked it clean, and then pushed one of those big fingers inside me. My toes curled.

"Winnie," he said. "You have work to do."

So I pressed the toy to my other nipple as Kallum searched and stroked inside me, his sharp gaze not missing a single squirm or shift in my seat. And the vibrator felt really good on my nipple, but I wanted to keep exploring, so I dropped it to my sex, running it around as much of it as I could reach around Kallum's hand.

And then it grazed my clitoris.

"Oh shit," I gasped, and Kallum gave a low laugh.

"Yeah," he said. "Oh shit. Want to do it again?"

"Hell yes," I said, Addison's bad influence showing through in my choice of words, and he laughed again. I felt that laugh in my stomach, in my lungs. It rolled through me like thunder.

I pressed it back to my clit. "That feels so good," I whispered, looking at him, and I didn't think I'd ever seen his face look so tormented, even in the angsty music videos for his INK ballads.

"I know, baby," he said. "I know."

Why had I bothered doing anything else with this? Having the vibrator here was *fucking incredible*, and I couldn't sit still, it felt so good. I was arching and moving and Kallum watched my face as he added a second finger.

"Fuck," I managed, and he gave me a devasting smile.

"That word sounds good coming from you, Winnie Baker. Why don't you try turning the toy up?"

That was an amazing idea, and I immediately obeyed, the toy going from *bzzz* to *BZZZZZ*, and then my body practically arched right out of the chair. "Holy *shit*," I cried. "Holy shit!"

Pleasure skated up my ribs to my breasts and throat; my thighs quivered; my pussy was the center of my entire world. Kallum's fingers filling and pushing—not thrusting and jabbing like Michael used to—and the vibrations . . . the *vibrations*!

"I want to do something dirty with you," Kallum said, and I stared at him through a haze of vibrator-induced fever. His eyes were hooded and his chest was flushed under the gold fleece of his hair. "Can I?"

There was something dirtier than this? Dirtier than riding my costar's hand while using a sex toy?

"Yes," I breathed. "I want it. I want it." I wanted every filthy thing. I wanted it done to me, and I wanted to do it to him. I wanted to go as far as our imaginations could take us. Even further.

"Keep using your toy," he rumbled, and then used the two fingers currently fucking me to paint a line of slickness down to my—

"Kallum!" I squeaked as his fingertips grazed against a spot that . . . well, let's just say it was a spot that had never been *grazed* before.

He looked up at me, his fingers going still, but not moving away. "I think this will feel good," he said. "I think you might like it. But this is just for you, Winnie Baker. We don't have to do anything you don't want to."

"No, I do," I said quickly.

I wanted to try everything. I didn't want sex fenced in by my old ideas of *should* or *should not*. I knew where that got me: not having had a single waking orgasm by the age of thirty-two.

"Or I want to try it, at least. If I don't like it, then we can stop, right?"

"Of course," said Kallum. "And I'll go slow. Promise."

"Okay," I whispered.

He pressed his first two fingers back where they were before, and at the same time, he pressed his pinkie finger down below, and then he leisurely, *tantalizingly*, began pushing in. A bare millimeter at a time, it felt like, and it was so wrong, so taboo, to have someone touching me there, but it felt so good too, a twisted little secret that my body had been keeping from me, that there could be pleasure in a place that definitely had nothing to do with making babies.

And then all three of his fingers were fully inside me, working in and out in slow, yummy drives, all while I kept the toy against the swollen bud of my clitoris. I looked down and saw the picture it made: my thighs framing the view of his broad chest and rounded belly, of one hand planted on my thigh and the other hand fucking me, stretching me. Filling me in two different places. His fingers shined every time he dragged them out; there was a slight tremble to the hand on my leg, as if some powerful need was running through him.

I hoped so. I hoped this was affecting him too, because it was well beyond affecting me. I was currently on the edge of the chair, trying to meet his fingers with my hips, trying to screw myself onto his hand.

"What does it feel like?" he whispered, and I was panting so hard I could barely answer.

"Full," I eked out. Each time he stroked in and out of *that* place, I could feel it everywhere. My chest. My throat. "It's like the feeling of having the wind knocked out of you, but it doesn't hurt. I never want it to stop."

"Mmm," he said and bent forward to suck on my nipple again. I didn't know what noises I was making, what I was babbling, but I knew that everything inside of me felt wonderful and strange. I felt like I was at the edge of something massive, and I was abruptly terrified of falling. Like it would be too much, somehow, like I wouldn't survive it.

And then Kallum did something with his hand, some deep curl of his finger in that untouched part of me, and it was no longer a choice. With a low, ragged moan, I fell over the edge, a moment of breathless agony followed by an explosion of pleasure, pleasure that kept growing and growing, until there was nothing but the hard, hot pulse of my core—my sex and my anus—clenching around Kallum's expert hand. Until there was nothing but the surges of bliss so intense that I couldn't think, couldn't *be*, all I could do was mindlessly move my hips for more, more, more.

And it lasted forever, for my entire life, or for at least the last decade or so that I should have been feeling this, and when I could finally drag in a real breath again, my lips were tingling and I felt dizzy, dizzy, dizzy.

I blinked Kallum's face back into focus. Hooded blue eyes, tight jaw. He was looking at me like he wanted to eat me alive.

I had just enough strength to pull the vibrator away from my crotch and turn it off. It dangled limply from my hand as Kallum and I looked at each other. His fingers were still inside me, and I was so sensitive that I felt every inch of them. I wanted them to stay where they were.

I bit my lip, and Kallum's face changed. If he'd looked hungry before, then he looked *anguished* now.

"You're the only person who's ever seen me come," I said, not knowing why I needed to say it. "You probably guessed that since I told you about all this back in LA, but just in case you didn't know."

"Yeah, Winnie Baker," he said hoarsely. "I know."

Our gazes were still locked, and I abruptly remembered this was supposed to be research, this was for the movie. "How did

I look?" I asked. "When I came?" Maybe Kallum would be able to give me detailed notes for our next love scene.

But Kallum just responded with, "Beautiful. You looked beautiful."

And then he looked down, past where his fingers were still wedged in my vagina, to his lap. And then he pulled his hand free and leapt to his feet.

"I, uh— I gotta go."

"What? Why?"

He leaned down and kissed my forehead. "You're perfect," he said, and then he straightened and left the room at a very brisk powerwalk.

But not so brisk that I didn't see the giant erection currently straining his jeans.

After the door closed, I wondered if I should have offered to help him get off. If there was some sort of etiquette to this situation that I'd breached. But I was still so buzzy and floaty and *smiley* . . . I couldn't stop smiling! I wanted to laugh. I'd grown up thinking that sex outside of marriage was something that would stain me and haunt me. But it turned out that getting off with a sex toy and a thick finger in my ass made me feel lighter and cleaner than I'd felt in years.

Still smiling to myself, and humming one of Addison's top-ten hits, I got up from the chair, scooped up the shirt that Kallum left behind in his haste to leave the room, and carried it to bed. I meant to fold it and leave it on the end table, but somehow I ended up falling asleep with it crushed against my face. It smelled like warm bread and soap, like Kallum. And when I dreamed, I dreamed of him.

CHAPTER EIGHT

Kallum

I slept like a fucking baby last night.

And I wondered if I should feel guilty about that, but kneeling there in front of Winnie Baker with her legs spread for me, knowing that I was the first and only person to have ever seen her come . . . And it was because *I* helped her . . .

I raced out of there the moment my brain caught up to what I'd just done. Mostly because if someone had dick tapped me, they'd have broken their hand.

My hotel door slammed shut behind me and I was unzipping my jeans and reaching for my erection. I sunk to my knees and it only took a few quick jerks before the warm release hit my hand.

She was so perfect and cute and ferociously sexy in ways she didn't even know. The moment my pinkie had pressed against her pretty little asshole and she'd let go of every inhibition would be painted inside my skull for the rest of my life.

So yeah, I slept hard. And dreamed of Winnie. I dreamed of all the things I wanted to do to her and even of the things I wanted her to do with me. And I dreamed I was the kind of guy who could take Winnie Baker on a date. I dreamed that she had a toothbrush at my house or her own drawer in my bedroom full of sweatpants and sports bras and the kind of underwear I could tear in two.

When I finally did roll out of bed for my nine A.M. call time, I already had a missed FaceTime from my sister. I shot off a quick text in response.

> **Me:** Just woke up. Call you back during one of my breaks.

After a quick shower, I reached for a fresh pair of jeans and faded Royals T-shirt from my suitcase. My phone rang again as I slipped on the wool hipster sneakers Tamara had gotten me for my birthday, which Topher referred to as my sheep-fucker shoes.

I swiped to answer. "Hey there—"

Tamara's face filled my screen, and she was flustered with a panicked expression I knew well.

"What happened?" I asked. "Is Toph okay? What about Mom and Dad?"

"Everyone is fine," she mercifully admitted as her nostrils flared. "Well, almost everyone."

"Is it Tucker?" I asked, wondering if the Vasectomy King of Kansas City had done something to set my sister off. "Did he . . . cheat?" I whispered.

"Kallum Lieberman, you should be one to talk. My husband would never. You on the other hand . . . you . . . you . . . HOME-WRECKER!"

My jaw dropped as I sprung to my feet, meeting my sister's energy. "What are you talking about? I don't even have a home to wreck!"

"You fuckface!"

I swear to God, if ever a woman could smack someone on the side of the head through FaceTime, it was my sister.

"And! That's not even what *homewrecker* means!"

"Oh." I swiped away from the screen for a moment and Googled *homewrecker definition*.

"Did you pause the camera?" she asked through the little phone speaker. "How dare you? How dare you not show me your face, you coward? What are you even doing? What is more important than you absolutely demolishing someone's personal life with that stupid dick of yours?"

"Calm your tits, Tammy Cakes! I'm looking up the definition of *homewrecker* so I can know what the hell you're talking about." And there it was, at the top of the search results page:

home·wreck·er

/ˈhōmˌrekər/

noun

DEROGATORY • INFORMAL

a person who is blamed for the breakup of a marriage or family, especially due to having engaged in an affair with one member of a couple.

"she was accused of being a homewrecker"

"Oh. *Ohhh*. But . . ." I swiped back over to the call so Tamara could see my face. "Not that it's any of your business who I sleep with, but just to be clear: I've literally never slept with a married person."

"It is my business when it involves one of my oldest friends," she spat back.

"Tam, what are you even talking about?"

"Payton," she said. "You hooked up with Payton. She got engaged—"

"That's great!" I said, and I really meant it. Being her stepping-stone was an easier pill to swallow when I'd just had the best night of my life. "Tell her I said congratulations. Who's the lucky guy?"

"His name is Adan, and he was her boyfriend of seven years."

I blinked once. And then again. "Is that in human years or dog years?"

"That wouldn't make it any better!" she said. "How are we even related?"

"Well, Mom and Dad fell in love and prayed for a son, but then they had you and knew they had to try again."

She shook her head and I could see her deciding that my dumbass response wasn't worth entertaining. "Adan proposed after coming back from a two-month-long business trip in South Korea, and he surprised her with a huge party afterward. She cried the moment she saw all of us waiting for her there in the private room at the Jack Stack downtown—"

"God, I love that place."

"I know, right. Did you know they can do kosher events?" she said before morphing back into her Mighty, Mighty, Angry

Sister Power Ranger mode. "So she's crying and she can't stop, so finally Adan is like, 'Baby, what's wrong? I thought this is what you wanted?' And, Kallum, do you want to know what Payton Ballenger, my oldest friend, said in front of her family, her future in-laws, our parents, at least thirty-five of her closest friends, and God?"

A pit formed in my stomach. "Nope. I'm good."

"Oh, that was a rhetorical question, because, by the way, there are these little things called consequences."

"Just pull the trigger, already," I told her as I grabbed my jacket and room key before making my way to my door.

"She said, 'I slept with Kallum Lieberman.' And then she tore that fat honking diamond off her finger and put it in the hand of the most sad, stunned man I'd ever seen in my life before running out into traffic and getting hit by a bus."

I froze. "Oh my God. No. Is she okay?"

She shrugged. "That last part was a lie, but she did steal some random girl's Uber."

"Sis, I had no idea." My voice dropped as I turned down the volume on my phone and stepped into the hallway. "I swear. This Adan guy sounds great, but I've never even heard of him."

"That doesn't fix the situation, Kallum," she said, her voice more gentle than I expected, making her words sting even more. She didn't sound angry anymore. She was disappointed. "This bridesmaid thing has to stop. These are people's lives we're talking about. Maybe you don't ever want to settle down and maybe start a family, but this is embarrassing. Not just for me, but for Mom and Dad too. Even if they don't say it. They shuffled out the side door of the barbeque restaurant. Mom was crying when I called to check on them."

The elevator doors opened, and I stepped into the thankfully empty lift. "This isn't their fault. I'll call and talk to Mom—"

"Of course it's not their fault, you pumpkin head. But you can't just go around Kansas City swinging your dick around like King Kong."

"Don't talk about my son like that."

"Can you please for once in your life take something seriously?"

"I take pizza seriously," I told her. *And Winnie Baker*, I thought to myself.

"You know, I was pissed about you up and leaving to do this movie, and I still am if I'm being honest. But it's probably for the best. You'd make this worse, and I'm already trying to help Payton get into damage control mode. But if you're going to be flouncing around Vermont for a few weeks, can you at least take some time to get your shit together and think about what it means to be an adult?"

"I'm sorry," I finally said, even if I believed this wasn't entirely my fault. I hated the thought of embarrassing Mom and Dad and ruining a good thing for Payton. I didn't want to be that guy.

I stepped off the elevator and into the quiet lobby. "Please tell Payton I'm sorry. Maybe I should call this Adan person—"

"No," she said firmly. "No. But I will tell Payton. And you should check on Mom. Tell her you're sorry and that you're done sleeping your way through every Jewish bridal party in town."

"It wasn't just Jewish bridesmaids," I clarified. "There were a few Catholic and Hindu weddings in the mix too. Oh, and then there was that Unitarian wedding out in Lawrence."

"I don't need to know this," she said.

"You still love me?" I asked sheepishly, despite the muddy feeling in my chest.

"I couldn't stop if I tried," she said. "And I have." Her head swiveled. "Tristan—no, Theo—no, wait—Toby! Get down from there! You're going to break your arm—again!"

"I'll let you go," I told her.

She opened her mouth to say one last thing, but the video cut and she was gone, probably trying to catch a kid in midair.

I stuffed my phone into my pocket and walked to the fifteen-passenger van waiting to take me to the movie set.

Tamara wasn't right about everything. I knew that. I couldn't be responsible for Payton's short-lived engagement—at least not completely. But maybe if I'd just talked to her for five minutes and caught up with her for a little bit before we started boinking in the bridal suite, I might have known. And if I'd known, I never would have hooked up with her . . . right?

And poor Mom. First the sex tape, then the sexy Santa movie. Now this.

What bothered me most, though, was knowing that this was how people saw me. I felt like a total hypocrite pretending to be a leading man when back home I was nothing but a home-wrecker, apparently. No matter how hard I tried to be a responsible business owner or a good son or a reliable friend or the best uncle, I'd always be the guy with the bridesmaid sex tape who broke up someone's engagement. And that just wasn't the kind of guy who saved the day and got the girl.

"Okay, so we're going to run you two up and down the ski lift a few times to get some B-roll for the skiing montage. And this is Ralph. He's our ski lift consultant and operator," Gretchen said as we stood on a deck next to a grouchy-looking old man with the most wiry and impressive eyebrows I'd ever seen.

"Nothing much to consult on," he said with a grunt. "You use the lift. I hit the buttons."

"Well, it sounds like you know exactly what you're doing," Winnie said brightly, her eyes briefly darting to me.

Since the moment we got out of hair and makeup, she'd been swallowing back a smile and biting that damn lip of hers. Every time our eyes met, her chest would bloom with a deeper shade of pink and she'd look away again. It made my mouth water.

Today we were filming at an old ski resort an hour outside of town. It was a family-owned operation that was a little rough around the edges, but nothing the camera couldn't hide.

"Great," Gretchen said with a nod as her walkie crackled with some sort of craft services emergency. "You two hop on and we'll probably stop the lift a few times for a few different shots. Do either of you have a phone on you?" she asked. "You can just call down if you need a break or anything. I can get a walkie too."

Winnie patted the pockets of her very tiny red velvet skirt. "I couldn't fit it in my pockets."

"I've got mine," I said, digging into the very ample pockets of my jeans.

Gretchen nodded with a sigh. "The fucking patriarchy," she said before turning back to Luca, who stood holding the skis to fasten to our feet. "Luca, can we do something about getting Winnie some pockets on her other costumes?"

He sniffed. "I'll see what miracles I can work. In the meantime, Winnie, I'm so sorry to say this, but I'll need your puffer."

"Right," Winnie said as she shed the floor length puffer coat she wore between scenes to keep warm. Underneath, all that was left were her hunter-green tights, the red velvet mini skirt, and a short white fur coat that looked about as warm as the fancy but thin throw blankets Tamara had on display in her house. (She had a secret stash of real blankets that actually did the job of keeping you warm, of course.) Winnie looked like the kind of fluffy holiday dessert that made me glad Nolan's mom, Mrs. Kowalczk, always invited me over for Christmas. But there was no hiding the way she gritted her teeth against the Vermont chill, especially up here in the mountains.

I steadied the bench for Winnie as she sat down, and I easily filled the space beside her, so that the only place my left arm had to go was behind her. "Is this okay?" I asked.

She smiled with a nod as she let her shoulder lean into my side. "You're like a radiator."

"Or a pizza oven," I supplied.

"This is great," Gretchen said. "You two just talk and look like you're enjoying each other's company and give us a few fake laughs if you could. Winnie, if you could lean on his shoulder every once in a while, that would be good too."

Luca squatted down between us, latching skis to our boots. "I love it," he said. "Big snow bunny energy."

Gretchen gave Ralph a thumbs-up, and we were off. The decades-old lines above us were rusted but intact, and I had to force myself not to think too hard about what might happen if this thing just snapped under my weight. I was a Kansas boy. I didn't really do heights.

"This thing is a little sketchy," I said to Winnie.

"It's not nearly as bad as this Fourth of July movie I did one time. I played a small-town girl who was supposed to climb down a Ferris wheel to stop the hero from leaving town forever. The hero, by the way, was the CEO of a corporate sno-cone chain that was stamping out all the mom-and-pop sno-cone stands."

"That was a good one," I said. "I was really sweating it when you climbed down the side of the Ferris wheel, but Nolan swore you had a body double."

"No, sir. I do all my own stunts—or as many as they'll let me do. To be fair, I was strapped into a harness and there were safety nets everywhere," she said in a way that made me think there were some things about Winnie's job she truly loved.

"Well, I believed every second of it. Did they get you to do the song they used for the montage, by the way? I swear it sounded just like you."

She blushed as we began to move above the tree line. "Wait. Go back. You've watched my Hope Channel movies?"

"As many as I could catch," I said. It was true. Winnie's movies were the perfect thing to turn on when I was lying in bed with Bread and just couldn't fall asleep. It was better than scrolling endlessly on dating apps or watching infomercials. There was also the fact that when Winnie's face lit up my TV, I couldn't look away. I stuck to her Hope Channel movies though. Seeing her in *Treasures in Heaven* with her creep of an ex-husband was not exactly relaxing.

"Huh. So you're a Hope Channel fan?"

I squinted. "I'm more of a Winnie Baker fan. Even your old TV show! I used to watch *In a Family Way* every day after school. How many kids were in that family by the series finale?"

"Believe it or not, there were nine kids by the end. They started with three and added one per season, except for the time they added twins." She smiled for a moment, before her plump lips slipped into a slight frown.

"What is it?" I asked.

She looked over her other shoulder, like it was easier to look away. "Are we just going to pretend like it never happened?"

I didn't need any further clarification. "I don't think I could even if I wanted to," I answered immediately. "Winnie, look at me. Come on."

She huffed as we caught a glimpse of a drone they were using to film, and then leaned her head against my shoulder. "I just—I don't want to feel embarrassed. In fact, I refuse to."

"Good," I said as I beamed with pride at her determination and also at the sight of her curled into my side, our skis dangling in the air below us. "It was research and you fucking nailed it, Baker. A-plus! You're like the valedictorian of orgasms."

She made a face. "I wouldn't go that fa—"

The ski lift wrenched to a screeching halt, and I instinctively threw my arms out in front of Winnie like my mom used to do when I sat in the front seat of her minivan and she was slamming on the brakes.

"Are you okay?" I quickly asked, my eyes scanning every inch of her, making sure she was all there and in one piece.

"I'm good," she said through a gasp. "I'm good."

"Let me see what's going on down there." I pulled my phone out of my pocket and dialed Gretchen.

A robotic voice on the other end of the line said, "Please leave a message after the beep."

"Dammit. I should have asked for the walkie."

"It'll be okay," Winnie said. "They've got the drone up here, and it's not like they won't notice that we're stalled and just hanging in midair."

I nodded. "You're right."

I shot off a text to Gretchen and hoped we'd hear back soon.

"I just hope I don't freeze to death before they get this relic of the past moving again," Winnie said through a shiver.

I could practically hear her teeth chattering. Some Tarzan-like urge inside of my brain said, *MUST KEEP WINNIE WARM*. I slithered out of the fleece-lined puffer jacket I wore and held it out for her. "Here," I said. "Take this."

"What about you?" she asked.

"I'm a pizza oven, baby."

She burrowed even deeper into me, pulling the jacket up to her chin. "This is just about survival, by the way. I don't want you to think that, like, I always expect you to save the day . . . or night . . . but I am freezing, so thank you."

"I don't know how else to say this to make you understand, so I'm just going to be perfectly blunt here. Last night was the hottest thing I've ever seen in my life, and I've seen . . . just about everything, Winnie Baker."

"But I didn't . . . *You* didn't—"

"Oh," I said with a rueful smile. "I did. Back in my room."

She tried not to smile. "Good."

"I don't think you understand what seeing you watch my sex tape did for my ego. My head can barely fit through the door at the inn."

She began to pull the coat up over her face.

"Oh no you don't," I told her as I tugged it back down.

She sat up straight, and I felt her absence immediately in every bone in my body. Her face shifted to serious and determined. "I just—I've never watched porn before. And you're the only person I know with a—a sex tape. So it felt somehow safe for my first experience with pornographic material to be with someone I knew. And I thought . . ." She paused to clear her throat. "I just thought that if it was you who turned me on that maybe I could use that in our scenes."

My pride swelled so much I had to stop myself from puffing my chest out. "I'm honored," I said. "Relieved, in fact, that my sex tape is finally being used for good."

"Finally?" she asked. "I'm pretty sure that tape is bringing happy endings to people all over the world. I mean, judging from your Instagram comments, it's pretty safe to say I'm right."

"I guess that's one way to look at it," I said. "And it has been weirdly good for business at Slice, Slice, Baby. Which is nice, because I wasn't even the one who leaked it. Reagan, the bridesmaid, drunkenly put it online to get back at her fiancé for cheating on her."

She gasped. "Oh my gosh, that's awful. I—I assumed it was a PR stunt. You had no idea?"

I shook my head. "It's okay. I wish she'd talked to me first, of course. And she apologized profusely. If I'm being honest, I think she's single-handedly funded the payroll at my Overland Park location with the amount of guilt-trip pizza she's ordered. And we split the licensing deal, which helped her get on her feet and leave that dumpster-fire fiancé, but according to my sister, I'm an embarrassment to my family."

A sad smile. "I may not have a sex tape, but I do know what it means to disappoint your family."

"You? Winnie Baker? An embarrassment? How is that even possible?"

"I threw it all away when I left my husband," she said simply. "They thought I should mend things, but I just couldn't."

"I'm glad you didn't," I said a little too quickly. "Not that I wanted you to get a divorce. But that guy didn't deserve you. So I'm sorry, but also congratulations, because you're better off without him."

She leaned her head against my shoulder again, her chin tilted up to me. "How can you be so sure?" she asked.

"Well, last night was pretty good proof, if you ask me." My voice grated in my throat. There were a lot of things I could do to Winnie Baker on a bench in the sky with a skirt this short.

She blinked slowly, like she was savoring the memory of it. "I feel like a fourteen-year-old boy," she admitted. "I woke up soaked all over again."

I bent down toward her, and she tilted her face up to me in response, so bright and wide-eyed. Slowly, taking my time, I dragged the pad of my thumb across her lower lip, eventually letting my hand cradle her cheek as my fingers braced the back of her neck. Somehow the cold white puffs of air between us felt hot and needy.

Just then, the ski lift jerked to life, dragging us up the mountain once again.

My phone began to ring.

"Hello?" I answered.

"You're both okay?" Gretchen asked.

I looked down at Winnie, still under my arm, even though the mood had changed from *I want to kiss you until we can't breathe* to *Thank God we're not stuck up here anymore.* "We're okay."

"Good, we're bringing you down, and Ralph is going to look at a few things before we send you back up."

"Sounds good. See you in a minute," I said.

"Next time, you're taking a radio."

"Oh, and Gretchen, could we get Winnie a real coat?"

CHAPTER NINE

Winnie

"Winnie, that was fabulous!"

It was the next morning, and Kallum was carefully setting my foot back on the floor, only letting go of my thigh when it was clear I had my balance again. I laughed a little at his considerate gesture, given that he'd just been fake-railing me against the wall hard enough that half the set had been shaking.

Gretchen hopped up on the stage with her headset around her neck and her face stretched in a wide smile. It was a genuine smile, but I could see the relief in her back and shoulders too. "You two nailed that take."

"Ha, yeah, we *nailed* it," said Kallum gleefully. "Up top!" And then he held up his hand for a high five, which Gretchen— sighingly—gave.

"Winnie, I'm not sure what Pearl managed to impart to you the other day, but I can tell that it's had an effect."

My cheeks burned a little; as much as I wanted to sing to the rooftops that the Peppermint Stick and I were ready to announce our engagement any day now, I wasn't sure I was ready to admit it was a vibrator that had given me my breakthrough yet. Although, heck, Gretchen probably already knew, since Pearl was her girlfriend and all.

The important thing was that I'd held my own with this love scene. Thanks to Pearl and the Peppermint Stick, and Kallum coming in for the assist the other night.

But this was an easy one. A quick scene, straightforward choreography. And half my face had been hidden by my mussed hair, meaning I had a little leeway in how well I was selling the getting-plowed-by-a-young-Santa-Claus vibes.

So yes, I'd passed the test today with flying colors, but we still had so much movie left, and the trickiest sex scenes yet to shoot. This was only going to get harder, and I needed to be ready; I needed to be great. For the first time since coming here, the new Winnie was once again within reach, and I wasn't going to back off now.

I was going to launch the new Winnie into the world with the sexiest, wildest splash possible, and I knew exactly how.

"KALLUM!" I HISSED from behind a bright red trolley two hours later. "Psst!"

Kallum, who'd been about to walk into the inn, turned on his heel. When he saw me, he immediately trotted over. The corners of his mouth pressed in, like he wanted to smile, but also was trying to be cool about how much he wanted to smile, and that made *me* want to smile.

Kallum Lieberman, the catalyst for my most traumatic tabloid shitstorm, made me want to smile. I didn't think the Winnie Baker of just a few weeks ago would have believed it.

"Winnie Baker, we have to stop meeting like this," he said as he reached me.

I glanced around us to make sure we were out of earshot of anyone else walking into the inn, and then said, as quickly as I could so I wouldn't lose my courage, "I want to ask you something. Um. A favor."

"Whatever you need," Kallum said without a second's hesitation. He looked like he meant it too: his mouth was curved in real smile now, soft and inviting, and his eyebrows were lifted in something like gentle concern. "Just say the word."

"It's more than one word," I mumbled and then took a breath. "I want you to help me again. With . . . research."

He blinked once, a long sweep of eyelashes the color of honey. His forehead was still etched in curiosity, but his smile had faded into something else. Something that reminded me how he'd looked the other night, kneeling in front of my chair.

"Research," he said. He made the word sound utterly filthy, and my stomach flipped right over at the sound of it.

"Yes," I managed to say. "I feel like—there's so much more I need to know, and you're a very good teacher." The last few words came out breathlessly, and his tongue slicked slowly over his lower lip.

"Do you mean *again* like one more time, or *again* like until we're done filming?"

His voice was still low, still husky.

"The last one," I said, my own voice now rough too.

"And would it be what we did before?" He stepped closer, his shadow blocking the light from the inn's front door. "Or more?"

Be a brave little toaster, Winnie. "More. Lots more."

He sucked in a shuddering breath, like I'd just hit him. "Fuck," he said, taking another step closer, and we could touch now if we wanted; we could slide our hands together, press our chests together.

But then he squeezed his eyes shut. "Steph wouldn't like this. We could get caught by the press like Bee and Nolan did. We could fuck up our professional relationship to the point where it affects the movie. I could wreck things."

"Why would you wreck things?"

He opened his eyes and glanced away. "It's a specialty of mine. Look, Winnie, you have no idea how badly I want to say yes right now. Like, sign me up to be your sex scene professor right the eff now." He met my gaze, torment stamped all over his face. "But is it a good idea? Will it make things weird? I don't know."

"It didn't make things weird today," I pointed out quickly. "It made things amazing. Seriously, Kallum, I had so much more confidence, and I *knew* what to do, how to move, what noises to make, all of it. Just imagine if I had a whole repertoire of movements and noises! Imagine if I knew what all sorts of sex felt like!"

He looked away again, and then it hit me.

"I know there's not really anything in it for you," I said, trying to think fast. "Other than hopefully the movie being better, but maybe—"

"There's plenty in it for me," cut in Kallum, glancing back. "That's not it."

I studied his jaw, which was flexed under his beard, and his eyes, so vividly blue in the fading dusk light. If there was plenty in it for him, then why . . .

"Okay, I know you're more of a casual sex kind of guy, and I promise this will be as casual as it gets," I said, raising my hand in testimony. "I'm not repeating the mistakes of my past, and that includes feelings and relationships and all the things that inevitably lead to divorce." I gave him my brightest smile. "So we're the perfect pair, see? You only do casual, and I'm never dating anyone again! We could even shake hands on it. No feelings, and over and done when we leave Christmas Notch."

Kallum took a step to the side, raked his hand through his hair. When he did, the T-shirt and Henley he wore under it lifted the tiniest bit, revealing a slice of curved, hair-dusted belly. I wanted to drag my fingertips across it.

"No feelings and over and done when we leave," he said, more to himself than to me. "No harm done. No messes made."

"Please?" I asked again, tucking my lip between my teeth, and then he let out a ragged groan.

"Okay, Winnie Baker," he said, voice gone a little hoarse. "You have yourself a sex research deal."

We shook hands, his hand covering mine, warm in the chilly night, and then he flashed me an abrupt grin so big that a dimple appeared under his beard.

"And luckily for you, we can start some low-key research right now," he said and gestured to the trolley, which was now being boarded by Luca, Jack, Gretchen, and Pearl.

"In the trolley?" I asked, confused.

"Nay, madam, but where the trolley will take us. A magical place they call the North Pole."

I'd seen the matchbooks in a bowl at the inn's front desk. "A strip club?" And then I heard so much of my old self in that question, so much of my old fears and judgments, and I wanted to put myself in a time-out corner with no snacks. "Actually, forget what I just said. What I meant was *yes*. Yes, let's do it."

The dimple grew deeper. "Then our conveyance awaits, milady."

THE NORTH POLE was what would happen if a straight teenage boy were put in charge of Christmas. Yes, there were vintage blow molds of candles and Santa and his reindeer; yes there was a toy train choo-chooing across the top of the stage and plastic tinsel everywhere—brittle and faded enough to make me think it was purchased back in the original plastic tinsel heyday.

But also there were so many boobs.

Like.

So many.

There was a dancer on each of the two stages, nipples covered with pasties made of fake white fur, and the cocktail waitresses were either topless or wearing outfits that meant they were essentially topless.

It was more boobs than I'd ever seen in one place—other than that time on a mission trip when four of us had to shower at once in the converted motel they used to house Habitat for Humanity volunteers. And that wasn't even getting into what was going on *down below*, which seemed to be the finest iridescent thongs that money could buy.

In addition to the boobs, there was a nacho cheese machine behind the bar, lots of domestic beer, and a box of Fireball on every table.

That's right: *a box*. With a little spigot. Like wine.

We were sitting at a large table, a pitcher of bright green Grinch Punch between us, and several plates of appetizers being passed around. Kallum sat in the chair next to me, and I swore I could feel the warmth radiating from him in this chilly room. ("It's to keep the nipples hard," Jack had said knowingly when I'd first mentioned how cold it was.) But Kallum was like a furnace, and even though we were touching, the side of my body that faced him rippled with warmth, awareness, electricity.

Gretchen sat with an arm draped along the back of Pearl's chair while Pearl was giving a soliloquy about finding poetic inspiration in sticky floors and bright yellow cheese, and Luca and Jack were fighting about the institution of marriage while Jack watched Miss Crumpets snoring on his hotel bed via a nanny cam app on his phone.

"I can't believe you're buying into this white-picket-fence bullshit," Jack said, eyes still on his phone. "Marriage is a sham. He'll dump you and then try to give your dog a new father and then all you'll be is a bitter divorcé."

"Joke's on you," Luca said with a sniff. "Bitter divorcé is the brand I've been cultivating for years."

"You doing okay?" Kallum asked me. "You've barely touched your loaded potato skin."

I nodded and took a bite of the potato skin, my eyes returning to the dancer on the stage. Vixen was pale and blond and wide-hipped, with a vibrating tongue piercing that she would come press against your neck for a five-dollar bill. While we ate cheese-drenched food, she flashed us her vulva to an Aly & AJ Christmas song. She had a piercing down there too.

Okay, I was maybe not doing so okay. I was overwhelmed— and maybe not just by the ambient sex or how casual everyone seemed around it all, but by how much I liked it.

We came here like this place was an X-rated Topgolf, a place just to hang out and have fun, but right now, I was having a little more than a good Topgolf-y kind of night. By the time Comet took the stage and began giving us teasing little glimpses of herself, I was wet enough to slide right off my chair.

And while I'd slowly, shyly, been wondering over the last two years if the reason I'd always called myself straight was because I was given no other option growing up, it was disorienting to realize *Oh I really do want eeeeveryone to have sex with me* here in a sticky room filled with Santa blow molds and congealed nacho cheese. And even more than that, it was disorienting to be so brutally turned on while everyone around me was laughing and chatting and playfully spanking the dancers whenever they presented their very spankable backsides. Couldn't they see my flushed cheeks, my hard-and-not-just-from-the-cold nipples, my fast breathing?

Oh God. This was embarrassing. We were here for grown-up fun, and I wasn't mature enough, I was actually getting wildly horny from all of it, and I swore my clit was now pulsing in time to the music, and I had to get out of here, I had to find somewhere to get my body under control.

Mumbling a frantic excuse, I left our table and hurried down the long hallway to the side, lined with ATMs, condom machines, and flyers for local concerts, and ducked into the first door I found. The room beyond was dimly lit, with padded benches lining the walls, a throne-looking armchair in the middle, and a tall trifold mirror standing at one end.

It was a private room.

I pressed my face in my hands, grateful for the chance to catch my breath. *Lust isn't actually a sin*, I reminded myself.

The door swung open, and I jumped back, like I'd been caught doing something naughty.

"It's just me," Kallum said cheerfully, stepping inside and shutting the door behind him. "Thought I'd give you the nickel tour."

I hugged myself, hoping he couldn't see the hard tips of my breasts poking through my thin boatneck shirt. "Have you been here before then?"

He laughed. "Actually no, but all private rooms are the same. Chair, mirrors. Maybe some black lights to get a glow-in-the-dark effect."

An absurd twist of jealousy took root inside my chest. And then curiosity too. "You've been in private rooms at strip clubs?"

"Oh yeah," Kallum said, strolling over to the mirror and giving it an approving once-over. "Nolan basically had a strip club punch card at one point. And it was impossible to avoid a private session anywhere we went, since every dancer wanted to say they had an INK boy in their private room. Even if it was only Kallum Lieberman."

I didn't like the way he said *only Kallum Lieberman*, like he wasn't as fascinating or sexy as Nolan Shaw or Isaac Kelly, but he spoke again before I could ask him about it.

"And you want to know my favorite thing about a private room?"

"Yes," I said. My voice had gone quiet. Distantly, I could hear the music from the rest of the club, and a lone horn from a truck somewhere on the highway.

"Attention," he said softly. "No other patrons, no other friends. Just you. The sole focus of someone's attention."

His words dragged over me like slow, wet kisses, and I was trembling. "And what does attention look like? In a private room?"

He turned to face me, and even though it was nearly dark in here, I could see the wicked grin spreading across his face. "Are you asking me to show you, Winnie Baker?"

Brave Little Toaster.

"Yes," I whispered with a slow smile of my own.

"Well, then. Have a seat."

I sat in the chair, clearing my throat. I wasn't sure what to do, what to say, when someone was about to give me a lap dance, but I remembered watching Pearl get one earlier, and she'd basically sat back and let the dancer do all the work. So I relaxed into the chair, eyeing Kallum with my tongue pressed to the roof of my mouth.

Kallum made a noise. "You look at me like that, and we're going to break the rules."

"There are rules?"

"The big one is no sex stuff." Another wicked smile. "For employees and patrons at least."

"A good thing you're not on the North Pole payroll then," I observed, and he laughed as he pulled his phone out of his pocket.

"But for the sake of the experience, we should pretend, my sex scene padawan," he said, moving over to a table in the corner of the room. I wasn't sure what he was doing over there—his back was to me—but then a rich, mellow beat began to fill the room. A song.

Kallum set his phone down and turned to me, and suddenly I wasn't in the room with my playful costar, but with a performer, with a man who knew how to captivate an audience, even if that audience was just one woman who used to think she could get pregnant from a hot tub.

He walked toward me with measured, arrogant steps, his eyes entirely on me, his body somehow utterly fluid and also utterly under his control. When the beat pulsed, his body did too, and when the melody rolled, so did his hips. I'd never thought that *walking* could be sexy, so filled with the idea of sex, but sex was in every step and shift, every gesture, every look.

And the *looks*. At first, I couldn't suppress the nervous smile on my lips as he came closer, feeling abruptly self-conscious, even though, if anything, Kallum was the one in the room who had the most claim to self-consciousness. But that was the thing I'd noticed about Kallum over the last few days on set—he was possibly the least self-conscious person I'd ever met. Everything he did, he did with that same earnest, easy attitude, and I'd never met someone who was both wholehearted and also absolutely relaxed about it too. Like it didn't matter if some blocking wasn't working or if we had to do another take or if a joke fell flat. He would just shrug and grin and then try again.

It was captivating, infectious. It made me want to be more like him, both easier and more eager; living in the moment but also not needing the moment to bear the impossible weight of perfection.

And so my self-consciousness gradually dissolved as he stopped in front of me and moved to the beat of the song. There was only me and him and the music.

No one had ever looked good taking off any shirt without buttons, but somehow Kallum did just then, making it look easy, making it look natural. Inevitable. And still moving to the music, he started unbuckling his belt, the tendons in his hands and forearms flexing as he loosened the leather and worked it through the frame of the buckle. He dropped the belt and unzipped his jeans. And even though it was regular old boxer briefs underneath—patterned with pizza slices to boot—it was still like a punch to the gut to see his thighs and hips with nothing but the thin cotton between his skin and my gaze.

And his penis—his—his *dick*—was clearly outlined in the fabric too. Thick and heavy and halfway hard, and I wanted it so much. I wanted to touch it, I wanted to taste it.

The thought consumed me, the idea that I could hold it in my hand, that I could watch him get all the way erect as I explored him with my fingers. I could measure with my fingertips how plump the head was, I could see if there were any veins for me to trace . . .

I bit my lip hard, feeling so wet and achy inside that it hurt, and then a groan ripped from Kallum's chest.

I looked up to see his eyes blazing down at me, and then he was on his knees in front of me, shoving my skirt up to my waist and hooking his fingers around the sides of my panties.

"You said there was no sex stuff in a private room," I said, half laughing, half whimpering as I lifted my hips and he pulled my underwear down to my ankles and then dropped it on top of his discarded jeans. "And that we should pretend for the experience."

"Fuck the experience," he growled. He looked up at me with his hands on my bare thighs. "I want to eat your cunt. Can I?"

I'd only ever heard the *C*-word from Addison's lips—usually while she was driving on the 101—and it knocked the breath right out of me with its blunt obscenity.

"God, yes," I groaned, spreading my thighs so he could see me. My cunt. "Please. Please."

He grabbed my bottom with his hands, hands big enough to splay easily around my cheeks, and yanked me to the edge of the chair. "God, you're so fucking wet," he said, his voice a groan of urgent awe. He pressed his nose to me and inhaled, and I closed my eyes, quivering. "Open your eyes, Winnie Baker," he said. "Watch me."

I did as he asked and opened my eyes. In time to see him smell me again, to see how his eyelashes rested on his cheeks as he leaned in and planted a soft kiss on my swollen clit. I was squirming without meaning to, and he moved his hands from my bottom to my hips, clamping me down to the chair and holding me still for the first long, hot lick of his tongue.

"*Kallum.*" My breath was shuddering in and out. "Oh God. Please."

"Mmm," he responded, already diving back in. His tongue was warm and strong and slick, and he found my entrance and began licking in earnest.

I arched against him, already dizzy with pleasure. This was more than being primed for sex. This was because of *him*, because of the eager, greedy noises he made, because of the way he would pull away to spread my pussy with his thumbs and then stare at it with a wet mouth and heaving breaths. Michael had only done this a handful of times, and every time had been unsatisfying and short, and then when I wouldn't react the way he wanted, he would tell me that it was okay that I didn't like it and stop.

Meanwhile, Kallum was eating me as if he'd snarl and snap like a trapped animal if someone tried to pull him away.

The music was a dark, thrumming beat now, a song I didn't recognize because it was music I wasn't allowed to listen to growing up, and he was fluttering the tip of his tongue and sucking and letting me twist my fingers in his hair and hold his face harder and harder against my sex. And his shoulders were wide between my thighs, spreading them apart, and when he looked up at me, I finally knew what he meant by *attention*.

I was the only person in the world for him right now.

Just as he was for me.

The orgasm ripped through me like I was made of paper, and I crumpled over him, still holding his face against my pussy, still rocking against his mouth as much as I was able. The music was loud enough that it took a moment for me to realize I was making wild, indecent noises, that anyone who heard them would know Winnie Baker was having A Very Good Time. But who could care? When Kallum had a mouth this wicked? When his shoulders pried me open, when his eyes were that intense and glittering in the near dark?

The pleasure kept tearing through me, a pleasure I wouldn't have thought possible before now, because even my betrothed, the Peppermint Stick, couldn't hold a candle to this. And Kallum kept eating me through it all, these gorgeous noises rumbling from his throat, like my climax was his favorite meal and he would happily eat it forever.

And then as the song ended, the climax ended too, each wave growing smaller and shorter until I was nothing but a limp wreck on the shore of it, breathing hard and fast in my chair.

Kallum sat back on his heels, licking his lips like he'd just finished an ice cream cone and already wished he had another one. There was a glisten of sweat at his hairline and on his chest, and in his boxer briefs, his cock was a colossal bar. It stretched all the way to his hip, and he'd adjusted himself so that the wide head of it peeped above the elastic band of his briefs. Something glistened along the slit. Pre-come.

"I have an idea," I blurted, and he stared at me as he slowly wiped his beard with the back of his hand. "For another lesson."

CHAPTER TEN

Kallum

Winnie looked down at me with heavy eyes. "I want to see it," she said.

I rocked forward onto my knees, spreading her legs again. "See what, Winnie Baker?"

"I showed you mine," she said cutely. "You show me yours."

"We use our big-girl words," I told her even though I was pretty sure the sight of her just looking at my naked erection would bring me to the finish line.

She braced herself on the arms of the throne and kicked off one of her flats before dragging her toe up the inside of my thigh, over my hungry dick, and up the trail of hair leading to my chest. With a little bit of bossiness in her tone, she said, "Show me your cock, Kallum Lieberman."

And I just sat there, frozen in place. Winnie—sweet, whole-some, darling Winnie—was filthy. And not only that, but she was my exact flavor of filth. She'd stunned me with her naughty little foot, tracing its way up my body, and my brain couldn't make words.

She dropped her foot and leaned forward. "Did I say it right? Did I sound weird? How does everyone else sound so sexy when they say things like that out loud? Saying it in my head is getting easier, but—"

I held a finger up to her lips as I stood to my feet. With my free hand, I guided her fingers to the waistband of my boxer briefs. "You can see it all you want, baby."

She inhaled deeply, her breath fluttering as she exhaled, and began to tug down on my waistband before reaching in and pulling out my fully thickened length.

Holy *fuck*. Seeing her delicate fingers wrapped around me was so obscene, I let out a gravely grunt.

"Wow," she whispered. "I'd seen it before—you know, because of the sex tape thing, but it's just wow. I've only ever seen one other penis in real life, but I feel like I can say with certainty that you have a very good penis."

I couldn't stop myself from glowing with pride. "Can you put that on a certificate or something so I can put it on my fridge? I never did make honor roll."

With her free hand, she took my right hand and covered it with hers. "Show me how to give you what you've given me."

I couldn't help but wonder if all of this was one sort of elaborate good person test. As tempting as it was to give in to her, this definitely crossed the research line. "You don't have to, Winnie. This—this research—is for you. You've made someone come before. You don't need my help with that."

Her grip tightened and I moaned. "It's never felt like this before, though. I've never been so turned on at the thought of making someone else come. But with you . . . it's like I could eat you up if you'd let me."

"Don't say it if you don't mean it. The list of things I wouldn't let Winnie Baker do to me is nonexistent. Nicolas Cage in a *National Treasure* movie couldn't find it."

She bit down on her lower lip with a slight smile. "I love those movies."

"Me too."

"Show me," she demanded.

I'd said no once already. That had to count for something. The thought of saying no was just as scary as the thought of saying yes.

As much as it pained me to do it, I removed her hand from my dick for just a moment, and brought her palm up to her mouth. "Open," I said.

She obeyed.

Oh God. I was in trouble.

"Lick," I told her.

And she did.

"Good girl."

Her hips lifted as she squirmed in her seat a little at that, and it made *me* want to lick her from top to bottom.

I brought her hand back to my erection, and her palm was warm, soft, wet, and ready.

She stood and turned us around until the back of my thighs hit the throne and I sat down.

"I want to sit on Santa's lap," she said as she straddled me, hovering above my crotch like a tease, her skirt hiking up around those juicy hips. Watching intently, she tentatively tugged on my shaft. "Is that good?"

I tightened my grip around hers. "Tight is good," I said. "You don't have to be gentle with me." I pulled her hand roughly along my length. "That's good."

A determined smile curled across her lips, like now that she knew what felt good, she could replicate it. She ran her hand up and down my cock, finding the perfect rhythm.

My toes curled as tension coiled in my belly with every pull. I let go and reached up to cradle her face in both my hands. "You're such a diligent student, Winnie Baker." I loved holding her like this, like my whole world was right there at the tips of my fingers.

With her eyes hooked on mine, she ran her tongue along her hand before picking up the pace. She pulled her gaze away to watch her work, to see what she was doing to me. How she could control me with one simple motion.

I was torn between that perfect fucking face and the red flush crawling up her chest and the sight of my cock seeping onto her hands.

"I—I'm gonna come, Winnie, I—" I wanted to be polite. I wanted to come into my shirt or at least warn her, but before I could say another word, her fist jerked and the head of my penis brushed the lips of her bare pussy, and I came un-fucking-done.

Warm ribbons of ejaculate painted the insides of her thighs and the image of it dripping against her porcelain skin made me wonder if someday I'd have the honor of watching my come leak from her.

Ecstasy tore through me as she continued to jack me off, milking every ounce like she'd get goddamn bonus points for it.

I threw my head back against the padded throne, my chest heaving in this dank little strip club private room. "You're a quick study, Mrs. Claus."

She leaned forward and kissed me on the cheek before standing up and licking my fluid off the tip of her finger. "Let's do that again."

LITTLE WINNIE BAKER was a horndog. And I was living for it.

That night, after we took the trolley back to the inn, she pulled me into the alleyway to dry-hump me like a teenager, bringing herself to a shuddering orgasm against my thigh.

Watching her fall in love with pleasure was turning out to be one of the greatest delights of my life. It was like when someone took a bite of my pizza for the first time, and they had a giddy, blissed-out expression on their face. Except witnessing Winnie compete in the Orgasm Olympics was way better than any slice of pizza.

The next morning as we walked to set, she buzzed with energy. "It's, like, all I can think about! How do people get anything done like this?"

"It's why I almost flunked out of tenth grade," I said. "Pretty much rubbed this little guy raw. So many sticky bedsheets and missing socks. My poor mother. And I thought I was so smooth—like she didn't know exactly what I was up to."

Winnie covered her mouth, but it didn't hold in the relentless laughter.

"Finally my dad told me that I had to do my 'business' in the shower, but that only pissed off my sister, because suddenly my showers were three times as long. There was no winning!"

"I finally get all those jokes about humping pillows and stuffed animals. I feel there's a constant game of Can I Hump It? playing in my head." The word *hump* came with a very sweet pink blush on her cheeks.

"Well, for the sake of research, my body is a hump-friendly zone."

"Kallum?" she asked as we stopped at a crosswalk near the production office. "Thank you."

"For letting you jack me off in the back of a strip club? Uh, not a problem."

She punched my arm gently. "Well, for that, yes. But also for being so nice and not teasing me for all the things I don't know . . . and for just letting this be fun. I didn't know this could be fun. I didn't know what I was missing."

I threw an arm around her shoulder, and for some reason it felt friendlier than I wanted anything between us to ever feel. "It's an honor. Before you know it, you'll be strutting around that set with uncontainable big dick energy."

"BDE!" she said proudly. "One of the secret company pillars of Wishes of Addison."

"My mom loves the shit out of her, by the way."

"As she should," Winnie said as I held the door open for her. "As she should."

THE NEXT FOUR days felt like lightning. The cast and crew were totally in sync—especially me and Winnie. I even got a call from Steph, telling me how happy Gretchen and Pearl were with how things were going.

"That's great to hear," I told her as I sat at the diner nursing a pot of coffee. "Hopefully Teddy feels the same way when he gets here later this week." Winnie was shooting some scenes on her own, so I had the day off.

"Teddy's visiting set, you say?" she asked over the sound of her virtual Peloton instructor aggressively shouting mantras and words of encouragement. "I've got to get the fuck out of LA, and I really should check on Winnie . . ."

"You should come! The air here is unreal and—" The phone beeped.

"Kallum, I gotta take this call. It's my gyno. He and my dermatologist just broke up and I keep trying to tell him that I can't choose him over her. Anyone can stick a speculum up your vagina and poke around like an orchestra conductor, but dermatology? Now, that is an art form."

The line cut out, and I shrugged. There was something I liked about Steph, something that reminded me of my sister.

My screen lit up with a text from my nephew.

Topher: how's the sexy santa gig going?

I smirked to myself as I typed back.

Me: So sexy they had to halt production yesterday because crew members kept fainting.

Topher: 🙄

Me: Seriously, though. Sorry I haven't checked in for a few days. We've had some long days. I'm free today if you need anything.

Topher: The pizza biz is good. I hired a new delivery driver for the Lawrence location.

Me: Is it that guy I saw you making eyes at who asked for an application the week before I left?

Topher: He was highly qualified.

Topher: And highly hot.

Topher: But I'm keeping it profesh. I swear.

Me: Who am I to stand in the way of young coworkers in love?

Topher: Uh, my boss?

Me: Right.

Topher: By the way, some Australian dude called. Said he was some sort of representative for an investor who's interested in expanding Slice, Slice, Baby.

Me: Just put his info to the side. I get all kinds of calls about franchising, but it's too much to think about.

Topher: The Australian dude said to tell you his client is famous and you've definitely heard of him. He owns a sports team and is on a TV show that rhymes with Tark Shank.

Me: Oh, damn. I love that show. Get me his contact info.

Me: Just for shits and giggles.

Topher: On it, boss.

Me: How's Bread holding up without me?

He sent back a photo of Bread yowling at his phone. She was a gray tabby and hated everyone who wasn't me because they weren't me. She did, however, tolerate Topher.

I polished off the rest of my coffee, then opened up my phone again to text my mom. She wasn't mad at me when I spoke to her about Payton's engagement party. Or at least she wouldn't fess up to it. I could hear the disappointment, though. It was drilled into my brain.

I opened a new message and selected a picture of the view from my room—snowy mountain tops and a glistening blue sky. Real-life postcard shit.

Me: Miss you. You would love it here. Dad would hate it.

Mama Mia: The man is half lizard.

Mama Mia: Love you too all the way from KC

She sent back a picture of Dad asleep in his recliner with a half-eaten deli sandwich on his chest.

Even when they were disappointed or embarrassed . . . I'd always have home.

OVER THE LAST week, Winnie and I found ourselves sneaking into nooks and corners to rub our bodies together. We were like two high school kids looking for any excuse to be alone.

Winnie's hand job game was getting so good that it took actual mental fortitude to last longer than a minute or two.

But it was all over this afternoon when she lured me into the makeup trailer during lunch and locked the door behind her.

After I tore off her panties and ate my lunch right then and there, she pulled down my pants and sank to her knees. "I want to suck your dick," she said. "Can I?"

"Uh, does Nicolas Cage and *National Treasure* ring a bell?" I said as I ran my fingers through her hair, before holding the back of her neck and gently pulling her toward me.

Her lips slipped over the head of my penis, and I saw fucking stars. What Winnie was lacking in experience, she made up with enthusiasm.

After cleaning up, we thought we were being so sneaky as we slipped out of the trailer.

"There you two are!" said Jack as he walked toward us with Miss Crumpets strapped to his chest in the doggy version of a BabyBjörn.

"We were running lines," Winnie said just as I said, "We were looking at lipstick."

Winnie's gaze darted to me as she swallowed back a smile.

"Both of those things," I said with a nod. "Lipstick and lines."

Jack arched an eyebrow before spinning on his heel and heading back to set. "Sure."

"How do you raise one eyebrow like that?" I called after him. "I've never been able to do that without looking like I have to take a shit."

"Maybe I do," he said over his shoulder.

"Did he just make taking a shit sound cool and mysterious?" I asked Winnie.

"I'm pretty sure he did," she confirmed before pinching my ass. "Let's go make some fake-sex movie magic."

I LEANED ON the hood of the red '57 Chevy parked at the center of town.

"I think we just need a few more takes of this one," Gretchen said as Winnie walked back over to her mark.

My character was supposed to be picking up Winnie's character for a date at a tree farm outside of town, but our car would break down before we even made it to the farm and then we'd get stuck at an inn with only one bed available—a scene I was looking forward to a little too much.

"Winnie, play it a little sweeter and more coy this time if you could. You're doing great," Gretchen told her. "We just need options for the cutting-room floor." She turned to me. "And Kallum, husky yet jolly as usual."

I crossed my arms over my chest in the most lumberjack-esque pose I could strike. "You got it, G."

"From the top!" Gretchen called, and then to Winnie, "Ready when you are."

Winnie closed her eyes and then shimmied her shoulders like she always did when she was getting into character. It reminded me of late nights sitting on the couch with my mom watching *I Dream of Jeannie*. Watching the shows that Mom used to watch with her mother was always a guaranteed way to get out of bedtime. That's how I started watching Winnie's movies. When I outgrew Nick at Nite, I needed another comfort watch, and Winnie was comforting in more ways than one.

Winnie dipped her chin down and smiled with her lips closed in a bashful sort of way as she walked toward me and the car. Her blond hair rustled behind her in a gentle breeze.

Sometimes I just had to remember I was supposed to be in character, but I guess that wasn't so bad when my character was falling harder than a Jenga tower, because I was too.

Winnie was the kind of girl I would risk it all for. But I'd never been the kind of guy that girls felt that way about.

I was the funny one. The sweet one. I was the one *before* The One. Especially if you considered my string of bridesmaids. And that had been fine—as much as I'd wanted to find true love every time I tumbled into bed with someone I barely knew, I also didn't begrudge them for using me as their soul-mate lucky charm. A stepping-stone to their true love.

But I couldn't handle the heartbreak of being a stepping-stone for Winnie. And even through the last week of romping through Christmas Notch—and fooling around in every spare moment—the fear that I was going to be her lucky charm took root in the far corner of my brain no matter how hard I pushed it away.

So as Winnie strode toward me, I forced myself to remember this was my job, and all the sex stuff Winnie and I had done over the last week was in the name of research.

Nothing more.

Oh shit. My line.

I ran over to the passenger door and held it open. "Your chariot, milady."

Then Winnie froze.

Her shy smile dropped.

Her shoulders tensed, and the Winnie I'd come to know since our time on set slunk back into her shell.

And the sight of it made me want to tear a damn hole in the sky just for her.

"Michael," she said.

No. Surely she didn't mean who I think she meant.

Gretchen stood from her chair, clearing her throat. "Let's take five."

"Five *days*," Luca mumbled from where he sat beside her. "This could take a hot minute."

I turned around to see for myself, and there he was. Winnie's slimy piece-of-shit ex-husband, his pale cheeks pink with the chilly breeze and his thousand-dollar scarf draped uselessly around his shoulders instead of wrapped around his neck.

My whole body coiled into one big muscle, and I felt like I could arm wrestle a polar bear. Really evolved of me, I know. But what the fuck was this guy doing here anyway? Not that it was any of my business, of course.

But I wanted it to be. I wanted all of Winnie's business to be my business.

I hated Michael Bacher for lots of reasons, but in this moment it was because he was a reminder that this wasn't real. Christmas Notch was like living in a snow globe, and it was too easy to forget that there was a whole-ass world outside of this place when all I wanted to do was wrap Winnie in my arms and live in our perfect snowdrift moment forever.

"Babe," Michael said. "Can we talk?"

"I'm kind of busy," I answered in a super high-pitched voice.

The whole crew laughed. A few even snorted.

Winnie looked at me, but there was no smile or secret nod telling me that we were on the same page.

I was an asshole.

She turned back to Michael, her gaze studying the ground, just like she had the first day at the Hope Channel offices when she was so tense with shame and embarrassment. "Um, sure."

I watched with a metallic taste in my mouth as she walked toward him, only turning back to hold a finger to Gretchen, who nodded in response.

Nothing about this felt good or right.

Jack strode up beside me. "At ease, lover boy."

Something in my chest twisted, and I couldn't help but feel like she was dragging my heart on a string behind her, tethered to her wrist like a deflated balloon.

CHAPTER ELEVEN

Winnie

Michael looked good, but then again, he always looked good. Sharp jaw, Roman nose, hair waved perfectly back from his face. Like he'd just stepped out of the J.Crew winter catalog with pristine boots, pressed chinos, and quarter-zip sweater. A scarf hung smartly from his shoulders—though not doing him much good, guessing by how he hunched against the breeze.

As we walked away from the square toward Caroler's Creek, a narrow stream that ran through the north end of town, he took my hand.

Just reached out and wrapped his fingers around it, like it was still his hand to take.

It took me a minute to listen to what my body was telling my brain, and then another minute for my brain to remember that I didn't have to hold his hand if I didn't want to. Which I didn't! We'd been separated for a year and a half! We'd been officially divorced for two months! What the heck!

I pulled my hand away as we turned onto Sugar Plum Avenue and glanced longingly back at the set. Back to Kallum, who was still standing next to the Chevy, his hands shoved in his pockets. Watching me.

I spun back around, cheeks burning, not sure what to think. Kallum had looked pissed when Michael first stepped on set, but then he'd made a joke and hadn't seemed to mind when I left with Michael.

Did I want him to mind?

What did it mean if I did?

Stupid. Whatever Kallum and I were doing, it was just for the sake of the movie, and it came with an expiration date. I wasn't that doe-eyed girl looking for fairy tales anymore; I was smarter than that now. The proof was sitting in Addison's pool house in the form of a notarized divorce decree.

Michael noticed me looking back, and his handsome jaw tightened. His displeasure had always been a subtle thing—he'd never yelled, never touched me in anger. But then again, he didn't have to. One heavy sigh, one slow look into the middle distance, and I would be desperate to make him happy again.

And I could feel it now, that desperation, that lonely panic. My shoulders were pulled in, my head dipped down, the low headache I sometimes got from my narcolepsy medicine pulling at my temples. I wanted to be small, invisible; it was impossible to think of who I'd been just ten minutes ago, laughing on set with Kallum, my belly molten just from one heated glance. Feeling so tall I could touch the sky.

"Have you heard from your parents?" Michael asked, and I was so relieved he wasn't saying anything about the movie or my costar that the words didn't hurt right away.

Until they did.

My parents hadn't spoken to me since my divorce had been finalized. And they only spoke to me before that to remind me—gravely—that remarriage after a divorce would be adultery and that hard-heartedness was a sin. I didn't think they'd believed me when I told them Michael had cheated on me, and even when they'd pretended to believe it, it still hadn't mattered. I should have forgiven him, they said. I should have at least played the part, so I didn't ruin everyone's lives merely to satisfy my own wounded ego.

Divorce was a sin, but to them divorce was also something much, much worse.

An embarrassment.

"They want you to come home," Michael said when I didn't answer.

"They wouldn't let me come home before now," I replied numbly. The Victorian houses on either side of us were giving way to snow-clumped trees, which then gave way to the ice-crusted slopes of the creek. Just beyond the bridge, I saw Holy Night Chapel, a small, steepled church frequently rented out for Hope Channel productions.

"They want to make things right," Michael said.

I stopped at the foot of the bridge. "Then why aren't they here?" I asked, but my voice was trembling, my face was ducked. For so long, I'd imagined myself a pillar of strength if I had to talk to Michael again, so confident and cool. The same with my parents.

But instead I was still that sleepy teenager who felt guilty for having narcolepsy, who felt guilty for not being as energetic and hardworking as girls like Addison. The teenager who'd been putting in medication-enabled sixteen-hour days since she was in the sixth grade. Who'd had to hide her disability as much as she was able because her parents were terrified it would ruin her career if the world knew her secret.

Michael had stopped, turning to face me with something in his expression I couldn't name. Regret, maybe? Determination?

"Because I wanted to be the one to come," he explained. "I wanted to be the one to talk to you."

"Talk to me," I echoed.

"Yes," he said, reaching out like he wanted to take my hand again and then stopping. His eyes were silver in the weak sunlight, and I'd once been so in love with those eyes. Had written poetry about them when we'd started courting.

Blue eyes flashed through my mind now, but I pushed the image away. They were temporary blue eyes. On loan from the bridesmaids of the world.

"I miss you, Winnie," Michael said. His face was earnest, his voice was earnest. Whatever his faults, he'd always been a decently good actor. "Getting those divorce papers was a wake-up call. I need you in my life."

Anger sluiced through me, as cold and jagged as the ice fringing the creek. "You should have thought about that before Olivia," I said, straightening up.

Michael had the grace to look ashamed. "I'm not proud of that. But I've truly repented, and now I'm called to make things right with you—"

"You can make things right by telling the media that you were the one who cheated, not me."

When I saw the horror on his face, I gave a quiet, mirthless laugh. "That's what I thought."

"I know I've sinned," he said. "But God has forgiven me. As for the media—maybe we can approach them together, as a couple, and say that we were both led astray by our sins—"

"Both led astray? I *never* cheated on you. Not once."

"No, but you must have known we were unhappy," he said, reaching out to me again. I stepped away and walked onto the bridge, not able to look at him right now. "And unhappiness in a marriage is the responsibility of both the husband and the wife to fix," he called after me as he followed.

I turned and gripped the railing of the bridge. I imagined it was his neck. "I did everything for you, Michael. *Everything.* And it was never enough."

He snorted. "You call that everything? You barely tolerated sex with me!"

"What do you think *everything* is to someone who grew up the way we did? What do you think it's like to be a girl and hear over and over again that any breach in purity will stain you forever, and then be expected to flip a switch the moment you get married? Sex *hurt* at the beginning, and then when it stopped hurting, it still never felt as good for me as it seemed to feel for you. I didn't even have an orgasm until—"

I stopped. That wasn't his business.

But his eyes flashed with some intense emotion. "Until when, Winnie?" he said softly. "Until you started filming pornography?"

I groaned. "This isn't pornography, Michael."

"It might as well be!" He pulled his phone from his pocket and woke it up to show me a screenshot from Dominic Diamond's website. There was a picture from the *Santa, Baby* set the other day, of Kallum pretending to screw me against a wall. Despite everything, a surge of lust arrowed to my belly. I knew it wasn't real, that it was just a shot from a take—and a slightly blurry one at that—but Picture Me looked like she was having the ride of her life.

And Real Me remembered exactly how it felt to have Kallum's warm body crowded against mine, his beard tickling my neck.

"'Winnie Bacher-Baker Back on the Naughty List,'" Michael read aloud from the screenshot. He read his own last name with the German pronunciation and accompanying throat-clearing noise on the *ch*—like Bach the composer.

"I'm not Winnie Bacher-Baker anymore," I interrupted, but he kept reading.

"'This troubled child star is baring it all for the Hope Channel's risky venture into the world of smut, and sources from the set tell us that viewers can expect to see a very bold side of Winnie Bacher-Baker that will leave no doubt she's no longer the sweet role model from *Treasures in Heaven.*'"

Ugh, I really needed to have Steph put out a press release about my name being plain old *Winnie Baker* again. And *role model*??? My character had been sick in *Treasures in Heaven*, suffering and dying (and then miraculously living) as prettily as possible while the neighborhood bad boy, played by Michael, found redemption through her sweetness and goodness. The only *role* she modeled was how to hide as much of your pain as possible—and also how to repeatedly forgive crappy people.

But that role, and the movie along with it, had been beyond huge—the kind of success that spawned tie-in books, a platinum single, and years of speaking engagements.

It had also been fifteen years ago.

"Maybe it's about time that people know I'm not the girl from *Treasures in Heaven*," I said tightly. "And you're not the boy."

"But people want us to be," Michael said, dropping the phone. He exhaled like he'd just lost a pawn on a chessboard and faced me, his face full of gentle understanding.

"I know I hurt you, Winnie, and I have to live with my weakness forever. But is it worth all this? Hurting your parents with this kind of behavior?"

His words stirred up all kinds of old shames, but I was tired of letting shame inform every decision I made. "My parents don't have to watch *Santa, Baby* if they don't want to."

"But it's hurting you too, babe. Because"—he put his hand over mine and squeezed—"True Vine wants to make a *Treasures in Heaven* sequel. A *sequel*."

His eyes were shining now, and he couldn't stop the smile pulling at the corners of his mouth. He was excited about this. He thought I would be excited about this too.

And all the pieces slotted together to make a very clear picture.

"So that's why you're here," I said slowly. "You want to make a *Treasures* sequel, but you know the True Vine studio execs will never go for it if I've released *Santa, Baby*."

"Winnie, think of how big it would be. People have been asking for this sequel for over a decade. We'll couple it with a book deal of our own, license out the journals, workbooks, all of that, and then? If it's clear we're together, that the movie brought us back together? Then the sky's the limit! A book deal every year, a production deal with a major streamer, a company to rival Addison's—you name it and it's ours, because the only thing better than a success story is a redemption story."

He stepped closer, close enough that my white costume boots bumped against his gleaming ones. "We can have it all, and we can have it *together*. All you have to do is come back." He took my hand off the railing, held it between us. "I know you wanted a family, Winnie, and just think of it—you and me, together and making movies again, you sleeping as much as you want."

"It's not about *wanting* to sleep," I murmured reflexively, with no real heat. I'd given up trying to explain narcolepsy to him years ago. Even my parents, who'd organized all the sleep studies and doctors' visits and medication refills, still seemed to think my narcolepsy was about being too lazy to stay awake.

"And," he added softly, "a baby on the way . . ."

Funny how things change. Up until a year and a half ago, I would have sworn to anyone who would listen that this was all I wanted. Michael and me, together, starting a family.

And I still wanted a family. I wanted it so badly it hurt sometimes. A child to hold and love and give the entire world . . .

Michael spoke before I could answer, pressing his forehead to mine. "I know I'll have to earn your trust again, but I know I can, if you'd only give me a chance." He let out a breath; it was warm against my lips. I didn't know what I was feeling. "And I can't lie, Winnie, seeing that picture of you, even if it was with another guy—I had no idea. No idea you were like that, that you could *look* like that, and I . . ."

He moved the hand he was holding down between us and pressed my hand to his groin. Where he was undeniably hard as stone.

I snatched my hand back, staggering backward. "Michael, what the *fuck?*"

"Language, Winnie."

"No, not *language.* You just—you just—" I was so pissed, I couldn't find the right words. "You think that I want to have sex with you ever again? We're divorced! You cheated on me!"

His eyebrows pulled together in confusion. "Yes, but like I said—"

"Did my parents even tell you they wanted me to come home?"

He sighed, like I was being unbelievably childish right now. "Look, they *will* want you to come home once you've stopped this little rebellion of yours."

"Go home, Michael," I said, turning back toward the town. "Make your *Treasures* sequel without me."

"You'll change your mind," my ex-husband said. When I looked back at him, he didn't seem angry or worried or anything other than contained and handsome. "There's only so far you can go alone."

CHAPTER TWELVE

Kallum

After Michael had waltzed onto set, we took a break, which turned into an early wrap on my scene with Winnie.

I watched her walk right back into his arms, their hands clasped with the stupidly picturesque mountains behind them. I should have taken a photo for them to use for their next Christmas card.

I wasn't off the hook so easily though. I filmed a North Pole (Santa's North Pole, not the nacho cheese–scented den of vice outside of town) scene of the young Santa writing a letter to his parents, the original Mr. and Mrs. Claus. He was letting them know he was going on his Santa sojourn to sow his wild oats and maybe even find his soul mate. Gretchen called cut over and over because I was grinding my teeth or furrowing my brow too much. One time I even gripped the pencil so hard it snapped.

Finally, Pearl came over and held some purple crystal to my chest and coached me through breathing exercises. I wasn't sure it worked, but it worked well enough for us to call it quits on such a car crash of a day.

I spent the whole night channeling my inner sad boy. I even shot off a text to the original sad boy, Isaac Kelly, who'd holed up in his Malibu mansion after his wife's death and hadn't come out.

Me: Wanna be sad together?

When he didn't message me back, I got angry. And maybe had a few beers, so I texted the safest person in my phone who could handle me when I was sad and angry and a little drunk.

Me: Fuck Isaac, by the way.

I expected a text in reply, but instead I got a FaceTime.

With a groan, I threw myself back against the tiny love seat in my room and covered my face with a Christmas tree–shaped pillow before answering. I didn't want him to see me like this.

"Kallum?" Nolan asked. "Is that you or a body-snatching Christmas tree pretending to be you?"

"It's me," I said. "You could have just responded with a text."

"Yeah, well, a Tuesday night *Fuck Isaac* really called for more than a text. So did I miss something?"

I peered out from behind the pillow. "I just . . . I feel for him and stuff. But why is he the only one who gets to be sad?"

"Kallum, are you crying?"

I sniffle for a moment. I feel like I *could* cry. "No, man. I'm pretty buzzed though. Winnie's husband showed up today. Well, her ex-husband. The ink on the divorce papers probably isn't even dry."

"I'd be shocked if it's even signed," Nolan said.

I let the pillow fall to my chest with a whimper. There was certain shit you could only do in front of a guy who'd known you since you were in sixth grade and helped you hide a surprise boner with his KC Royals binder. "You think she's still married?"

Nolan wore a shiny gray blazer with tissue paper tucked into his T-shirt collar. He was definitely in the middle of a makeup retouch. I forgot about the time difference between here and California. "Sounds like you got it bad for Winnie."

I shrugged. "It doesn't matter anyways. She knows what she wants and it's not me."

"One minute, people!" someone behind him yelled.

The makeup person ripped the tissue from his collar, and Nolan held his face closer to the phone. "Listen, man. Winnie and Michael have been together since they were teenagers. Sure, people can change, but this whole divorce could be a publicity stunt for all we know."

"It's not. Why would she even do this movie if it was?"

He shrugged. "I don't know. Let me ask the Christian media gods."

"Don't they only have the one?" I reach forward and take a swig of my Nutcracker IPA from a local brewery here in town. "I don't know, the trinity thing confuses me, man."

Nolan ignored me. "All I'm trying to say is you've had a crush on Winnie since we were kids, and crushes are fun . . . until they're not."

I didn't want to tell him about everything Winnie and I had done and how we were way past *crush* status now.

"If you're taking her ex showing up this hard now, imagine how much worse it will be when she leaves the movie to get back with him."

"She wouldn't leave the movie," I said. I might not know Winnie as well as I wish I did in some ways, but she would never cut and run on a film shoot in process with tons of people relying on her.

"You think Michael, Jesus's homeboy, is about to let his wife release a soft-core Christmas movie?"

"Ex-wife," I clarified. "You're right. It's just a crush. I'm not husband material. Fuck, even boyfriend material." Preparing myself now for disappointment would make it easier when it eventually came. It was better than letting myself have hope.

"Nolan!" someone said. "We're ready for you."

"I gotta go," he said. "But just pop a couple ibuprofen, eat something greasy in the morning, and let's talk about this for real."

"Okay," I said, knowing full well that I didn't have it in me to go down to the lobby and find some meds.

"And Kallum Lieberman?"

"Yeah?"

"If you were even a little bit bi, I'd have taken you off the market a long time ago."

"Don't tell Bee," I said with a grunting laugh.

"Oh, she'd be so into it," he said. "In fact, let's just count that as an open invitation. Gotta run. Love you, pizza boy."

"Love you back."

The phone went dark, and I polished off the rest of my beer before falling asleep right there on the couch. The warming amber liquid dulled me enough so that I didn't have to think about why or how this could hurt so bad.

WHEN I WOKE up the next morning, three things immediately became apparent:

1. I should have taken the ibuprofen.

2. I was too fucking old to sleep on a love seat. Or really anything that wasn't a bed.

4. I forgot what number 3 was.

I splashed cold water across my face, hoping it would have the same effect it did when we were touring and partying our way across the world through our teens and twenties.

But it was just cold water.

I needed coffee. And bacon. That was how you survived a hangover in your thirties.

Well, really, it was cold pizza, but I didn't think that'd be on the continental breakfast menu downstairs.

After a quick shower and forcibly ignoring my morning wood because the only way to get off at this point was to think of Winnie, and thinking of Winnie made me sad, and sad jacking off would make me even more sad, I got dressed and went downstairs in search of food.

Some small part of my brain knew that I was being an unreasonable mope. But the caveman in my brain only wanted Winnie.

And cold pizza.

After going downstairs and chugging a cup of coffee, I settled in with a feast of bacon, eggs, and a cherry cheese Danish that was definitely a day or two old, but my stomach didn't care.

"I need to check out," a voice said.

I looked over my shoulder to see Michael Bacher in a pair of khakis and a cable-knit sweater with another useless scarf draped over his shoulders. Who packed not one but two useless scarves for the same trip?

But he looked like a Ken doll, and I decidedly did not in my worn, flour-stained jeans, Slice, Slice, Baby sweatshirt, and sheep-fucker shoes.

"Checking out early?" the woman behind the counter asked.

My chest swelled with joy.

Michael's lips puckered with annoyance. "I said I needed to check out, didn't I?"

"Leaving empty-handed, huh?" At least I could officially tell Tamara that she wasn't the only person I loved to antagonize.

Michael slapped his credit card on the counter and marched over to me.

I dropped my fork and stood. That was one thing about being the biggest guy in the room—it gave me a chance to set the tone, especially with assholes like this.

But Michael wasn't intimidated or slowing down on his approach. His hand curled into a fist at his side.

Oh shit. I was a wiseass, for sure, but I was not the kind of guy who just punches people—even if I really wanted to. So as much as it killed me, I couldn't whale on this dude.

With just two steps between us, he reared his arm back, and I braced for impact.

"Oh no, you don't," Gretchen said as she walked through the front doors of the hotel, decked out in cold-weather running gear.

She held an arm out and caught Michael's fist before it collided with my face.

"The Hope Channel would just love to sue your ass, Michael. Do you know what kind of damages you're looking at for stalling a production like this?"

Michael snarled at her and pulled his fist back.

It was true, though. The Hope Channel and Michael's family's company, True Vine Productions, had been at odds for decades. They would jump on a lawsuit like this even if it cost them much more than it would recoup.

"Like your punch could even sting," I muttered.

Gretchen slapped my meaty shoulder. "You're not really helping the situation here."

Michael looked me up and down with a sneer. "It was you, wasn't it?"

"What are you talking about?"

"You ruined her then and you've ruined her now."

"Ruined her *then*?"

"The moment you snapped that picture of Winnie at the Chateau Marmont. She'd just won the surfboard for *Treasures in Heaven* and you took a picture of her passed out like just another LA party girl. Like a little whore."

My fingers twitched, begging to form a fist, and beside me Gretchen clenched her jaw.

"The media got their grubby little hands on that photo, and it tainted Winnie's reputation. And now, you think you can just— what? Give her a little carnal pleasure and think that's it? You made her look like a slut then and you're turning her into one now."

"Leave," I growled. "Now. You better pray I never see you again."

"Oh, brother Kallum, I'll pray all right. I'll pray for my dear Winnie and that she sees you for what you truly are—a washed-up celeb with nothing to offer. And even then, you were just the funny fat one who no one ever seems to remember. You're forgettable, which is just as well, because soon you'll be a memory Winnie would rather forget."

"It's time to go," Gretchen said. "You're disrupting my production." She crossed her arms and sniffed. "And you're a bigoted, woman-hating piece of shit."

Between us all, a credit card skittered across the floor. "You're all checked out," said Stella from behind the check-in desk. "You were charged for your full reservation due to our cancellation policy. Oh, and the printer's broken, so I can't get you a statement either."

Michael rolled his eyes and then bent over to pick up his matte black credit card. He turned to Gretchen. "To be clear: I plan on doing more than disrupting your production."

He left with his ass clenched—or maybe his butt was just that muscular.

Stella chuffed. "Good riddance."

I turned to Gretchen. "Coffee?"

"Please," she said before sitting down at my table as I fetched her a cup of coffee and a random selection of breakfast foods.

"Thanks for defending my honor back there," I told her once she'd had a little bit of caffeine.

"Well, I can't have Santa walking around like he just got in a donnybrook."

"Did you just say the word *donnybrook* like a 1950s gangster?" I asked.

She sighed. "It was my word of the day on some app Pearl had me download that teaches you a new word every day."

"So a dictionary?"

Gretchen grinned, and she had one of those toothy grins that could have gotten a decade of modeling contracts after her years as a child actor if she'd wanted that kind of life. "It's better than the meditation app she had me on last year. I got so enraged by the calming Englishman telling me to pretend I was in a meadow that I purposefully dropped my phone in our pool."

"But phones are basically waterproof now," I told her.

"Well, I know that now." She looked up over her mug of coffee. "But Pearl didn't and still doesn't."

"You remember that picture Michael was talking about?" I couldn't ignore the way it was gnawing at my brain. I ruined Winnie? How could that be?

"How could I not? 'Purity Princess Passes Out After a Long Night of Partying.' 'Abstinent? Not from the LA Party Scene.' 'Winnie Baker Lets It All Hang Out.'"

"God," I said, wincing. "I can't believe we survived that shit as teens." I knew it was bad back then, but time had taken away some of the sting. And I couldn't shake the fact that, in a way, this was my fault.

"Not all of us did, Kallum. Don't you think it's a little too perfect that Winnie and Michael got married just days after her eighteenth birthday? I can't say for sure, but the rumor was Winnie's team and parents basically strong-armed her into getting married to save her reputation. People were literally talking about whether or not she was still a virgin on morning talk shows."

My stomach curdled and it was more than the hangover. "I took that picture. I thought . . . she was so cute . . . just snoring there in her car while everyone else was trashed inside. I thought it was so sweet. I posted it as a joke."

Gretchen picked apart a muffin and gave me the most pitying look, like somehow in all of this, she felt bad for *me*. But I wasn't the one whose parents basically married them off to maintain social capital.

"Winnie went on an apology tour, and then she and Michael announced their engagement on *Ellen*. You remember that last part at least, right?"

"Painfully," I said. "We were on tour in Germany, and Isaac and Nolan took me out to lick my wounds, but I just sat in the black SUV waiting for them in the alley, drinking tiny bottles of liquor."

"That's sad," Gretchen confirms.

"I did end up hooking up with a German bridesmaid at the hotel bar," I admitted, which, thinking back, was probably when my little bridesmaid habit started.

"Lucky bridesmaid." Gretchen took a bite of hash browns and kept talking. "So you and I got to have some semblance of a teenage experience, even if it was delayed, but Winnie grew up as a child star and was basically married off before she could probably even go on a real first date or hang out at the mall."

"I have to talk to her." I grabbed my last two pieces of bacon and downed the rest of my second cup of coffee before getting up from the table and jogging to the elevator. Technically, the tabloid storm that followed my picture wasn't completely my fault, but I still felt like I owed Winnie something. An apology. An explanation. I wasn't sure.

"Kallum?" Gretchen called across the tiny lobby. "Good job not punching Michael, but if he shows up here again, I might beat you to it."

"We'll make it a real donnybrook," I told her as I jabbed the elevator's Up arrow three times in a row.

I PACED IN front of Winnie's door after knocking for a solid two minutes. Either she wasn't in there or she was really, really good at pretending she wasn't.

I wanted to apologize. I wanted to take her on a date—the kind of date I would have taken her on if we'd been just two normal teenagers when we first met and not living under some kind of intense microscope.

Trying once more, I rapped my fist on her door. "Winnie, can we talk?"

But it was totally silent, not even a creaking floorboard.

I sent her a quick text.

> **Me:** Hey, my call time isn't for another hour. You have time to talk?

A message appeared at the bottom of our text thread that said: Winnie has notifications silenced.

"Dammit," I whispered before I went down a few doors to my room and grabbed some Edelweiss Inn stationery and a pen.

Winnie—

Will you go on a date with me? A real one. Not a North Pole one.

—Kallum

I trekked back to her room and knocked once more just in case, but like I knew there would be, there was no answer. Squatting down, I slipped the note under the door, and immediately wanted to take it back. What if she said no? What if she just wanted whatever was going on between us to quietly die off and now that I'd asked her out on a date, I was forcing her hand?

Just then my ringtone filled the empty hallway.

Maybe it was her.

An unknown California number flashed across the screen.

"Hello?"

"Mr. Lieberman?" the person on the other end asked in an Australian accent.

"Speaking," I said, my shoulders broadening as though the person on the other end could even see me. "You must be the investor my nephew mentioned."

He laughed dryly. "I am his representative, yes."

I started walking back to the elevator in the hopes I'd run into Winnie on my way to hair and makeup.

"My client," he continued, "who you might know from—"

"He's a celebrity. He owns a sports team. He's on *Shark Tank*. But what does he want with me and who exactly are you? Is this whole mysterious vibe, like, part of your branding?"

"My name is Ian and my client was recently in Kansas City visiting family. I am legally obligated to say that he was not there in support of any local professional sporting leagues."

"We don't even have a basketball team," I told him. "Can we stop pretending I don't know who this guy is?"

Ian cleared his throat. "He and his family ordered your pizza and he was impressed. When he learned who owned Slice, Slice, Baby, he thought there was a real opportunity for expansion there. Texas and California to start. We'd want to discuss rebranding and diversifying the menu, but my client wants to meet in person."

"I need to think about it," I told Ian as I stepped back onto the elevator. I'd had several offers to franchise Slice, Slice, Baby and even sell it, but none of them felt right. And not that this did, but if this guy's client was who I thought he was, it might just be the real deal.

The truth was, though, I could barely think about the business. The machine was on autopilot and Topher had things under control. So I found myself almost resenting this Ian person for trying to take up real estate in my brain when all I could think of was being here with Winnie.

But soon this would be over, and Winnie would go back to LA where she'd start her new life. Or maybe even go back to that shitbag.

"I'll send over some preliminary numbers," Ian said.

"Great. I love math," I said.

"Oh, lovely. As do I."

"That was a joke," I told him, trying to hold back a laugh. "But yeah, thanks. I'll keep an eye out."

"A joke. Right."

We hung up and when I stepped back out into the lobby, Gretchen was gone.

Stella, though, sat there with her printer humming in the background as it spit out paper after paper.

"Got your printer up and running?" I asked.

Her white hair and bedazzled sweater vest were very misleading. She smiled as she pulled the pages from the printer and slid them into her filing cabinet one by one. "The Lord works in mysterious ways."

CHAPTER THIRTEEN

Winnie

I stood in front of my hotel door, holding the folded piece of paper in my hands.

The paper swam in front of my eyes, and I braced my shoulder against the wall, narcolepsy lapping like a thick tide at my feet, despite being passed out for the last sixteen hours. Even though I didn't have cataplexy, and the sudden loss of muscle control that came with it, the sleep attacks were sometimes just as sudden, just as overpowering. I just had to make it long enough for the meds to kick in, though, and then I'd stand a fighting chance of making it through makeup without falling asleep on the stylist.

But I was awake enough to know that the paper in my hands wasn't some kind of wonderful dream. It was real, and my cheeks were burning just reading it, and it was absurd given all the stuff that Kallum and I had already done, but this wasn't research; this wasn't for the movie.

This was something else.

Before I could talk myself out of it—before I could remind myself I was still feeling fragile after Michael's visit yesterday, that I'd rather pluck out my left eye than get romantically involved ever again—I pushed off the wall and walked over to the desk.

Yes, I wrote underneath his question, and then added a little heart next to it.

And then felt very silly.

I was thirty-two! This man probably knew his way around my cervix better than my gynecologist! Why was I drawing hearts on someone's note like I was in middle school?!

But I was humming to myself as I folded the note back up. Humming as I grabbed my bag and coat, and then actually singing an old INK song as I left my room to slip it under Kallum's hotel room door.

"Greetings and salutations," said Kallum as I opened my door later that evening.

He was wearing a zipped sweater with a peacoat open over it, nice jeans, and those sustainable wool sneakers he liked so much. His dark blond hair looked tousled, but his beard was perfect, like he'd groomed it and then made a point not to touch it again.

"Hi," I said a little breathlessly, looking up into those lovely eyes. There were times when he was like a bearded Peter Pan, all boyish mischief, and times when he looked like he just stepped off the set of a History Channel show about warriors or something. And then there were the times when he didn't look like anything but himself. Just Kallum Lieberman, who gave me his coat when I shivered between takes and who wrote me date requests in neat, blocky handwriting.

"You look—" Kallum flushed and cleared his throat. "Really cute."

I laughed. "You've seen me naked, and it's the jeans and long-sleeved shirt you think is cute?"

He was still flushing. "Yep."

It was strange how backward this was, especially since earlier this afternoon we snuck off between takes and I rode his fingers to a quaking orgasm, but my heart flipped over to see the way he looked down at the floor, the toe of his sneaker tracing the tiniest crescent in the red carpet over and over.

My own cheeks were hot as I shrugged on my wool trench and grabbed my purse. "Well, it would be a shame to deprive the world of my be-denimed cuteness." I approached him and he extended his elbow for me to take, gallant as always.

Together, we went downstairs and stepped out into the night. For the first time since we came to Christmas Notch, the dark didn't bring sharp, biting cold with it. Only a regular kind of chill that was warded off easily enough with our coats and gloves. The town was lit by lights strung along the treelined streets and in the storefront windows, and in the center of the town square, a giant Christmas tree shined like a beacon.

We were headed to the Mistletoe Theater, the little cinema in the middle of town that played exclusively winter holiday movies all year long. Kallum was taking me to see *The Holiday*, which was my favorite Christmas movie, because I was convinced that I was Iris. Minus the adorable cottage. (Actually, minus any kind of house these days.)

But the walk there was so lovely and Kallum's arm was so nice to hold on to that it was almost a shame we were going to the movie at all. I would have happily walked with him for our entire date, like we were in a Jane Austen book, promenading up and down the length of some drawing room.

"I'm sorry about the picture," he blurted, and I was still mentally imagining him in Regency-era breeches and a tailcoat, so it took me a second to catch up.

"The picture?"

"You know, the picture. The picture of you in the car after the Teen Choice Awards, the picture that ruined your life. The picture that I took. That picture."

"Oh," I said, and then added automatically, "It's okay."

He looked over at me, but I kept my own gaze resolutely on the salted sidewalk ahead of us.

"Gretchen told me about the fallout after I posted it. About the headlines."

I didn't want to talk about this. Not when the night was so pretty and Kallum was so handsome and when the ugliness from those years had mostly died off on its own. "It's okay, Kallum. Really."

"She told me that's why you were pushed into marrying Michael, and I wanted you to know that I'm sorry. I thought you were cute taking that nap and that everyone would find it as cute and silly as I did, and knowing that it's the reason you had to get married so young just kills me."

I looked to the side, blinking fast. I used to blame Kallum for everything that had gone wrong—or if not blame, then something like it. It was easier than blaming myself. But the truth was more complicated than that.

"The picture was the catalyst," I said, trying to keep my voice as neutral as possible. "But I was always going to end up where I did—Michael just happened to be there, because of *Treasures in Heaven*, because his parents owned the largest inspirational media company in the country. And it made the perfect story, you know? The princess who'd lost her way, redeemed by her prince's steadfast love. The *Treasures* story, but in reverse."

"Winnie." Kallum sounded miserable. I finally looked over at him and gave him as much of a smile as I could.

"I chose it with my eyes wide open. I chose to let my parents take control of my life; I chose to court Michael; I chose to say yes when he proposed. I wanted to believe that I'd found my prince charming, and that I was on the verge of living happily ever after. And yes, there are so many things I wish I could change, but even if I could go back and warn that younger version of myself, she wouldn't listen." I smiled for real. "She was so convinced that she knew everything. That she knew the right way to live. In fact, she'd be shocked to know I was going on a casual date with someone."

"Because she—you—weren't allowed to date?"

"Yes. But—"

I stopped, struggled for the right words. I had only talked at length about this with Addison, who already knew the world we'd grown up in, and my therapist, who got paid to listen. How could you explain something that took years and years just to even name?

"The end goal was purity," I tried again. "Always. And dating? That was just tempting impurity. Not to mention being a distraction from living fully for God's will."

"You can't live fully for God and date?" Kallum guided me over a dark slick of ice on the sidewalk. "That seems made up. Don't you have the Song of Songs in your bible? It's super horny."

"Yeah, well . . ." I laughed. "That one was un-horned for us. We were told the real point was about not awakening love until the proper time. And of course, the proper time was marriage. Which was really where the lingo became important, because *dating* was frivolous, and maybe even dangerous, but *courting*? Courting was about marriage. Spending time with someone to see if God wanted you to marry them. So as long as you were courting, you could spend time with someone."

"So you and Michael did this courting thing?"

"Yes. Marriage was on the table from the beginning. It *was* the table."

"And it didn't scare you? Thinking about getting married so young?"

When I glanced over at him, mild horror was sketched all over his face. "Almost everyone I knew got married before their mid-twenties, so it didn't seem so young, and I . . ." I cleared my throat. Kallum had given me a literal lap dance not too long

ago, one that ended with his semen spattered across my vulva. If
I could say this to anyone, I could say it to him. "I was having a
lot of physical feelings. Um, *desires*, I guess. Paul says it's better
to marry than to burn, and I was burning alive by then. Getting married would mean that all the hunger I had for Michael
and all the things I wanted to do with him didn't have to be
bad anymore."

"Winnie," Kallum said, voice almost pleading. "What you
wanted was never bad. Tell me you know that now."

"Yes," I replied. "But you can't imagine how scared I was of my
own feelings back then. How terrified I was that I was secretly
sinful. Because if I gave in, if I slipped just once . . ."

Kallum made a face.

"I know, I know." I made the same face back. "But that's how
I was raised to think about it. If your purity was tainted—by
lustful thoughts or kisses or more—then you were forever
smeared by those sins. I remember one time in youth group, my
pastors passed around a glass of water and had each person take
turns spitting in the glass; when they were done, the pastors
held up the glass and asked if anyone wanted to take a drink."

"*Gross.*"

"We were told it represented what happened to a girl when
she gave her purity away before she got married. We also did
the same thing later by passing around a rose and plucking
off all the petals—and once we did the exercise with a piece
of tape until it lost its stickiness—anyway, my point is that I
grew up thinking purity was this binary thing that you had
or you didn't, and once it was marred even the tiniest amount,
there was no going back. You would go to your future husband

cloaked in shame, and always know that he would be the bigger person for accepting you, even though you weren't fully pure." I tried to remember how I'd started talking about this part. "So I was excited to get married, because the sooner I was married, then the sooner I was free from worrying about it all the time."

I'd been so desperate for my wedding night, thinking it was the answer to everything, and then sex had hurt so much I'd snuck into the bathroom after, crying silently in the dark. Wondering if God was punishing me for some sin I couldn't remember committing.

Kallum seemed to know which way my thoughts had gone. "But it's not like getting married means you made it to sex Valhalla."

"No. Sex was . . ." I shook my head. "I guess you already know how it was for me, given that I didn't have my first real orgasm until a couple weeks ago."

His arm tensed under my hand, and from the press of his mouth, I could tell he was trying very hard not to say whatever it was he was thinking.

But he didn't need to. I'd already said it all to myself, a million times.

"I know, believe me," I said quickly. "The orgasms just—they didn't happen at first, and the longer they didn't happen, then the harder and harder it got to ask for them to happen. And asking was already really hard, because godly women are supposed to automatically love sex with their husbands, and if I didn't, maybe that meant I wasn't godly enough. And maybe *that* meant Michael would be able to see I wasn't godly enough, and I couldn't bear the idea of that. So I started faking it, faking feeling good, and hoping that at some point it would take. Like, maybe if the dinner was romantic enough, if I lit the right candle, if I just *tried* harder, it would happen."

I glanced down at where my hand curled over Kallum's peacoat-covered forearm, swallowing. "And then I eventually gave up. I thought maybe I was supposed to be taking pleasure in *his* pleasure instead. Maybe that was the 'joy in the marriage bed' married women talked about, and the idea of having an orgasm at all was selfish. Michael's joy would be in my body, and my joy would be in his . . . love. I guess. And that would have to be enough. That, and children."

Children that never appeared no matter how many basal body temperatures I recorded or how many ovulation test strips I peed on. In fact, I'd been about to see a doctor when I saw a text come through on Michael's phone. From Olivia, sent with an awkwardly angled selfie of them having sex in a Tahoe hot tub. Miss you and miss this 😊, read the text.

So anyway. I hadn't had to make that appointment after all.

"Winnie, you weren't stupid," Kallum said. "And I could punch Michael in the taint for making you feel that way."

His fierce defense of me made my stomach jump.

"Thank you," I said, looking over at him. We were in the middle of town now, the Christmas lights from the tree catching the gold in his hair. "Thank you for never making me feel, I don't know, weird. Or prudish."

His eyes when they looked at me were soft, as dark as the sky above us. "I get it, though. I didn't have the purity stuff going on, but I know what it's like to be pushed out of childhood too early. Except for me, it wasn't being pushed toward marriage, but toward this sort of 'being nineteen forever.' Old enough to be hot, but no older. Mature enough to know how to handle fans and their moms constantly hitting on me, but not so mature that I was allowed a steady girlfriend." His lips quirked up, although it wasn't really a smile. "Not that there would have been time, anyway. If we weren't touring, we were recording. If we weren't recording, we were doing press. If we weren't doing press, we were rehearsing for the next tour. Every minute was filled with INK, and while we made time for getting into trouble, there wasn't time for anything else. Much less a date like this."

"Then I'm glad we can go on a date like this now." I squeezed his arm as I thought of those sheltered or overworked teens who never had a chance to do something as simple as go to a movie with someone cute.

"Me too." His dimple flashed. "This is exactly the kind of date I would have taken you on too. So long as there wasn't an arcade in town, at least. Nothing is more romantic than getting your ass handed to you in Skee-Ball."

We walked up to the glassed-in ticket booth at the front of the theater, and Kallum bought our tickets to the movie.

"So what happens next on our teenage movie date?" I asked as we walked inside and handed an employee our tickets.

"What's next is I buy you some popcorn, and also fill up a little cup with butter to make sure we appropriately drizzle all the geological layers of the popcorn."

"I do that too! Well, now, I do. Before the divorce, I only ate popcorn without butter."

Kallum, now in the midst of paying for our snack, swiveled his head to look at me, like I'd just admitted to eating sawdust in my spare time. "What?"

"You know," I said, waving my hand around my body. "To maintain the official Winnie Baker image and all that." It had only been after Michael and I had separated and I'd lost my Hope Channel work that I'd learned how to feed myself—*actually* feed myself. To enjoy food, to eat when I was hungry, to learn what feeling full felt like.

"But I have a new official Winnie Baker image now," I said, and Kallum grinned, holding the popcorn butter cup as if to toast me with it.

"I'll drizzle to that."

Maybe not so surprisingly, we were the only ones seeing a twenty-year-old Christmas movie in March, and my heart gave several quick, jumpy beats when I realized that Kallum and I would be alone in here during our grown-up teenage date.

Kallum seemed to be thinking the same thing, because he shot me a wicked grin over his shoulder as he led me up the shallow ramp to the seats in the back. This was an old theater, without stadium seating, and the back was shadowed enough that if anyone did come in, they wouldn't be able to see us.

Peeling off our coats felt like a striptease; when Kallum first put his hand palm up on the armrest of the seat and I grazed his pinkie with mine, it was on par with the buzz of the Peppermint Stick.

By the beginning of the movie, we were palm to palm, our fingers laced with each other's, and by the time Iris and Amanda decided to switch houses, Kallum's free hand was stroking my knee over my jeans. I felt each circle of his fingertip like it was on my breast—my pussy—and it felt *good*. Not shameful, not chased with guilt.

Just . . . good.

I finally couldn't take it anymore. "Kallum?" I whispered, even though we were alone with Cameron Diaz and Jude Law at the moment.

"Yeah?" His eyes were dark enough to reflect part of the movie—cottages and snow.

"What else would we do on our date?"

"Well." His Adam's apple moved up and then back down again. "I think I'd try to kiss you."

Kiss. For as much as we'd done—lap dances and orgasms galore—we still hadn't kissed. Because we both knew that kissing wouldn't be for research. If we kissed, it would be because we wanted to kiss each other for the sheer hell of it.

If we kissed, we couldn't keep up the pretense that what was happening between us was only about our movie.

Panic flared at the idea, at someone else being able to touch a heart that had taken so much work and anguish to claw back into my own rib cage again, but there was more than panic inside me, there was craving and lust and the chest-fluttering feeling and then I was leaning forward and our mouths brushed together.

Soft and warm.

Slow.

His beard did tickle, but in a way that made me want to rub against him like a cat, and when he parted my lips with his own, I tasted mint and ChapStick and the faintest bit of popcorn. His tongue was silky against mine, slick and skilled, and I whimpered, which earned me a rough groan. Abruptly I was hauled out of my seat and dragged onto his lap.

I parted my thighs to straddle him, and the minute my center came into contact with the hard-on trapped in his jeans, we both grunted, our mouths crashing together once again as I began grinding on him. He shoved a hand up my shirt to find a breast, which he squeezed and fondled and stroked over my bra.

This is all backward, I thought as I pulled back to stare at his half-hooded eyes and his kiss-swollen mouth. Kisses were supposed to come before lap dances. Chest flutters before orgasms. Movie dates before marriages and restaurant chains.

But I couldn't find it in me to care. Maybe this was the wrong way around, maybe I should be embarrassed that I was thirty-two and making out in a movie theater like I was seventeen, but Kallum had that way of making anything even close to embarrassment melt away. Of making everything fun and perfect and *light*.

And even though it was temporary, I couldn't help feeling like it was a gift. A gift I'd never forget, even after we left Christmas Notch, and each other, behind.

CHAPTER FOURTEEN

Kallum

I sat in a glistening red sleigh wearing furry red pants and an unbuttoned Santa jacket, and I had my bits tucked into a flesh-colored pouch and ready for action as a snow machine whirred to life behind me. Ya know, just normal pizza mogul shit.

It'd been two days since my date with Winnie, and all I could think about was kissing her. It gave me foolish hope. We shared the kind of kisses that made me want to make playlists and over-think about birthday presents. But we only had four measly days left. And then that would be a wrap on *Santa Baby*. What could possibly change in four days?

Jack held a hand out for Winnie as she stepped into the sleigh. "It's just like we rehearsed the other night," he said. "Choreography. That's all it is."

Winnie nodded confidently as she straddled my thighs. The short buffalo check dress she wore was tailored so perfectly to her chest that it gave me a semi. She leaned forward and the scalloped lace of her red bra—which was part of her costume today—peeked out the edge of her bodice.

Today was the big sex scene. All the others had consisted of short and simple choreography or had been snippets for montages, but this was the first (and longest) sex scene in the whole movie. Even though Winnie was putting on her brave face, her nerves were in the details. Her trembling fingers. The way she bit the inside of her lip so she didn't ruin her makeup.

"You good?" I asked under my breath.

She gave me a small nod as she let her inner thighs settle around my lap, but she still didn't sit all the way down, which irritated me just a bit.

"Get comfortable, Winnie," Jack said. "You're not going to hurt Kallum." He chuckled to himself. "He might actually like that."

Winnie laughed and let herself fully settle in my lap.

I studied her expression, looking for a hint. She'd been in this exact same position just the other night in the dark movie theater. Why was this so different now?

Sure, there were the lights, camera, and crew. And this scene really was a doozy, but I still took it a little personally . . . and then promptly hated myself for it. This wasn't about me. Or even us.

This was work. Winnie and I were doing our job. That was it.

"Just signal if either of you need to come up for air," Jack told us before he rejoined the bare-bones crew waiting to get started.

Miss Crumpets was in a portable playpen next to him, snuffling around for her favorite stuffed carrot.

"We're rolling," Gretchen announced, "but you two ease in and take your time."

"You okay?" I asked Winnie.

She braced herself on my shoulders and looked up from under her pre-mussed curls courtesy of the hair department. "I'm really hoping all my research pays off."

I cradled her left cheek in my palm just like we'd rehearsed, and she nuzzled into my touch before dipping her head down and parting her lips.

My body lit up, reacting the way it always did to her. Except this wasn't anything like the kiss at the movie theater. Our tongues danced, but just enough for the camera. I wanted more, and pulled her to me just as she was pulling back for her little choreographed striptease, and our foreheads smacked together.

Winnie let out a soft *oof*.

"Are you okay?" I asked as I gently pressed my fingertips to the site of impact on her head. "Sorry, I just—"

"Medic!" Gretchen called.

"I'm fine," Winnie told her.

"My bad," I said. "I got turned around on the choreo."

Hair and makeup quickly ran up to re-powder both of us and fluff Winnie's hair.

Winnie motorboated her lips and bounced her shoulders like she was a football player waiting for the coach to put her in.

I waved my arms around and whispered, "This energy is really sexy."

"I'm trying to hype myself up," she said.

"Well, you're definitely hyping me up," I said, glancing down to my crotch.

She giggled and guided my hand to her cheek before resting her hands on my shoulders.

"Rolling," Gretchen called.

We ran through all the motions. The kiss, her leaning back as she seductively unbuttoned her dress, and then showing off the luscious lace underneath.

I gripped her waist before letting my hands sweep up her rib cage to cup her breasts.

Don't get a chub. Don't get a chub. Don't get a chub.

Just like we practiced, Winnie leaned forward so that her pillowy chest was right in my face. Winnie wasn't going topless in the movie, but the bra was sheer, and I had been instructed to *lick*. Don't mind if I do.

"Hot," Winnie said with a gasp.

I couldn't help but smirk as I traced her cleavage with my tongue. I guessed I wasn't the only one mixing business with pleasure.

"Smoke," she said, her voice a little frantic, like she was about to—

"FIRE!" she yelled.

I jerked my head around to see the snow machine in flames. Shit! My whole body went into emergency response mode as I threw Winnie over my shoulder and gunned it out of the sleigh.

Crew members armed with extinguishers swarmed the set as I delivered Winnie to her director's chair.

She gripped the arms of her chair and just stared at me, her eyes wide and stunned. "I'm sorry but did you just throw me over your shoulder like a bag of potatoes?"

"Umm." I glanced down to see my belly poking out from my open Santa jacket. "I just . . . when I was a kid I was really scared of my house burning down, and I always imagined myself throwing the family dog, Coop, over my shoulder as I ran out of a burning building."

We both glanced over to the snow machine, the flames now contained, but the warehouse was filling with residual smoke.

Winnie's lips twitched with a smile. "So you thought of me like your dog?"

"Hey," I said. "Coop was my world until he got doggy cancer."

"Is doggy cancer different from regular cancer?"

I shrugged. "I'm not a doctor, but yes. Yes, it is."

"Okay, people," Gretchen said. "We've got another snow machine on its way, but it's coming from somewhere in Massachusetts, so it's going to be a few hours. Normally, I'd send everyone home for the night, but our schedule is tight and we've got to get this scene in. Head back to the hotel if you want. Grab a bite to eat. Cammy will send out an email when we have a firm ETA on the new machine."

I grabbed my phone from where it sat on the chair next to Winnie's. One missed call from Topher, three missed calls from Tamara, and twelve text messages. I needed to figure out what the hell was going on.

Winnie still sat there, a little dazed as she buttoned up the front of her dress.

"Hey, Winnie?" I said.

"Yeah?"

"I wasn't thinking of you like my dog," I told her. "More like the first thing I'd grab in a burning building."

She blinked a few times, looking stunned.

Fuck. I shouldn't have said that. I wanted to fold the words back into my mouth. But instead I held up my phone. "I gotta deal with a few things. Let me know if you want to go over our scene or anything before the new snow machine swoops in to save the day."

She nodded again, her knuckles turning white as she gripped the arms of the chair even harder. "Sure."

"HAVE YOU TALKED to my mom?" Topher asked. He'd picked up the phone before I could even get through one ring.

I paced back and forth in front of the gumball machine assembly line. I'd snuck into the fake Santa's workshop that we'd used for the opening of the film when I announced to all the workers at the North Pole that I'd be going on my journey. It was mostly dark except for the strip of safety lights overhead.

"No," I said. "Why?" I tried to not sound suspicious. Topher wasn't a teenager anymore, but I still didn't want to risk my status as the Cool Uncle.

He sighed into the phone. "Thank God. Okay, so Mom opened a letter from UMKC confirming that I dropped out this semester."

"You did *what?*" I asked, losing my Cool Uncle status in three little words.

"Dropping out makes it sound so much worse than it is. I'm taking a gap semester. People in Europe do it all the time."

"Toph, I never went to college, but I'm pretty sure your mom doesn't give a shit about what college students in Europe do."

"And that's the problem!" he said, as though he'd just made the most profound statement that I definitely did not get.

"Okay, back up. Why are you not in school right now?"

He took a breath. "I just figured that with you being gone for a little bit and me being in charge of the place . . ."

Shit. I could see where this was going.

". . . that I could take some time away from school. I don't even think college is for me, honestly. You didn't go to college," he said. "And look at you. You're, like, a pizza mogul."

"Bud," I said. "I'm flattered, but this really should have been a discussion between you and your parents."

"Yeah, because my mom is so good at discussions."

Nope. I was not going to fall for it. He would not con me into shit-talking his mother in front of him, no matter how right he was. The thing was that Tamara could do discussions. She just loved so big and so hard that sometimes the discussions got . . . loud.

"So now your parents think you dropped out of college to run a pizza parlor?" I asked.

"I mean, you're missing a few details, but that's the gist of it."

"And Tammy thinks I know?" Of course she did. She'd called me three times in the span of four minutes.

"Well . . ."

"Topher," I said in the same way I'd said his name when he was little and about to do something he absolutely should not do, like bite Crusty the cat's ear. "What are you not telling me?"

"I might have said it was your idea."

I held my hand to the bottom of the phone, blocking the receiver, and hissed a string of swear words. "You're going to have to tell them the truth at some point," I finally said when I was done.

"But not today?" he asked.

I hated the thought of lying to my sister, especially considering her current opinion of me, but Topher was already in hot water. I knew what it felt like to be the family fuckup, and if I could save him from that—or at least delay it—I would. "Just text me everything you told her so we can get our stories straight."

"Oh my God, you are legit the best uncle of all time. Texting you right now!"

"I bet that's what you tell—"

The line cut out.

"All your uncles," I mumbled.

I hoisted myself up onto the workshop table with my phone at my side. Moments later, I received a text from Topher that was so detailed it could have been a police report.

Now, I just had to psych myself up to call my sister. No FaceTime. She'd be able to tell I was lying before I even opened my mouth.

I needed to hype myself up like Winnie had done in the sleigh. I let my lips fly, blowing air out, as I shook my shoulders like Rocky Balboa.

"Hey, Champ," Winnie purred as she stepped into the soft glow of the safety lights.

"I didn't hear you come in," I said.

"You were busy doing my pump-up routine," she said. "Got something big you need to tackle?"

I held my phone up. "A phone call back home."

"To whom?" she asked as her heels—shiny and bright red—clicked against the floor. I'd never been into the idea of someone stepping on me in heels, but her legs moving lazily one in front of the other made me wonder. And then there was the thought of her foot pressed to my chest back at the North Pole. Did I suddenly have a foot fetish? Or was it just a Winnie fetish?

"My sister," I finally answered.

"You mean to tell me there's someone out there who actually intimidates you?"

"You've never met my sister," I told her. "She's amazing. Don't get me wrong. But I guess you could say she and I aren't seeing eye to eye right now." I shrugged. "But anyway, you're here, which means Tammy Cakes can wait."

"Tammy Cakes?" she asked. "No wonder she's got it out for you. That's an awful nickname. I don't even want to know what you call me."

"You don't require a nickname," I tell her. "You're Winnie Baker."

"Well, Kallum Lieberman."

"Yes, Winnie Baker?"

"I have a proposition for you."

My dick twitched as I tucked my phone into my back pocket. She had my full attention. "Your propositions always seem to involve me getting into trouble."

"For the sake of artistic research," she said, and then took a deep breath. "Fuck me. Please."

CHAPTER FIFTEEN

Winnie

I mean"—I needed to clarify, because we'd already done so many kinds of sex—"intercourse. Penetration. That."

The words left my mouth along with all the air in my chest, because for an awful, certain second, I absolutely knew he was going to say no. He was going to say no because we were costars and we were actively shooting a movie together and Steph would literally shred us like cooked chicken if she found out. He was going to say no because it was very apparent after our theater date that whatever was happening between us was more than research. And also he was Mr. Bridesmaid and also I had no interest in rehashing my teenage mistakes when it came to romance and relationships.

And anyway, we'd agreed that this would end the minute we left Christmas Notch.

But Kallum didn't say no. He didn't say no at all.

In fact, he looked like a kid who'd just been told he was going to Disney World.

"You want to do that? With me? When? Right now?" He swiveled his head around the barely lit set, as if already scouting potential coital locations in Santa's Workshop. And then he grabbed my hand and started pulling me impatiently to the table where elf extras had been pretending to assemble toy race cars.

A happy, fragile gratitude bloomed in my chest, right where the panic had been. He hadn't said no! And I didn't feel gross or tawdry! I was light as air as Kallum spun and tugged me into him, as warm as a sunbeam as he dropped his mouth to mine and gave me a hard, quick kiss. Overflowing like the proverbial cup when he lifted me and put me on the table and then stepped between my thighs.

Kallum kissed me again, this time like he was going off to war, with his lips moving hot and urgent over mine, and his tongue delving into my mouth. His hands were in my hair, tilting my head back so my mouth was more available for his plunder.

"Winnie," he mumbled against my lips. "I'm ruining your makeup."

Luckily, years of hiding unscheduled naps and sleep attacks had made me a very creative liar when it came to ruined makeup and mussed hair. "I'll tell them I had an allergic reaction to my lunch and it made my lips itchy," I mumbled back.

A grunt and a harder kiss told me that he approved of the little allergy fiction, and he dropped a hand to my breast, squeezing and molding until I could feel my nipple grow stiff against his palm. He stroked his tongue against mine, all slick and strong and seeking, until I was panting underneath his mouth and arching my chest against his touch.

I wanted more, and *more* was this giant, pulsing need beating in time to my thudding heart, and I wrapped my legs around his waist to lock him against me as I fisted my hands in his open Santa coat. His bare chest under the coat was warm to the touch, pelted in that light golden hair, and oh my God, why were hairy chests so sexy, why did I want to spend the rest of my life draped over his bare chest and purring?

Okay, maybe not the rest of my life, because I could feel the thick bar of his erection between my legs, and I wanted it in my hands, in my mouth. Inside me. I moved a hand down to tug at the waistband of his pants, and he let out a ragged groan.

"Wait," he said, although he did sound pained as he said it. "Winnie, wait."

"I locked the door behind me," I muttered, still yanking at the shockingly well-tailored waistband of his Santa pants. That Luca person was not joking around when it came to costumes; these seams were Savile Row quality.

"No," he said, pulling back enough to break our kiss but gently pressing his forehead to mine. I could feel his rough exhales against my wet lips. "I meant: Are you sure? Are you sure you want to?"

Did I want to?? Was water wet?? Was peppermint lube a bad idea??? *Yes*, yes, I wanted to; I'd wanted to since those first clumsy takes in the sleigh, when all I could think about was how awkward I must have looked and how *un*awkward and wonderful I felt whenever Kallum and I were together in private. I needed a fresh hit of that, a quick infusion of whatever sex magic Kallum carried inside himself, because as it was, I'd been about as yielding and sexy as a bag of broom handles during our takes today.

Okay, and maybe I wasn't being entirely truthful with myself. I'd wanted this since our date two days ago, when Kallum had left me at my hotel door with a kiss that seared both my heart and my lips. I'd wanted this since I crawled into my bed after and felt the empty space next to me like an affront, a void. I'd wanted Kallum there with me, and I didn't want it because I was supposed to want it or because I thought it would make him happy.

I just . . . wanted it. Free from any worry about what it meant for me, Winnie Baker. Free from any thoughts about whether it made me good or bad. No courting or discerning required.

Only both of us choosing it, together.

"I'm sure, Kallum," I murmured. "I think I've never been more sure about anything in my life."

He closed his eyes, a wounded noise coming from his chest. But he didn't speak, and when he opened his eyes again, there was nothing but heat simmering in their depths. He dragged his mouth over mine once, slow and hot, and then I was being pushed backward onto the table, plastic wheels scattering to the floor and rolling away.

Kallum bent over me, stamping his kisses along my jaw as he slid one of those giant hands up my thigh and all the way under the skirt of my dress. He moved his lips farther down.

"Are you wet for me?" he asked, the words rumbling right from his mouth and into my throat. "Does this pretty cunt need to be played with?" A blunt fingertip sanded over the lace covering my seam. He was half on top of me, and I couldn't arch, couldn't buck closer. I could only lay there, panting, while his fingers ran torturous lines up and down my sensitive center, my panties a hideous barrier between my body and his touch. Just as I was about to blurt that they need to come off before I died of whatever the vaginal equivalent of blue balls was, Kallum nudged the crotch of my panties aside. He slowly stroked his fingers up the slickness he found there to the hard pearl of my clit at the top.

"I could feel how wet you were through these," Kallum said, biting my throat before straightening up and tugging the lace down my hips and off my legs all together. "You must have been hot and bothered for a while now, hmm?"

"Since the sleigh," I said as Kallum spread my thighs wide and stared at my naked pussy with the look of a starved man. He dropped gracefully to his knees and pressed his hands to my thighs, his thumbs reaching to my center and opening me up for his avid gaze.

"Fuck, Winnie," he mumbled. "This pussy could bring about world peace."

My laugh broke into a moan as he licked a hot, velvet stripe up my center and then slowly began mapping every contour and dip of my sex, swirling into my channel until I was squirming, and then moving up to knead at my clit until an orgasm shimmered through me, gentle and quivering and sweet.

He stood up and wiped his mouth with the back of his hand, but even as he was standing, he was looking at my cunt like he needed to dive back in.

"Kallum," I whispered. "Fuck me with your cock now."

"That mouth of yours is killing me," he groaned. His hands dropped to the waist of his pants and he fumbled to unfasten it. "Can't wait to feel you around me. Can't wait to slide into that wet— Oh shit."

He'd frozen, his hands still on his pants, his eyes wide on mine.

"I don't have a condom," he said, in the tones of someone doing a reading at a funeral service. "I wasn't planning on . . . well, you know. My wallet is back at the costume department with my clothes."

I could have laughed if I wasn't about to experience the world's first death due to penis deprivation. "Can't we find one somewhere? I don't know, maybe Jack has one in his Caboodle?"

Kallum's face lit up. "I could do a Caboodle heist. Like *Ocean's Eleven*!"

A heist would take too long, and I didn't actually know if Jack had one in his kit, anyway, since the kit was technically only for *fake* sex. "Or maybe it would be okay?" I suggested, knowing I sounded desperate, and not even caring at this point. "If you pulled out? I'm clean. And I trust you."

He closed his eyes again, the picture of a man at war with himself. But then: "*Wait*," he said, eyes popping open. "I got this! We're saved!"

And proud as a Boy Scout, he reached into the back pocket of his Santa pants and pulled his phone free.

"Are you going to Instacart a condom?"

He gave me a giant grin as he shook his head and pried the case off his phone, revealing a condom wedged inside. The little foil wrapper had an anthropomorphic pizza slice with a blond pompadour printed on it . . . an anthropomorphic pizza slice I recognized.

"Is that a—"

"Slice, Slice, Baby promotional condom? Why, yes it is." Kallum tapped his temple. "I saved one for an emergency smash."

"Your pizza place made promotional condoms?"

"Sure did. Pizza and Chill: order a pizza for two and get a free condom." He sighed. "It didn't take off like I thought it would, so we ended the promotion early. I've got a lot of condoms left over."

"Well, I'm glad you had this one left over," I said, not even caring that it was a freebie pizza condom coming to the rescue.

"How right you are, mademoiselle," he said, tossing his phone onto the table and clamping the edge of the condom packet between his teeth. I squeaked as he scooped me up and carried me to Santa's big red chair at the front of the workshop.

He gave me another grin as he turned and sat us both down, him in the chair and me straddling him. I pulled the condom from his mouth and leaned in to kiss him, both of us grunting as my full weight settled against his erection.

He reached up and started undoing the top buttons of my dress, his hands pushing inside the moment they could, rough and demanding as I found his tongue with mine. I knew my lipstick was fucked, and probably all the makeup around my mouth too as his beard rubbed against my chin and cheeks, but

I didn't care. I'd tell them I fell into a pond, that I was attacked by a bear or a maple syrup poacher, because I wanted to be smeared and marked by him. I wanted to look in the mirror and see *Kallum was here* scrawled in my beard-chafed inner thighs and ruined makeup.

Condom dangling from my fingers, I pushed open his Santa coat so I could pet his bare chest. "Kallum," I breathed, scratching a hand down his sternum. "Please."

He knew what I was asking for. He took the condom and I rose up on my knees so he could shift underneath me. And then he laughed so hard that I shook along with him.

"I forgot," he managed between his deep giggles, "about the pickle pouch." And sure enough, his hand emerged with the not-so-little beige pouch he'd been wearing for our sleigh scene. The sheer ridiculousness of the moment slammed into me, and I was giggling too; here we were on Santa's chair, in our red velvet costumes, our sexcapade helped by fire-prone snow machines and hindered by pickle pouches, and oh my God, this was the most fun I'd ever had in my entire life. This moment, this movie. These last few weeks with Kallum.

Kallum tore open the packet and then our giggles subsided into quick, deep breaths as he adjusted his erection so that it was free of his pants. It was thick and heavy looking, a dark, needy red color, with a swollen head and pre-come already smeared at the tip. I watched as he pinched the top of the condom and then rolled it over his length with deft, easy movements.

"I've never seen someone do this in real life," I murmured, fascinated. "It's really hot."

"It's hot to me too. Knowing I'm getting ready to be inside someone . . ."

Our eyes met, both of us clearly thinking the same thing. He was about to be inside *me*. We were really doing this.

Not breaking our gaze, he curled one hand around my hip and used his other to hold his penis upright. He guided me down, so that he pushed at my opening.

The skirt of my dress hid everything from view, but it was almost a blessing, because I didn't know if I could handle the sight of what was happening along with the feeling. The sensations were already so much—the heat of him through the latex, the shudder-inducing way he began stretching me as I slowly impaled myself.

Inch after thick inch, I sank down, having to pause twice to adjust, to take a breath. He was big and I was out of practice, and when I looked up from his chest to his face, his expression was one of pure agony. His eyes were closed, his head tilted back against the throne. His jaw was tighter than I'd ever seen it.

And I realized he was trembling. No, not trembling. *Shaking.* His thighs underneath mine, his hand on my hip, his other quaking hand now sliding up my thigh. With my hands braced on his bare chest, I could feel the heavy, near-violent pumping of his heart inside his rib cage.

All of him, shaking, shaking, shaking—muscles, heart, body, and bone. Like he was coming apart, coming undone, and all that was left between him and death was me.

And when I finally managed to take all of him inside me and

whispered his name, he groaned like I'd just buried a dagger in his chest.

"Baby," was all he said. "Baby."

His eyes were still squeezed shut, and I was grateful, because I suddenly felt on display, straddling him like this. I'd tried being on top a handful of times before now, and every time, I'd felt like I was doing something wrong, and even now, I wasn't sure what to do.

Bounce up and down? Circle my hips like I was playing with a Hula-Hoop?

He didn't open his eyes, but he squeezed my hips and grunted, "I promise I'm going to look at you again, but I'm half a second away from blowing my load, and I need a minute."

"Really?"

His firm lips quirked—half smile, half tortured grimace. "Really. You could start recapping the plot of *The Phantom Menace* to me and I'd still go off like a rocket."

"Because it's a boring movie?"

"Because it's a cinematic tour de force!" he exclaimed. "Have you ever seen the 'Duel of the Fates' fight scene? It's the seminal creative achievement of our time!"

I laughed and then he sucked in a breath. "Babe," he managed. "Seriously. I'm dying here. You feel *so fucking good.*"

And just like that, all my anxiety was gone. It didn't matter what I did, because Kallum loved all of it, was in agony just from being inside me. I didn't need to impress him or please him—I didn't need to put on a show. This was for both of us, and as if he knew which way my thoughts were going, he opened his eyes a sliver and murmured, "Do what feels good to you. It all feels good to me."

So while Kallum watched from under hooded eyelids, I experimented. I tried lifting myself up and down, the way I'd had when I'd tried being on top before. It felt good, but *only* good, so I stopped and tried swiveling my hips next, moving in slow circles and feeling Kallum's rigid cock move inside me in turn.

His hands were tightening and loosening on my hips—out of pleasure or the effort of restraint, I didn't know—and then he groaned again as I tried moving forward and backward on his lap, grinding as hard as I could. Sparks shot hot and bright into my stomach every time I did.

"Holy shit," I breathed, bucking my hips even harder. His erection felt bigger than ever inside me, filling me up, choking the breath out of me. The swollen bead of my clit had the gravity of a supermassive black hole; my soul, my entire being, was being pulled down, down, to where we were joined. To where it was wet and hard and tight and urgent, and I was shaking now too, trembling, an orgasm looming over me like a threat, like the shadow of a tidal wave ready to pull me under.

Kallum leaned back a little and lifted up my skirt, his eyes hooding even more as he watched me fuck myself on his lap.

"That's it, baby," he said, his voice nothing but gravel. "That's it."

"Kallum," I whispered, almost panicked. It was too much, too good, too hot—one person couldn't endure the force of pleasure this intense. I was going to die when I came, I was sure of it.

Kallum's hands moved to my ass, and he urged me on, moving me over him, his eyes roving everywhere—my face, my bra-covered tits, my eager cunt—while he murmured a litany of absolute filth.

Your pussy feels so good, baby, so fucking good.

Spent so many nights jerking off thinking of this.

God, you're wet. Make me wet too, babe.

And then one of his hands moved, a fingertip finding the tight, pleated circle behind my pussy and grazing the sensitive skin there. I shivered as he traced the place where my cunt stretched around him and then trailed the slick moisture back up to my hole.

"I want to fill you up everywhere," he said, leaning forward to drag beard-rough kisses along my throat and collarbone. "I want to feel the inside of you while I'm fucking your cunt. Can I?"

"*Yes.*" The word fractured into a moan as he began pressing his finger inside. It was a sweet pressure, a shudder-inducing invasion. It made everything feel tight and full and filthy.

"I'd love to put a toy here someday," he grunted. "Would you like that?"

"Only if I can return the favor," I whispered and then blushed as he pulled back to give me a burning look.

"Don't say it unless you mean it," he warned.

"Would you . . . would you do that? For me?"

A dark grin, crooked and quick. "I'd do it for *me*. It would be so hot to have you fuck me there." He leaned in to nip my jaw. "Who knew Winnie Baker harbored such dirty fantasies?"

I sure didn't until I came here to Christmas Notch—and now here I was riding Kallum Lieberman like I was in the Kentucky

Derby, our Mr. and Mrs. Claus costumes half torn off, my makeup smeared, repeatedly fucking myself not just on his erection, but his finger too. And it felt so good, and more than just good, it felt *right* and gorgeous and sublime. Like my body was made for this . . . and how strange was it that I used to think of sex like I was giving parts of myself away? Because there was nothing subtracted here, nothing stained or marred. There was only Kallum and me giving gifts to each other—the same gift multiplied many times, the same gift made more and more wonderful by our sharing it together.

And what if *this* was virtue? What if this was purity? The raw generosity of sharing space and pressure and pleasure, the honesty that came with each moan and every breath? What if good sex only made me *more* like Winnie Baker in the end . . . happier, more hopeful, closer to my own soul and the soul of the person I was with?

I wasn't soiled by this. I wasn't dulled. If anything, the sex I'd had before—within those all-important bounds of marriage— had done that.

But this. This made me brighter, shinier, a lamp with the bushel basket pulled right off. And when the orgasm finally tore through me, clawing up from my belly to my chest and to my throat, I felt downright incandescent. A burning sun right there in that Santa chair, in Kallum's lap, glowing with pumping blood and joy and life and love for the person right here with me.

Love.

The word burned brighter than the pleasure even, and—as my center seized and released and my belly fluttered and my hips jerked in instinctive, eager movements to wring every last second out of my climax—my heart was on fire with it.

But no . . . that couldn't be right? I couldn't be in love after only three weeks; I couldn't be in love with my costar who was also my sex tutor who was also the king of short-lived flings. It didn't matter that he was sexy and silly and warmhearted, or that when I was with him, all the ideas of Old Winnie and New Winnie melted away, and there was only *Now* Winnie and she was enough.

No, I couldn't be in love, because I wasn't ridiculous enough to believe in all that anymore. This was just hormones and affection and maybe some kind of lingering surfboard-injury-induced Stockholm attachment. It was just being here in Christmas Notch, where everything was sparkly and unreal and filled with artificial hope and wonder.

But the fire in my chest never stopped. Not when I slumped against Kallum after my body finally went still, spent and panting. Not when he grabbed my hips and fucked up into me like I was his brand-new toy from the Toy Shop 2 and I climaxed a second time, screaming into his Santa coat.

Not when he said my name in a voice that curled my toes all over again. *Winnie*, as his cock pulsed inside me; *Winnie*, as he held me flush against him and gave me every last throb of his release.

Winnie, baby, as we both came down together, his arms so tight and warm around me and his lips in my hair.

No, my heart still burned, and the flames weren't flames, but echoes of that one absurd, childish lie of a word.

Love.

I ENDED UP nailing the next take in the sleigh.

And then Kallum nailed me that night in his hotel room, my hair still damp from the snow from the new snow machine, my core still wet and slick from earlier in Santa's Workshop.

The next three days after that were a blur of fake sex and not-so-fake sex, and I couldn't get enough of it. And despite the *significant* amounts of fornication, the sky didn't fall in on me. I wasn't riddled with diseases, I wasn't scandalously pregnant. I was just happy.

Deliriously so.

And so maybe my guard was starting to slip. Maybe that burning in my chest didn't scare me so much anymore.

Maybe, I thought on the second-to-last night in Christmas Notch as I lay nestled against Kallum's shoulder, petting the hair on his naked belly and feeling him rumble like a pleased bear, *maybe this doesn't have to end when we leave.*

Maybe . . . maybe we didn't have to say goodbye after all.

CHAPTER SIXTEEN

Kallum

Winnie lay back in bed, fully nude with the blankets draped across her hips and her arms folded behind her head. We were both spent, but I'd be ready to rebound in no time at all. For Winnie, my body could recharge faster than a fucking Tesla.

I lay there next to her, propped up on my side, memorizing every freckle and birthmark and the way her breasts spilled gently to the side. She sucked in a laugh as my index finger circled her belly button and the faint scar just above it.

"What's this from?" I asked.

She peered down to see. "Oh . . . that. A navel ring."

I nearly choked. "What? Did you say a belly button ring? Rebel, rebel, Winnie Baker."

"For a full seven hours," she said. "I was sixteen and Addison convinced me to pierce my navel with a sewing needle. But then it got red so quickly after, and I was terrified it was infected, and then I broke down and confessed it all to my parents. My dad was so mad he put my cell phone in his gun safe and my mom cried like I'd been murdered."

"Wow. There's just so much to unpack there."

"The gun safe, the belly button piercing, or the fact that my work was actually paying all of our cell phone bills?" she asked.

"Are you close with them now?" I asked. "Your parents."

She turned her head to look at me and then gently ran her fingers through my hair. "I thought so." She exhaled, her brow furrowing, and I wanted to reach up and smooth every worry from her forehead. "They were upset that I left Michael. Given what Michael said to me the other day, I'm pretty sure they're losing their minds over me doing this movie, but I wouldn't know for sure because we haven't spoken in months. It doesn't matter, though. I don't know if I could bring myself to take their calls even if they were talking to me."

Her gaze drifted to the window behind me and the snowy early morning sky visible just beyond the glass. "It's funny— I've spent my life pretending to be part of these perfect families for TV, and now here I am, basically without a family of my own, even though that's all I've ever really wanted. Just like in the TV shows and movies: big dinners, crowded houses, everyone talking and hugging and teasing and cooking." A small smile. "Kids everywhere."

Her words carved a hole in my chest. I wanted to give Winnie everything her heart ached for, but the idea of giving her a family . . . I was drunk on the very thought. Even though everything in me knew that could never be us. I wasn't exactly father material. Tamara's kids had hated me as babies. Just making eye contact with me was enough to make them scream their heads off.

But I couldn't ignore the feeling that had been ballooning in my chest since the moment I saw Winnie in the Hope Channel offices just last month.

I loved Winnie Baker. And it wasn't the floaty, fuzzy kind of love. It was the kind of love that made my bones ache with want and sadness at the thought of her not being near.

I wanted to keep her forever. I wanted to steal her away and introduce her to my mom. God, my mom would love Winnie. Dad too. She'd charm the hell out of them. Tamara would probably try to see if she was being held against her will or something.

On the other side of the room, my phone rang, but there wasn't a chance in hell I was leaving this bed. "Growing up," I told her, "it was just me, my parents, and sister, but we always felt like a big family. I was never alone. I think that's why Nolan hung around so much too. In fact, our family sort of just absorbed his at some point. Maybe it was when INK really blew up. Our moms got close. No one else knew what it was like to be the mothers to two global pop stars. At least not anyone else in Kansas City."

"Your family sounds great. Maybe one day I'll meet them. Especially the famous Tamara. I've got to witness her for myself."

I pulled her close to me and pressed my smiling lips to her temple. "My mom loves your movies," I admitted. "She and Dad watch them every year. She's really hoping the Hope Channel finally makes a Hanukkah movie."

"How is that not a thing yet?" she asked.

"I don't know. But if they can do sexy Santa, I'm pretty sure there's a market for a Jewish holiday rom-com."

She yawned as she placed a hand to my chest and rested her cheek there. "I can't believe the shoot is already over."

"You still technically have one more day," I reminded her. I'd wrapped last night and Winnie had just a quick scene before the whole thing was done.

"Sure, sure," she said. "But it's basically done. We made a sexy movie." Her voice began to fade as she drifted to sleep. "Yay."

I kissed her again on the forehead.

We made a sexy movie.

I was in love.

It hurt like hell.

Yay.

MY PHONE RANG over and over again until I forced my eyes open to see sunlight spilling in through the window of my hotel room.

The ringing stopped.

And then it started again.

"All right, all right, all right," I muttered as I delicately untangled myself from Winnie and replaced myself with a feather pillow for her to rest her head on.

I tugged on a pair of jeans and a Slice, Slice, Baby hoodie before stepping out into the hall just as the call went to voicemail.

"Well, if it isn't Santa himself," called a voice.

I spun around to see Teddy Ray Fletcher stepping off the elevator. He wore flannel pajama pants, a Dave Matthews Band T-shirt, and a corduroy blazer, with two paper cups of black coffee in his hands.

I stumbled forward with my hand outstretched. "Uh, Mr. Fletcher—or is it Uncle Ray-Ray? I'm a huge fan of your work, sir."

I had yet to meet the producer of *Santa, Baby* in the flesh. Even though we'd spoken over a few video calls, it was hard not to be a little starstruck. Teddy was responsible for some of my all-time favorites. *Tightanic*, *A Tale of Two Titties*, *Sext in the City*, and *MILF Super Bowl XXII*.

"My work?" he asked with a snort, waving my hand away. "You'll always be the one who got away for me. Do you know how hard I tried to license that sex tape of yours?"

I was blushing like a damn schoolgirl. "The bidding war was pretty intense," I said.

"I didn't expect Steph to give me any special treatment, and she definitely didn't," he said, a shiver rolling through his body. "Seeing her in action is always a treat in and of itself." He threw back an entire cup of coffee like a Jell-O shot. It was impressive.

"Yeah, she's always out for blood, and as her client, I'm not complaining."

Teddy peered past me like he might see her there. "She didn't make it to set, did she? I'd, uh, hoped we could get together. To talk business, of course."

"No," I said, "There was some sort of client catastrophe on the set of the next *Fast and Furious* movie and she had to go to Dubai."

"That's a shame," Teddy said. "About the catastrophe. Not Dubai. I've never been. Maybe one day. When I'm done bleeding money out of my ass for art school and sustainable sex toys."

This man was a goddamn onion. "Right."

"I hear the first few days here were a little touch and go. I guess Winnie was having a hard time getting into . . . character. People think selling sex is easy, but it's not. It's a real art form. You get it. You're a natural," he said. "Gretchen said your tape is looking solid. That's not easy when your costar isn't really pulling their load."

Teddy Ray Fletcher, the porn king of my adolescence, had just called me a natural. Holy fuck. My brain pulsed, suddenly remembering that it needed to make words. "I just did the best I could with what I had, sir," I managed to sputter.

"It was good of you. It's the kind of thing that can tank a movie, awkward sex scenes." He shook his head. "I saw some of the early stuff. Ouch."

"Well, I mean, we were all embarrassed for her," I said, thinking back to how stiff and stressed Winnie had been, and how much we'd all wanted her to succeed, how much we hated seeing her struggle. I was about to tell Teddy how she'd been blowing us all away ever since she'd found her sex-scene feet, but my phone started ringing again before I could.

I glanced down to see Topher's contact number illuminating my screen. "I better get this," I told Teddy.

He stepped aside, and I got onto the open elevator. If Topher was calling me this early in the morning, I was going to need a coffee. Or maybe a stiff drink.

The phone rang again just as I was about to hit the little green button to call him back. "Hey, Toph, what are you doing up so early?" And as the words came out, I realized just how bizarre this was, especially since he was in a different time zone.

"Uncle Kallum?" he said through hiccups.

For a moment, I thought he was definitely drunk, but then I heard that same little sniffle he'd made when he was a kid and crying because he'd fallen down. "What's wrong?" I asked quickly.

"The restaurant . . ." Another hiccup.

"Slice, Slice, Baby? Which one?"

"It's the—the Lawrence location. I went to pick up the deposit last night and I accidentally fell asleep in the back office while I was waiting for everyone to close. The guys who closed up forgot to check the oven and—and I don't know—the fire department thinks that maybe a stack of boxes caught on fire—"

"Topher, listen to me. Are you okay? Was anyone else inside?" Frantically, I began to push the buttons in the elevator to get back to my floor. Forget coffee. I had to get home.

"I'm—I'm okay, and I don't know. I think I was alone, but Paul, the new delivery driver, was supposed to meet me there and I can't get a hold of him and—"

"Kallum," my sister's cool and even voice said. "We're heading to the hospital so they can check him out for smoke inhalation. He's okay, but we're still trying to get in touch with Paul. The place . . . well, it's a total loss, I think."

"I'm coming home. Right this minute."

"To what?" she asked. "You're supposed to fly home tomorrow anyway. Besides, the damage is done. There's nothing you can do here."

She wasn't being mean or sarcastic or teasing. She was just being honest, and that's what stung the most. "I need to be there," I finally said. "I have to see Toph with my own two eyes. See if you can get as much info as possible on Paul. Full name, address, emergency contact. I'm walking back to my hotel room right now and then I'm on the first flight back. I'll take a fucking cargo plane if I have to."

There was some commotion in the background. Metal clanking, wheels squeaking, voices barking. "Okay," she finally said. "Okay. They just loaded us in the back of the ambulance. I'll text you all the info I can find."

"Thanks," I said. "Thanks. And Tam?"

"Yeah?"

"I love you. I love Topher. More than anything. You know that, right?"

"We know," she said. "We love you too. Let me know when you get a flight."

I know there was so much there we both wanted to say. I should have been there. I shouldn't have left her kid in charge of an entire restaurant chain. And she should have been angrier, but she wasn't and I had to find a time to thank her for that.

The elevator doors opened again and I was already searching for the first flight. It was in an hour and a half and I was forty-five minutes away from the nearest airport. I had to haul ass if I was going to make it.

"Winnie," I said the moment I opened the door. "Winnie, this is wild, I know, but there was a fire and . . ."

My bed was empty. I could still see the imprint of her body

on my sheets. She was gone. I'd have to run down to her room to say goodbye.

I threw everything I could find in my suitcase and zipped it up, not even bothering to check the bathroom for toiletries. One of Winnie's hair ties sat there on the nightstand and I shoved it into my pocket.

After hitting a few buttons on my phone, I called an Uber and ran down the hallway to Winnie.

My knuckles rapped against the door so hard it shook. "Winnie," I called. "Hey, Winnie . . . uh, something's come up. Can you let me in?"

A few seconds passed. I looked at my phone. And then a full minute.

I tried knocking again. "Winnie," I said her name more firmly this time. "I really don't want to say goodbye through a hotel door."

I pulled out my phone again and shot off a text in case she was in the restroom or somewhere else.

The minutes ticked past, and I got an alert that my ride was here. If I had any chance of making this flight, I had to go now.

My stomach tensed into a knot. I'd spent the last three weeks trying so hard to make our time together last that I hadn't let myself consider what it might feel like to say goodbye.

But now that it was here and I was being robbed of my moment, all I could think of was the things I hadn't said.

And she didn't know.

She didn't know that I loved her.

A text from a random Vermont number popped up.

Your Driver: Hey, the app says I should only wait for three minutes. Are you coming down or not

And then one from Tamara with a contact card attached.

Tamara: They've admitted Topher for observation. Working on Paul's emergency contact info, but here's his cell number.

I looked at Winnie's door once more and reached into my pocket to leave her hair tie on her door handle. Like an addict, I held it up to my face and inhaled the scent of her. Orange and cinnamon and a sweetness that always seemed to linger in her hair and along her skin.

With a growl, I shoved the little piece of fabric back into my pocket and stormed off down the hallway with plans to text her and tell her all about the fire and why I had to leave early. With each step, something inside of me stretched thinner and thinner until I walked outside and realized that I'd left an entire piece of me up there on the fifth floor of the Edelweiss Inn.

I'd go home to take care of my family and my business and once that was settled, I'd get my Winnie. I'd cook for her every night and let her fall asleep nestled next to me on the couch and tear her clothes off with my teeth and I'd make her laugh so hard she cried and I'd be the kind of man she deserved.

This wasn't the end of our story.

It couldn't be.

CHAPTER SEVENTEEN

Winnie

We once filmed an episode of *In a Family Way* at an amusement park, and the actors got to ride all the rides for B-roll footage. I loved most of them—the roller coasters and log flumes and bumper cars—but there was one I'd absolutely hated: a giant barrel that spun fast enough to pin me against the wall while the floor lowered farther and farther down. I couldn't stand the feeling of my stomach smashing back against my spine; I'd hated looking down to see my feet floating above the dropped floor, like the entire world had fallen away and there was nothing left but some invisible, crushing force to keep me from falling into nothing.

But I didn't need the horrible barrel ride to feel that way, it turned out. All I had to do was listen to Kallum agree with Teddy Ray Fletcher out there in the hallway.

We were all embarrassed for her.

And yep, there had been that sick, about-to-vomit feeling, that pressure on my chest. The sensation that there was nothing but vacant air under my feet.

It was what I got for eavesdropping, I supposed, but it hadn't been on purpose! I'd woken up to find him gone, and then I'd heard his deep rumble outside the door, and I'd been so groggy, so very groggy, and my narcoleptic brain was only capable of two thoughts, which were: *more sleep* and *more Kallum*. So I'd stumbled over to the door, meaning to open it and demand he continue snuggling me—and that's when I'd heard Teddy mention my name.

I just did the best I could with what I had, sir.

We were all embarrassed for her.

The world had spun; the floor had dropped. I could barely breathe.

And now I was back in my room somehow, my hands shaking, my pulse pounding in my ears. It was stupid, *so deeply stupid*, to be upset about something that had been obvious from the moment we'd all started *Santa, Baby*, but dammit, I was upset. I was embarrassed. It was one thing for Teddy Ray Fletcher, an expert in on-camera sex, to declare me mediocre, but Kallum had known how much I'd had to overcome even to *try* acting in this movie. He knew I'd had to rewrite years of shame and fear—and he'd also known that my professional life had been about as provocative as an episode of Bob Ross's *The Joy of Painting*! It wasn't as if I'd come to set with any experience in on-screen sex. Much less with a young, hunky Santa Claus!

I pressed the heels of my hands to my eyes and tried to breathe in and out like my therapist had taught me to do. For so long, whenever something had hurt, I'd told myself that I'd maybe deserved it, that if only I was better or sweeter or tried harder, I could make sure someone couldn't ever be disappointed in me again. But that outlook had changed after Michael's affair, because it didn't matter how good I had or hadn't been, it had happened anyway. And for the first time I could remember, I had let myself be truly angry. I had let the anger burn away the idea that I needed to be perfect in order not to be hurt, because even imperfect people didn't deserve to be treated like trash cans.

And what Teddy and Kallum had said about me? It felt like a trash can thing.

A sudden knock shook the door, and I dropped my hands, staring at the red-painted wood. *Rap, rap, rap* went the knuckles on the door, and then Kallum called my name in that toe-curlingly deep voice.

I realized I was still only wearing his T-shirt and my panties, and suddenly that floor-dropping feeling was back, because just ten minutes ago I'd been cuddled in his bed, in his arms. Just last night I'd been panting his name and purring on his chest. Thinking about how I'd never been safer or looser or happier than when we were together.

Thinking that maybe I'd been overzealous in my decision never to fall in love again.

"I really don't want to say goodbye through a hotel door," Kallum called, and I sealed my lips together, barely breathing. If I spoke, I knew my voice would come out all shaky and weird, and I knew if he heard it, he wouldn't leave me alone until he knew why.

And my battered pride simply could not bear him knowing that he had the power to hurt me with such a casual, careless comment. He could never know that he'd conjured up my ugliest fears—that I was laughable, pitiable, embarrassing—and confirmed them to be true.

I took another step back and pressed my mouth shut, tamping down the urge to speak, to open the door, to make him explain himself. Because I wasn't about to compound the sin of being embarrassing by also being naive. I knew exactly what this had been: a deal. A deal to help me with *Santa, Baby*'s sex scenes, which meant that once *Santa, Baby* was done, we would be done too. So maybe Kallum didn't owe me some sort of gallant verbal defense . . . but then neither did I owe him a goodbye.

We'd each gotten what we wanted out of the last three weeks, and now it was over, and clearly he would be grateful that it was done, anyway. He'd walk away from my hotel room door feeling relieved I hadn't made a scene, that I hadn't clung to him, that I would no longer expect him to shoulder the burden of the ridiculous Winnie Baker.

And then I would finish the last of my scenes here today and go home and forget about him forever. I would bury the version of myself that had started to imagine more with him, a future with him, because from now on, it was just Winnie Baker on her own, with no ties or responsibilities to anyone else.

And when I heard Kallum's reluctant footsteps echo down the hallway, I let out a long, determined breath, and started to get ready for my last day on set. My eyes were dry the entire time.

Part Two

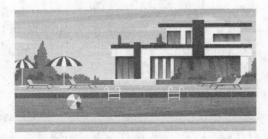

CHAPTER EIGHTEEN

Winnie

Six weeks later

"R ise and shine, and give God the glory, glory!" called a loud, horrible voice. A shaft of sunlight hit my face, and I squirmed away from it like an ant under a magnifying glass, clawing at my comforter to pull it back over my head.

"The Lord said to Noah," sang the voice, "there's gonna be a floody, floody!"

I squeaked in protest as the comforter was ripped away and my dark little cocoon became a blear of sunshine and blond hair.

"GET THOSE CHILDREN OUT OF THE MUDDY,

MUDDY!" Addison sang-yelled as she jumped on my bed. "CHILDREN OF THE LORD!"

"Go away," I moaned, trying to roll over. I was stopped by Addison flinging herself on top of me, like I was the door from *Titanic* and she was Kate Winslet.

"How do you have so much energy?" I mumbled. Sleep was like liquid concrete around my limbs and in my chest. "It's basically six in the morning."

"Correction, it's almost noon, I'm already on my third double shot of espresso, and also I just got done with my weekly B-vitamin infusion, you non-bio-hacked crone. Also you need to wake up."

"I *don't* need to wake up," I said and closed my eyes again. I knew I'd been sleeping more than twelve hours a day since I came back from Christmas Notch, but I didn't *care*. I was un- employed and unemploy*able*—now that everyone knew how bad I was at filming fake sex—and all I had left in this world was naps. And sleeping in. And going to bed early.

And more naps.

"Don't you take medicine for your narcolepsy or whatever?" Addison asked. Her face was fully pressed to the side of mine now, and it was so nice to be snuggled by another person that I didn't even mind that it came with a side of Trying to Wake Me Up.

"It's not a magic cure," I mumbled defensively. Which was true—even on its own, my narcolepsy medicine wasn't perfect at keeping me awake, but treating narcolepsy was also about insomnia and fractured sleep cycles and hypnagogic hallucinations so scary that even the idea of sleep sounded terrifying and miserable.

At any rate, I hadn't taken my medicine for the last few weeks, because every time I tried to swallow the gigantic and very bitter pill, I'd gag. I needed to go to a compounding pharmacy and have them mix it into a foam that tasted like something yummy. Maybe a pizza . . . or the maple sugar candy from my Edelweiss Inn gift basket, which was about the only thing that sounded good to me these days.

"Okay, well, I'm about half a second away from making you a narcolepsy-medicine-cream cold brew and funneling it down your throat, because you *have to get up*. Someone's here for you."

My heart—my ridiculous, traitorous heart—surged, pumping several hard, urgent beats in rapid succession. I was officially awake.

"Who?" I managed to ask, forcing open my eyes to see Addison looking at me with a soft expression.

"Not him," she said. Her voice was gentle. "Not Kallum. I'm sorry."

My heart deflated. It felt as flat and flimsy as a raw flank steak in my chest. I closed my eyes again.

"You could text him, you know," Addison suggested. "Before you watched that YouTube video about tech-detoxing and turned off your phone, he was texting and calling nonstop."

I remembered the long text he'd sent me the day I got home, telling me about a fire at his restaurant and how his nephew wound up in the hospital. I'd responded and told him I was sad to hear about the fire, but glad his nephew was okay. I'd said nothing else after that, and he must have sensed that there was something deeper to my silence, because then the never-ending waterfall of texts and calls had commenced.

"I have nothing to say to him," I said. "We were just an on-set thing. We're off set now, and it's over, and that's all. The end."

"Winnie," Addison said, "you know I support your choices—even when you do completely unhinged things like star in a sexy Santa Claus biopic—but can it really hurt to hear what he has to say? At the very least, you have to turn your phone back on. You've missed, like, twenty Wordles, and it's really stressing me out."

I made a noncommittal noise. It wasn't just Kallum I wanted to avoid. Michael had been trying to call too, and I didn't have the energy to tell him to back off *again*.

I didn't have the energy for anything, really, which was why I would've loved to go back to sleep right about now . . .

"Anyway, your manager is in my living room," Addison said, giving my cheek a Glossier-sticky kiss and levering herself off me. "And there's only so much stalling I can do and still keep it profesh, so you need to get dressed and come see her."

"Steph is *here?*" I asked. My heart thumped again—half in fear, half in hope. Either she was here to fire me for being bad at fake sex, or she was here to give me another job. Which I couldn't afford to say no to at this point—my *Santa, Baby* paycheck and *Treasures in Heaven* residuals only went so far—and eventually, I had to stop trading on Addison's goodwill and get my own place.

With a noise like an awakening bear, I crawled out of bed and staggered to the bathroom to brush my teeth.

STEPH STOOD IN Addison's living room, her eyes on her phone as her thumbs moved rapidly across the screen. She looked up as I walked in and flashed me a quick smile with an unnerving amount of teeth.

"Winnie Baker," she said. "You haven't been answering my calls."

"I'm so sorry—my phone was off," I said, sinking down onto one of Addison's modern farmhouse chic couches. "I've been . . . under the weather."

I didn't like lying, but it seemed like an easier explanation than *My hot costar made me feel like a joke, and so now I'm hiding from him and the rest of the world.* Plus, it wasn't completely untrue; I had been feeling crappy lately. My narcolepsy was the worst I could ever remember it being, and I'd been feeling so groggy and gross that the only things I could choke down were peanut butter sandwiches and the green smoothies I sometimes begged off Addison's personal assistant.

"Well, it's time to get over the weather," Steph said crisply, "because people are asking for a piece of that sexy Winnie Baker pie."

I stared. "Really?"

"Really. And they're willing to pay good money for each gooey slice. Haven't you seen Gretchen's *Vogue* interview?"

I shook my head wordlessly, and Steph heaved a dramatic sigh. She handed me her phone after a few impatient taps, and I scrolled through the article while Addison read over my shoulder from behind the couch.

"She talks about how amazing and unsung you are, yadda yadda, but what really matters is that this is just the beginning,"

Steph went on. "As the buzz builds for *Santa, Baby* and then after it releases, people will wake up to what they're missing, and we want to make sure we have some projects in the queue before that happens. So I have a few scripts for you here, some proposals . . ."

But I was barely listening by this point. Because *oh my God* Gretchen Young said in this article that I was good in the movie!

More than good—incredible. Sexy. Provocative!

And maybe she was lying to protect the future of *Santa, Baby*, but Gretchen struck me more as the *diplomatic sidestep* rather than the *outright lie* type when it came to this sort of thing.

Which meant she probably believed it.

Which meant that I hadn't been a total disaster on the set of *Santa, Baby*, and Kallum and Teddy were wrong about me, those facial-haired jerkwads.

". . . after reshoots, of course," Steph was saying, and my brain skidded into the present.

"Reshoots?" I repeated.

"Yes, reshoots, and you'd know about them if you'd kept your phone on," Steph said, plucking her own phone out of my hands and then using it to point at me. "You, missy, are due back in Vermont in a few weeks for reshoots. Pearl changed the ending of the film. There's *a lot* of boning in the new ending, so brace yourself, but the intimacy coordinator with the mangled-looking dog will be back to help you with it."

I must have gone pale, because Steph came up and patted my cheek. "Turn on your phone," she said. *Pat, pat.* "I'm emailing you the scripts and proposals tonight. Let's make some money, Winnie."

And then she waltzed out, leaving the scent of cherries behind her.

I stared at the shiplapped wall in front of me until Addison's concerned face replaced it.

"You okay, boo bear?" she asked.

"I don't know if I can see him again," I confessed. "Much less do love scenes with him."

"Oh honey," she soothed, pulling me to my feet and into a tight hug. Which was really nice until she squeezed and pain shot from my breasts to everywhere in my body. I yelped.

Addison let go of me with a worried look as she prodded at her side boobs. "Did my underwire poke you or something?"

"No, it just hurt having my boobs smashed— Ow! Shit!" Addison had just reached out and given one of the boobs in question a thoughtful honk.

"What the heck?" I demanded, rubbing the abused breast protectively.

"How long have you been mega-sleepy?" Addison suddenly demanded.

"I don't know, a while, I guess? Since I got back from Christmas Notch?"

"And the whole peanut butter sandwich and green smoothie diet? When did you start that?"

"Also when I got back, but I just haven't felt good enough to eat much else—"

"And have you had your red badge of courage this month?"

I scoffed. "Of course I have; I always have it at the end of the . . ." I trailed off as I realized that in fact the crimson tide *hadn't* come this month. It had finished up right as I'd gotten to

Christmas Notch, and then had stayed un-crimson ever since. Which didn't mean anything. People had fluctuating periods for all sorts of reasons!

"I'm late sometimes when I'm stressed," I insisted. "That's what it is. I've just been stressed out about being bad in the movie. That's all."

Addison was eyeballing me like I was a teenager trying to argue that I hadn't replaced the gin with water while Mommy was on vacation. "Winnie, I hate to sound like a high school counselor right now, but did Kallum wrap his willy before he got silly?"

I dropped my face into my hands. "Addison!"

"*Well?*"

"Yes! We always used a condom—even the first time when we thought we didn't have one, and it turned out Kallum had an emergency condom in his phone case."

"In his phone case?" Addison repeated. "Like trapped against a hot battery every hour of every day for God knows how long?"

"Phones don't get *that* hot," I said. "Plus no one gets pregnant the first time they have sex together. That's a lie we were told as teens, Addy."

"I think it's less of a lie if you've sous-vided a condom to death with a phone. I bet it was an Android phone too. Stupid boys," Addison muttered, disappearing from the living room and then coming back with a pink box. "Here. My sister left these here a million years ago when she was in town doing IUI."

"What—no, I can't be pregnant. I was going to have to see someone to get pregnant with Michael!"

"And had Michael ever seen anyone about having children? About making sure his loins were well seeded?"

"Gross, Addy."

"Well?!"

"We hadn't gotten to that point," I admitted. And I wasn't sure if we ever would have. I'd known Michael wouldn't take the suggestion that he needed to have his sperm count checked very gracefully, and so I'd been too nervous to bring it up. "Anyway, it was just one dicey condom one time. I can't be pregnant. No way."

"Yes way. Oui way. Ja way." She pushed the box of tests into my hands. "We need to know if you've got a joey in the pouch so we can make plans."

I stared down at the box. It was a giant multipack that had expired last year. "Plans," I said.

"Yeah, baby girl. Plans." She wrapped her hands around mine, all thin gold rings and almond-shaped nails. Even for a day at home getting her IV infusion, even in leggings and no makeup, she looked perfectly put together. "And you *do* have options, Winnie. This doesn't have to be the beginning or the end of anything. If you don't want to stop your career before it's gotten started, if you don't want to have a baby with a pizza parlor magnate who talked trash about you, then you don't have to. I'll help."

I met her soft silver gaze and felt my chin dimple.

"Are you sure?" I asked.

She squeezed my hands and gave me a banner-in-Target-worthy Addison Hayes smile. "I'm in this with you. Whatever you need, we'll figure out. One shitty condom doesn't have to be your destiny, Winnie Baker."

I looked back down at the box, not even sure what I was feeling. Dread? Guilt?

. . . hope?

"And if I *want* to have a baby?" I whispered. "Even single? Even when I'm trying to launch a new career? Even if Kallum is a gaping dickhole?"

"Then I will be your baby's godmother and give them their first-ever stiff-brimmed hat and be their Cool Aunt Uber when they drink too many White Claws at the beach. You won't have to do this alone, Winnie Baker. Forget Kallum and your awful parents, you've got me." She tossed her hair with a sniff. "I mean, what baby wouldn't want to be raised by us anyway?"

I smiled—a smile that was dangerously close to watery. "Addy . . ."

"Shut up and go pee on a stick already."

And so I did.

And when the little digital readout said PREGNANT—and the digital readout of the second test said PREGNANT—and then when the unexpired tests we Instacarted *also* said PREGNANT, PREGNANT, PREGNANT, Addison held me in her arms while I cried into her inhumanly nice-smelling hair and leaked snot all over her eight-hundred-dollar flannel shirt that looked like it was from a thrift store.

"It's okay," she crooned as I let myself feel every single ribbon of terror and hope and excitement. "Aunt Addy is here. Aunt Addy is here."

And even though this was unplanned, was horrible timing, was nothing like I ever pictured around having a baby, I couldn't help but feel something almost like happiness. Like joy.

Sometimes the things we wanted most came when we least expected them, when we weren't prepared for them, when we thought we didn't want them anymore. And maybe this shitty condom *was* destiny, because now this baby was getting a mother who knew herself, who knew how to get through hard times without crumpling into a ball like a used Taco Bell wrapper. Now this baby was getting an Aunt Addy and a father who wasn't Michael Bacher and a childhood free of words like *purity* and *stumbling block* and *shame.*

We were in it together, this little bean inside my tummy and I, and even if I couldn't find acting work after this, even if Steph fired me for being unhirably pregnant, even if I had to live in Addison's pool house forever, it was going to be okay, *we* were going to be okay.

For the first time in a long time, I knew I had the power to make it so.

CHAPTER NINETEEN

Kallum

"Kallum?" Nolan called through the closed door of his guest bedroom in the perfect little Los Feliz house he and Bee shared. "Isn't your call time in, like, three hours? Shouldn't you take a shower?"

"Showers are for happy people," I told him as I pulled the covers over my head.

"Uhhh . . . I like to think showers are for just . . . people. And the people who have to live with them."

"Offer him leftover waffles," Bee whispered.

"He's not a stray cat we're trying to trap," Nolan said to her.

"I'm not hungry," I called back gruffly.

Without warning, the door swung open and Nolan stood

there, dressed in clean clothes, rubbing his happiness in my face, with Bee on her tiptoes peering over his shoulder.

"You literally haven't left this room since you got here two days ago," Nolan said. "And you even called in sick to your preproduction meeting for *Shark Tank*."

"What were they going to tell me that I didn't already know?" I asked. "I already have the investment secured for the new locations. This TV gig is just for show."

"Uh, I'm pretty sure when you called me two weeks ago to tell me you'd be crashing here, you said it was part of your contract with Mark Cu—"

"I'll get there. I'll give them the pizza pitch. Feed 'em a slice or two and that'll be it. I'm charming. It'll be fine."

Bee stepped forward and waved her arm in my general direction. "I don't know that I would call this current version of you charming."

Nolan turned to Bee. "You said that way nicer than I was going to, babe."

She kissed him on the cheek. "Thanks, babe."

"*Babe* this," I muttered. "*Babe* that."

They both looked at me the same way my mom looks at one of the grandbabies when they're crying for no reason.

"I've got to get to work," Bee said. "Are you good to handle this?"

Nolan nodded. "I peeled this guy off the floor when he fell in love with our tour manager who had a husband and two kids at home."

"Michelle was a crush. This was love," I moan.

"Oh boy." Bee sighed. "I really wish I could stick around for this." She looked to Nolan. "Did you talk to Gary next door about checking on my tomato plants while we're on set for *Duke the Halls 2?*"

Nolan smacked a hand to his forehead. "No, but I will."

They shared a quick kiss and then he whispered something in her ear that made her growl like a deranged little kitten.

Once she walked down the hall, and he watched her go for a moment, he turned back to me and clapped his hands together like a mechanical monkey. "Okay, bud. It's time to get out of this bed, take a shower, and get your ass to the studio. I took your Slice, Slice, Baby apron to the dry cleaners yesterday, so if we can just wash the feelings off of you, you might not look as depressed as you feel. Then when you get home, we can order a pizza from every good place in town and make a pizza flight. We'll talk about your feelings and get you in with a therapist back home first thing in the morning."

"I never said you could plan my life," I told him as I dug myself out from the pile of decorative throw pillows that I'd used to shield my body from the world for the last two days. "But I am sorry for coming here and turning your guest bedroom into a black hole."

"It's cool, bro. That's what your best friend's guestroom is for. Plus it's always sunny and seventy degrees here, and it's been raining since you arrived, which feels ominous, but is sort of nice. I was starting to feel like I was living in one giant simulation."

"I just wasn't prepared for how much it would hurt to be near her, but so far away."

Nolan clutched his heart. "God, that hurts. Why didn't they ever let you take a stab at our lyrics?"

"That's not really how boy band factories work."

"You really got it bad for her?"

"She's my person," I told him. It had been ten weeks now since I'd left Christmas Notch, and I'd spent all of it falling asleep to her old movies and reaching for her every morning. "I love Winnie Baker. And I thought when I found my person, I'd just be overjoyed that they existed and that there actually was someone out there for me. But this fucking hurts, Nolan. I'm terrified that this is how our story ends and the only future out there for me is pizza and being a semi-okay uncle."

And after one of our locations burned to the ground when Topher was in charge of the business, I wasn't even sure I could say that. Thankfully Paul the delivery driver was alive and fine, despite hot-boxing his own car before dozing off in an old Dillard's parking lot before he could make it over to the Lawrence location. When the cops found him he was high as hell, but alive.

"She won't answer her phone," I said. "And now it just goes to voicemail. I've tried getting to her through Steph, Teddy . . . hell, even Gretchen. But no one could help me."

Nolan scrubbed a hand up and down his face. "I'm about to give you some shitty advice."

"My favorite kind," I told him.

"You're here. In Los Angeles. Go get her. This is your moment. Profess your love. Do the big gesture. Get the flowers. Sing to her if you have to. But this is your shot, man. So go take a shower and become human. Film *Shark Tank* and then go get your lady."

"Yeah?" I asked, feeling hopeful for the first time in months. "How do I even find her? Last I heard she was living with Addison Hayes, but that was back when she was talking to me."

Nolan took my phone off the charging dock on the night-stand. He held my phone up to my face to unlock it and mumbled, "Not that I don't know your passcode. It's been the same since we were kids."

"Not true." I stood up and began to dig through my bag for beard oil and whatever other toiletries I'd thrown in during my depression brain fog.

He locked the phone again to prove his point and then tapped out *6969*.

"It's a classic for a reason, okay?"

"There," he said as he held up Addison's Instagram for me to see. "This makeup store in Burbank tagged Addison in a promo post for some kind of event she's doing for her new perfume line tonight. Winnie probably won't be there, but maybe Addison could answer some questions for you."

He kept scrolling. "Oh shit, this juice bar tags her like twice a week. You could try there too."

My heart stopped.

Right there in a post from last week was Addison sipping on a cup of red juice, along with a blurry Winnie. A cup full of dark green juice dangled from her fingertips and her hair covered most of her profile, but I knew the slope of her nose by heart.

"What's this place called?" I mumbled as I clicked on the profile. "Got the Juice. It's near Culver City."

"Now, go clean that body," Nolan commanded as he slapped me on the butt.

NOLAN LEFT FOR work before I got in the shower, so I turned on my "Pump Me Up" playlist, which started out with Bonnie Tyler's "Holding Out for a Hero," at least six Kelly Clarkson songs, "Pony" by Ginuwine, "Man! I Feel Like a Woman!" by Shania Twain, and a healthy amount of Destiny's Child and Queen . . . and of course a little bit of INK.

We were pretty good back in the day, okay?

By the time I got into my rental car, I had thirty-five minutes to travel six miles, but Google Maps told me it was going to take fifty minutes. Shit.

I took a quick second to shoot off a text to the contact number one of the PAs sent over before reversing out of the steep driveway so quickly that my rented KIA SUV, which was too small to actually be an SUV, got some solid air.

As I did my best to politely haul ass across town, I waved and nodded to anyone who let me pass and it was mostly returned with a honk or the bird. I just wanted to scream, "I'M FROM THE MIDWEST!"

After I passed Fox Studios, I got stuck in a mini traffic jam along a palm tree–lined road dotted with little shops and—a juice bar!

Oh shit! Got the Juice! Right there in front of my face.

I checked the time on the dashboard and then the time on my phone—like the two might somehow be different. In the end, though, it didn't matter. I was already swerving over into an open spot on the street that had a very complicated parking sign above it. But signs were for people who had time to read them!

There was no way she was here.

But what if she was? Everything about me and Winnie had been so impossibly unbelievable, so who was to say she wasn't sitting in a trendy juice bar waiting for me?

I locked the car and dropped the keys in the front pocket of my apron. My apron! I nearly doubled back to take it off, but there was no time. The *Shark Tank* producer had told me to show up in my Slice, Slice, Baby uniform, which was an apron, jeans, and white ringer T-shirt with the company logo—a cartoon slice of pizza with a blond pompadour.

I jogged down the block and swung open the door of Got the Juice.

Everyone in line and the whole staff turned to look at me, but not a single one of them was Winnie or even Addison.

"Uhhhh . . . keep up the good work, guys—I mean people. There are more than guys here. I can see that now. Not that I can just see anyone's gender or anything, but I was just assuming and uhhhh . . ." I held up two thumbs. Maybe if I just shut my mouth, words would stop coming out. "I gotta run, but I'll be back for juice. Or several! Several juices soon."

"Kallum?" a soft voice asked from behind me. "What are you doing here?"

I spun around and there was Winnie. Her hair was swept into one of those messy buns with a few loose strands hanging down around her neck and she wore sage-colored leggings with a big baggy sweatshirt.

"Winnie?"

Addison stopped short behind her. "Kallum Lieberman, it's been at least a decade." She looped an arm through Winnie's. "Should I verbally eviscerate him? Say the word."

Winnie sighed and shook her head. "You go ahead and go inside."

Addison leaned toward me and then barked like a dog before going inside where the entire staff sang out her name.

"That woman is feral," I said.

"If you're going to compliment her, you should say it to her face."

I smiled and reached for her hand, but she stuffed both of them into the front pocket of her hoodie.

"What are you doing here?" she asked again, and then fully noticed my getup. "And in your Slice, Slice, Baby uniform?"

"I'm here filming an episode of *Shark Tank* . . . It's a long story."

She stepped forward to open the door. "Cool. Break a leg."

I stepped into her path. "Winnie, what did I do?" I said, my voice desperate. "Will you just talk to me? One minute you were in my bed sleeping next to me and now you won't even return my calls."

She crossed her arms over her chest, her nostrils flaring.

God, she was sexy when she was mad. My heart was mangled and my throat was dry with grief, but that didn't stop me from wishing I could drag my nose up her throat and along her jaw until I reached her lips and kissed her for so long that our bodies melted into one.

But talking. Talking first. Professing my love second. And then making out like teenagers in heat.

I pulled the chair out from the little table outside of the storefront, and she sat down.

Once I was pretty sure she wouldn't make a run for it, I sat down across from her.

I wanted to check the time on my phone and maybe text the PA again, but no. I was here with Winnie and there was no telling if I'd ever get a second shot.

"So talk," she said.

"I've called. I've texted. I even tried reaching out to Steph and Teddy. But nothing. Is it because I had to leave so abruptly? You got my text, right? About the location burning down. I'm so, so sorry, but my nephew . . . I had to get home and check on him and the—"

"You were embarrassed for me," she said.

"Huh?"

She shrugged. "You were embarrassed for me."

Her words sounded vaguely familiar, like they were from a movie . . . or maybe even from our script. "I'm sorry, Winnie, but I'm not really following."

"That's what you told Teddy, wasn't it? About me and the movie and our scenes? Our intimate scenes."

Teddy. Oh God. The conversation came back to me like an anvil falling from the sky. "Winnie . . . I was just . . . It was, like, five in the morning. We'd—we'd been up all night." My voice dropped to a near growl. "I'm pretty sure you remember that part."

She swallowed as her cheeks flushed. But then she shook her head, like she was physically trying to clear away the memories. "You made me feel silly. And *then* I felt ashamed for all the things I didn't know. Kallum, do you know how much of my life I've spent in shame? I'm sick of it."

"I . . . but I love you, Winnie." The moment the words were out of my mouth I knew it was the wrong thing to say at the wrong time, no matter how true it was.

Her lips parted . . . but it only took a split second for anguish to furrow her brow. "You're not hearing me, Kallum."

"*Shame,*" I said, forcing my brain to drop the mission I came here with. "I'm listening, I promise. And I might not know fully what it was like to grow up with the constant need to be everyone's good girl and to be so pure and—but I do know that you've fought so hard to come out of it, Winnie. I know you're so goddamn brave and that you left everything you knew to escape the shame. And what I said to Teddy was dumb and careless. I know how it sounded. It sounded bad, but, Winnie, you have to know that I'd been about to say more, to say how awesome you'd gotten, and you have to know that to me, they were just silly, pointless words."

"But to me they weren't," she said.

Behind her, a parking attendant approached my rental and began to type in my license plate number.

Winnie began to look over her shoulder to see what I was so distracted by, but I needed her to know she was my universe, so I reached across the table and enveloped her hands in mine.

That snapped her head back around, and she watched our hands for a long moment. I didn't know what she saw there, but I hoped it was a future and all the right words that I couldn't manage to say. Because when I thought of losing Winnie, my brain turned into endless static.

I took a deep breath. I needed a do-over. Dear God, let this perfect creature give me a do-over.

"I never say the right things," I finally said. "Ask my whole family. Ask Nolan. Literally anyone. And with you it's even harder, especially now that we're back in the real world and all I want is for what we had to be real. I said a stupid thing to Teddy. I—okay, this is embarrassing—but I was sort of starstruck when I saw him. That guy is a porn king, and let's just say his work was very formative to a young Kallum. So what I should have said was 'You let me star in a movie with the girl of my dreams and the memory of this experience will be the last thing I think of every night for the rest of my life.' I would have said that we're all just lucky to work with Winnie Baker, who is kind and smart and clever and surprisingly filthy. But I said an awful fucking thing, and I will never stop regretting it."

She looked at me and then back to our hands. Our perfect hands, cradled in front of us like they were meant to grow old together.

"I like you so much, Kallum. Too much, even. You're funny and warmhearted, and you've made me feel things I didn't know I could feel. In, ah, more ways than one. But we don't fit." She shook her head before I could interrupt. "You know it's true. You're easygoing and fun and have a great life full of bridesmaids and pizza, and I'm someone who has to have emergency lessons in sex—and we just don't make sense. So thank you for your apology. Truly. I feel ridiculous about how hurt I was, but your apology means so much to me, and just knowing that we're on okay terms will make our reshoots so much easier."

"Reshoots?" Of all the earth-shattering things she'd just said, the one thing I heard was *reshoots*.

She pulled her hands back into her lap and my empty palms felt cavernous without her. "Yeah, we're headed back to Christmas Notch next week? Didn't Steph call or email you?"

"I wouldn't say I'm the best at checking my emails."

She grinned slightly. "Well, surprise?"

Addison walked out of the juice bar with two cups in her hands and her upper lip snarled in my direction.

Winnie stood. "I better go, but I'll see you back in Christmas Notch." She bit her lip, which had a predictable effect on my nether regions, and then added, hesitantly, "We should talk while we're there. About some things."

But before Winnie could say more, Addison handed Winnie her drink and then slung an arm over her shoulder before barking at me once more.

I watched her with confusion, knowing that if this were any other day, I would think she was hilarious.

"See you in Christmas Notch!" I called to Winnie.

She glanced over her shoulder and gave me a small smile.

I turned and walked back to my car where there was a ticket waiting on my windshield. Fine, I deserved that.

Shoving the ticket in my pocket, I walked around to the driver's side door when I noticed a huge yellow boot on my front wheel. What the—

I spun around looking for the parking attendant. She was a few cars ahead, pacing in front of a Range Rover.

"Ma'am!" I called.

She held up her hand to stop me before I even got started, but I had to get to the studio and surely LA County didn't pop a boot on your car for one simple ticket.

"Ma'am, I'm so sorry, but I think there's been a mistake."

She shook her head. "No mistake. You've got nine outstanding tickets."

"Nine! Nine? This is a rental car. I've had it for two days."

She turned to move on to the next car. "Sounds like a problem for the rental company."

I opened my mouth to argue some more, but I knew it wouldn't get me anywhere.

Pulling my cell phone out of my pocket, I called an Uber. Just as Dylan confirmed he was on his way, I got a text from Justin, the *Shark Tank* PA.

> **Justin** 🦈: We're wrapped for the day and not back for another month. I called you four times.

I checked the time. I was supposed to be there an hour ago. Another text came through.

> **Steph:** How was Shark Tank? And did you see my email about reshoots?

I leaned back against the hood of my rental.

I screwed up today. I missed the shoot. I told Winnie I loved her in the worst possible way.

Everything should have felt hopeless. But all I could see was Winnie turning back to look at me and her delicious lips curling into a faint smile.

We were going back to Christmas Notch. A place full of movie magic and Winnie-Kallum history.

I'd told Winnie I loved her, and if there was any place I could convince her I meant it, it was in Christmas Notch, Vermont.

CHAPTER TWENTY

Winnie

The first thing I noticed when I walked through the door
of the Dirty Snowball the following week was how awful
it smelled. The very air was a poisonous stale-beer fume, and
the ghost of every half-eaten basket of nachos, wings, and fried
pickles lingered like a fog.

My mouth did that weird watering thing that happened
whenever I was about to throw up, and I pressed my lips firmly
together. Uh-uh. Not here. Not in *those* bathrooms.

The second thing I noticed was the absence of a certain tall,
bearded person—not that I cared, of course I didn't! I only
cared for logistical reasons, because we needed to talk about
this dang baby, and it would be easier to do it tonight, during
our "welcome back to Christmas Notch" mixer, rather than

while we were having fake Santa sex in a chimney or something.

And the fact that Kallum had told me he loved me at Got the Juice . . . the weird skip in my pulse whenever I thought about his pleading blue eyes as he'd said it . . . that had nothing to do with anything. It didn't change things. It didn't change that for all his boyish charm, he could hurt me again.

It didn't change that from now on, my heart was reserved for the little lemon-size creature growing inside of me, and for no one else.

"Winnie!" said a voice from next to me. "Welcome!"

I turned to see Gretchen and Pearl standing by the door, Gretchen holding a craft beer and Pearl holding a kombucha bottle in one hand and a basket full of mini-Fireball bottles in the other.

"I would offer you a Fireball, but Steph told us about the bambino," Gretchen said. "Congratulations, by the way."

"Make sure you drink lots of red raspberry leaf tea now that you're in your second trimester," confided Pearl. "It makes the uterus strong."

"Thank you," I said, mostly breathing through my mouth to avoid smelling the horrible air in here. "It's still early on, so you're in a pretty small group of people who know. And I'm hoping this won't impact the reshoots too much."

"Not at all," Gretchen said briskly. "You're barely showing, and it's nothing we can't work with when it comes to angles and costuming. And besides, people get pregnant. It's something we need to stop punishing actors for." Her face softened a little, a small smile curving her mouth. "Also babies are great. I can't wait to meet this one."

"Thank you for being so understanding," I said, and I meant it. So far, everyone had been so much nicer than I'd planned on—even Steph, who I'd been certain was going to fire me, because there was *sexy* chaos like Nolan Shaw, and then there was *unsexy* chaos, like being a pregnant former child star. But she hadn't fired me; in fact, she'd been weirdly delighted. ("Do you smell that?" she'd demanded. "Smell what?" I'd replied, confused, because I couldn't smell anything bad, despite now being a human sniffer dog. "All those freshly printed *People* magazines, Winnie!" she'd exclaimed with unbridled glee. "With your glowing, maternal face on the front!")

Turned out that Steph D'Arezzo's new position on clients was *the messier the better*, and she already had a couple projects in mind that would dovetail with my visibly gravid lifestyle. And now that Gretchen, Pearl, and Teddy had been formally told, along with Jack Hart and Luca, who needed to know for inti- macy coordination and costuming reasons, there were only my parents and Kallum left to tell.

I was doing a very good job not thinking about how my parents would react. Kallum? Not so much. I wanted to give him a chance to be a part of the baby's life . . . but I also won- dered how much a carefree guy like Kallum would want a baby and its neurotic, narcoleptic mother messing up his world.

Surely not, right? Surely the guy famous for slinging pizzas and boinking bridesmaids wouldn't want to be bogged down with spit-up and mastitis and all the other unglamorous parts of parenting?

So I had to prepare for it being mostly—if not entirely—me, and I had to let go of all the fantasies I'd once held so close to my heart. Fantasies of being cuddled while I nursed a tiny newborn. Of my now-estranged parents coming to stay and my mother rocking the baby while I napped nearby. Of a house full of people ready with a hug or a clean binky or open arms to take a beloved baby who hardly ever knew its crib because it was held so much.

But that was okay; I was a brave little toaster, and even though I wasn't about to make Addison do three A.M. diaper changes just because Past Winnie hadn't been smart enough to wait for a condom that hadn't been baked like a pizza by a cell phone battery, I still wasn't alone. I had Aunt Addy, and Steph hadn't fired me, and I had Gretchen's support, and things were going to be completely fine.

I just had to tell Kallum, that was all.

"Of course," Gretchen replied, right as someone bumped into me from behind. I turned to see Nolan Shaw with his arms full of red plastic baskets, lined with paper and filled with things like jalapeño poppers and Tater Tots covered in a gluey, bright yellow cheese.

My stomach promptly climbed into my throat and prepared to jump off my tongue like a diving board.

"Winnie Baker!" Nolan shouted, the tousled hair emerging from his beanie hanging just so over his forehead. "Welcome to my favorite Vermont dive bar, where the martinis are dirty and the floors are even dirtier."

"Hi, Nolan," I said, a little confused. "What are you doing in Christmas Notch? I thought you lived in LA?"

"Nolan—and Bee—are here for *Duke the Halls 2: A Ducal Wedding*, which is kicking off after our reshoots," Gretchen said from behind us. "So we thought it would be fun to have the whole family here tonight."

"Also the Dirty Snowball is booked all next week for a Disney Channel Original Movie trivia tournament, so we couldn't do separate cast mixers," Pearl chimed in.

"Ah, DCOM," Nolan said with a wistful sigh. "I was almost in a DCOM with a Jonas brother once. But I got caught making out in a Disneyland bathroom with Prince Eric right before the movie was set to start filming, and the Mouse doesn't do scandal. Even deeply, deeply understandable scandal."

He gave a shake of his head and then flashed me a grin so crooked and mischievous that I flushed. No wonder Bee Hobbes had fallen for him while shooting a movie together. If he was this charming in a dive bar with a beanie jammed down around his ears, I couldn't imagine what he was like dressed up like Mr. Darcy and smoldering at me.

"But where are my manners?" he asked suddenly. "Do you want a jalapeño popper?" He shoved one of the plastic baskets in my face, and a miasma of cheese and pepper fumes engulfed me.

Saliva flooded my mouth as my stomach gave the first shuddering lurch upward. With a squeak, I clapped my hand over my mouth and bolted past Nolan to the women's bathroom, where thankfully a graffitied stall door hung open.

I didn't have time to shut it behind me as I dropped to the floor in front of the toilet and began puking, my hands braced on the seat and my hair sliding perilously close to the action.

This was a rough one at first, lasting much longer than it had any right to, and when it finally subsided, I was crying a little, which was ninety percent a physiological reaction to vomiting and ten percent feeling very sorry for myself. I hated throwing up *so much*, and there wasn't much that my mother had done well when it came to parenting, but taking care of me when I was sick was one place where she had been truly motherly. And I wished she was here right now, holding back my hair, force-feeding me cola syrup, sitting with me until it was all over. I wouldn't even care that it was so I'd get well enough to work, which had always been the end goal when I was younger; I was so desperate for comfort that I didn't care if it came attached to ulterior motives, which my therapist wouldn't approve of. But she also didn't have flat knees from hunching over a toilet for an entire trimester.

"Hey there, couldn't help but notice you're doing the Technicolor yawn," chirped a voice from behind me, and I whirled, trying to push the tears off my face at the same time.

A tall goddess stood in the stall's open doorway, chestnut hair waving over her shoulders. She wore a baby-blue dress with very puffy sleeves and a very short skirt, which revealed thick thighs with a handful of freckles dotting her suntanned skin. She tugged idly on her gold septum ring as she looked down at me.

"You're Bee Hobbes," I said. My voice was hoarse from throwing up. "Hi. I'm Winnie Baker. I would shake your hand, but . . ."

"But it's been touching the grossest floor this side of I-91?" supplied someone else, popping up beside Bee. I didn't recognize her—although I was sure if I'd seen her before, I would have remembered, because she was stunning. Black hair, light olive skin, tattoos peeking out from fishnet tights and a sweater that was falling down around one shoulder. Giant black boots and bright green gum snapping around her mouth completed the picture. "It's okay, Winnie Baker," she added, "if there's any place where normal etiquette is suspended, it's on the floor of a bar bathroom."

"I'm okay," I said, a lifetime of trying to assure people I was fine taking over. "Totally fine. And I'm sorry I didn't close the stall door. And that you had to hear me . . . you know."

"Doing a visual burp?" the woman offered. "Hakuna matata, baby. We're here to be your bathroom fairy godmothers."

"That's really not necess—" But before I could finish demurring, I was bent over the toilet again, heaving.

Except this time my hair was pulled back for me. And someone flushed the toilet, so I at least had clean water while my pregnancy hormones did their thing. A warm hand rubbed soothingly along my back, and it was so nice that even after I was done throwing up I didn't move, just kept my head on my arm and my eyes closed while they petted me.

"Did you eat the shrimp quesadillas?" Bee asked kindly. "They really should take those off the menu."

"No," I rasped. "It's the hormones." And then I wanted to immediately rewind the tape and try again, because I hadn't meant to say that. I opened my eyes and turned to see two sets of wide blinking eyes, one set bottle green and the other a very dark brown.

"You're pregnant?" Bee said.

"Yes, and it's a long story, and not very many people know." Feeling a little better, I managed to sit all the way upright and turn to face them properly. A sudden worry darted through me. "You won't tell Nolan, will you?"

"Of course not," Bee assured me. I saw the question in her eyes, but I wasn't ready to explain everything right now, not when I was still on the floor of the Dirty Snowball.

A few more minutes passed, during which the other woman left and then returned with a cup of ice from the bar, which I slowly munched on until it became clear that my stomach had taken enough revenge for the night. I made my way to my feet and then offered them both a thin smile. "Thank you," I told them. My eyes were still watering and I had to sniffle, and they both made crooning noises at the same time. I was pulled into a squeezing hug, and then abruptly released.

"You are our baby now," Bee announced, and the other woman nodded.

"You can call her Mommy. I'm Daddy, obviously."

Bee rolled her eyes. "Sunny, you can't just *call* Daddy. That's not how it works."

Sunny snapped her gum. "Tell that to Jack Hart's mom," she said and then threw me a shameless wink.

Jack Hart's mom?

I gaped, and Bee shook her head at her friend. "He's never going to forgive you if you keep bringing it up."

"I don't know why he's still so fussy about it," Sunny huffed. "Rebecca is his *step*mom, and actually his *ex*-stepmom if we're getting specific, and also have you seen how tall she is?! This is not my fault!"

Bee was clearly not impressed by Sunny's defense, but she dropped the matter to dig invasively through Sunny's giant purse, which seemed to be something that happened a lot, judging by how unbothered Sunny was by it.

Bee emerged with a paper-wrapped object and handed it to me. It turned out to be a disposable bamboo toothbrush.

"You just had one of these in your purse?" I asked Sunny, but then added a heartfelt, "I'm glad you did. Thank you."

"You're welcome, and obviously I have an emergency toothbrush in my purse. I have several, along with baby wipes and condoms, because you never know when a content opportunity is going to appear!"

"Sunny is a porn star," Bee added, seeing my blank look at the words *content opportunity*.

"Ohhhh."

"Except for the next few weeks, when I'm doing makeup for *Duke the Halls 2*," Sunny said cheerfully. "I wear many hats, you know. Mostly while naked."

BEE AND SUNNY helped me finish cleaning up and then shepherded me out to the main room of the bar, making lots of noises about getting me back to the hotel and also getting me *fully horizontal*—or *full H* for short—on my bed so I could rest. But as the bathroom door was swinging shut behind us, I saw him.

Kallum.

Kallum looking so casually handsome in a zip-up pullover and jeans, his beard a little longer than usual, and his eyes reflecting the flashing lights of the grandma-and-reindeer-themed pinball machine next to him. Kallum searching the room, almost as if he were looking for me, as if all of his attention was bent on finding me.

My heart was swelling, soaring, taking up my whole chest

and stomach, and I couldn't breathe for it, and he was so handsome, and his baby was inside me, and oh my God, this was too much, all so much more complicated than I could have imagined. How was I supposed to tell him calmly and neutrally I was having his child and that we could navigate a platonic coparenting relationship when all I wanted to do was pull him on top of me and bite his neck while he sank that giant dick between my legs and rode me ragged?

Nope! I was *not* ready to talk to him tonight, not until I got my feelings in order, and definitely not until I got my unruly vagina in order.

"I, um, need fresh air," I blurted to Sunny and Bee, and then bolted for the back door of the bar without another word, not caring how strange it must look. I had to get out of there *right now* before he saw me. Before he talked to me in that rich baritone, before he told me he loved me again. Before all the feelings I'd been pushing down surged to the surface and I told him I loved him back.

I shoved the creaky old door open and slipped into the quiet alley behind the bar. It was early June and the night was mild—cool enough to feel nice on my flushed cheeks, but warm enough that my thin sweater and jeans kept me comfortable. The fresh mountain air immediately cleared away my sour stomach, and I thanked God and Sunny for that disposable toothbrush, because with zero nausea and a clean, minty mouth, I almost felt like a human again.

I took a deep breath, tilting my face up to the moon and trying to gather the energy to slink off to my hotel room like a good little coward, and then the creaky door opened again.

I turned to see Kallum standing in the alley, his face partly in shadow, his hands jammed into his pockets.

We didn't speak.

After a long moment, he came forward, slowly, and I backed up until my heel hit the brick wall of the building behind me. He stopped just in front of me, his blue eyes black in the moonlight.

"Winnie," he said roughly. And then he brought his forehead to mine, his breath coasting across my lips. I was trembling.

He was trembling too.

I can't fight this, I realized dizzily. It was too much, it was a blitz, a cavalry charge ready to run me right over, and with him so close, so warm, so *Kallum*, I didn't even want to fight it. I wanted him, and who cared what he'd said in a hallway last spring, he was right here and shaking just to be near me and when I pressed both of my hands to his chest, he made a noise deep in his throat—half plea, half growl.

"Kallum," I whispered. "Take me back to your hotel room."

I felt how much he wanted to say yes. I felt him lean forward, felt his arms come tight around my shoulders, felt him shudder like he was already imagining being between my thighs.

Then he ripped himself away, jamming his hands into his hair as he turned back to face me. "No," he said. "No, I'm not touching you until we get our shit sorted out."

He was right, but I didn't care.

"Not even a kiss?" I said, knowing it came out sounding pouty as heck.

Kallum's face was a study in agony, and I went in for the kill. I bit my lip.

With a rough groan, he was against me again, his hands in my hair and his mouth moving hot and urgent from my lips to my jaw to my neck. I rubbed against him like a cat in heat, and then practically purred in his ear when one of his hands moved from my hair to my breast and gently pressed. I was still a little tender there, but with his hands so large and warm, it still felt good, and the goodness was seeping down to my belly now, down to the ache between my legs, and I knew it was shameless, but I did it anyway. I grabbed Kallum's hand and guided it to the waistband of my jeans.

"What about this?" I murmured, and he pulled back to look at me.

"Don't think I don't know what game you're playing, Winnie," he said darkly as his fingers made easy work of the button and zipper. "Don't think I still won't win."

I whimpered as his fingers pushed into my panties and found my clit, circling it until I panted and then sliding his fingers farther down until he could enter me. We both exhaled as he pushed them inside, working expertly until I was chasing his touch, eagerly trying to ride his hand. I hadn't had the energy to masturbate since I'd left Christmas Notch the first time, and my body was abruptly aware of how long it had been since I'd last had an orgasm. Forever, it felt like, and I needed to pay off my orgasm deficit right the eff now. Ideally with many, many orgasms.

"Fuck, this is hot," Kallum grunted, his other hand still tangled in my hair.

"Please," I moaned, not even sure what I was asking for. To come? To be hauled back to his hotel room for a more thorough sexing?

It didn't matter, though, because Kallum didn't give me either one. Instead, he waited until I was shivering *right* on the edge of my climax, my feet planted apart, my chest heaving, so wet where Kallum was fingering me that my panties were soaked, and then he pulled his hand free.

I stared at him as he pressed his fingers to my mouth and I obediently sucked them clean, my body in a state of shock. And when he didn't go back to fingering me—when he instead stepped back and adjusted the very obvious hard-on tenting his jeans—I made a very unladylike splutter.

"You—you—but—"

He nodded, like a wise sage with a giant boner. "I told you, Winnie. We need to figure out our shit first. And maybe this will give you some incentive."

Incentive! This was torture!

I glared at him and then, like a pissy kitten, nipped at the fingers still in my mouth.

He pulled them back and then gave me a stern look that made my toes curl. I had a very vivid fantasy of being draped over Kallum's lap—my jeans pulled down and my bare bottom awaiting some Stern Kallum punishment—play out in my mind.

Did I really want that? For Kallum to spank me sometime?

All signs from my erogenous zones said *YES, YES, YES.*

"Careful, babe," warned Kallum. "Next time, I might bite back."

The erotic threat in his words was intoxicating—maybe to us both, because he suddenly shook his head and rubbed his non-bitten hand over his face. "Okay, I might have to find a different talk-to-me incentive, because this one is getting me all worked up too, and that's the exact opposite of what we need."

Guilt crept in, thick and heavy. I didn't need hostage orgasms as incentive; not when all the incentive we needed was currently growing its genetically blessed vocal cords somewhere vaguely north of my bladder.

Kallum was right. I was horny and selfish and Kallum was right.

"No," I said as I started doing up my jeans. "I think you're right. We should talk first."

His voice had softened a little when he added, "I *want* to figure this out. I meant what I said in LA, babe. I love you."

My throat went tight; I blinked and kept my eyes on my hands as I hiked my jeans up over the barely there swell of our lemon-size baby.

"You don't have to say it back," Kallum said, and he said it so gently, so vulnerably, that I pressed my face into my hands.

"I want to say it back," I murmured. It was the truth. The horrible, glorious truth.

I loved him back.

But how could I say it when I still had to tell him about the baby? When I still wasn't sure if I could count on him not to hurt me with some throwaway comment or thoughtless moment? Because if he'd thought I was embarrassing before, God only knew what he'd think of a frazzled Winnie panicking about car seat installation appointments with cabbage leaves stuffed in her bra . . . and I didn't know if I could handle him being careless with me then.

Or God forbid, careless with the baby.

Maybe it wasn't fair to either of us to say it until there were no more secrets, until I knew for sure that I was ready to take the leap.

I looked up to see Kallum watching me like a starving man.

"Tomorrow," he said suddenly. "We've done enough tonight. We'll sleep and then start fresh tomorrow, and then we'll get the two of us sorted out."

The reshoots schedule was pretty brisk, and even when we weren't on set, we'd be working with Jack and Gretchen on choreographing the new love scenes, so I wasn't sure how much time we'd be able to carve out.

But there wasn't a choice—not when the two of us had a future where there would be three of us instead.

CHAPTER TWENTY-ONE

Kallum

I sat in my room wide awake. It was nearly one in the morning and all I wanted was to relive that hot little moment in the alleyway. Until I ended it like a painfully responsible adult.

It'd been two hours since Winnie and I walked back to the Edelweiss Inn and I was still rocking a moderate chub. But I was trying to think with my brain, and my brain knew that there was no path forward with Winnie without us hashing our shit out like grown-ups. With the way the rest of the world turned to silence any time our bodies collided, part of me wondered if we would have better luck talking through a wall.

I sent off a quick and way-too-late text to my mom, telling her that I'd made it here safely, and another to Tamara, promising to check in on Topher several times a day.

Shockingly, after my *Shark Tank* no-show, the investors were still interested. They were disappointed—and fuck, that was a word I'd heard too much lately—but they were interested in restructuring their expansion plan, so until then I was sort of in a holding pattern. I kept telling myself that once I had all that squared away, I could get Topher back in school and talk to Tamara about his (hopefully) brief college dropout status.

Just as I flipped the switch on the bedside lamp, a knock tapped at my door.

I looked up at the dark ceiling and inhaled deeply. If that was Winnie banging on my hotel room door in the middle of the night, I'd tell her the same thing I told her just hours ago. And secretly, as much as I hated leaving her unsatisfied, I relished it too. But if we could just talk. If we could just straighten things out, there'd be a lifetime full of naughty little games for us to play.

Another knock sounded from the hallway.

I fumbled for the light and slipped on the jeans I'd left on the floor before pulling the door open. "Hey," I said in the deepest growl I could manage. I told her we'd talk first, but I never said I'd play fair—especially not after that lip-biting action she served tonight.

"Are you feeling ill?" the person in the hallway who definitely was not Winnie Baker asked. "Because I haven't left my house in six months for more than an hour at a time, and I didn't come all this way just to catch whatever it is you have."

"Isaac?" I asked. "Is—is this real? Am I hallucinating?"

Isaac Kelly, my reclusive friend and the third member of INK, stood there wearing slouchy jeans tucked into black boots and white V-neck tee that teased at a silver necklace worn underneath. His hair was different than when I'd last seen him, no longer the signature heartthrob tousle he'd had at Brooklyn's funeral but now thick, loose waves around his jaw. It was as careless and broody as the rest of his outfit, and of course, like everything else on Isaac Kelly, it looked unfairly good.

I peered down the hallway to see a tall bodyguard with her hair pulled back in a low ponytail and sunglasses pushed up over her head even though it was the middle of the night. Beside her was Donna, the assistant he'd had since INK broke up and he went solo.

"What's up, Donna?" I called down the hallway.

She didn't look up from her phone as she sighed and said, "Kallum."

"Cool," I said to Isaac. "So she still hates me."

He glanced down to Donna and shrugged. "Not just you. Nolan too."

"Oh, that makes me feel so much better." She'd wanted Isaac to stay clear from us both, especially after Nolan's big scandal. "So what the hell are you doing here?"

He tilted his head to the side. "You asked if I wanted someone to be sad with."

I blinked. Once. Twice.

"In the text you sent," he added.

"Isaac, that was months ago."

"Well, I'm here now." He walked past me and into my room. "And I'm ready to be sad with you."

I leaned out the door. "I promise not to besmirch his name, Donna. You can go to bed."

Donna rolled her eyes and turned down the hallway with a key in her hand as the very intense-looking bodyguard strolled down the hallway toward my door.

"Uh, is your bodyguard going to be joining us?" I asked Isaac, who had already opened my mini fridge, retrieved a toasted pecan beer, and was propped up in my bed.

"Krysta will wait in the hallway. Or scope out the floor or some kind of tactical thing. I don't know. Do your thing, Krysta!" he called to her.

I saluted her before closing the door. "That woman looks like she could knock me on my ass."

"Because I could," she said through the door.

"Good to know!" I told her as I came to sit down on the other side of the bed beside Isaac.

"So what is it that we're sad about, Kallum? I didn't even know you could be sad."

"That's it?" I asked. "We're not going to talk about what the fuck you're doing in Vermont? Or how you haven't answered a phone call from me in over a year? Shit. Shouldn't I at least drag Nolan down here?"

"He's here?" Isaac asked.

"Filming *Duke the Halls 2*."

"Well, that explains why I couldn't rent out the mansion."

"You tried to rent out *the mansion?*"

"I saw it in the first *Duke the Halls*. It looked very . . ." He waved an elegant hand. He wasn't wearing his wedding ring, which I couldn't decide was a good sign or not. "Very quiet up there on the mountainside. Secluded. Anyway, don't tell Nolan I'm here just yet. He's so happy and in love right now." He lowered his eyelids until his dark gold lashes rested on his cheekbones. "I don't have the stomach for it tonight."

I tilted my head back against the headboard. "Same, man." I bumped his fist. "Sad boys for life."

"So what is it?" he asked again. "What in the world could ever make Kallum Lieberman sad?"

So I told him. I told him every detail of me and Winnie. I told him about the picture from the Teen Choice Awards and Michael showing up on the *Santa, Baby* set like he was hot shit and how I've been falling in love with Winnie Baker slowly for the last twenty years and yet suddenly all at once. And how I fucked up and said the wrong thing and how I needed to prove to her that I could be the man she deserved.

When the whole story was laid out there crystal clear, he turned to me with watery eyes. "Addison Hayes really barked at you?"

"Yeah. It was terrifying."

He sniffed. "I always liked her."

"What about you? Nolan and I have been worried. The last time he had eyes on you was a year and a half ago. If you hadn't picked up when I called on . . ."

"Brooklyn's death day. You never forget," he said.

"I was fully prepared to book a flight to LA and climb over your gate to check on you."

"You would've been electrocuted," he said simply before setting his beer on the nightstand. "I was feeling restless. And then I felt guilty for feeling restless. Shouldn't I just be happy to be alive? I'm breathing. I can see her favorite view every morning. Should that be enough? But sometimes I wake up in that house and I can't catch my breath. It's like . . . grief is sitting on my chest. I couldn't leave, but I couldn't stay."

I gripped his thigh. "I'm glad you're here."

"I saw your text and yes, I know it was from months ago, but I fucking hate having a phone. For so long, every time I looked at it, I expected to see a text or a call from her, and then when I stopped feeling those expectations, I felt like an ass. Like I was letting go of some part of her . . . but anyway, I got your message and I thought to myself, 'Vermont sounds like the kind of place where you could just disappear.'"

"You're not a shitty person for moving on," I told him. "I mean . . . if anything ever happened to Bee, Nolan would probably cope by fucking his way through the San Andreas fault line. You basically entered a monastery and took a vow of silence."

"I did actually consider that," he mumbled.

"I'm probably not in a position to give anyone advice right now . . . but Brooklyn would want you to get out there and live. She was all about the drama, of course, so your level of mourning would be fully appreciated by her, but she'd also want you to go out there and find a hottie or something."

He pushed a hand through his hair, which went right back to being a lush, magazine-worthy mess when he was done. "Brook did love hotties . . . and I did download some dating apps."

"Maybe be careful with those. Even on the invite-only ones, you never know who people really are and—"

"I know how stranger danger works, Kallum. I've seen *Catfish*."

"I don't know, man. The internet has changed the dating game, and you got together with Brooklyn when we were kids." I changed the subject. "So if you're not staying at the mansion, where are you staying while you're here?"

"Here. Donna booked me a presidential suite, I believe."

I laughed. "I'm pretty sure the only thing different about the presidential suite in the Edelweiss Inn is a foldout sofa."

He stood with the kind of grace that reminded me he'd had the best dance moves of us all. "Well, I suppose I should see what luxuries await me. I'm sure you have an early morning. I'm wide awake. Still on California time." He smiled to himself. "The boys of INK all under one roof."

"Donna must be losing her damn mind."

As he placed the empty craft beer can in the recycle bin—he'd always been painfully conscientious about recycling while on the road, and Nolan and I had never had the heart to tell him that most hotels just pitched everything into the trash—the necklace he was wearing under his shirt slid free and I saw what was on the end.

His wedding ring. Slender, platinum-bright. Glinting, like it had just been cleaned.

He saw me looking and gave me whatever passed for a smile from him these days. "I promise to listen to your advice—both about the hotties and being careful. And I don't have any advice for you, but maybe don't be sad forever, because that's *my* brand."

He walked out into the hallway where—sure enough—Krysta was waiting for him.

"M'lord," she said with a smirk.

That got a little laugh out of Isaac, and with Donna being such a hell demon, I was glad to see the bodyguard bring a smile to Isaac's face.

THE NEXT MORNING, Winnie and I sat on opposite ends of an endlessly long velvet sofa across from Jack Hart on the second floor of the old Victorian house–turned–production office.

Jack took a huge sip from his cup of steaming hot water, gargled it, and then swallowed. "Sorry . . . I just have this awful taste in my mouth I can't get rid of."

Winnie made a sympathetic sound. "I understand completely."

Jack walked over to the coffee station and refilled his cup of hot water before sitting back down on the hearth of the large brick fireplace. "Okay, you've seen the rewrite from Pearl?"

We both nodded. The original script was interesting enough, but this new version . . . well, things had taken a turn.

"So we've got to stage this blow job scene. And Winnie, we're going to have to make it clear that you swallowed," Jack said as his dusty, Swiffer-looking dog searched for the perfect patch of sunlight to lay in.

"Because of the magical peppermint semen?" Winnie asked.

"Exactly. Which is how we'll discover that Santa's semen is the blah, blah secret sauce that can fuel Santa's sled for an entire Christmas night," Jack continues.

"Wait," I said, "so it's not the belief in Santa Claus that fuels the sled?"

"Well, yes, it was that." Jack looked to be doing mental gymnastics in his head as he flipped through the new pages. "But not enough people believe in Santa and part of you taking over the role of Santa Senior is finding a way to power the sled when belief is at an all-time low."

"So that's why we added a sex marathon to the end?" I asked.

Jack nodded. "I mean, the only reason anyone is watching this thing is to see you two bone all over this winter wonderland, so if peppermint semen is how we get there, then that's how we get there."

"Sounds good to me," Winnie squeaked.

"It does?" I asked. The new script had gone so far off the rails that I was fully prepared to push back on anything Winnie wasn't comfortable with.

"And Winnie," Jack said, "I hear we need to work around—"

"I'm good," she said briskly.

Jack paused for a moment. "Okay, then. Now, I brought a kneeling pad for you, Winnie, which you'll also have on set and—"

"Knock, knock," a voice called from the doorway.

I turned to find Sunny Palmer hovering over the entry into the room. We'd only met a few times, but she was funny and stunning and I'd be lying if I said I hadn't enjoyed her content from time to time.

"Sunny!" Winnie and I both said in unison.

"How do you two know each other?" I asked, confused.

The color vanished from Winnie's cheeks.

"We go way back," Sunny said, and Winnie nodded.

Huh.

"Out," Jack demanded before swallowing back more scalding water. "This is my place of business."

"Your place of business?" Sunny asked from the hallway. "You're not, like, some mom-and-pop intimacy coordinator. And need I remind you that this is also my place of business for the next four weeks? Besides, we should talk about last night. Well, technically, this morning."

Winnie and I shared a quick glance. She shrugged, so I was guessing we were both in the dark here.

"Um, we can wait," Winnie offered.

Sunny curtsied. "Thank you, Winnie."

Jack threw back the rest of his hot water and then made a gagging sound as he stood up and stomped his fancy, pointed-toe boots right out the door.

"You have any idea what's going on?" I asked Winnie as the two disappeared down the hallway.

She shook her head. "I feel like I vaguely remember hearing something about Sunny hooking up with Jack's ex-stepmom."

My eyes bugged out. "I have to know more," I told her.

"Kallum Lieberman?" she whispered. "A gossip?"

"I got my bloodlust for it from my mom's side," I admitted as I stood up and tiptoed to the door.

"It's not like you had to stick around," I heard Sunny say. "I was happy to handle him on my own."

"Don't feed me that bullshit," Jack spat back.

Winnie was leaning so far over the couch as she strained to hear that she was about to fall off, so I waved her over. After a moment, she conceded and came to stand behind me, with her ear pressed to the wall.

I could feel the warmth of her breath on my back, and if I didn't have to watch the door, I'd spin around so I could at least look at her even if I couldn't touch her. Not yet at least.

"He was so sad," Jack said. "How could I deny him a three-some?"

"It's not like he was magically happy afterward," Sunny told him with a huff.

My eyes bulged even farther out of my head.

"He was happy for a little while there though," Jack countered.

"See! It wasn't so bad," Sunny said. "We're like the Red Cross, but sexy. Sexy do-gooders bringing joy to one sad celebrity at a time."

"That doesn't change the fact that I scrubbed the taste of your vag from my mouth and I can still taste you. It's disgusting."

"I'm not going to make a *your mom* joke. I'm not going to make a *your mom* joke. I'm not going to make a *your mom* joke."

"You know what, Sunny? Fuck you. I hope you have only mediocre sex for the rest of your life."

Sunny scoffed. "Don't pretend like you didn't have fun."

"Of course I had fun," Jack said. "Who doesn't love a hate fuck?"

"So what you're saying is you had a good time? With me?"

"Enough already. I have an actual job to do, okay?"

"Jack Hart had fun with me," Sunny sang to herself.

Jack groaned and we heard the stomp of his boots as Winnie and I ran back to the couch.

She looked at me and I looked at her just as we realized we were in each other's spots and scrambled to swap places.

As Jack walked back in and refilled his cup of hot water, I pulled out my phone to text Isaac. Who had officially been in Christmas Notch for less than eight hours by this point.

Me: Ummmm

Me: When I said find a hottie, I meant have a fun little hookup. Not have a threesome with two porn stars??

Three little dots appeared as I waited for his response.

Isaac: I'm new to these apps. I swiped and suddenly they were both there and group sex was one of the options and . . . Brooklyn always wanted to have a threesome.

I began to type, So you had a threesome in honor of Brooklyn? But then I backspaced. Isaac had not only left his house, but he'd left the state of California. Who was I to rain on his three-some parade?

"Everything okay?" Winnie asked me.

I looked at Jack, who was staring off into the distance beyond us, like a changed man.

I grinned at Winnie. "Great."

Jack opened his script again with a sigh. "Back to fictional peppermint blow jobs."

CHAPTER TWENTY-TWO

Winnie

I'd always been good at making plans—a little gift from having narcolepsy, I supposed, since I had to be eternally ready to salvage a day derailed by oversleeping or an emergency nap— and I'd gotten even better at it during the divorce. Any task, no matter how existentially terrifying, could be broken down into the smallest steps when you thought about it. Stop crying. Walk into the next room. Pick up the phone.

Et cetera.

So this evening, I finally made a plan for telling Kallum about the baby: choose a spot where I would absolutely, *absolutely*, have no way to climb him like a tree, no matter how much I wanted to, text him to meet me at said spot under the pretense of talking about *us*, and then walk all the way there without chickening out.

Not that I was going to chicken out. It was going to be totally fine! Kallum was easygoing to a fault. He'd probably absorb the news in the same casual way he'd absorbed the fact that Santa's semen was more potent per ounce than liquid rocket propellant, and then tell me that whatever I wanted to do was cool by him. He'd say exactly what I'd emotionally prepared for him to say, that he wasn't ready to be a father but would gamely pony up money to help, and that would be that. Secrets all revealed, my pregnant person duty discharged, and then maybe he'd agree that it wouldn't do any harm to have as much sex as possible while we were here in Christmas Notch together. (I would of course bravely and maturely explain that another temporary sex fling wouldn't induce me to expect more than he wanted to give on a parenting level, and he'd be so charmingly grateful.)

Mustering as much optimism as possible, I left my room and headed to the lobby, rubbing my belly as I waited for the elevator.

We got this, kiddo, I told my little bump. *No matter what, we have each other.*

Funny how love worked, sometimes fast, sometimes slow; sometimes exactly like the idea of love you had in your head, and then sometimes not at all. All my life, I'd wanted to be a mother, and I'd assumed the moment I learned I was pregnant, I'd be glowing with love like a little maternal star, but that wasn't how it had been. It had taken longer, been interrupted by nausea and exhaustion, been threaded through with worry about money and perception and how I was going to manage narcolepsy and a baby at the same time.

But it was here. Different than how I'd expected, maybe, but here.

And we would have a beautiful life together, whatever happened with Kallum tonight.

I passed a woman checking in at the front desk, and then did a double take. She had on giant sunglasses and a silk scarf wrapped around her head like a 1950s movie star, but I'd recognize that pearl-and-pantsuit combo anywhere.

"Steph?" I asked, confused.

She turned away, ducking her head and tapping her fingernails on the battered wood of the counter, until I stepped closer, and she spun back to face me.

"Winnie, hello," she said, taking off her sunglasses like she'd just walked inside the lobby. "Just the person I was looking for."

"I am?"

"Ye-e-es," she said, not very convincingly. "I wanted to let you know that I've decided to come to Christmas Notch for the week, what with you and Kallum being here, and *Duke the Halls 2* starting. Made sense to be where so many of my clients are."

"Lots of sense," I responded. "I had no idea you were planning on coming up?"

"It was a spontaneous decision. A spontaneous business decision. About business."

My phone buzzed in my hand, and I looked down to see a text from Kallum.

> **Kallum:** Just got cleaned up from filming the sauna jerkoff scene! Be there in ten!

"Ah, I need to go," I said to Steph. "I'm glad you're here though!"

She put her sunglasses back on. "Me too. More soon, Winnie Baker." And then Stella the innkeeper approached and handed Steph her room keys. *Keys.* Plural.

Hmm.

FROSTY'S DINER WAS empty when I got there—June being too early for most of the through hikers, and way too early for the leaf-peepers, apple-eaters, and Christmas enthusiasts—and I picked a booth in the far corner, grabbing a menu and reminding myself to breathe. I'd been with Kallum this morning! He'd had his fingers inside me last night! It was all going to be fine!

The bell rang over the door, and I looked up to see the young Santa himself striding toward me in jeans and a flannel shirt with the sleeves rolled up to expose his forearms. His face was faintly pink and glowing, like he'd just gotten out of a hot shower, and when he came closer, I realized that at some point between our coordination meeting and his sauna scenes, his hair and beard had been trimmed a little shorter, a little neater. I could perfectly see his lower lip now, soft, curved temptation itself.

I wanted to lick it. I wanted to feel it dragging over my clit.

I dragged my eyes up to his, my cheeks warming when I saw his raised eyebrow. So he'd noticed that I was already a horndog tonight. Great.

He slid into the booth and grabbed a laminated menu from where it was tucked between the ketchup bottle and the napkin dispenser. "I'm glad you were game for meeting tonight," he said, beaming down at the menu. It was one of those classic Kallum smiles, a smile like there could be no better day than today, no better moment than right now. I blinked and looked away. His warmth and sweetness were sometimes almost painful to me, in a way I couldn't even explain to myself. They made me feel worthy and unworthy at the same time; they felt like gifts when I'd given nothing in return.

"So what are you going to get?" Kallum asked, oblivious to his effect on me. His eyes were still on the menu. "I've only eaten here a few times, but everything I've had has been good."

I looked back down at my own menu, and my stomach sloshed unhappily as I scanned through the options. Nothing sounded good because nothing had sounded good to eat for months now. Even peanut butter sandwiches and green smoothies had lost their luster for me—I'd been choking down bananas and protein bars to get by. (So much for morning sickness getting better in the second trimester.)

"What's wrong?" Kallum asked, and I realized I was visibly pouting at the menu.

I made an effort to be mature about becoming the world's pickiest eater. "I think I'm not that hungry, actually. I'm just going to have some ice water. But you should get whatever you want."

"*Winnie*," he said, with the gravity of a brain surgeon. "What sounds good to you?"

"Really, I just—"

"Not on the menu," he clarified. "Like at all. If you could eat anything right now, what would it be?" His tone was very firm for Kallum: less cinnamon roll and more *I'll keep you bent over my lap until you're a good girl.*

And holy heckballs, Bossy Kallum really, *really* worked for me, because that voice was making me squirm in my seat.

I decided to obey Bossy Kallum. I closed my eyes and thought about it. "Maple syrup," I said. "And, um. Bacon. String cheese, maybe? And a pear! A pear sounds delicious."

I opened my eyes to see Kallum pushing out of the booth and standing. He gallantly extended a hand to me and then pulled me to my feet.

"Wait, what are we—"

He didn't answer, but started pulling me to the back of the diner, past the empty tables, past the low red counter and to the kitchen, where a bored line cook was flipping a water bottle onto the stainless steel prep table.

Kallum pulled several bills from his wallet and pressed them into the line cook's tattooed hand. The cook—somewhere older than college but younger than twenty-five—blinked at us both with hazy-eyed confusion and then blinked down at the money in his hand.

"I think you deserve a break," Kallum suggested, and then the kid got the hint.

"Yeah, sure," the cook said, stuffing the money into his pocket and stripping off his apron. "But if someone comes in while I'm gone, you gotta make their food. And probably serve it too, because I haven't seen Linda around for a while. Sometimes she leaves to go check on her parrot when it gets slow."

With that he left, and Kallum picked me up and plonked me onto the prep table.

"Stay put," he told me, and then went and found a clean apron, tying the strings with the intensity of a knight readying himself for battle. And then he began rummaging through the glass-doored commercial refrigerators, and then the open shelves nearby.

"Now can you tell me what we're doing?" I asked.

"*You* are going to sit there looking adorable," he said, pulling a plastic-wrapped ball of dough off a shelf and pressing on it with his knuckle. Whatever he saw made him sigh, but he still set the dough on the counter. "And then *I'm* going to make you dinner."

"Oh, Kallum, you don't have to—"

"I want to," he said firmly. The look he gave me was somewhere between Bossy Kallum and the Kallum who gave me his coat on the ski lift. "You need dinner. And I want to see you eating my food. The worst part about being on set is never having time in the kitchen. So hush."

Smiling, I pressed my lips together in a visual promise to do as he said. Satisfied, he turned back to the kitchen, and— whistling—began assembling ingredients. A bottle of syrup. A package of bacon and two containers of cheese in different shades of white.

And a pear. Pale green and mouthwateringly pretty.

Kallum dusted a nearby counter with flour and dropped the dough in the middle, deftly flattening it into a disk with his fingers. He then used his fingers to slowly work and stretch the dough open—in a way that wasn't intentionally suggestive, but in my orgasm-denied state was practically pornographic. (Also pornographic? The way the muscles and tendons in his forearms flexed as he expertly tossed the dough into a familiar shape.)

"Are you making me a custom pizza?"

"Yepperoni pepperoni, baby." He moved over to a stove, and with a few easy movements, had a skillet over a burner and was draping pink ribbons of bacon over the surface. They started sizzling.

"Ah, the sound of the delicious forbidden," he said, cleaning up the package and going to a sink to wash his hands.

I felt suddenly oblivious that I'd never asked Kallum about food before. "Do you keep a kosher kitchen at home? I guess it would be hard for a pizza place to keep kosher, because it wouldn't just be the recipes themselves, but the equipment and ingredients too?"

"Down to the raisins for Raisin 'Em Right, my second best-selling breakfast pizza," Kallum confirmed. "But nah. Lots of reform families are observant, but it's just never been part of our family life. And so I decided not to start my new path as a pizza-wizard with a kosher restaurant, because it is pretty complicated to get started and do it right. But I do have a meat-free kosher pizza truck that makes the rounds to my different SSB locations one night a week. It's called There's Something About Dairy. A rabbi came in and kosherized the truck's equipment with a blowtorch. It was awesome. And my mom likes to brag about it, so a win all around."

He flipped the bacon and then hit the switch for the smallish electric pizza oven nearby, giving it a baleful look as he did so.

"I prefer wood-fired," he said when he noticed my questioning stare. "Although this is *fine*, I guess." He went back to the pizza dough, humming a little as he sprinkled cheese over it, and then went over to the bacon, drizzling maple syrup into the pan to great, sizzling fanfare, and then dumping the whole lot onto a wooden cutting board.

He kept humming as he chopped the bacon and then spread the pieces over the pizza, adding a second kind of cheese, and then slid the whole thing onto the pizza oven's metal conveyor belt and set the timer. Ten minutes. I watched as he put all the ingredients away, scrubbed the pan, cutting board and knife, his hands, and then wiped down the counter.

Finally, he washed the pear and came back to me. He nudged his way between my legs with his hips, and with a paring knife, began slicing a wafer-thin piece of fruit.

"I was wondering when the pear would make an appearance," I murmured as he held up the slice.

"Open," he said, his voice a warm rumble, and I obeyed without thinking, parting my lips and letting him place the pear on my tongue.

It was sweet, bright, that perfect texture between soft and crunchy that ripe pears were, and I sighed with happiness as I ate it.

"Thank you," I said, and he smiled down at the pear as he cut me another slice. His hands were so sure with the knife and the fruit, exerting just enough pressure, cutting at just the right angle, and it occurred to me that Kallum was so much more than silly jokes and nice cuddles and lap dances in private rooms. I'd just watched him go to the trouble to make me a custom pizza because nothing else sounded good to me; he'd not only made it, but cleaned up after, even the messy, greasy bacon pan. And now he was feeding me a pear like it was a privilege to do so.

And maybe . . . maybe I'd been too hard on him with the whole Teddy thing. Maybe it had just been a onetime slip—like Kallum had said, a blunder born of the early hour and being starstruck.

Maybe I could trust him to be careful with me. That was why I'd refused to even entertain the idea of a relationship before, right? Because I'd been scared of someone being careless with me again?

Kallum fed me another slice, and something in my chest broke like brittle ice under a warm spring sun.

I chewed, swallowed. Met his eyes with mine.

"I'm pregnant," I whispered.

The moment stretched into silence, his lips parting as he drew breath, his eyes like sapphire mirrors reflecting my own nervous, hopeful face.

"It's yours," I added, maybe pointlessly.

"I . . ."

He trailed off. Behind him, the pizza oven dinged with a sharp noise that made us both jump.

Clearing his throat, he pushed away from me, setting the pear and knife down and then sliding the hot pizza onto a square of red-and-white-checked paper, and then using the rocking pizza cutter to slice it. It smelled divine; I'd forgotten what it felt like to smell something and want it immediately in my mouth.

Well, except for Kallum, of course. Who still wasn't looking at me.

"Kallum," I said, my voice trembling, a little hoarse. "Say something."

He took a breath and then lifted his eyes to mine.

He was crying.

Panic tore at my throat, but before I could say anything, he was back between my legs and wrapping those strong arms around me. He buried his face in my neck: all wet cheeks and scratchy beard.

"Oh my God," he breathed. "Oh my God."

"Are you—" I couldn't even think. Was he that devastated? Was he imagining his whole life ruined, his future crushed? "Kallum, I should have led with this, but I don't expect you to help me, I don't expect you to be a father or anything like that, I just thought you should know—"

"What are you talking about?" he asked, pulling back. His thick, straight brows were bunched together, his expression genuinely confused.

"I'm saying"—I took a steadying breath—"that I'm not trying to trap you into responsibility or anything. I'm not asking you for anything."

"Winnie," he said, shaking his head and then making a sound that was something like a laugh, something like a choked plea. "Why wouldn't you ask me?"

I didn't have a good answer to that. Because what seemed like *noble, clear-eyed maturity* just a few minutes ago was starting to feel like *assuming the worst of someone.*

He took in a shuddering breath and then straightened up. He took my hands in his and looked directly into my eyes. "I've never heard better news in my entire life. And just so we're clear: I want to be asked, Winnie. I want nothing more than for you to ask me to be a father to this baby."

I might as well have been on that floor-dropping barrel ride, hanging in midair, no safety net in sight. "Really?" I asked in a whisper.

He gave me an emotional smile, tears sparkling on his eyelashes and in his beard. "Yes. Really."

"You're not . . . upset? Disappointed? Grieving the ghost of your future self?"

Another puzzled expression. "Huh?"

"You know, because this wasn't planned, and we're not—" I struggled for the right words. Because even though it was easier to say what we *weren't* than what we *were*, I suddenly didn't want to say any of that out loud. I didn't want it to be true that we weren't together, that we had no future, that the thing between us was only about sex or research.

I loved him.

He loved me.

Why couldn't that be a start?

"Because we're not sure what we are yet," I finished softly. "This is a giant thing to throw into the middle of that."

"A giant, beautiful thing," he said earnestly, bringing my hands up to his lips and kissing my fingers. "The best thing."

"The best thing?"

He nodded solemnly, and then his tear-wet face broke into a huge grin. "A baby," he said, almost in wonder now. "*Our* baby."

I knew my smile was more tremulous, more full of uncertainty, but it still felt good to smile back at him, like we were two kids just getting into trouble together, and not two grown-ups who were about to be responsible for a real, living, breathing person.

"Oh!" he exclaimed. "Your pizza!"

He dropped my hands and then selected a slice for me. It was still hot when he put it in my hands, and when I bit into it, it was the most delicious, gooey, maple-y thing I'd ever eaten.

I moaned around the slice. "Oh my God, this weird pizza is the only thing that's tasted good to me in months."

Kallum's eyes went wide with awe. "It really is my baby," he breathed, and then he reverently watched me inhale three more slices of his pizza while he pressed his hands to my stomach. I'd tell him later that the baby was only barely above my pubic bone and he definitely wouldn't be able to feel it move yet.

"I know that we have so much more to talk about," he said as I set down the crust of my last slice and gave a dreamy, full-bellied sigh. "But I really, really want to bone your brains out right now."

It should have sounded terrible—I'd just eaten a whole bunch of maple syrup and bacon pizza and we still had *so much* to figure out—but instead I felt energized and brave and I was still so viciously horny, I could scream. Boning our brains out seemed like the only logical next move, really.

"Lead the way, Daddy Kallum," I said, and he groaned before yanking me bodily out of the diner and back to the inn.

CHAPTER TWENTY-THREE

Kallum

The elevator doors closed behind us, and I'd already pinned Winnie into the corner, pulling both of her thighs around my hips. I'd been hard as a rock for the last two blocks as we tripped toward the Edelweiss Inn, dipping in and out of shadows and panting into each other's mouths and kissing every bit of exposed skin.

As we fell into our hallway, Winnie frantically shoved a hand to her purse. "My room is closer."

A laugh barreled through my chest as she pulled out her key, rocking her hips against me. "Winnie, I'd fuck you in this hallway if I could." Sweeping her hair back over her shoulder, I kissed along her neck and pulled her closer to me, reaching around to undo the button of her jeans, until finally the key clicked and we tumbled into her dark room.

She turned to me as the door shut behind us, and it hit me all over again as I watched her swaying in the narrow slant of moonlight creeping in through the window. Winnie was pregnant with my child. *Our* child.

I reached up and held her face in my hands. Her head tilted to the side as she leaned into my palm and we walked backward slowly toward the bed. The room was thick with her scent. Thick with cinnamon and orangey citrus.

"I want to tell everyone," I told her. "I have to call my mom. You have to meet my mom. And my dad! Can we send out one of those announcement postcards with the little baby skeleton?" I must have had at least five of those things on my fridge from friends and family.

She laughed quietly. "You mean an ultrasound?"

"Yes! That."

She bit down on her lower lip, and I couldn't resist any longer. Our mouths collided, my tongue mingling with hers before I pulled back just enough to bite down on the supple lip myself.

Her fingers tugged at the waistband of my jeans, and with one hand, I circled my fingers around both her wrists.

"Not before that pussy sits on my face."

She writhed against my grip and let out a whimpering moan.

My cock strained at that beautiful little sound, and I practically ripped the zipper out of her jeans and yanked them down her hips. I stood back for a moment as she pulled her sweater over her head to reveal a sheer lace light blue bra and a matching pair of panties.

Running a mindless hand over her stomach, she looked up to me, and my chest felt full, like my eyes could spill over with tears again at any moment. Nothing about Winnie looked all that different and if I didn't know to look, I'd never notice, but there was just the slightest rise to her stomach.

I stepped forward and sank to my knees.

A soft gasp escaped her lips as I wrapped my arms around her hips and nuzzled into her stomach. "You are perfect," I whispered to Winnie and the tiny magic inside her belly.

She ran a hand through my hair, and I loved everything about this moment. Kneeling in front of this woman as she looked down at me. I'd never been religious, but this moment was as close as I'd ever come to believing in a higher power.

I wanted to toss Winnie over my shoulder and fuck her until this bed broke, but a warring part of me wanted this to be slow and steady and never-ending.

Dragging my nose down her belly, I breathed in the scent of her waiting and ready and already soaked through her delicate panties.

She let me undress her as I tugged down on that pretty lace until it pooled at her feet. I sat back on the floor and pulled her down on top of me.

"Sit on my face, baby girl," I said, my voice rasping in my throat.

She blinked for a moment, the slightest panic flashing in her eyes as her bare pussy straddled my hips.

I thrusted upward so that the hard ridge of my jeans would brush her eager clit. "Winnie, I said sit on my fucking face."

She threw her head back with a whine as she tried to hump

back, but I was already reaching under her thighs and pulling her up my body as she rocked forward and braced herself on the floor just above my head.

Her glistening seam was right there hovering above my lips. All I had to do was drag my tongue along that slit and take it, but I could feel her body tensing, unwilling to settle on me.

"Why sit on Santa's lap when you could sit on his face?" I asked.

A giggle hiccupped in her chest as her cheeks flushed.

With a growl, I dug my fingers into her hips and pulled her to me, my mouth hungry and ready as I devoured her.

"F-fuck," she said with a grunt. "I've missed this." She moaned so deeply, it vibrated against my tongue. "So much."

With her fully settled, I used my hands to open her even wider for me. With my thumb, I found the sensitive nub of her clit, pink and pouting and ready.

She leaned into me even more, removing her hands from the floor and digging her fingers into my hair, pulling hard enough that I almost came in my goddamn pants like this was some sort of teenage wet dream.

I moved my mouth to the side and away from her pussy just long enough to say, "Use me, Winnie. Ride my fucking face."

She looked down to me, a wild light in her eyes before tilting her head back and riding my tongue as I furiously circled her clit.

"I'm close," she said through a gasp.

With my one free hand, I swiped my fingers through her dripping wet cunt and reached up to slide two fingers into her open, moaning mouth.

"You taste so good," I told her. "You taste so good, baby."

She unfisted her hand in my hair and held my wrist, keeping

my fingers in her mouth and sucking as she came on my beard. She tried to lean back as the waves hit her one after another, but I held her firm as I sucked on her aching clit.

"I didn't think it was possible to come that hard," she said as she slid back down my body and settled against my denim-covered erection. I hadn't come, but I felt satisfied in a way I never had before. If the rest of my life was making this woman melt on my face, then so be it.

Winnie was already ready for more though. She purred as she reached between her legs and gripped my stiff cock through my jeans. Pushing my T-shirt up my belly, she left a trail of kisses.

I didn't think too much about my round belly—or dad bod as it was so often called in the media after the sex tape leaked. And while women loved the way I fucked them or "tossed the dough," my body had never been as fully appreciated by anyone until Winnie came along. She always wanted to see more of me. To touch my belly and run her fingers through the hair on my chest. Watching her hands explore me broke something inside that I didn't even realize I'd been holding on to. It was something that I'd lived with for so long that I thought it was just . . . me. But no. The feelings I had at being the third, lesser member of INK or being the husky one or the funny one or the guy you fucked before The One . . . Winnie sunk right through all of that and saw me for exactly who I was. Because, yes, every little thing that the world had defined me as was part of me but it wasn't the whole of me.

I sat up, with Winnie clutched to my chest, and held her as I stood up and tossed her on the bed.

She immediately scrambled to the edge. "I want your dick in my mouth."

"Next time," I promised her, even though the sight of her looking up at me as she reached for my zipper was pornographic. "Or the time after that or the time after that, but right now, Winnie Baker, I need to fuck you good. Now get on all fours and show me who's a good girl."

Finally, I unzipped my jeans and my cock sprung free as Winnie flipped over, showing me her porcelain bottom.

"Winnie, one day when you're nice and ready, I'm going to take this ass and make you see stars."

She looked over her shoulder, her eyes dark and ravenous as she leaned down, giving me the perfect view of every little thing that belonged to me. "Right after I take yours."

With a growl, I kicked off my jeans and laid kisses from the top of her ass up her spine. "How did I get this lucky?" I brushed my cock against her slit. "Let me just grab a condom. I came prepared this time."

"I haven't been with anyone else," she said as she sat up on her knees and rocked back against me. "And it's not like you can get me pregnant again . . ."

"I haven't been with anyone else either," I told her, as one hand cupped her pussy and the other pulled her bra cups down so I could give her stiff nipples the attention they deserved. Honestly just the thought of fucking anyone else made my stomach turn. It had probably been my longest dry spell since high school.

"Then what are you waiting for?" Winnie asked.

I wrapped her ponytail around my fist and guided her head to the side so that I could bite her lower lip as my cock sunk into her slick, needy pussy.

"Deeper," she begged.

With her hair still in my grip, I pushed her forward, so that her cheek pressed into the mattress and I could slide every inch inside of her.

My eyes rolled to the back of my head as she clenched around me and began to slide forward and then back, fucking herself on my dick.

As hot as it was, I needed her to stop. I needed to remind her of what she'd missed for the last few months. I gripped her hips, stilling her. "My horny little girl can't help herself, can she?" I asked as I thrust into her.

She arched her back and whimpered as I sawed into her, finding the perfect pace.

"Play with yourself, Winnie."

Obediently, she reached between her legs and made circles with two fingers. My balls tightened as she groaned and our bodies made wet, filthy noises that I'd never be able to forget.

Without warning, I flipped her over onto her back, and as my cock left her briefly empty, she made a pained, frantic noise. "Fuck me, fuck me," she pleaded.

I knelt between her open legs. If I didn't see this image every day of my life, I didn't know what I'd do. I leaned forward, my cock dragging along her opening as I pushed a stray lock of hair from her damp forehead. Our lips hovered so closely that we were simply sharing oxygen back and forth, like the only thing keeping each other alive was our shared breath.

"Fill me," Winnie said as she draped her arms around my shoulders.

I pounded into her and she muffled her scream with my neck. "Don't stop, Kallum. Please."

I rutted into her in short quick pumps so that my cock created constant friction against her clit.

"I'm—I'm coming," she said between labored breaths.

Her muscles spasmed around my dick as her fingers dug into my biceps. "Keep going," she told me as her body convulsed. Her eyes locked on mine. "Come inside me."

The pregnancy was completely unplanned and a total accident, but I couldn't help but feel like at that moment she was choosing me.

Then my dirty little girl reached down between us and got her fingers nice and wet before reaching around my hip to let her fingers skate down my back crevice and between my cheeks until one little devious finger pressed against my asshole.

"Oh my fucking God, Winnie," I said as she wrapped her legs around my hips, somehow pulling me even deeper as her finger penetrated me.

With that, I erupted inside of her, my gaze bouncing from her hooded eyes to where our bodies were joined as I continued to slowly pump in and out. She clenched around me, milking ejaculate until it leaked out of her pussy.

Still inside of her, I pulled her up into my lap. "I love you, Winnie Baker. I love the pizza-hungry monster inside of you. I love us."

"Oh, Kallum," she said as draped her arms around my neck. "I love you too."

My eyes blurred with tears, and my heart brimmed with gratitude and joy and a little bit of fear too, because this was too good and I couldn't picture a version of myself without Winnie. It terrified me, but in the most thrilling way.

WE SPENT AN hour, or maybe two, in the tiny shower of her hotel room just touching each other and cleaning one another until I was hard again, and we fucked quietly and slowly like someone was on the other side of the bathroom door. I wondered briefly how often we would fuck like this once our baby wasn't a baby anymore. Quiet, needy sex in stolen moments. The thought made me nostalgic for a time I didn't even know yet.

Once we got out of the shower, Winnie draped towels all over the bed.

"What are you doing?" I asked. "You ready for an especially messy round three?"

"No, no . . . I mean, talk to me in the morning, but this is so we can lay naked in bed while we dry off."

"Is this an everyday shower ritual thing?" I asked.

She laid on her side and patted the space beside her. "Oh yeah. Sleepy post-shower naked time is a Winnie Baker special."

"I can get behind that," I said as I leaned back on the pillow and pulled her into my side. "I wasn't kidding about the skeleton postcards," I said again.

"Ultrasounds," she reminded me. "And I know."

"Can we call my parents in the morning?"

She tilted her head up to me. "I think that would be okay."

"What about Steph? We should ask her about making an announcement."

"We should." She breathed a heavy sigh against my chest. "At some point."

"What's the deal, Winnie?" I asked, refusing to ignore her hesitation. "You're being shy. What's there to hide? We're two grown adults."

She nodded. "I know. I know that. Logically, that makes perfect sense." She sat up and scooted up the bed a little so I could wrap an arm around her hips.

"Then what is it?"

"I know purity culture is trash," she said after a minute. "But there's still something inside of me that feels hesitant about making some big splashy announcement that I got pregnant out of wedlock."

"We can talk about marriage, Winnie. That doesn't scare me."

She looked down at me with a grateful smile. "I know that, Kallum. At least, I do now. And maybe we can talk about that at some point, but there are so many little things to figure out. You live in Kansas, first off. That's where your family and business is. I live in Addison's pool house for goodness sake. And those are big things, yeah. But we haven't even talked about what kind of parents we want to be."

I was ready to be everything Winnie needed me to be, but I couldn't ignore the uncomfortable weight settling on my chest as reality came into focus. "We take it one step at a time," I said. "You would love Kansas and California could probably use some Slice, Slice, Baby."

She nodded, but didn't look at me directly. "And what about religion?" she asked. "I don't think I could go back to church anytime soon, but I still feel a personal connection to God. I think I want my child to experience that too."

"I don't believe in Sky Daddy," I said. "But for me, being Jewish has always meant tradition, and family, and this—I don't know—connection with grandparents who died before I could know them and even the generations of Liebermans who came before me."

"I think that's beautiful," Winnie said. Her voice was soft as a tear rolled down her cheek.

I reached up to wipe it away. "So why can't our child experience both? Maybe they'll want both or neither or something completely different. My sister's oldest became a Satanist for a month last year."

Winnie laughed. "You know they don't actually believe in Satan."

"I didn't know that until he explained it to me. They're just kind of like trolling everyone in the name of free speech."

She laid back down beside me and my heart settled a little just to have her near. "It's kind of genius," she said through a yawn. "We don't have to have all the answers tonight."

"Thank God," I said.

"Don't you mean Sky Daddy?" she asked.

I pulled the blankets over us with the towels still beneath us.

"I love you," she whispered again. "I think I knew it was true the moment you blurted it out back in LA, but I couldn't say it then."

I pressed a kiss to her forehead. "That's okay. It was worth the wait."

"*Badum tss*," she said lazily, making a drum sound. "That purity culture pun gets ten out of ten."

CHAPTER TWENTY-FOUR

Winnie

"How'd it go?" Kallum asked from the makeup chair. He was waiting for temporary white dye to set in his hair and beard, his long legs kicked out in front of him and crossed at the ankles, his phone in his lap and open to a YouTube video about plant-based meat.

The makeup and hair team were nowhere in sight, so I sat down in the chair next to him and answered honestly. "I think it went as well as telling your religious parents that you got pregnant can go."

I set my phone on the makeup table and tucked my hand over my lower belly, feeling the small, firm curve there. "Which is to say that they didn't answer, and so I left them a voicemail breaking the news instead."

Kallum reached over and squeezed the hand closest to him. "Yeah?"

"Yeah. I didn't apologize or make excuses though. I simply told them I was expecting and that I wanted them to know. And that if they wanted to know more, they could call me back and we would talk, but I wasn't going to listen to any blame or judgment about it."

"Your therapist would be so proud. I am too!"

I knew *I* should be proud too, because communicating boundaries had been a parent-project of mine for two years, and I'd finally done it. But I didn't feel proud or mature. I felt weirdly like I was playing all those things on TV rather than actually being them.

I squeezed Kallum's hand back and smiled at him. "I'm glad your parents were nice, though." Just remembering the squeals and shouts coming from the end of Kallum's phone after he'd told his parents made me smile even bigger; listening to their happiness had made me feel like I'd just scooted up to a warm fire.

"They're over the moon," said Kallum, letting go of my hand to dab cautiously at his newly white beard with his fingertips. "My mom has known for a total of twelve hours, and she's already bought you lanolin ointment, whatever that is."

"She's amazing." It was how I wanted my own mother to react, but that was a fantasy I needed to let go of.

He cracked a grin. "She kept talking about all these creams and remedies and I'm just like, slap a Pampers on the kid and call it good. It can't be that hard, right?"

"I think, very famously, it's supposed to be really hard," I said, the end of the sentence lilting up like a question. This wasn't the first thing Kallum had said over the last couple of days that made me wonder if he thought of a baby like a Nintendo Switch—something to play with when you're bored, something that you might take a nap with on the couch, but not something that would change the entire way you lived your life.

But I shook it off. Kallum and I were still learning each other. He was probably a lot more dependable and mature than he came off while he was making a sexy Santa movie. He owned a business! That meant taxes and payroll and finding out how to buy those giant rolls of toilet paper for public bathrooms! I was making something out of nothing.

"Hey, you okay?" Kallum asked. He leaned forward, his eyes a bright, concerned blue. "I know parent stuff can be weird."

Despite the Pampers comment, he seemed so wise right now, with the white hair and beard, and it almost felt like I was telling the *real* Santa. If the real Santa were Viking-size and loved having me sit on his face, that was.

I opened my mouth to speak and then stopped, because I wasn't even sure how to say what I wanted to say.

Kallum waited silently, his attention never leaving me, and I decided to just try, no matter how little sense my feelings made. "I got to be part of a perfect family on TV, this fictional family that people *still* talk about, twenty-odd years later. A fake family that was twenty-two minutes of adorable kids and loving parents, of pep talks and kitchen hugs, of people messing up and being forgiven, all in the predictable container of a single episode. It was my job to make sure everyone watching the show got to live vicariously through me growing up in this wholesome, loving family—but *vicarious* is the wrong word, even, because it wasn't like I was living it either."

"You should have been," said Kallum. His voice was deep, warm. A little frustrated, which was so, so validating. "I don't think any family is perfect, but every kid deserves pep talks and hugs in the kitchen, Winnie. I hope you know that."

"I do, I do," I assured him. "But I'm still mourning it a little. That no matter how much my parents *looked* like TV parents— shiny hair and big smiles full of veneered teeth—there weren't any kitchen hugs for me. There never will be. I spent my childhood creating something that I myself never got to have. I guess it makes it lonelier, in a way, because I can imagine what it would have been like. Because it makes me wonder if everything is fake, in the end. If no one actually gets to live out the fantasy of the loyal, loving family. And I'm thirty-two, and it's time I just accepted that."

"No family is a sitcom family," Kallum told me. "And mine is a mess sometimes, and totally chaotic, and constantly in each other's business, and we definitely don't fix problems in twenty-two minutes. But, loyal?" he added. "Loving? Yes. And I just want you to know that you're officially a Lieberman now. It's as good as notarized as far as my mom is concerned."

I smiled. I couldn't wait to meet her, and the rest of Kallum's family, even if I was a little nervous too. What if they didn't like me? What if they *did* like me, but Kallum and I broke up and then I would have lost another chance at a family?

"And hey," said Kallum, gesturing around to the toy shop, and to Christmas Notch at large, "this is kind of a family too, isn't it?"

I thought of Kallum and Gretchen and Pearl and even Jack Hart and Luca and Sunny and Bee. I thought of late nights on set and jostling shoulders at the craft table and the layers of inside jokes that built and built over the days. I thought of how it felt to be here, to be the Winnie who wasn't Old Winnie or New Winnie, but Now Winnie, and I thought of how happy Now Winnie was with the zany, melodramatic, oversexed Christmas Notch gang.

"Yes," I agreed, happiness unfurling a little in my chest, like a flower in the sun. "It is like a family here."

THREE DAYS LATER, and I was sweaty and yawning as the shuttle stopped to unload several bathrobed elves and me at the toy shop to change out of our costumes. (Not that there was much *costume* for the elves to change out of—the backdrop for Santa and Holly's big fight was an eggnog-fueled elfish orgy, and the extras had been wearing nothing but modesty patches and waterproof foundation.) Kallum had ducked out of the back lot the minute we'd wrapped today, needing to take a call about a missing shipment of pizza boxes, and I was hoping I could get changed and back to my room in enough time for us to have sex before I crashed face-first onto a bed. We'd been working non-stop to get all the new scenes and transitions filmed for Pearl's rewrite, and this pregnant narcoleptic was exhausted.

My obstetrician had recommended going off my narcolepsy meds since the research around their fetal impact was limited, and had prescribed me "as much coffee as you want" in its place. Even though pregnant people were often advised to stay away from caffeine, in my case it was safer than the alternatives, and medically necessary to keep me upright while I was working.

Not that it mattered—even sucking down coffee as fast as craft services could brew the stuff, I was still so tired that I sometimes fell asleep between takes. Once, memorably, with Kallum half naked on top of me while they reset the lights. (He had to wake me up by blowing raspberries on my neck.)

I yawned hard enough that my jaw hurt as the elves trooped into the toy shop and I staggered out of the van and onto the sidewalk. Jack Hart, who'd used the shuttle to get back to town from the back lot, was getting ready to strap Miss Crumpets into her BabyBjörn-esque carrier when the toy shop door banged open and Luca strode out.

"You're so tall," Jack complained, squinting up at Luca. "Stop it."

Luca pointed a finger with no less than three rings on it. "One of the elves has a modesty patch stuck in their pubes. You need to fix it."

"Me?" Jack said, his Ken Doll face full of irritation. "Why?"

"Because they're your weird little patches!" Luca said. "If anyone would know the best way to get them off, you would!"

"What am I, an adhesive expert? Try peanut butter or something!"

Luca sniffed. "I have a peanut allergy. And if you don't come inside, I'm bringing the elf out here to you, and then all of Christmas Notch can see what you do to people's pubes."

Jack glared.

Luca glared back.

"I still can't believe Angel agreed to marry you," Jack relented with a grumble.

Luca gave him a beatific smile. "Just wait until you see my wedding dress. Now *inside*."

Jack turned to me and before I could speak, gesture, or consent, Miss Crumpets was put into my arms like a baby. She settled in with a fart, gave my upper arm a half-hearted lick, and then fell asleep.

"Don't feed her macadamia nuts," Jack instructed ominously— and unnecessarily—before disappearing back inside the toy shop with Luca, leaving me alone on the sidewalk in a red velvet dress that was practically lingerie.

With another yawn, I started pacing Miss Crumpets back and forth on the sidewalk, letting the warming evening breeze ruffle her fur and dry some of the sticky sweat still in my hair. It was a little preview of having a baby, maybe, of being exhausted and having to rock and sway with a little farting bundle in my arms—

"Winnie?" an alto voice said from behind me.

My spine stiffened, my shoulders set. My heart gave a series of quick, sharp beats, as if my body wanted me to run away. Which was ridiculous, because of course I didn't want to run away, of course I was happy to hear that voice.

I turned and saw my mother and father for the first time in two years.

Joy—it must have been joy—crashed through me, hot and shaky, and suddenly all the stuff I'd said to Kallum earlier was bullshit. All the hopes and dreams and fantasies of my thirty-two years were still rooted deep inside me, still trying to push their way to the surface.

"Hi, Mom," I said, a little shyly. "Hi, Dad."

"Hello, sweetheart," my father said in his deep baritone. I'd always thought he looked and sounded like the perfect father. Even more than my *In a Family Way* father had—but then again, my TV father had been more than someone who merely looked like a dad. He'd also been silly and playful and kind to everyone on set. In my darkest moments as a child, I'd wished my TV father *were* my real father . . . and then I'd beg God for forgiveness for thinking such a horrible, ungrateful thing. How could I when my real father so perfectly looked the part? Even now, years later, my father's face was folded in an expression you could find under *paternal love* in the dictionary.

"We got your message," Mom said. Her expression was similar, so full of love, and she was so pretty, with her soft blond bob framing her face and her smile. It faltered a little when her eyes ran over my body—with a flush, I remembered how skimpy my costume was, how much I must look like a fallen woman to them—but then her smile came back. "Winnie, we came because we hate this distance between us. We want to be with you."

"You do?" I asked, shifting Miss Crumpets in my arms. She gave a little snorfle and went right back to sleep. "I thought you'd be mad."

"It's not our place to be mad," Dad said. "And this is a gift. A blessing."

"And we just want to make sure that this blessing knows how much he or she is loved," Mom added. "Have they done the blood test to find out yet? The sex?"

"Um." I felt disoriented, almost dizzy. The scraggly dog in my arms was strangely the only thing that felt real and good, and I cuddled her closer. "I'm not sure if I want to learn the sex yet."

"Hmm." My mother's *hmm*s were legendary. So much information in such a small sound. "Well, at least it's nice to be here in Christmas Notch again. Vanessa over at the Hope Channel was able to book our usual room at the inn for us. Is that little gourmet marshmallow shop around the corner still in business? I always loved their stocking stuffers."

Memories of when they would visit me on set or when Mom would stay with me for a whole shoot ran through my mind. Our time here had been like a little capsule where—for a brief moment—we were almost the family I'd dreamed of. But then there'd also been all the times when Mom accused me of being lazy for sleeping through a call time or when I'd have to beg her to cancel a dinner reservation or a shopping trip because I was too tired.

In this moment, though, it was easy to forget all of that. I studied their expressions, chewing on my lip. They seemed earnest, kind. They were saying all the things I wanted to hear.

They both stepped closer, and all the little details of their faces revealed themselves to me. The silver at my father's temples and the hitch in the middle of his left eyebrow. The blue veins in my mother's temples and the always immaculate line of her lipstick—a subtle, pink hue that made her look ever so slightly younger without being flashy about it.

"We know we have a lot of ground to make up with you," my father said. "We know there's a lot of bridges to mend. But we're committed to putting in the work if you are."

"We want to know the baby," Mom added softly. "But we're not going to push. We came to show you that we're here when you need us. And when you go back to LA, it will be the same thing. We'll be there when you're ready."

The door to the toy shop swung open, and Jack Hart stalked out. He plucked Miss Crumpets from my arms, and I had the surreal moment of watching a porn star strap a sleeping dog to his chest while my parents looked on.

"Mom, Dad, this is Jack. He's, um, part of the production team."

"Nice to meet you, Jack," my father said. "We need to check into the inn, but don't hesitate to call us, Winnie. We're here for you, to help in any way that you need."

They came forward and they each gave me a hug—a textbook hug, with a squeeze and everything—and then left.

"They seem nice," Jack offered. Miss Crumpets was snoring right beneath his chin.

"Yeah." I watched as my dad helped my mother into their rental car and then walked around the front to get into the driver's seat. "They do seem nice. I mean, they are. They are nice."

And they said that they were here for me. Here to help.

I wanted nothing more in the entire world than for that to be true, but this time, wanting wasn't enough. If they meant what they said, then they needed to show me. They needed to prove they'd changed.

They owed me that much.

CHAPTER TWENTY-FIVE

Kallum

N olan and I sat next to each other on the trolley to the North Pole while Winnie sat a few rows behind us next to Bee. Sunny was leaning in between them from the next row back.

"Is this what we missed the last two years of high school?" I asked Nolan.

He glanced over his shoulder with a smirk. "I don't remember girls that hot on the bus." He rustled a hand through my hair. "You're going to be a fucking dad!"

"It's cool," I said, unable to hide the absolute dorkiness in my voice. "It's cool, right? Like I'll be good at it, right?"

"I don't know anything about being a parent, but I think you fuck up your kids no matter how hard you try."

My shoulders slumped a little as I nodded.

"But," he continued, "I think knowing that is half the battle. If we know that going in we're not perfect and can't make little perfect human beings, then maybe just trying your best is good parenting. And then when your kid is an adult in therapy, they can come home over the holidays and give you the lowdown on all the things you did wrong—and just maybe some of the things you did right."

I shook my head in disbelief and gave him a big kiss on the cheek. "Dude, you're a fucking parenting scholar. You need your own TV show."

"I don't know. I think we might have pregamed pretty hard at the inn bar."

"Are you telling me Nolan Shaw is feeling it after three beers?" I asked.

"Three beers, a Moscow mule, and two Tipsy Elf shots."

I slapped a hand to my forehead. "The shots! I forgot about those."

Turning back again, I waved to Winnie at the back of the trolley. She was mid-laugh as she waved back. I pointed to my belly and then to her and then shrugged before flashing two thumbs. Surely she would understand my miming Morse code which definitely translated to: *Baby in your belly feeling good, hot stuff?*

She laughed again and gave me the double thumbs-up.

I couldn't wait for the rest of our lives, and I was also terrified for it to all happen too fast. My mom was ecstatic. She'd been digging through all my old baby clothes and photos and sending me and Winnie both a constant stream of blurry cell phone pictures. She'd texted me and asked for Winnie's number the moment we got off the phone, and Winnie happily agreed even after I told her Mom often FaceTimes everyone when she's meaning to make a regular call and holds the phone up to her ear and that we'd all tried to help her understand the difference but there was no use.

Tamara cried when I told her and had been sending me a constant stream of names used by friends and family for their newborns so that whatever name we chose was original. She also sent me the names of her doctor of choice and a list of which Kansas City hospitals were on her shit list and why. And Dad, well, he sent me a seven-word text that I screenshotted for when I didn't know what the hell I was doing. *That's going to be one lucky kid.*

Life was good.

"My girlfriend is so fucking cool," I said as I turned back around.

"Your girlfriend, huh?" Nolan said through a burp that he caught with his fist.

"I mean, we never said it was official, but I'm her baby daddy and she literally owns this dick. If you look along the bottom it says: *Made in the USA, property of Winnie Baker.*"

"That sounds pretty permanent."

"Forever kind of shit," I confirmed. "Look at us! Just a couple of former fuckups who are all settled and spoken for. We're basically a Home Depot commercial."

"Speaking of forever," Nolan said as the trolley chugged up one of the last steep hills before we reached our destination, "what's the plan after this cast party tonight? Your sexy Santa movie is *done*-done."

"Why'd you have to go asking me real-life shit on a night like tonight, man?"

"You're the one out here looking for parenting advice!" he yelled over a shrieking Luca as he reenacted some story for Teddy and Steph, who sat as far from each other as two people on the same bench seat possibly could.

"Okay, okay, okay," I said and then took a deep breath. Fuck, I really was drunk. "Real life. I'm going home to KC. She's going back to LA. I'm going to settle some shit . . . and I don't know . . . find someone to run the restaurants for me, because I don't know if Toph is up for it. Especially not with a location that still needs to be rebuilt after the fire. And Winnie really wants to book more gigs after the baby, so I'll fly out to LA and be with her as long as I can. Hell, maybe I'll sell the whole Slice, Slice, Baby franchise and just start a food truck in LA or just be a full-time dad and—"

Nolan gripped my shoulder. "Bro, you love SSB. You've poured your heart into that company."

I nodded. "I know . . . and it's all a big maybe, ya know? But I'll do what I have to do. I'm not just, like, some pizza daddy anymore. I'm someone's father. And I'm Winnie's—whatever she wants me to be, I guess. Future husband, I hope."

The trolley lurched to a stop and the driver, whose name tag read Ronald, pulled the lever next to the steering wheel to open the door.

Nolan turned to me and grabbed my cheeks, squishing my face a little. "One day when Isaac isn't sad—or as sad as he has been—we're going to reunite and—"

"Holy fucking shit. An INK reunion," I said through my puckered lips.

"We're going to do a new album called *Grown Men* or something and we're doing it on our terms. Just don't tell Isaac. Yet."

"We gotta write this down," I said frantically.

"It's in my dream journal." His hands dropped and he began to stand up as the rest of the cast and crew filed out.

"You have a dream journal?" I asked. "Is that something I'm supposed to be doing?"

"Yes, I have one and if you ask me about it when I'm sober, I'll probably lie. And yes, you should have one. It's life-changing."

I followed him out of the trolley and the neon lights of the North Pole lit the dark summer sky.

"You know what's beautiful?" I asked. "We've been best friends since middle school and we still surprise each other."

He threw an arm around my shoulder. "I love you and will definitely not lie about that when I'm sober. Now, let's go fuck this place up like we're twenty-one again."

ME, WINNIE, NOLAN, Bee, Sunny, and Luca all sat in a huge half-circle booth with a feast of appetizers and table full of drinks. Steph, Jack Hart, Gretchen, and Pearl were at another table, and then two more tables were filled with our secondary cast and some crew members, including a very strange man they called Tall Ron.

"Has anyone tried fried pickles dipped in honey mustard?" Winnie asked. "It sounds good to me and I can't drink, so I feel like I have to be a little wild." She smiled and then yawned.

She'd been so sleepy with the baby, and I was a little surprised we'd managed to coax her out this late.

"Follow your heart, babe," I told her. "The sixth baby sense will tell you when it's the wrong flavor combo."

"The sixth baby sense?" Luca asked.

"You know, like when the baby makes you nauseous and is like *Oh no you don't* when you smell or eat something," I explained.

Winnie laughed a little and pulled my arm closer around her, causing something in my chest—and pants—to rumble.

Luca sipped his cherry limeade margarita. "Sì, certo. That actually makes sense."

"If people knew how smart I was, it would scare them," I told him without a funny bone in my body.

"I really appreciate this unearned confidence," Sunny said as she bopped her head to the music. "Also, you don't have to speak Italian to us, Luca; you're not in Italy right now."

A desolate sip of margarita. "Don't remind me. My beloved is there, pining away for me."

Sunny was still bopping. "Did you tell your beloved in Italy that while he's toiling away at his new animation studio, you're at a strip club with his *dad*?"

We all looked over at Teddy, who was standing at the bar getting a glass of white wine.

"I did," Luca said. "Angel asked me to chaperone. He thinks Steph might try to take advantage of Teddy's innocence."

"It's hard to think of the man who made *Camp Stepbrother* as innocent," I said, stroking Winnie's arm. Her head was now on my shoulder.

"You take that back!" Bee shouted. "Teddy is a giant Care Bear!"

"Good people of Christmas Notch," the DJ called from the side of the stage. "Tonight we've got a special treat in store for us in honor of the Hope After Dark cast and crew party! Give a hardy welcome to Donner and Cupid!"

Two girls in monster high heels and the kind of reindeer onesies people buy for their whole families to wear on Christmas sauntered out onto the stage.

"Hello, ladies!" Bee called before letting out a whoop.

"God, I love when they come out with a ridiculous amount of clothing on," Sunny said. "I have such a lady boner right now."

I leaned down and whispered to Winnie, "If this is weird, I'd be happy to take you back to one of the private rooms for an encore."

She giggled. It was a sleepy giggle, something I'd had the deep pleasure of becoming familiar with over the last several days. "Not that I don't always want a private dance from you, but I just went pretty hard on those Irish nachos and I don't know how long I'll be for this fully conscious world. Plus . . . it's kind of sexy to be here with you . . . as a patron."

"I like it," I nodded. "I like it."

"Seriously, though." She yawned. "I may need to get back to the inn."

"Aw, babe," I said, squeezing her. "The party's just getting started. See?"

Donner and Cupid each took a pole on either end of the stage, leaving the middle one empty as the music transitioned into a soft, sultry voice singing, "Santa, baby . . ."

The whole table gasped as though it was the most shocking thing in the world that two strippers named after Santa's reindeer in a Christmas-themed bar were dancing to a song that just so happened to also be the title of the movie we'd just wrapped.

The girls zipped down their onesies and effortlessly kicked them off and into the laps of eager onlookers to reveal Mrs. Claus outfits underneath, which consisted of sequined triangle bikini tops, matching thongs, and aprons so tiny they could fit on Tamara's old American Girl dolls.

"I might have to get myself one of those outfits," Winnie yawn-whispered.

"Oh, trust me when I say this one-hundred-percent Jewish guy has a bona fide Santa kink now."

She looked up to me. "You can be my ho, ho, ho."

I grinned and pressed a kiss to her lips. How could one person be so smart and funny and stunning and perfect all at once?

Bee leaned forward over her glass of Grinch Punch. "Come on, Santa! Show these girls what you got!"

"Santa, Santa, Santa!" our table began to chant. Except for Winnie, who was holding on to my arm.

"Did someone say Santa?" the DJ asked as Donner and Cupid slid up and down the pole. "Could it be that Santa is on a summer vacation to Christmas Notch and needs to let loose a little?"

"Get your hot ass up there," Nolan demanded.

I looked down at Winnie, and she gave me a tired smile. I stopped her before she could say anything. "I know you're ready to sleep, but come on, don't you want to see me up on that stage?"

"Like *on* the stage?" she asked, sounding surprised.

"Yes, he means on the stage!" laughed Nolan. "You've never seen Kallum the party animal, but trust me, he's a *beast*. One time he put a hockey stick through a door chasing after me during a poker game."

"What, like during your INK days?" Winnie asked, eyes wide.

"No, that was last year," I said proudly. We ended up leaving the hockey stick in the door, it was wedged in there so tightly.

"I see," said Winnie faintly.

Bee smirked. "You're going to be raising two children, Winnie. Have fun with that."

Winnie bit her lip, but not in a cute way. Well, it was still cute, but she looked a little worried now, like she was thinking there might be something to Bee's words

I lovingly flipped Bee the bird and then turned back to my beautiful baby mama. "Once Santa has a chance to meet his naughty boys and girls, we can go back to the inn, if you want."

"It's a plan." Winnie offered me a small smile. "Just no going down on anyone but me in a private room, capisce?"

"It's actually *capisci*," Luca cut in condescendingly.

I ignored him. "Winnie Baker," I said. "Did you just capisce me?"

"I guess I did," she said, looking rosy-cheeked and drowsy and so fucking perfect.

"God, you're so fucking cute," I said as I slid out of the booth. Luca groaned something about us not being allowed to visit him and Angel in Milan.

As I jogged over to the stage, a few people held out their hands for high fives, including Teddy.

Steph shook her head with a coy grin. I stopped for a moment and held her hand up and gave her a high five. "Didn't want you to feel left out," I told her right before sliding across the stage and thankfully stopping just shy of flying off the other side. I stood up and shouted, "I'm good!"

The whole crowd erupted in cheers and applause. Oh boy, I forgot what a drug adoration was. Even in a musty old gem of a strip club.

I squinted past the stage lights to see Nolan hold two fingers to his lips and let out a wolf whistle. I thought I could see Winnie smiling next to him.

And with more faith in myself than any rational adult should have, I began humping the open pole in the middle of the stage.

"Go Santa!" Cupid said as she untied her bikini top to reveal green glitter pasties. Or maybe it was Donner.

"Give us a twirl," the other said.

Maybe it was because my joints were nice and lubricated with liquor or maybe it was my INK days coming back to me, but I spun around that pole so hard it shook.

Feeling a little dizzy from my sweet moves, I stopped for a moment and then gripped the collar of my Slice, Slice, Baby T-shirt with both hands and tore as hard as I fucking could.

The audience roared and I ripped the rest of my T-shirt off and tossed it to Winnie, who was holding her hands up and screaming like I was a fucking Beatle.

"This one's for my very own Mrs. Claus!" I shouted.

I gripped the pole and did a nice slide down and a little twerk or two for my fans. *Shit. My knees aren't what they used to be.* After popping back up—literally, my knees were popping—I swung my feet up and gripped the pole and spun around a few times.

Okay, maybe I was actually pretty good at this. All those

years being a boss at the monkey bars in elementary school and my INK dance experience had led me to this moment.

I looked over to Donner and Cupid who were both hanging upside down by their knees from their poles. They made it look so easy.

Without much thought as to how, I shimmied up the pole, and let go so that my proud belly would be on full display.

Except gravity had different plans . . . and before I knew it, my body hit the edge of the stage.

Face-first.

Oh God.

I landed with a crunching *thud*. My head immediately began to spin and my mouth was full of coppery warmth.

With a groan, I rolled over onto my back to find two topless dancers hovering above me and Winnie rushing the edge of the stage.

"Kallum!" she said as she gripped my shoulders. "Kallum, are you okay? What day is it? Can you spell your name? Or count back from ten to zero?"

I sat up slowly as the rest of the cast and crew surrounded us. Nothing actually hurt, which meant I'd probably feel like a train wreck in the morning. "C-A-L-L-U-M. Uhhhh, Tuesday or maybe Wednesday, depending on how late it is, and ten, nine, eight—"

Winnie flung her arms around my neck. "You doofus, you can't even spell your own name now!"

I pulled her even closer and buried my bloody face in her hair even though I didn't want to get her dirty. "I wasn't kidding when I said that was all for you."

"Well, it was not Winnie approv—" Her grip around my neck tightened for a brief moment and then she pedaled back. "I need—I'll be right back."

"Winnie, what's wrong?" I asked as I stood up and immediately stumbled back onto the stage, Nolan steadying my grip.

The group of concerned faces closed in on me as the house lights came up and Winnie disappeared.

CHAPTER TWENTY-SIX

Winnie

innie?" Sunny's voice called through the bathroom door. "No, *you* get back," she said, presumably to someone next to her. "I was here first."

"Well, Nolan deputized *me* to figure out what was going on," I heard Bee say, "and it doesn't matter how hot you are, I'm the sheriff of Bathroom Town now."

"If anyone is the sheriff of this town, it's me," announced Steph's no-nonsense voice. Then there was a sharp, hard rap on the very hollow door of the North Pole's single-stall women's bathroom. "Winnie? Are you okay?"

I was most definitely not okay. I was sitting on the toilet, my Ralph Lauren dress hiked up to my waist and my panties around my knees. I was staring at something that only four months ago would have been completely normal, so utterly mundane: a wet bloom of blood on my panties. Crimson. Shining in the yellowish light of the bathroom.

Had I just been laughing? Cheering Kallum on? I couldn't believe it; I couldn't believe there was any version of myself that wasn't this one: staring at bloody panties with my hands shaking and my breath coming in short, arrhythmic bursts.

But I did everything right, was all I could think. *I did everything right.*

"Is Winnie okay?" came a gruff voice through the door. Even Teddy's voice sounded like it had a mustache, which made no sense, but what did make sense right now? Nothing. Nothing made sense.

But I didn't want to be a problem, that much I still knew. Narcoleptic messes only got so many second chances, and I couldn't have my producer thinking I was a constant catastrophe.

"I'm fine," I called through the door. I hoped they couldn't hear how thin my voice was. How much it shook. "Teddy, I'm fine, I promise. You can go!"

"Teddy's good in a pinch," Sunny informed me in a comforting tone. "One time when I was on set, a performer started bleeding from her butthole during a scene, and Teddy didn't miss a beat! He draped a towel over the seat of his Chrysler Town & Country and got her to an emergency room ASAP."

Her butthole??? Holy heck. "Was she okay?"

"Oh yeah," Sunny said. "Turns out she wasn't bleeding at all, she'd just eaten a lot of beets the day before. Anyway, my point is that Teddy is a good man to have in a crisis, aren't you, Ted?"

Teddy ignored Sunny and told me through the door, "Winnie, I'm right here if you need anything. Can you tell me what's wrong? Do we need to go back to the hotel? Is there someone I can get to help?"

There was something so bluntly fatherlike in his tone that I felt my face start to crumple.

"Can you get Kallum?" I managed to say. I was dangerously close to losing it now. "I just want Kallum."

There was a convocation of whispering and hissing, and the door thumped a little in the frame, like someone was jostling to go out into the main room. And then some more whispering—I thought I heard Nolan's husky voice in the mix now—and then Bee said, "Um, Winnie? Kallum's still out of commission a bit. I guess the reindeer are trying to get the bleeding on his lip to stop. But once he's not bleeding anymore, I can send him in?"

Right. Kallum was bleeding because he'd drunkenly tried to pole dance at a party. And I was bleeding because we might lose our baby.

I looked at the blood and tried to think. I wasn't cramping, I didn't have any pain. When I dabbed myself with toilet paper, the blood was bright and thin, no clots in sight. It might be okay. Everything might be okay. I just had to speak. I just had to ask for help because the person I trusted the most *couldn't* help right now.

"I'm bleeding," I whispered and then took a breath. I had to be louder. "I'm bleeding," I said again, louder, and I heard the worried murmur roll through the crowd on the other side of the door.

"Well, shit," Bee said after a minute.

"Shit," Sunny agreed. There was more murmuring, then the tap of Steph's heels receding into the distance.

"Winnie, we need to get you to a hospital," Teddy said. "Steph is checking to see if anyone has a car to drive you there. I think with as far out as we are, it'll be faster than waiting for an ambulance."

"Is anyone okay to drive?" I heard Bee ask.

"Oh God," Sunny said. "I know you and I aren't, and Nolan definitely isn't. Teddy?"

I heard the kind of heavy sigh that can only come from under a mustache. "I'm not sure if I'm good to drive or not, and if I'm not sure, that means it's not safe enough for me to feel good about. Maybe a crew member?"

"I'm looking for an Uber now," Bee said decisively. "In case Steph can't find a car and-slash-or someone to drive it."

"And I'm looking for Lyfts," Sunny added. Then: "Nearest Lyft is forty-five minutes away."

"Closest Uber is in Montpelier," Bee added. "Fuck me sideways."

"Have offered many times," Sunny responded. "Winnie, are you still doing okay in there?"

Was I doing okay? I was frozen on the toilet, afraid to move or even breathe, lest I bleed more. Lest I feel something worse than blood, like pain or cramps.

"I don't know," I said numbly. I could have been at the deep end of a pool; in one of those sensory deprivation tanks Addison swore by. Everything felt like it was coming from a million miles away.

"Okay, we're coming in," said Bee. "We promise not to let Teddy in unless you start bleeding from your butthole too."

"Actually, I've got an idea," Teddy said. "Be back in two shakes." I heard a quick, heavy stride pace away from the bathroom.

"Move it! Move it!" Sunny called after him, and then the door opened.

"Oh, honey," Bee said, seeing me with my panties around my knees. "Okay, okay. We've got you."

I looked up at her and Sunny, and their kind, concerned faces, and then promptly burst into tears.

"Shh," Sunny said. "Shh. We're here now."

And indeed in short order, I was stood up, my panties taken off and then folded into a paper towel to show a doctor, and then given a pair of sequined panties and a pad to wear.

"Vixen gave us the panties from her stash and Cupid gave us the pad," Bee said, straightening out my dress as Sunny held up a tissue for me to blow my nose in.

Teddy arrived at the door just then. "I have a ride to the hospital," he said. "But we should get going now."

"And Kallum?" I asked hopefully. "Will he be coming with us?"

"Yes," Teddy said kindly. "The dancers are getting him an ice pack and he'll be ready to leave."

Teddy's ride ended up being none other than the trolley, helmed by Ronald, and the ice pack Kallum showed up with was a prepackaged frozen cocktail that he was holding directly against his cut lip.

"Babe," Kallum said to me the minute he climbed onto the trolley. "Are you okay? Teddy said you were bleeding? Does that mean . . . ?"

The confusion on his face was so hard to look at, and I closed my eyes and pressed my face into his shoulder.

"I don't know," I whispered. He smelled like spilled beer, and since he had ripped his shirt, he was wearing one of the shirts the North Pole sold from behind the bar. It said I GOT BLITZED BY DONNER AT THE NORTH POLE.

He was about to speak when Sunny and Bee trooped onto the bus, followed by Teddy and Steph. They stopped by our seat.

"You don't have to—" I started. "I mean, I don't want anyone to miss their night of fun—"

"I'm going to stop you right there," Steph said crisply. "You are more important than discounted appetizers. We're going to make sure you're okay."

And then more people crowded onto the trolley. Nolan. Luca and Jack Hart. Gretchen and Pearl.

"You guys," I said. "Please don't miss the party just because of this. It's so silly, and it's probably nothing . . ."

"You need to be surrounded by good energy and loving kindness," Pearl said seriously. "And western medicine—"

"—is great for emergencies," Gretchen cut in. "We're here for moral support."

"You want me to call your parents, Mrs. Claus?" Jack Hart asked. He didn't have Miss Crumpets with him and was wearing a mesh shirt under a button-down with a few of the buttons undone. He also had red lipstick all over his neck.

"Your parents are in town?" Kallum asked, confused.

I flushed a little. I hadn't told him, and I'd rationalized it to myself by saying that we were about to leave Christmas Notch anyway, so there was no point in trying to arrange a meeting between him and the baby's other grandparents. And if I made us take the stairs up to his room, if I scouted out the hotel lobby before we walked inside, that was just a knee-jerk reaction.

It wasn't because I was terrified of the potential fallout of my parents meeting him.

"Yes," I told Jack, and then I handed him my phone. "My mom is under *In Case of Emergency: Jessica Baker.*"

"Taking no chances, huh?"

"And you should text rather than call," I said suddenly. The trolley was already getting rowdy behind us, with Luca kicking up a fuss about sitting next to Nolan and Pearl loudly humming a tone that was supposed to settle my sacral chakra. "I don't think you'd be able to explain this trolley to my parents."

"Oh honey, I can explain anything if you give me an hour, a dark room, and a fully charged Hitachi," said Jack. "But texting it is. Kallum, you're bleeding again."

Kallum looked down and then up and then finally thought to pull his hand away from his mouth, where blood had started dripping from the inside of his lip down the mojito packet to his knuckles. "Shitballs," he mumbled, and Jack sighed.

"There's a light above my seat," Jack said. "Come back with me and I'll see if I can get a look at where you're bleeding from now."

"I don't want to leave Winnie," protested Kallum at the same time I grabbed onto his arm.

"I'll sit with her," Gretchen said from behind us, standing up as the trolley rumbled to life. At my pathetic expression, she gave me a warm smile. "I'm very good at cuddling, I promise. At least as good as Kallum."

I looked up at Kallum, at where blood was running over his chin like he was a vegetarian vampire who'd just finished eating a fawn. "You should go with Jack," I whispered, even though I wanted him close. But it was also hard to relax against him when he was bleeding from the mouth and sticky with spilled beer and sweat.

He gave a pained groan, like it hurt him to move away from me. "Okay, babe, but I'll be back on this bench the moment Jack doctors me up."

I gave him a wan smile, and then he and Gretchen swapped seats as the trolley lurched forward.

Gretchen settled close and took my hand. "Are you doing okay?"

The problem with breaking the *I'm okay* seal was that once it was broken, it was hard to go back. "No," I admitted. "I'm scared. I want the baby to be okay. And I wish . . ."

I trailed off as I looked out the window. It was dark outside, save for the occasional house set between the trees, sitting in a small pool of yellow porchlight.

"Wish what?" Gretchen prompted gently.

"It's stupid," I said. "But I'd kind of wanted to leave earlier, and if I had, maybe I would have been back at the inn when this happened. With my parents, and not—"

I stopped. I didn't even want to say it out loud.

"Not a drunk-off-his-face Kallum?" supplied Gretchen.

I turned to face her. "I mean, I'm not mad that he drank or even that he got on the stage," I said, in a low enough voice that only she could hear. "It was a party! And no one could have predicted I'd have a bleeding emergency. But—but—"

I didn't know what I was trying to say, or what I even felt. Kallum had every right to enjoy his night; if I wouldn't have found blood on my underwear, we would have gone back to the inn with smiles on our faces and snored the night away in peace.

Gretchen squeezed my hand. "You know it's okay to feel two things at once, right? You can think it was okay for him to have a good time and still wish he was ready to help when shit hit the fan."

I sighed. "Yeah."

"And I didn't know Michael very well, but I'm guessing that he put himself first a lot of the time. It's understandable that after everything you went through before this that you want to be with someone dependable."

"Kallum's dependable," I said defensively. And then I had to add, because he was sitting in the back of the trolley with a frozen mojito packet and a broken tooth, "Sometimes."

"Winnie," Gretchen said with a smile. "We all grew up together, and I can tell you that Kallum might still be a giant nineteen-year-old inside. And that's great for him—he's living the dream nineteen-year-old life with his pizza parlor chain and his sex tape cred. He's funny and loyal and sweet as hell, and an amazing friend. I think he'll make a fun dad. But as a life partner? A boyfriend or husband?" She shrugged, still holding on to my hand. "Maybe it's just not his personality, you know? To settle down and take life seriously."

The hospital came into view, a blearily bright haven in the dark, and Gretchen squeezed my hand again in reassurance. But her words were rolling around my mind, crashing into the memory of his words to Teddy in the inn's hallway, into the memory of him ripping off his clothes and then careening drunkenly off the stage tonight.

I hated admitting it to myself, but tonight, I'd wanted Kallum to be . . . different. To have made different choices.

And that wasn't fair to him. He had every right to drink and dance and strip in public and do whatever he wanted. But the stakes were higher than just my own comfort now, and what was fair to me mattered too.

I just didn't know what that was right now.

Or what it meant after tonight.

It was chaos as we got to the hospital, all of us issuing from the trolley in a single clump, everyone jostling and talking over each other to try to explain to the bewildered triage nurse what was going on. Eventually Kallum and I ended up in the small triage room, and the nurse snapped on her gloves.

"Okay," she said in a brisk, I've-been-a-trauma-nurse-for-as-long-as-you've-been-alive tone. "Lower the frozen mojito and let me see what I'm working with."

Kallum just blinked at her, a picture of handsome, bearded bafflement, and I realized what was going on. Turns out that a horde of mostly drunk porn stars and former boy band members wasn't the greatest at communication.

"No, no, it's me who needs to be seen," I interjected. "I'm four months pregnant and I'm bleeding. He's the father."

The nurse paused, recalibrated. Then nodded.

"Okay, love," she said. "Let's get some vitals, some history, and then let's get you lying down. As for you, keep that frozen mojito right where it is."

Within just a few minutes, I'd been weighed, checked, and given a hospital bracelet, and then Kallum and I were taken to a room in the ER proper, leaving the horde behind to argue and pillage the vending machines for snacks.

"Your nurse and doctor will be in shortly," the person leading us back said, and then pulled a folded gown from a cabinet. It was blue, with a funky Memphis pattern that made me think of paper cups from the 1980s. "Once you have this on, please lay down. We want to keep you horizontal as much as possible."

I nodded. At this point, they could ask me to stand on my head while reciting the lyrics to Weird Al's "Albuquerque" and I would have done it. I would do anything, no matter how small or potentially pointless, anything to keep my little baby right where they belonged.

The nursing assistant left, and then I changed into my gown and laid on the bed, shivering on the chilly sheets. They'd put a chux pad down, to catch any bleeding—and cold, clawing fear threatened to break through my numbness. They were expecting me to bleed more. They need to keep track of how much I bled.

There was no universe where this wasn't scary.

Kallum saw me shivering and got up from his chair. He went to rub my arm to warm it, but his hand was approximately the temperature of a half-thawed frozen mojito and it just made me shiver more.

"I'm sure it's no big deal," he said. "It's going to be fine, Winnie. Promise."

"I'm scared," I admitted in a whisper. "I can't lose our baby. I already love them so much and I just—"

"Don't be scared," cut in Kallum, like not being scared was that easy. "You'll see. The doctor will be in and out, and it'll be like this never happened."

I thought he was trying to be comforting, to remind me that there was a strong possibility that everything could be okay, but right now with his slightly-too-loose voice and his North Pole T-shirt, it didn't feel comforting. It felt like he didn't want to be bothered with worrying; it felt like I was bothering him by worrying.

I *hated* feeling like a bother.

But also, if not now, then when?

And even if everything was going to be okay tonight, was this how Kallum was going to be whenever something went wrong? If our baby got sick? If they hurt themselves playing soccer or climbing a tree or riding a bike?

No. No, I had to stop catastrophizing. Just because Michael had been hurtful and selfish to me didn't mean Kallum would, and of course Kallum was taking this seriously. I could viscerally remember his joy when he found out I was pregnant, how eager he'd been to tell the entire world. He would be devastated if something happened to the baby.

There was a little bit of dried blood in his beard, and when he shifted the now-squishy mojito mix to another angle on his lip, I could see the sharp edge of his broken tooth. It made him look a little dangerous, a little piratical, and if I wasn't bleeding on a hospital bed, I would have found it endearing.

"Are you still doing okay?" I asked. "You took a huge spill on that stage."

Kallum lowered his makeshift ice pack and his face split

into an instant magazine-level smile. There was definitely no missing that chipped tooth, front and center. "I'm great, actually. I'm thinking this might be a new look for me. Hillbilly chic."

I tried to answer his smile with one of my own, but my face wouldn't quite work. My smile muscles were broken. "You don't feel woozy or anything? You did have trouble spelling your name up there."

A line dug itself between his brows. "What?"

Maybe when the nurse came in, I needed to have her take a look at Kallum too. "Remember? You spelled your name with a *C*? *C-A-L-L-U-M*?"

"Ohhh," he said, understanding lighting his eyes. "No, that's my real name. Emotionally, it's my real name, I mean. I was born Callum with a *C*, but then I swapped the *C* for a *K* when we formed INK, so that way our names could match up with the letters."

"Oh, like a stage name," I said. That made sense. I'd been born Winifred Baker, but had been credited as Winnie Baker since my very first gig (as a secret twin's secret baby in a long-running soap opera).

Kallum grinned—a drunken grin that looked all the more rakish for the chipped tooth. "See, I didn't actually get how stage names worked back then, so when our manager suggested I go by Kallum with a *K* instead, I thought that meant I had to go have it changed legally. So I did!"

"Ah," I said. My voice sounded faint, even to me. "Cool." And it was cool, or at least totally fine. Name changes were so common in our business!

But I couldn't shake the feeling that maybe I barely knew Kallum at all . . .

"This isn't a hospital, this is a glorified clinic," came a polished voice from through the door. It swung open to reveal my parents, my mom in a pressed sweater set and my dad in a button-down and blazer, even though it was near midnight.

"Darling," my mother said, coming forward to take my hand. She and my dad both ignored Kallum. "We're here now, and we're going to make sure you and the baby get the best care possible. And we're going to organize a transfer. Boston, maybe. Albany, if we must."

My dad came up and gave my foot a warm squeeze. "I'm going to make some calls and see how quickly we can get you to a real hospital, sweetheart," he said. "Be back in a flash."

"And I'm going to find you a blanket," Mom said, after *tsk*ing at me shivering on the bed. "This is ridiculous."

She bustled back out of the room, and Kallum stared after her. "Those are your parents?"

I nodded, but before I could say more, my mom was already back with a warm blanket. She draped it over me and tucked me in, and it felt so deliciously nice that a sudden wave of sleepiness washed over me. I had to drag my eyelids back open again and again.

Dad returned with a beleaguered looking nurse, who ran an IV under the watchful eyes of my parents, and then promised that a doctor and a sonographer would be in very shortly. After the nurse left, Kallum seemed to decide it was time to make his move. He unfolded himself from the chair in the corner, and approached my mom with his hand stuck out.

"Mr. and Mrs. Baker, it's a pleasure," he said. My mother hesitantly slid her slender, French-manicured hand into his, and then immediately yanked it back. I could see the mojito slime on it from here; Kallum's ice pack had been leaking on his hand, apparently.

He seemed to realize it at the same time we all did. "Oh shit, I'm so sorry," he said, laughing a hearty Kallum laugh, and then he tried to stride over to the sink in the corner to wash his hands—except he tripped over my new IV cord, yanking on the needle taped to the inside of my elbow and knocking over the pole with a loud crash.

At the very same moment, the doctor walked in, freezing in the act of pulling her hair into a low ponytail. She took in the scene: me clutching my elbow, the two parents looming over my bed, the man in the strip club T-shirt wrestling with an IV pole.

The mojito ice pack was in the middle of the floor, slowly leaking pale green goo onto the floor.

"Right," the doctor said briskly, finishing with her ponytail and then sticking her hands under the sterilizing foam dispenser and rubbing them together. "Only one person can be in here during the exam and the ultrasound." She turned her gaze to me. "Who would you like it to be?"

I glanced at Kallum, who was still trying to set the IV pole back on its wheels, his lip bleeding a little again after all the commotion, a shiny patch of sticky mojito goo lingering just above the line of his beard.

I glanced at my mom, who was the furthest thing from sticky, who'd already brought me a blanket when she saw that

I was cold. At my side, Kallum finally got the pole settled and then walked back to the chair, where he dropped himself down with a woozy, drunk-sounding groan.

"My mom," I said. "I want my mom to stay."

Kallum's head snapped up. "What?"

"She's been pregnant before, and you know, it'll be easier without . . ."

I stopped. I didn't want to spell out that he was drunk and a mess and not helpful right now.

Even if it was the truth.

His face fell. "Okay. If that's really what you want . . . ?"

My mother put her hand on my shoulder and gently rubbed it. The doctor said, "You can wait out in the waiting room. And once we know what's going on, we can open the room up to more visitors."

"I think he might actually need to be looked at too," I interjected. "He had a pretty big fall at the party we were just at, and I'm worried he might have a concussion."

"Well, then," the doctor said, just as Kallum opened his mouth to protest. "I think you should wait with the triage nurse instead, and have her take a look at you. And no arguing with me—you don't want to mess with the possibility of a concussion. Seriously."

Kallum gave me an inscrutable look and walked to the door, and I knew this was the moment I should say something, call out to him. But there was a burn in my chest, blazing there alongside the fear, and it kept me from saying anything to make him feel better.

I'd wanted to count on Kallum so much; I'd talked myself into trusting that he wouldn't be careless or selfish when it came to me and the baby . . . and this is where I was right now. Scared and bleeding on a chux pad while he was stumbling around and nearly yanking IVs out of my arm.

Maybe Gretchen had been right. Maybe taking life seriously was never going to be his personality. And if that was the case, then who was I to ask him to be any different?

"I'll call," was what I managed to say. He didn't turn back.

By the time the door closed, I was starting to sniffle again, with my mom pulling me into a tight, Chanel-scented hug.

"Now," began my father, patting my foot again, "about getting my daughter and my grandchild to someplace with a higher-level ER . . ."

Voicemail left by Winnie Baker on Kallum Lieberman's phone the next day, 9:13 A.M.

Um, hey. It's me. I'm sorry it took a minute to call—everything happened so fast. The initial exam and sonogram returned good news: I'm not in any kind of preterm labor, and the baby's heartbeat is still really strong. Dad ended up getting his way and having me transferred to a much bigger hospital in Boston, where they'll be doing a more intense ultrasound and running several tests, but right now, it looks like the reason I'm bleeding is that the placenta is resting over the cervix a little. As the baby grows, the placenta should move away from the cervix, so the only real treatment for it is time. And maybe some bed rest too.

I heard from Steph that you didn't have a concussion or anything worse than a chipped tooth. I'm so glad. I hope you're getting some much-needed sleep.

Look, Kallum, I know we didn't have a chance to say goodbye, but part of me wonders if that's a good thing. If maybe we need some space from each other, to think about what we really want our lives to look like. I don't want you to feel dragged into the biggest responsibility a person can have, and the more I think about it, the more I don't think it's fair that you have to be. You're an incredible friend and lover and I know you'll be really playful and kind with our child. But last night really made me realize that I'm not ready to count on someone who also isn't ready to be counted on. I've done it before, and it really sucked.

And I think . . . I think we might be mismatched, you know? Who we are, the stages of our lives. And that's no one's fault, that's just the way things played out. But maybe it's good that we learn this now, before the baby gets here, rather than after, when everything is messy and hard anyway. But I do wish—

It doesn't matter. And I'll call again when I know more about the baby.

Goodbye, Kallum. And I'm sorry.

CHAPTER TWENTY-SEVEN

Kallum

I slept off my hangover at the hospital and thanks to the IV drip they had me on, my body felt fine. (Besides the chipped front tooth, which felt like the universal sign for *fuckup*.)

When I got back to the inn, I had a text from Isaac.

> **Isaac:** I'm out looking at real estate today. Nolan caught me up on what I missed last night. I hope Winnie's okay. My jet is at the airport and I've called ahead to let them know you can take it wherever you need to go. Winnie. Home. Whatever.

At that point, I'd already listened to Winnie's voicemail, which sounded too much like she was ending things between us. But I just had to apologize. I was drunk and stupid, and a solid apology would fix it. Especially if I could see her face-to-face.

So much of that night was fuzzy, but I just remember her parents and their crisp clothes and wrinkle-free Botox faces. Hell, even I'd wanted to let them be in charge at that moment. I'd lost plenty of girls to their one true love, but never had I lost a girl to her parents.

When I got to the private airfield, I FaceTimed Winnie only to get a text response from her, saying that she was in the middle of being discharged and was cleared for travel. She was flying back to LA and we could talk more when she got home.

So I took Isaac's fancy jet, and couldn't even enjoy the fancy steak and ceviche they served me for lunch because my brain was racked trying to understand how things went from utterly perfect to a pizza oven engulfed in flames faster than my pole-dancing career could even fully begin.

HOME IS WHERE the pizza is. And for me, home was the apartment above the Slice, Slice, Baby flagship location in downtown Kansas City. When I first started it up, I dumped everything I had into this place. I bought the location outright. It was a good spot too. A corner space with decent square footage, so I bought a king-size bed, a couch, and a TV big enough to fit in a small movie theater. I've updated it since then and even hired one of Tamara's friends to decorate. I have art, matching sheets, and a bidet. Now I just need a nursery.

When I let myself in through the back room, the pizza oven was still warm, so I fired it back up again. I needed to get my shit together, but first I had to make a pizza. To knead my fingers into the dough and let myself get a little angry at it.

I wandered into the office and flipped through some mail as my computer came to life. Waiting for me were two emails from Ian. Just as I clicked on the latest one, something above me rumbled.

"What the hell?" I whispered before grabbing my dad's housewarming gift when I first moved in, a baseball bat I kept behind the door of my office.

I held the bat up, ready to whack an intruder, as I crept up the stairs.

It sounded like the TV was on. In fact . . . not only was it the TV, but the very familiar sound of *Mario Kart*. What the—?

I swung the door open.

"Eat my dick, goatmafia33."

"Topher?" I asked.

But he didn't turn around. Because he had on my huge-ass noise-canceling headphones. He lay sprawled out across my extra-long camel-colored leather couch with a half-eaten pizza on the ottoman that had to have one of every topping we offered.

I shook my head. That's one way to compromise the integrity of my impeccable crust.

Like the good uncle I was, I tiptoed behind him and slowly lifted a headphone off his ear. "Boo."

Topher shot into the air and spun around, hurling my Nintendo Switch controller right at my head. It hit with a *thud* before landing on the hardwood floor in more pieces than it should have been.

"What are you doing here?" Topher asked. He wore a pair of polka-dot boxers, one of the many free shirts I'd gotten for sponsoring some local 5K, and my flannel robe, which swallowed him. "And with the office bat? Whoa. Also what happened to your tooth?"

"Um, what are you doing here is the better question," I told him, "And this is my self-defense bat for, ya know, intruders."

"I'm not an intruder," he said innocently.

"Uh, you sure look like one to me. And the tooth is a long story."

I took a quick look around to see the state of the rest of the apartment. The sink overflowed with dishes and the Slice, Slice, Baby boxes were piled high enough to make a cardboard mansion.

Bread peered up from her cat bed on the window ledge and then leapt toward me. I scooped her up and let her nuzzle my beard before turning back to Topher. "Are you squatting in my apartment?"

He cringed. "Why do you have to say it like that? Bread needed the company!"

Knowing Bread, that was hard to believe.

"Remember how I dropped last semester and you took the hit for me?"

"I definitely have not forgotten."

"Very cool of you, by the way," he said. "Well, I might have promised my mom that I was taking a summer-mester. And I was about to sign up, but I got this really cool opportunity to invest. So I took the money for classes and I invested it."

"You invested your federal student loan money?" I asked. I

couldn't tell if this kid was a genius or not, but lately I was leaning toward not.

"It wasn't federal student loan money," he corrected. "It was a private loan."

"If you're going to scam your student loan money, shouldn't it at least be government money? And who gave you a private loan?"

"The Vasectomy King of Kansas City himself."

"And what did you blow your stepdad's cash on?"

"My friend Riley had this great idea to put hot tubs in the back of pickup trucks and drive people around downtown . . . like a horse and carriage but without the animal cruelty. And plus hot tubs."

I pulled out a dining room chair and slumped down into it as my body finally began to feel the shock of the last twenty-four hours. "Let me guess. Your mom found out?"

He nodded.

"And so you're hiding out here? Great."

"She knows where I am," he said. "She's got location tracking on my phone."

I could see how, if I were fourteen years old, I would want to dump a bunch of cash into a redneck hot tub company. But Topher wasn't fourteen. He was twenty. And blowing through cash that didn't even belong to him while other people—like me!—took the blame.

I knew what I had to do, but that didn't make it any easier. I was the fun uncle. Not the tough-love uncle. But I owed this to Topher. I loved him enough to know that.

"You're fired," I said.

"What?" Topher circled around the couch and rushed toward the dining room table. "Slice, Slice, Baby is my life! I basically ran the place for the last four months!"

"I know that," I told him. "And that's my fault. I asked too much of you. I should have done this sooner, but dammit, Toph, I'm doing it now."

He began to pace. "What am I supposed to do? I was trying to save up for my own place."

"You were?" I asked.

He shrugged. "I was thinking about it."

I pulled out the chair beside me. "Sit down, buddy."

He sniffed, his eyes glossy with tears.

Wrapping an arm around his shoulder, I pulled him in and planted a kiss on his forehead just like I'd done so many times when he was a kid. After a moment, I let go so he and I could see eye to eye.

"Tomorrow, you and I are going to see your mom. We're going to tell her everything. I'm going to own up to my shit and you're going to own up to yours."

His head lolled back. "This blows."

"Yeah," I admitted. "It does."

"And listen, I don't give a shit if you go to college—though your mom might and it might take some time and convincing—but I want you to find your thing, and I'm going to do whatever I can to help you do that. So if you want to be a chef, I'm sending you to whatever Michelin star culinary school you want. Or if you want to work as a mechanic or a choir teacher or—"

"Craft services," he blurted. "I've always wanted to work in craft services in Hollywood."

"Really?" I asked.

"I know I love working with food," he said as he rubbed his eyes and yawned. "And I've always wanted to work on movie sets."

His yawn set off my own and I stood to stretch. "I don't know if there's a school for that, but the offer stands, kiddo. Whatever you want to do, I'm going to help you get there. And that includes talking to your mom."

"That's the hardest part," he mumbled.

"Hey," I snapped as I went to investigate his everything pizza. "Your mom is an amazing parent. You know that, right? She's spent her whole life loving you and dreaming for you and fighting for you. Before your siblings and stepdad, it was just the two of you. She's not perfect, but you're growing in a direction she doesn't know how to handle."

He nodded. "I know. I'm not going to be some lawyer or professor like she wants, but I can still make her proud."

"I know that," I told him. "And she will too."

I scooped up a slice of his pizza and folded it in half before taking a bite full of pineapple, olives, and anchovy.

"Topher, this is fucking foul," I said as I took another bite.

He grinned. "But if you hadn't tried it, how would you know?"

After doing a little surgery on my game controller, we played a few rounds of *Mario Kart* and picked apart his Frankenstein pizza while Bread paced circles, waiting for me to go to bed.

Soon enough, Topher was fighting to keep his eyes open. I set him up on the couch with blankets and pillows before I went down to turn off the pizza oven, put my bat away, and check all the doors.

My phone sat there glowing on my desk with a message from Winnie.

Winnie Baker: Made it back to LA. I'm staying with my parents and I'm seeing my doctor tomorrow. Will update you after.

I wanted to write back and tell her I loved her and I loved our baby and I wanted to get on a flight to LA to be right there with her. But that wasn't what she needed from me right now.

Me: Good. I'm back home in KC. Let me know how things go tomorrow. I'm glad you and the baby are okay.

THE NEXT DAY, I stared at my open laptop, hardly daring to believe my luck.

Dear Mr. Lieberman,

I hope this email finds you well.

This correspondence is long overdue, but my client and I appreciate your patience while we reassessed our business plan. While my client was disappointed that you were unable to join him on the set of *Shark Tank*, he appreciates your apology and has ultimately come to the conclusion that this new plan is much more appealing and exciting for both parties.

Please see the attachment below for our official proposal.

Best,
Ian Ker

One hundred new franchise locations over the course of two years with me opening each of them in person. They'd help me get set up with a tell-all book deal. Slice, Slice, Baby merch. A whole pizza empire. But it would cost me fifty-one percent of my business. The business I started with what little INK money I had left. The business I turned into four busy locations that had earned me recognition as a trusted business owner. A Kansas City establishment. Something my parents were truly proud of. A business that was successful enough that I could buy Winnie a McMansion in the suburbs and send my nephew to whatever school or training it would take to make his dreams come true without being indebted to the federal government or his stepdad.

But the business forecasts in this proposal . . . Holy shit. Even if they were only half right, I could buy Winnie an island. I could give our kid every opportunity in the world. I could buy my parents their dream house. Two of them, even.

But it would cost me more than fifty-one percent or control of the company. It would cost me the first two—probably three— years of my child's life. But Winnie would never have to worry about leaning on her parents or doing projects she didn't fully love.

I sat there at my desk, memorizing every page of this pdf and dreaming about the life it could give me and everyone I loved.

Topher pounded down the steps, turning the corner into my office, his hair still wet from the shower and his whole body vibrating with now-or-never energy. "She's here."

THE PREP STAFF wouldn't be here for another hour and a half, but if we couldn't hash all this out in an hour and a half, our problems were bigger than time.

Tamara parked on the street and read the parking sign for a whole three minutes before coming in.

She gave us each a hug and an air kiss, which meant she was pissed. If we were in her good graces, we'd have both gotten actual kisses. But that was fine. We both deserved that. When I was back home after the fire, I'd been so wrapped up in insurance and inspections and investor drama that she and I never got to have the talk I'd promised her, so my sister was owed.

Tamara and Topher sat on either side of a booth, so I pulled up a chair to sit at the end.

"I fired Topher," I told her before her son could dig this hole any deeper.

She eyed me, and then him. "That's probably for the best."

Topher nodded like he knew he deserved that. "And I lied about the spring semester. It wasn't Uncle Kallum's idea. It was mine."

My sister looked at me, and I saw all the things racing through her head. *Why would he lie? Why would Kallum go along with it? Do I even know my son? Or my brother for that matter?*

She took a deep breath and the hard lines etched into her expression began to soften. "Start from the beginning."

I nodded to Topher and he took a sip from one of my coffee mugs. (It was full of root beer from the soda fountain.) And then he began to talk. He told us both how claustrophobic school had felt for him and how he felt aimless and like there was something out there for him, but he felt tethered to traditional education . . . and this city. That was a tough pill for Tamara to swallow. I'd seen the same expression on my mom's face when I left for LA for the first time. It was wonder and fear at the sight of your child finally realizing just how wide the world really was.

I told Tamara about my offer to help Topher find the thing that makes him tick. Her lip trembled, and that was enough to get me and Topher crying like babies because Lieberman men are fucking feelers. Dad might come off as chill and stoic, but you could turn on *Seabiscuit* and watch that man turn into a blubbering toddler.

As the prep staff trickled in, Reuben, my location manager, came over. "I'm short a worker today," he said. "We should be fine, but we have a big lunch order from that ad firm down the street, so I think I'll have to turn off online ordering until we get their pies out the door."

Topher looked at me and then Tamara, who gave a soft nod.

"Topher can help," I told Reuben, "but just FYI, I fired him last night and if you knew he was crashing in my apartment upstairs and didn't tell me, we should have a talk."

Topher waved his hands. "Reuben had no idea. I was sneaking back in after they closed up for the day."

Reuben laughed. "I like this kid, but not enough to risk my job for him."

I bumped fists with Reuben. "Good man."

Topher followed Reuben back to the kitchen and grabbed an apron on his way.

Once he was out of sight, Tamara sipped from her son's mug. "I swear, he's an eight-year-old trapped in the body of a man."

"What? You don't start your day off with a fizzy mug of root beer?"

She took another sip and smirked. "You might just be a pretty great dad one day," she said.

I clutched a hand to my chest. "I'm sorry. But did you just compliment me?"

"I wouldn't call it a compliment. More like a potential compliment."

I leaned back in my chair, letting it balance on the back two legs. "That's fair."

"But maybe you should get that tooth fixed before the baby comes. It's really making your face even more of a horror story."

"Your love is so warm," I told her, and then after a moment, I added, "I'm sorry." It was probably the sixth time I'd apologized since she got here. "Not just as Topher's uncle," I told her. "But as your brother." I let my chair rock forward again on all fours. "Winnie and I . . . I don't know. I don't know what we are. But she said something to me that hit me really fucking hard. She said she wasn't ready to count on someone who also wasn't ready to be counted on."

"Wow," Tamara said. "I gotta mentally bookmark that one."

"I feel like I've been kind of moving through life haphazardly. And sometimes I do shit that seems harmless, but nothing ever happens in a vacuum, does it? Everything affects something, and I think I'm starting to realize that sometimes being a grown-ass man means owning up for the shit you caused, but especially the shit you didn't mean to cause."

"Big lessons for a big boy," Tamara teased, but her voice was kind as her hand settled on top of mine. "Now what's all this about you not knowing what's going on with Winnie? Because you're having a baby together. That's what."

"I think she loves me in her own way. But I don't think she wants the life she would live with me. I don't know. Or maybe she just saw straight through me for the giant dope I really am. I mean, I make pizza for a living."

"Okay, enough with the self-deprecation. I hate hyping you up. It literally makes my skin crawl, but I will do it to remind you that you're a Grammy-nominated artist who has more accolades than I can count. You're a successful businessman and a good son and good brother. And I might gag saying this, but the ladies appear to be . . . fans. She would be lucky to live a life with you, Kallum."

"That's sweet of you—"

"Don't thank me yet," she warned. "Because here's the other side of the coin. You're both about to be parents. You think you've been tired or confused or frustrated before? Just wait until you're trying to heat a bottle on thirty-six minutes of sleep in forty-eight hours and working the bottle warmer feels like doing trigonometry. I want you and Winnie to be happy—and maybe even together, but the truth is: the two of you have to figure out a way to parent through whatever problems you're having. When it comes down to that baby, it doesn't matter if you two are trying to untangle feelings and history. You still have to find a way to communicate as adults about the real tangible things that matter. Doctor's appointments. Insurance. Day care. The fucking texture of baby poop for goodness sake!"

"Insurance," I said with a snarl. But she was right. Winnie and I had a lot to figure out. But one thing—one incredibly simple thing—we both knew. In just a few short months, we'd be parents. And whether we were living in romantic harmony or trying to coparent from two different states, we were about to have a brand-new, life-altering priority to consider.

I wanted to be everything for Winnie. The man she leaned on in every situation. But I would show up in whatever way she'd have me. So I'd give her time and space . . . when it came to us.

But our child? Give me some New Balance dad sneakers, a grill, a Home Depot credit card, and call me Dad.

CHAPTER TWENTY-EIGHT

Winnie

You'd think medically prescribed bed rest would have been awesome. But alas.

It was not awesome.

Instead of finally living my dream of sleeping all day without guilt, I was staring at the walls of my childhood bedroom—the pink of my teenage years now replaced with some expensive-looking Farrow & Ball shade of green—and thinking about how much I missed Kallum Lieberman.

I missed his smile and his deep laugh. The small hitches in his breath whenever I did the smallest thing: took his hand or kissed his cheek. Bit my lip.

I missed how easy he made the world to be in, how comfortable and happy he made the people around him. Where I'd grown up terrified of being too much for someone—anyone, the entire world—he'd seemed to see *too much* of anyone as a good thing. Like handfuls of candy at Halloween or piles of presents at a birthday party. As if everyone should be more of themselves.

As if the world would be a better, funner, sweeter place for it.

I couldn't think of something I wanted my baby to have in their life more.

But then I would think of that night in the hospital, of how lonely it felt to be the only one scared, the only one thinking straight, the only one *in* the problem, and my missing Kallum would granulate into something more complicated, something I didn't know how to put back together.

I'd told him we needed space, but I missed him.

I wasn't sure if I could trust him, but he might be the best father in the world to our child.

I loved him, but he let me down.

. . . And maybe it had been unfair of me to depend on him anyway?

I didn't know what to do with all those contradictory feelings, because what could I do? I couldn't forget that he had been a giant mess when I'd needed him the most—but also, he'd only been a mess because we'd all been at a function that was mess-appropriate. I couldn't fault him for partying at a party. But it wasn't just that he'd been partying at a party, because before that, there'd been the crappy thing he'd said to Teddy, and heck, even before that, there'd been the picture of me asleep in the car. And yes, each thing had extenuating circumstances, but how many extenuating circumstances were there going to be? How many times would there need to be explanations and apologies?

I didn't know the answer, and in this case, not knowing the answer was its own answer. No, I didn't think I could trust him with the scary, hard chaos that came with a baby. The only logical step was to figure out how to bring him into the baby's life . . . without also setting us up for failure.

But then why did *logical* still feel *shitty*? That was something my therapist had definitely neglected to mention when she'd explained setting boundaries to me.

The door to my bedroom opened, and my mom walked in with a cup of hot peppermint tea and a bottle of artisanal water for me. And, as she had every day since I'd come home, she brought a slice of maple bacon pizza, which was anonymously delivered every day to our house at the same time. We all knew that Kallum was responsible somehow; my parents tolerated it because it was the only solid food I would reliably eat.

Even if it came with a side of extra-messy feelings and miseries and hopes.

"We're going to have a visitor today," she said as I sat up and smoothed my hair. My parents had been big on me *staying productive* until the bed rest order expired next week, but their idea of productivity was journaling to explore what God wanted me to learn in this time . . . or reading through movie scripts they wanted me to consider. Since Michael and I had gotten married, they'd been working at the Bachers' media company, True Vine Studios, doing IP development, and I knew they wanted me to commit to a project with True Vine almost as much as they wanted me back together with Michael. In fact, two of the scripts they'd loaded onto my iPad were for different versions of a *Treasures in Heaven* sequel—one a direct sequel, and the other a spin-off about the hero and heroine's children.

I didn't know much more than that; I hadn't read them.

"Okay," I said, accepting the tray with my lunch on it. "I'll shower and dress after I eat." I was allowed to move some each day—enough to shower and shift from couch to bed and back again, but not much else. I was due for another ultrasound next week, though, and if the previa had gotten better by then, I'd be able to graduate from Bed Rest University. "Who is it?" I asked.

"An old friend," my mom replied cryptically, and would say no more.

THE OLD FRIEND turned out to be my old manager, Jackie Lipps, who had unceremoniously fired me not two years ago, and was now smiling up at me like we were old friends.

"Winnie, so wonderful to see you," Jackie said, standing up and extending her hand for me to shake, which I did automatically before we both sat down. Jackie looked virtually the same as the last time I'd seen her: Short hair dyed chestnut and aggressively styled. Light beige features with too much makeup. A smile so insincere it made my skin crawl. "I'm so glad you agreed to meet with me."

"I didn't," I said honestly. "I didn't know you were coming until I walked in the room."

"Winnie," my father scolded, like I was a teenager with bad manners. But that didn't work on me anymore. The disapproval, the guilting me into behaving a certain way.

Funny how it had taken less than a week for us to slip back into those old routines.

Jackie's fake smile didn't slip a millimeter. "That's perfectly all right. I know you've had a rough go of it these last few months, Winnie. Your parents care about you very much."

I didn't answer. They did care about me, I did believe that, but it had always been on their own terms. I'd thought maybe that had changed, that maybe a grandbaby would mean a different kind of love between us, but between the scripts and Jackie's visit, I was getting less and less certain.

"Now, I know we've had our professional differences," Jackie went on, "and now you've found yourself where so many young women find themselves when they stray from their parents' love."

I curled a hand protectively over the small rise in my lower stomach, as if I could stop her words from reaching my womb. "Our professional differences were that you fired me," I said. I hated that her words had the power to make me defensive, but they did.

Jackie sensed it too, like a predator scenting blood on the wind, and leaned forward. "Because I couldn't help you then. But I can help you now, Winnie."

"Help with what?" I asked warily.

"We," Jackie said, looking at both my parents and then back to me, "have found a way for you to move forward from this unpleasantness and give yourself a new chance at the career you're meant to have."

My hands tightened over my belly at *unpleasantness*. I was only just over the worst of the fatigue and the morning sickness;

I hadn't even felt the baby move yet. But I would fight an army for this child. I would cross deserts and climb mountains, and I would definitely throw a Crate & Barrel coaster at Jackie Lipps if she said more awful shit about me and my baby.

"Is this about the *Treasures in Heaven* sequel?" I asked. "Or switching back to the Hope Channel's usual movies? Because I think that door is shut after *Santa, Baby*."

Jackie's smile grew even wider; greed glinted in her pale green eyes. "That's where you're wrong. I've spoken to the Hope Channel execs, and they're willing to bury *Santa, Baby* if we give them something even better in return. Like an exclusive sit-down alongside Michael."

I stared. "I don't want to bury *Santa, Baby*," I said slowly. "I loved working on it. I'm proud of it. I'm proud of everybody's work on it."

My dad scoffed next to me. "You can't be serious."

"What he means," Jackie put in smoothly, "is that we are going to find you fulfilling work inside of your old brand. We know you want to feel proud of what you do, and that's why we'll make sure you have plenty of creative input on the projects you choose."

I shook my head. "No. I'm not shuttering *Santa, Baby*, and I'm not trying to squeeze my way back into True Vine's good graces. And as much as you might want me to fit back into my old brand, I can't now. I'm having a baby with someone I'm not married to. There's nothing more contrary to the old brand than that."

"Actually." My mother cleared her throat. "We have a way around that."

I laughed. And then stopped because she was completely serious. "There's no getting around the fact that I'm going to be a mother," I told them. "It's kind of inevitable at this point."

"What if," Jackie said, "you weren't going to be a mother, but rather, a sister?"

"I'm sorry, I think I'm not . . ." I paused, looked at my parents. They looked back, my father putting his hand on my mother's shoulder from where he stood behind her chair, and then it clicked.

"You want to take the baby," I said, hoping I was wrong. "You want to raise the baby as your own."

"An elegant solution to a thorny problem," Jackie said. "And then there will be no need for the world to know you're pregnant at all. We'll have anyone who already knows sign an NDA, and we'll make sure those agreements are ironclad. From the outside, it will seem as if your parents have decided to welcome a new child into their family, and you are its attentive, doting sister. And from the inside, well, you'll be able to see your baby as much as you want, play house as much as you want. The brand *and* the baby in your life. That's a win-win if I've ever seen one." Jackie sat back, satisfied with herself.

I was so upset I could barely breathe.

"And before you say no as a knee-jerk reaction, really think about this, Winnie," my mother said. "What would be better for this baby? Having a mother who will be famous for tawdry movies—and a father who makes his money with the same tawdry movies *and pizza*—or having us as his or her parents? When we could give this child so much more stability and guidance?"

"I don't want this," I said clearly. Without hesitation. "I don't want any of this."

Words I hadn't been able to say until just two years ago. Words that still somehow were a surprise to everyone hearing them. But at least they came easily. At least I didn't have to rehearse them, shape them in advance, scrape together every ounce of courage in me to speak them.

They came as naturally as breathing now. *I don't want this.*

My father stiffened, and when he spoke, his voice was filled with a tight, angry frustration. He hadn't been expecting me to have an opinion, and why would he? Until the divorce, I'd done everything he and Mom had wanted.

"Hasn't this rebellion run its course, Winifred?" he demanded. "How much further can you change—can you fall—before you admit that your pride has led you astray?"

I stood up, both hands shaking. All of me was shaking. But not with fear, not with uncertainty.

With sharp, angry clarity.

"And what about your pride?" I asked them. "You'd rather lie to the entire *world* than admit you have a daughter you can't control any longer? You'd rather see me unhappy than offer your love freely? This is how I know I've changed, Dad: I can't think of anything more *astray* than that."

And without another word, I left the room, left them alone with each other and their horrible plans.

"LA ROADSSS, TAKE me hooome," Addison sang as she pulled her G-Wagon into her driveway that afternoon. "To the place! Where I belong!"

She kept singing as she parked and the tall metal gates swung shut behind us. We had a brief fight about her carrying my bag, which she won, and then we trooped to the pool house, where she tutted at me to sit down as soon as possible.

"Thanks for picking me up, Addy," I said as I sank onto the sofa and pulled a throw pillow to my chest. "I couldn't stay there anymore."

I'd left the house by sneaking out my window, which was not very bed rest of me . . . or very thirty-two of me. But I figured in the long run, it was less stress for the baby if I was back home. My real home, however small and technically not mine it was.

"You betch," Addison said. She threw herself on the couch next to me and her iced pomegranate juice spilled on her hand. She licked it off her fingers like a cat. "You doing okay?"

Strangely . . . I *was* doing okay. "I'm still a little rattled," I admitted. "But two years ago, a day like today would have broken me. Instead, I feel . . . stronger? I had to say *no* to two people I never used to say no to, and I had to do it without any warning, and I was still able to do it."

"You're a *no* machine now," Addison said approvingly.

"I wanted them in my life so much, even before the baby." I looked down at the pillow. "And just when I'd learned how to stop wanting it, they showed up again. They were there when I needed someone to be there for me. I guess I'd hoped . . ."

"That you were going to get the family fairy tale after all?" asked Addison.

"They'd traveled all that way, and then they came to the hospital in the middle of the night, and I thought it was because they cared about me. And not because they wanted something from me."

"Relationships shouldn't be like high-pressure sales meetings. You shouldn't feel obligated to say yes to a time-share just because they gave you free champagne flutes. Except in this case, a time-share is literally giving up your baby, and the free champagne is the bare fucking minimum." Addison slurped her juice and then set it down emphatically. "But! You refused their hideous offer, and now you're here! With Aunt Addy where you belong! So what next, boo bear?"

What next, indeed. "I guess I'm back to where I started before reshoots. Steph thinks I'll be able to find plenty of work, especially leaning into the *good girl gone bad* narrative. And as for the baby and me, we'll figure it out."

"You know you can move into the main house anytime," Addison said, suddenly serious. "I've decided I don't care if people know you're living here. It was shitty of me to care about that in the beginning, and I'm sorry for it."

"But I need you to subsidize my single parenthood with that immaculate Wishes of Addison brand," I said with a smile. And then to show her I meant it, I curled my hand over her wrist and squeezed gently. "I understand, Addy, and I understood it then. I wasn't hurt by it. There are no good variables to work with when the answer to the equation is other peoples' idea of perfection."

"Still," she said with a little sniffle. "I want you and the baby to be where you feel best, and there's definitely more room in the main house."

"But it's cozy in here," I said, meaning it. "Plus I still don't know what coparenting with Kallum will look like. I might need to be in Kansas City quite a bit."

Even just saying his name made my chest hurt. Aside from Addison, Kallum was the only person who would understand all the webbed and tangled feelings I'd had about today. How hard it was to let go of wanting my family to be what I needed, and yet how freeing it was to know that I was strong enough to.

"Okay, but what's next for you, right now?" Addison asked. "What do you want right now?"

I only felt like I knew what I *didn't* want, and that wasn't very helpful for figuring out what came next in the immediate future. I sifted through all my feelings, about my parents, about Kallum, about the little baby currently growing organs and bones just below my belly button.

"I think I want to know for sure that my parents can't try again to woo me over to their side of things. I trust myself to say no, but—"

"But you've already said no once and you shouldn't have to again," Addison said sagely.

"Right."

"You know," Addison said, her voice pitched in a slow drawl that I knew from experience either spelled trouble, vodka, or both, "I know a way we can make that happen."

"Stopping my parents? Really?"

"It's as easy as an Instagram post, pickle pie. Do you have an ultrasound picture?"

My eyes grew round as I absorbed her meaning. "Are you saying I should just . . . announce that I'm pregnant?"

"Yeah, girl. Drop that baby news like Taylor drops an album. People will go ba-*na*-nas!"

And so forty minutes, four filter attempts, and one newly delivered red juice later, the deed was done. I had a post with a very cute picture of me in Christmas Notch dressed as Mrs. Claus with a swipe over to my latest ultrasound.

This year, Mrs. Claus will be hanging up an extra stocking! Thank you to the Hope Channel, @officialgretchenyoung and @steph darezzo for making Santa, Baby a safe place for this expecting momma, and thank you to my costar @pizzapartykallum and the whole crew for making this wacky movie a blast to film! More updates on my mini-Winnie coming soon!

I hit Share and then set my phone on the table. Addison and I watched as the first notification popped up on my screen, and then the second and the third, and then more and more until my phone was merrily vibrating its way across the glass.

There was no taking it back now. The world knew that Winnie Baker, former wholesome sweetheart, had not only divorced her husband amid cheating rumors, but now was pregnant without her husband anywhere in the picture. The scandalous descent was now complete.

I was so relieved.

Amid the incessant bubbling of the social media messages came a text message from Steph. It was a thumbs-up emoji and nothing else, but that was basically a five-minute-long hug with boob presses and everything when it came to Steph D'Arezzo.

And then a second text message popped up right after it.

From Kallum.

"Oh shit," Addison said with wide eyes. "Do you think he's upset?"

I grabbed my phone. "I'm not sure," I admitted. He'd wanted to shout it from the rooftops while we were back in Christmas Notch, but now that things between us were murkier, he might not be as excited. I'd taken care not to name him as the father or anything, but maybe mentioning him at all in the caption was bound to raise eyebrows?

"Ohhh, it's a voice memo," Addison said, leaning over to look down at the screen. "Do you want me to listen to it first for you?"

"No, no. It's totally fine." But I was glad she was there to listen to it with me.

I hit Play, and then Kallum's warm, deep voice filled the room. It was easy to forget, sometimes, how gorgeous that voice was. How it vibrated so rich and so low.

"Hey, Winnie," Kallum said. "I just saw your post, and I wanted to say that I'm proud of you. I know that with your parents and all the stuff they raised you with, it might have been hard to tell people, and that there are going to be some people who say the very things you're terrified someone will say. So I wanted to make sure, in case no one else said it, that you're this supercool, amazing, brave, really hot person, and I'm proud of you. And, um . . ." A pause, and he continued, "I'm here if you need me. Even if it's just to talk about what brand of car seat to register for. Or if you need someone to fight in your Instagram comments for you. Even my sister is ready to go if we need to tag team and fight some people on the internet. I'm just . . . I'm here . . ."

And right then, as he said *I'm here*, I felt a small, soft flutter below my navel. So small it was barely there, but it *was* there.

For the first time, I'd felt the baby move, and it had happened while I'd been listening to Kallum's voice. While we'd *both* been listening to Kallum's voice.

"I think the baby likes hearing Kallum," I murmured, pressing my hand to my stomach and closing my eyes.

"Then let's queue up the Spotify-sponsored INK playlist, baby girl," Addison said. "And get another red juice, because we've got registries to make."

CHAPTER TWENTY-NINE

Kallum

My phone lit up in my hand and sent my heartbeat galloping.

> **Winnie Baker:** Thanks. That means so much to me, Kallum.

I began to type back, but before I could send anything else, another message from Winnie appeared.

> **Winnie Baker:** I felt the baby kick. For the first time. Just now.

I gasped. I laughed. I was about to cry. And all I wanted was to see the way her face lit up when she felt that little stir in her belly for the first time.

> **Me:** Holy shit! What did that even feel like? It sounds so cool and exciting, but weird too. I can't believe you're just casually growing a human.

Reuben poked his head into my office. "Everything okay, boss?"

"Better than okay," I told him. "You ready to check out the other locations with me?"

Reuben nodded before disappearing to let the flagship staff know he'd be out for a few hours.

> **Winnie Baker:** I have an appointment tomorrow and if you want, I can try to FaceTime you during the sonogram?

> **Me:** I would love that. Consider my schedule cleared.

I stood and grabbed my car keys from the top drawer of my desk, pausing for a sec to send off a quick text to a friend and fellow pizza entrepreneur who I knew in LA. I'd struck a deal with him to send Winnie a maple bacon pizza every day, using my recipe. It probably wasn't exactly the same, but it was close.

I'd been home for a week and big changes were happening for Slice, Slice, Baby. After firing my own nephew, I knew that whether or not I took the investment deal, I'd need an area manager to keep things running smoothly. Even if it was just *Santa, Baby* promo or maybe other jobs that came up—or just spending time in LA with the baby, and hopefully Winnie too—I needed someone with a slightly more fully-formed frontal lobe than Topher could offer to run the place.

So I sat down and looked at my finances and put together an offer package for Reuben, who'd worked for me for the last six years now. The fact that I went to Topher in the first place was a mistake on my part. Reuben was funny and loved making people happy with good food as much as I did. He and his wife had a two-year-old daughter who they dressed as a pizza delivery driver for her first Halloween. If I couldn't be here to run my business, Reuben was the next best thing.

He countered my offer with more money and an extra week of vacation, and I said yes. He was dependable, smart, and knew the business. And he was standing right the fuck in front of me this whole time.

He was also the only person who didn't make fun of me for chipping my tooth, and that was the kind of love I was willing to pay for.

"How was your flight?" Nolan asked as I bustled around his kitchen making my signature non-pizza dish, ginger-lime chicken with coconut rice.

"It was great," Topher chimed in. "Except for when my own uncle ditched me for business class like those awful parents in *Home Alone*."

Bee paused for a moment and then pointed a serving spoon at him. "You're right. No one ever talks about how bad those parents were. Especially the uncle!"

"He was the worst," I confirmed. "Speaking of holiday content, I'm still bitter we never made a Hanukkah album. It's not right that Adam Sandler is the highest-ranking artist on the Spotify Hanukkah playlist."

I shoveled chicken from my frying pan into one of Bee's vintage Pyrex bowls and placed it on the kitchen table.

"What's the plan for the next week and a half?" Nolan asked as he popped a piece of chicken in his mouth and immediately regretted his decision once he realized how hot it was. "Hothothothothothot," he hissed.

Bee let out a little *hmph* and continued setting the table while I scooped the rice from the cooker.

"Well, I've got to find an apartment. Nothing too big. Just enough for when I'm in town and space for a crib and whatever other baby stuff I need. I'm going to an appointment and a class with Winnie. We're supposed to finalize the registry. And names. We have to talk about names, because I've got a couple new contenders." I set down the bowl of rice and then sat down next to Topher. "And then there's Topher shadowing your craft services crew while we're here and I'm looking at space for an LA location for Slice, Slice, Baby."

Nolan's jaw dropped to his plate. "Don't tease me, man."

"I'm just looking," I told him. "But it makes sense."

He slithered down in his chair with his hand to his stomach. "Slice, Slice, Baby in LA? It's all I've ever wanted."

"I don't know," Bee muttered. "I certainly had you begging for way more than pizza last night."

Topher's brow furrowed. The three of us weren't quite old enough and parental enough for him to feel grossed out by our sex lives, but it was a murky space in between.

"Well, we would love having a location down the street, Kallum," Bee said. "And I do mean down the street. Because anything else will take me forty-five minutes to get to."

I laughed. "Noted, madam."

"So this means the big investor franchise deal isn't happening?"

Topher huffed beside me. "Money left on the table."

"Yes, I'm currently taking business advice from my nephew who just blew his college tuition on hot tub trucks."

Nolan held up a hand. "Say more."

Topher sat up in his chair, fully ready to pitch this disaster to Nolan when I shoved a spring roll in his open mouth and said, "Nolan, keep your money. And yeah. I looked over the proposal with my lawyer . . . and Tammy Cakes too, because she's even sharkier than my lawyer. But I just couldn't imagine missing the first two years of little Kallum-Winnie's life. I want to be the dad who's around, ya know? I don't want to be the kind of dad who's just there for the big recitals or the important games. I want the little stuff. I want to know their friends and which kids at the lunch table are punk-ass bitches."

Bee made a heart with her hands. "I think I want babies."

Nolan took her hand and began to stand up with a sly grin on his face.

"Not, like, right this moment," she said with a laugh.

Nolan kissed her temple as he sat back down. "Didn't you see Winnie yesterday, babe?"

She nodded with a full mouth and then held up a finger while she chewed.

I couldn't help but feel immediately and deeply jealous of her. In the last four weeks since Winnie's announcement, I'd done everything in my power to think *baby first*. But Winnie was always my last thought at night and my first thought in the morning.

Thankfully, we'd gotten in the habit of talking every day. It'd been four weeks since Winnie had announced she was pregnant on social media. Since then, she'd send me weekly bump pictures and I downloaded an app to track the size of the baby. We'd stayed on the phone for hours at a time talking about names and what kind of sports our kid might sign up for or if they'd be into something bougie like dressage. We'd send each other *Consumer Reports* listings about strollers and car seats and recalls on crib mobiles we'd considered.

I'd been waiting for the perfect moment to ask her how much space was enough space, but I also didn't want to ruin this little bubble we were in right now. And maybe she'd be ready to talk some time this week. Whenever the time came, I'd be waiting.

"I did see her," Bee said finally with the kind of look you got from a girl's good friend that said *I know something you don't.*

And I loved Bee, but whoa, that made me feel totally irrational.

Nolan elbowed her a little. "Holding out on us, huh?"

"She's good!" Bee said defensively. "She's happy . . . ish." She took a huge bite of rice and added, "And that's all I'll say."

Nolan gave me a pointed look, his brows waggling.

I could have just stood up right then and there and raced over to Addison's and given Winnie some huge grand gesture of my love.

But I was being patient. I was playing the long game. And that was the biggest grand gesture I could offer.

And it was the one Winnie—and our soon-to-be child—deserved.

I LOOKED AT five apartments within three blocks of Addison's house and took the only one with a shower I could stand in without crouching over like Gru from *Despicable Me*. The real estate agent, who drove a Porsche so small I opted to drive myself to our listings, looked at me like I was playing an elaborate joke on her when I told her this place would do the job.

After I signed my lease and put down my deposit, I met with Steph's cousin who happened to be in commercial real estate. It was like meeting Steph if Steph were a fifty-eight-year-old man named Lenny in Danny DeVito's body. Turned out that finding a location for Slice, Slice, Baby's West Coast debut was a hell of a lot more difficult than finding an apartment.

We toured properties for three days straight. If I saw another poorly maintained kitchen, I was going to just get a van to sell slices out of.

On the third day, we ended up in a familiar place just across the street from Got the Juice. I couldn't tell if it was a good or bad omen, to be honest. Either way, I read the parking signs this time.

"So your pizza," Lenny said as he typed in the door code. "It's not that Chicago shit, right? People in LA want their pizza to be gluten-free, taste-free, and with a sprinkle of microgreens and Twitter threads or whatever on top."

"Now, Lenny," I said as we walked into the vacant space. "That's not entirely true. Carbs are universal. Besides, I make a killer side salad."

He grumbled about something under his breath. I'd never met a real estate agent who tried so hard not to sell real estate and that actually made me trust him even more.

The space was small. Just enough room for a couple booths, some barstools by the window, and a carryout line. I flipped the light switch as I stepped behind the counter where there was an old slicer and a moldy-looking drinks fridge. It was gross, but definitely one of the least offensive things I'd seen in the last few days. "What was this place? A deli?"

"What wasn't it?" he said with a grunt. "A deli, a gluten-free bagel shop, a kebab place. Nothing's really made it more than a year in this space."

"The location's good, though."

He shrugged. "If it's a commercial listing in LA and it's not structurally compromised and there's not a rodent problem, the location is prime."

We walked through the kitchen, which needed work, but was usable. "What's back here?" I asked as we walked down a narrow hallway past a single-stall restroom.

Pushing through the back door, I expected to find a dark alleyway, but instead, there was a huge overgrown patio with vines crawling up the backside of the building.

"Oh," Lenny said. "A beer garden. Whatever the hell that means."

I took a look around. Broken furniture. Weeds. String lights hanging dangerously low.

But I could see exactly what this space could be. I could practically hear my family right here. The sound of little feet running down the hallway and out onto this patio where I'd put in a little swing set and a playhouse for kids while adults sipped on a cold beer over one of my pies.

Back here you could barely even hear the chaos of the city. It was perfect.

"Ya know, it's not smart business to open up in a place that's been a revolving door of companies. I've got one more place to show you today."

"I like this one," I told him. And he was right about the revolving door. People's eyes started to glaze over when a location constantly changed hands, but in a way, it reminded me of my constant stream of bridesmaid hookups. Every time I thought it would be different and that maybe I'd found The One. But if I'd just given up on love, I never would have opened myself up to Winnie and the thought that we could be more than a good time.

And sure, Winnie wasn't ready for me. But I was building a life for us . . . and I would be here, serving up pies, when she was ready.

I turned back to Lenny. "Let's put together an offer."

CHAPTER THIRTY

Winnie

"Is that cold? It sounds cold," observed Kallum as the sonography tech squeezed a clear goo onto her transducer and pressed it to my stomach.

"It's been warmed," the tech assured him right as she dug into my very full bladder. She must have noticed my thighs tense under the sheet, because she said to me, "You're at twenty-four weeks now, this will be the last ultrasound we need a full bladder for, I think. Oh look! There we are."

On the screen, flickers of staticky baby emerged—head, legs, spine—until finally we could see almost all of them at once.

"Oh my God," Kallum breathed, his eyes glued to the screen. "And that's really the baby? Right now? That's what the baby is doing right now?"

The baby was doing nothing but kicking its legs right into my cervix, but Kallum looked like he was watching his first-born paint the Sistine Chapel inside my uterus.

"Look at them kicking!" he said excitedly, pointing. "You can even see their toes! And oh my God, is that their heart? Their tiny, little heart? Doing tiny, little heartbeats?"

"Sure is," the tech said, with the fond air of someone who'd listened to many parents squeal over shit she saw for eight hours a day every day. "Oh, honey," she said, reaching back to hand Kallum one of the tissues they kept for wiping the ultrasound gel off my stomach. "Here you are."

He took the tissue but still wiped at his eyes with the sleeves of his Royals T-shirt. "Thank you. It's my first time."

The tech's face stayed neutral—I was guessing she'd seen stranger antepartum relationship configurations in her time—but she did scoot her chair over a little so Kallum could see the screen better. And he leaned forward with unabashed tears running into his beard and stared at the screen like he was watching the most intense sports game in history.

For my part, I couldn't decide what I wanted to look at more, our baby or Kallum looking at our baby, and I wished I had a photographic memory, so I could forever recall the way his eyes widened when the baby started sucking their thumb, or the way his mouth split into an infectious grin when the tech confirmed that the little twitches were baby hiccups.

The last ultrasound he'd seen via video call, and the signal had been so bad that I didn't think he'd seen much of anything, and it was hard not to regret that. Not to regret that he'd already missed moments we'd never be able to get back.

And it had nothing to do with the baby, or maybe it had everything to do with the baby, but he was so tall and handsome sitting there in the chair, the tissue looking so small in those lumberjack-size hands, which could so easily hold a newborn or the handle of a car seat or assemble a crib, and then he'd look over at me with those shining eyes, his face open in wonder, and I would think about how easily he gave of himself, of his own feelings, his own vulnerability. How easy it was for him to be kind, to give me coats or custom pizzas or lap dances, to bestow those gifts of time or care or playfulness so freely, without ever expecting anything in return.

"Well, I'll leave it up to the doctor to say for certain," the tech said, pausing to capture some images, "but I think you might finally be in the clear, previa-wise."

"Oh thank God," I mumbled. This meant no more bed rest for real, and also a chance at a vaginal delivery.

"Good job, babe!" Kallum cheered, like the placenta clearing my cervix was a personal achievement of mine and not just uterine mechanics. It did feel good to be encouraged though, and I smiled back at him.

"Now, I saw in the notes that you haven't learned the baby's sex yet," the tech said. "Do you want to keep it that way? I can mark in the file not to offer."

I glanced at Kallum. "Actually, I do want to know," I admitted. "But it didn't feel right to learn it without you. If you want to learn the sex at all, that is."

"I'm happy either way," Kallum said and I knew he meant it.

Whatever Kallum's flaws and foibles, he always meant what he said. "I love the idea of learning it with you now, and I love the idea of waiting until the baby is born too."

I chewed on my lip. "I want to know, but I don't want it to change how we think about anything. Is that okay?"

Of course, the baby's biological sex would never guarantee their gender. But girls had to bear the brunt of purity, shame, and perfection in the world I'd grown up in. The gravity of the way I was raised . . . A part of me would always be a little frightened of it. That it would pull me back in; that I'd find myself not only folding my own life into a rigid, shame-filled box, but also folding a child into it too.

That gravity had been even stronger since I'd posted the pregnancy announcement. My parents had stopped talking to me—again—but had sent me one short email, signed by both of them, saying that I could always come home when I was ready, and that they would be happy to be part of their grandchild's life once I did come home. From the outside, it seemed like a nice enough email, but I could very easily read all the things they didn't say—which was of course part of the gravity I was so afraid of. It could be so invisible, so subtle. Present in what *wasn't* said as much as what was said, and it could steal the air from your lungs if you weren't careful.

The social media comments, magazine headlines, and gleefully scandalized Dominic Diamond articles—they were bad enough. But having people who were supposed to love you put conditions on that love . . .

Well, it wasn't the kind of parent I wanted to be.

Kallum reached over and took my hand. "It's more than okay. And my nursery is going to be pizza-themed anyway."

I gave him a shy smile. "Thank you."

"Ready?" the tech asked, bobbing her head from side to side, like she was excited too.

Kallum smiled back at me and squeezed my fingers. "Yes," he told her, but he didn't take his eyes from mine. "We're ready."

"MAN, I CAN'T wait to meet the baby cousin," Topher said a month later, inside the mostly renovated space that was the in-progress LA location of Slice, Slice, Baby. "That's so rad. We have way too many boys in the family right now. Do you know about the triplets, Winnie? Has Kallum told you? They're like the triplets from *Brave*, except they're always in their bear forms. It's terrifying."

I was sitting in a newly delivered vinyl booth—still wrapped in plastic—while Kallum supervised the installation of a new pizza oven in the back. He'd planned on dropping me by Addison's after our latest baby appointment, but when he mentioned the installation, I'd offered to come to the new location with him so there wouldn't be a chance of him being late.

And just now, he trotted back into what would be the dining area to check on me. "Do you need water or anything?" he asked, coming up to the booth.

"Yeah," Topher said, "you peed so much when you got here. Like so much. I'm worried you're going to look like the guy at the end of *Last Crusade*, you know? The old guy who drinks from the fake Holy Grail and then looks like a mummy?"

"Sometimes," said Kallum, who'd gone to get me a bottle of

water from the refrigerated case behind the battered counter, "I wonder why you don't have someone you're dating. And then you open your mouth."

"Like you're so smooth," Topher retorted. "Remember that time—"

"Kallum!" I broke in, waving him over. "She's kicking! You should be able to feel it this time!"

It had only been in the last few weeks or so that I'd been pretty sure I could feel her kick from the outside, and Kallum still hadn't had a chance to feel it. He rushed over, practically dropped the water bottle in the process, fell to his knees, and pressed both hands to my stomach.

"Down here," I laughed, guiding his hands to a spot below my belly button. "Feel that?"

"Yes," Kallum said. There was awe scrawled all over his face. "I feel it."

He lifted his eyes to mine just as she kicked again, and I pressed my hands over his, and suddenly it was like none of the messy stuff had ever happened. It was just him and me and our baby, it was just pure joy . . . and then we both seemed to realize at the same time that this was the most he'd touched me since that fateful last night in Christmas Notch.

I didn't want him to stop.

And from the way his eyes dipped from my face to where our hands tangled over my stomach, I got the sense that he didn't want to stop touching me either.

"I never thanked you," I murmured.

"Never thanked me for what?" he said as he tore his eyes away from our hands.

"The pizzas," I said. "The maple bacon ones. I have no idea how you managed to send me a fresh one every day, even while you were in Kansas City."

"The pizza mafia owes me a few favors," he said, and I laughed, although I noticed his answering laugh was a little strained. I added that to the small but fascinating mental bucket of Kallum Lieberman mysteries.

"Kallum," I said, having no idea what I was going to say or why, but knowing that I had to tell him how his touching me made me feel. "I think that maybe I—"

"We need you in the back, boss!" called a voice from the kitchen. "The natural gas hookup isn't where you said it would be!"

With a heavy groan, Kallum got to his feet. "Hold that thought and hold still," he said.

"I can't go anywhere without you, remember? You are my chauffeur today."

A bright grin. "Oh yeah. Sometimes my foresight amazes me." And then he trotted off to go deal with the gas hookup crisis.

Topher plopped down on the booth next to me after Kallum had disappeared through the brick opening to the kitchen. "He's trying really, really hard at this whole baby thing, you know."

"I know," I replied with a smile at Kallum's nephew. He'd been at Kallum's new apartment today when Kallum had swung by with me to show the new crib he'd built himself. Topher and Kallum had been jostling with each other to show me all the baby things Kallum had stockpiled already—a bottle warmer and an entire Target aisle's worth of baby bottles, a diaper pail with enough bags to last a nuclear winter, and a mobile for the baby's crib that had dangling pizza slices.

("It's custom," Kallum had told me proudly. "From an Etsy store. It even plays the Slice, Slice, Baby jingle when you turn it on.")

Topher had seemed to be equally proud of all the baby stuff—he'd helped Kallum pick out all the stocking caps—and had helped put the crib together. He'd been staying at Kallum's while he waited for his first couple paychecks from his new job to roll in, but he already had his eye on a place out near Studio City and was getting a decent amount of overtime as a catering attendant for the TV studio that produced Nolan's show *Band Camp*.

"And I'm so glad he was willing to move to LA, even part-time," I added. "Although this location for Slice, Slice, Baby seems to need a lot of elbow grease."

"Yeah, just imagine if he'd taken that *Shark Tank* deal or whatever," Topher said, stretching out his legs. With his height, scruff, and dark blond hair, he could have been a younger Kallum, and it made me wonder what any sons of ours would look like one day.

"*Shark Tank* deal?" I echoed, still thinking about sons and how I maybe wanted them. With Kallum.

"Yeah," Topher said. "You know. They were going to funnel *so much money* into SSB to expand it. All fifty states and then internationally too."

"They were? I had no idea." Kallum hadn't said anything about it, which was strange. Yes, our new routine was growing slowly and carefully, with both of us cautious about how much we leaned on each other and shared, but over the last eight weeks, we'd become something like . . . well, like friends. Which probably should have come *before* the lovers and coparents part, but Kallum and I seemed destined to do things out of order, I guessed. Either way, I was still surprised he hadn't mentioned such a big opportunity to me. "That sounds like it could have been huge."

"It would have been epic," he pronounced with solemnity. "He would have been a pizza emperor! But it would have meant a lot of time away from you and the bambino, so he couldn't do it. He told that tank of sharks no thank you, and decided he'd expand whatever way would give him the most time with the baby. And you."

And you.

And that was it, wasn't it? When I'd told Kallum I'd needed space, he hadn't pressed me and he hadn't crowded me. But he hadn't run away either. He'd let me know he was there to help with anything I needed—that he was there to be a father when the time came—and that took so much patience and generosity. And that wasn't even factoring what he'd given up for Slice, Slice, Baby, which, however metaphorically, was his baby too.

He'd given all that up for a *chance*. For the hope that we'd be able to mend things and peaceably coparent. For the hope that I would learn to trust him again.

And I was startled to realize that I *did* trust him. It had come slowly, quietly, a gentle tide coming with each call and text and ride to the doctor's office. With his signed leases and diaper pails and *Consumer Reports* listings. With his sweet, happy, surety that everything was going to be okay, because he'd make it that way.

I'd been so afraid to give him grace because so many people in my life had been grace-eaters—they'd devour any grace I'd given them and still needed more and more, endlessly, eternally. But Kallum devoured nothing. He gave and gave and he tried.

I wanted to be more like him, actually. And I wanted more of him in *my* life, not just our child's life, and it was so obvious it could have been kicking me in the stomach along with the baby:

I still loved Kallum Lieberman.

And it was time to find out if he still loved me.

CHAPTER THIRTY-ONE

Kallum

My family didn't believe in hotels. For as long as I could remember, any time we visited a city or country with even a distant relative in a fifty-mile radius, we stayed with them rather than getting a hotel. In fact, in advance of our INK tours, my mom would send me a list of names and numbers of every last relative she could think of and the corresponding city they lived in no matter how many times I reminded her that we had hotels booked and a literal tour bus with beds for sleeping.

So I guess I shouldn't have been surprised when my sister called the day before she and the rest of the family were flying out to LA for the grand opening of Slice, Slice, Baby to see if I had a hair dryer.

"No," I said, "but I'm sure your hotel will have one."

"If I could reach through this phone, and smack you, I would," she said. "You know Mom would die if we stayed in a hotel."

"Tam, my apartment is a two-bed, one-bath. And I use the word *bed* loosely. It's more like one-bed and a closet."

She sighed over the sound of a screaming child. "You don't think I don't want to stay in a hotel where nice people bring you endless fresh towels and my gremlin children can belly flop into a pool and eat free waffles?"

"Well," I said, sounding more smug than I deserved to be, "I guess it's a good thing that I went to Target and bought every air mattress and towel they had. I also put my Keurig away and bought one of those ancient Mr. Coffee machines Mom loves."

"Did I tell you she's packing one to take on the cruise?"

I groaned. Of course she was. I was still bummed to miss the family on Hanukkah, but at least the baby would be here by then and I'd be knee deep in diapers and onesies. And Bee and Nolan would totally spend a night lighting the menorah with me. Maybe even Isaac.

"Is Winnie coming to the opening?" Tamara asked.

"She's invited," I said. My sister had done a great job of deflecting our parents' questions about my relationship with Winnie, but I knew they were all curious. I wanted to give them some kind of answer, but saying the truth out loud, that we were just friends, wasn't something I was quite ready to do.

The whole family flew in, and sure enough, we all crammed into the cozy little apartment I currently (and temporarily!) shared with Topher. I got a tent for the kids to "camp" in the living room. I took the couch. Topher took an air mattress while his parents took his room and Mom and Dad took my room. The sleeping arrangements were the easy part. It was the bathroom that concerned me, but honestly I was too busy getting the new location ready to spend much time at home.

Topher played tour guide, taking Mom to see the tar pits and Tamara on a celebrity home tour. He even got to drive everyone by the culinary school he'd be attending part-time. Mom cooed over the crib I'd built and Dad chuckled at the pizza mobile hanging above.

"Can't wait to meet our new grandbaby," Dad said as he clapped me on the back.

"Me too," I whispered as I watched over the empty crib, with laughter, family, and one very grumpy cat behind me. The apartment was full of all good things, but it still felt empty.

I GOT TO the restaurant early in the morning to prep. I didn't actually have any more work to do, but I couldn't sleep. It was either the nerves or the triplets nearly lighting my microwave on fire when they decided to see how flammable my remote control was.

Still, I headed to the restaurant and checked on my dough before chopping extra toppings and triple-checking the soda fountain. By the time my staff showed up, their work was done for them.

As I sat down in the office, my phone chimed with a text.

Winnie Baker: Good luck today!

Disappointment settled in my chest. She wasn't coming. That was fine. It would be busy hopefully, and I'd hardly have a chance to even talk to her. And she'd still be able to meet my family before they left.

"Uh, boss?" Samantha called as she poked her head around the corner. Her double nose rings glittered in the dim light. "We've got a line. Like a major line. And some paparazzi are here too."

"What? Are you serious? Must be a slow day for gossip." I'd never been happy to hear paparazzi were waiting outside of a building for me, but I knew enough to know that sometimes tabloid attention wasn't always bad.

I stood up and took off my flour-dusted apron before walking out into the kitchen. I'd hired a staff of twelve, and they were all on the schedule today. They were good and smart and hard-working and way too young to give a shit about INK, which was for the best.

"Okay, team, I'm not very good at inspirational speeches," I said as I eyed the digital clock on the wall. "But I am great at pizza and so are the rest of you. Our only job today is to make people happy with great food. It's going to be a little chaotic, so just take it easy. Ask for help when you need it. Don't let customers bully you, because in this house, the customer isn't always right."

That got a few dry laughs.

"I might be from the Midwest, but I have a no-jerk policy." I pointed to the rules painted on the wall of the dining room that we could see from the kitchen.

The Pizza Commandments:

1. Don't like it? Let us fix it.

2. Pineapple? Ranch? Eat your pizza how you want it. No pizza shaming zone.

3. NO JERKS.

After everyone had a second to settle into their stations, I jogged over to the doors and let myself have one quick look at the place before it was too crowded and busy for me to even think.

Like all my other locations, we had the logo painted on the wall with red vinyl booths and checkered floors, but we'd also added some palm tree accents, including an incredible palm tree lamp I found on eBay.

I opened the door to an excited crowd and quickly ushered in my family, followed by Bee and Nolan, who gave me a good smack on the ass for encouragement.

"Thanks for waiting out here so patiently, folks! Now, let's get you some Slice, Slice, Baby!" I waved to the cameras, feeling silly and out of practice, but the moment was gone in a flash as the crowd snaked inside and formed a steady line.

I rushed to the back and called in an order for my family and friends while Topher led them back to the little section on the patio I reserved for them.

Once their pies were ready, I brought them back myself to find Dad absolutely charmed with Bee while he told her embarrassing stories about me and Nolan in the height of puberty.

"You gotta shut your old man up," Nolan said as I placed his favorite, pepperoni and banana peppers, down in front of him.

I smirked. "Dad, don't forget to tell her about the time Nolan got drunk at homecoming and peed in Mom's birdbath."

Dad slapped his hand to his chest, laughing so hard he was wheezing.

"He did what now?" Mom asked in shocked disgust. "In my birdbath?"

"Oh, I'm pretty sure that's only the tip of the iceberg," Bee said. "Especially based on what I saw at the *Santa, Baby* cast party."

"A night we don't speak of!" I told her, only half kidding.

The triplets were playing a serious game of keep-away on the jungle gym with one of the promotional foam pizza hats I had made for today. "Bubbie Jo!" one of them screamed at my mom. "Poppy! Look over here."

We all turned to see Toby shove Tristan down the slide head-first. Tucker, with his arms full of a sleeping Talia, ran to catch Tristan, but I beat him to it, throwing him over my shoulder and giving him a quick spin.

Tristan gave a delighted squeal as he began to pound his meaty little fists against my back. Theo and Toby shot down the slide, landing on my feet at the end and then tugging on my legs.

To their absolute thrill, I walked with them clinging to my calves and Tristan still in tow before depositing them next to Tamara, who was waiting to serve them slices of the best cheese pizza in LA.

"Again!" shouted Theo.

"Not until you three put away some of that pizza!" Mom told them.

"I better get back inside," I told them.

As I opened the door, a small hand pressed to my lower back.

"My sweet boy," Mom said as I turned back around.

Customers filled in all around us and Mom wound her arms around me, her head resting against my chest for a moment before looking up at me. "Your dad and I are so, so proud. You know that right, baby?"

I nodded silently, my throat burning and my rib cage expanding. I knew they were proud. They'd said it plenty of times before, but in this moment I felt like someone worthy of their pride.

"Now, go make some dough!" she said with a wink.

"Ma! Look at you with the pun."

She grinned. "Don't you forget where all that charm and humor comes from. It certainly isn't your dad."

"Boss!" Samantha called. "We need you!"

Mom waved me down and obliged so she could give me a kiss on the cheek and send me on my way.

I jogged into the kitchen, expecting to find chaos, but everyone was doing their job, jamming to the kitchen playlist I'd made for them.

Preparing myself for a disgruntled customer instead, I stepped out into the dining room. "What's going—"

"Hi, Kallum," Winnie said as she sat perched on a stool between diners. She bit down on her lower lip and stood with one arm resting on her belly, like she'd done so often lately.

"Winnie." My heart raced the way it always did when I saw her lately. The last month had passed in what felt like glimpses. We talked so much, and I'd been spending more and more time in LA, but at times we felt like best work friends and our job was the baby. Seeing her here now outside of baby business felt thrilling and a little bit against the rules.

She wore a soft pink sundress that perfectly matched her lips and the blush in her cheeks . . . and other parts of her body that were definitely not on display. Okay, maybe the grand opening wasn't the best time to rock a semi for my baby mama, who was definitely only a friend.

"Can I, uh, get you something?" I asked her.

"I already ordered one," she said. "But I like the addition to the menu."

I glanced over my shoulder to the huge menu above the counter that was basically a shrine to pizza. Right there under specialty pizzas was the Winnie. Mozzarella, maple syrup, sliced pears, and bacon. "I had to name it after you," I told her.

"I'll take a daily lunch order as my royalty payment," she said very seriously. "I want the grand tour of the pizza palace."

I held an arm out for her and she kept her hand on my biceps as I guided her through the very small dining room and then to the office that would be mostly for Samantha but also for me when I was here. Winnie had been in and out several times over the last month on our way to appointments or hospital tours, but showing it to her now, I felt a little inadequate. Winnie's ex was a slimy fucker, but he had power in this town in a way I could never offer her, and here I was showing off my little pizza place wedged between a tax prep business and a nail salon.

"It's perfect," Winnie said as she looked all around the office, her sights settling on the sonogram framed on the wall.

She took a deep breath like she had so many times on set to calm herself. "I need you to sit," she said suddenly. "Can you sit?"

I settled into the chair just as Samantha knocked on the doorframe.

I opened my mouth, about to ask her if everything was okay, when she turned to Winnie and said, "Small pepperoni for Baker."

"Your timing is perfect," Winnie said as she took the small Slice, Slice, Baby box.

"Pepperoni, huh?" I asked as she placed the box down on the small folding chair across from my desk.

She rubbed her belly nervously and then sat on the edge of the desk in front of me.

I looked up at her and was reminded that I liked this view way too much.

"A few months ago, I asked you for space. For—for room."

"I know," I said. "And I know the apartment and setting up shop here . . . it probably feels like a lot. I don't want you to feel crowd—"

She shook her head and bent down, her lips colliding with mine so hard she might leave a bruise. Fireworks exploded inside of me and instinct took over as I pulled her into my lap.

My brain caught up after a moment. "Wait, Winnie, wait. What's going on? I don't want . . ." I pressed my forehead to hers, trying to breathe. "I don't want to be friends with benefits. Or a hookup."

"No, no," she said frantically. I could feel her exhales against my lips. "No, I—I need you to shut up. Because I have to just get this out and all I want to do is kiss you." She took another deep breath as I tucked a lock of hair behind her ear. "I wanted space, but not anymore. You gave me what I asked for and somehow still found a way to be here for me and the baby. You gave me what I needed without any obligation or expectations. You loved me, Kallum. You loved me in the exact way I needed."

"I still do," I said, the words catching in my throat. "Winnie, I love you. I never stopped."

"I love you too. It's true now more than ever. Kallum, I want everything with you. I want kids. And a house. And vacations to Disney and weekends at gymnastic meets or debate competitions. And I'm so sorry for— Oh, oh, wait!"

She left my lap to run around and reach across the desk for the pizza box. Her lips curled in a hopeful smile as she opened the lid. There on one of my own pizzas was I'M SORRY spelled out in pepperonis.

She was the perfect woman for so many reasons, but damn, she knew how to speak my language.

"I'm sorry," she said again. "I'm sorry I pushed you away and didn't give you the . . . the grace you deserved. The grace you give others so freely."

"Grace," I said with a smile and tears beginning to brim. "Grace."

It was the name we'd finally settled on. Grace. The name Winnie had fought so hard for.

"Grace," she whispered with a knowing smile.

I stood and took the pizza from her, dropping it on my desk. "I have to show you something."

Taking her hand, knowing she was mine forever, I led her out back to where my family sat.

Winnie gasped, recognizing them all immediately, but before we could make introductions and share hugs, I turned Winnie around to see the back wall of the restaurant. I'd planned on showing her no matter what, but this moment couldn't be more perfect if I tried.

In beautiful hand-painted letters taller than me, the wall read: GRACE'S BACKYARD.

Because, sure I was in a tiny little apartment for now and Winnie was still in Addison's pool house, but this place would always be for our daughter. For Grace.

Winnie's hand drifted to her mouth as the realization set in and tears began to flood her wide blue-green eyes.

"For her." I turned Winnie around to this little oasis with its bistro tables and picnic benches and playground with twinkling lights strung across that always reminded me of Christmas Notch, where it all began. "For us," I said.

Winnie threw her arms around my neck as she turned to me and my arms slid up her back. I pulled her even closer to me, her belly round and full between us and bigger than it had been the last time I'd held her this closely.

She looked down and laughed. "You learn to work around it."

"I'm a quick study," I said with a soft growl before bending down to kiss her good and thoroughly. My hand traveled up her neck, guiding her even closer to me.

Her tongue danced along mine, and she gave my lip a soft tug with her teeth. I drew back just enough to whisper, "If we don't stop, my whole family is going to see me dry humping you right here right now."

She squeaked, her cheeks blushing.

She attempted to step back, but I only tugged her closer into my side as we turned to my family, who were all glassy-eyed—even Dad. But definitely not the triplets. They looked like they might puke.

"Mom, Dad," I said, truly prouder than I'd ever been in my life. "Meet Winnie."

"Mr. and Mrs. Lieberman," Winnie gushed. "I've been dying to meet you for real."

Mom squeezed past Nolan and gave Winnie a warm, tight hug, and I watched as Winnie melted into her arms, an indescribable joy on her face.

"I'm Mom or Bubbie Jo," my mom whispered. "And that bozo back there is Dad or Poppy."

"Or Josephine and Jacob are fine," I said.

Winnie wiped back a tear. "Our little Grace can't wait to meet her Bubbie Jo and Poppy."

Tamara weaseled her way in and stole Winnie from me, but I didn't mind. I loved watching my rambunctious family pull her in like she'd belonged there all along. Because she did. She always did.

I didn't know what would happen with Winnie and her parents, and I knew there'd always be a hole created by their absence and that the pain they caused her would always live in her like an echo, but I would do my best to fill in the gaps and ease the hurt. Winnie had a family now. She always would.

Tucker passed a wriggling Talia to Mom and came over to give me an awkward fist bump. "You got it all, man. The biz. The girl."

"Yeah," I said, for the first time not annoyed by his Dr. Bro energy.

"Tamara and I are so happy for you, and hey man, when you're ready for that vasectomy, it's on the house."

I threw an arm around his shoulder. "I'm pretty sure Winnie and I are only getting started."

Teddy Ray Fletcher

Three months later

Teddy set his baby shower present on the foyer table of Addison's Sherman Oaks mansion and dithered for a moment. He could hear laughter and chattering from the living room, where most of the baby shower festivities were taking place, and he knew he should join them . . . but what if *Steph* were in there?

What if she were in there, and once again, Teddy had to figure out how to say hello after several awkward months apart? Could his crusty old heart handle going through all that again?

Before he could decide one way or another, he heard a massive *thump* at the front door, and since he was the only one in the foyer, it fell to him to investigate.

He opened the door to see Sunny Palmer balancing four boxes of diapers in her arms, and he only barely caught the top box as it toppled from the stack.

"Do you think you brought enough diapers?" Teddy asked mildly as she shuffled inside and finally managed to deposit her payload onto the floor.

"Teddy, you ignorant slut," Sunny panted as she used the toe of her platformed Mary Jane shoe to kick a diaper box closer to the wall. "This is only the beginning."

Teddy didn't even have a chance to say *beginning of what* before a line of jumpsuited men came into view of the front door, each one wheeling a dolly piled high with boxes of diapers, in every size from newborn to pull-up. He held the door open, speechless, as they rolled in one by one and lined the hallway with boxes until it looked like a trench from World War Diaper.

After three trips, Sunny briskly thanked the men and they left, going back to whatever diaper freight train they'd come from.

"Are all of these diapers from you?" Teddy asked. "Where did you even get all these?"

"Don't worry about it," Sunny said, taking off her jacket and scarf and hanging them on a Wishes of Addison coat-tree. (Only $129.99 on QVC.com.)

Teddy stared at what had to be tens of thousands of dollars' worth of diapers. "Don't worry about it?"

"I don't ask how you're paying for dinner," answered Sunny.

"Come on, or they're going to eat all of Bee's pimento cheese dip without us."

And there was very little Teddy could say to that, because he did really like Bee's pimento cheese dip.

Once inside the living room, Teddy was both relieved and miserable to see that Steph wasn't there.

It wasn't that he expected Steph to be as delusionally obsessed with him as he was with her. It would just be nice to know if she even *liked* him, that was all.

The first two times they'd hooked up, he understood the ghosting afterward, because they could have been any old hookups born of convenience. But they'd spent a week together in Christmas Notch during the *Santa, Baby* reshoots, barely leaving the hotel room, subsisting only on sex and room service, and it had been like something from a dream. Lazy conversations, delightfully bad TV. Cuddles while a breeze blew sweet-smelling air into the room and they both ignored their phones.

Maybe Teddy was getting old, or maybe he'd always been a little old-fashioned, but surely leaving without a word after all that wasn't a cool thing to do?

Ah, unrequited love. The drug that hit the hardest, even in one's late forties.

Not that Winnie and Kallum would know anything about it. They sat squashed together on the sofa, a little baby burrito nestled in the crook of Kallum's arm while Winnie opened presents. Bee had told him that Winnie had moved into Kallum's apartment this fall, and that they were looking for a house in LA together. Mostly to accommodate Winnie's upcoming production schedule—she was slated for another Hope After Dark movie in the coming year and for a new, edgy sitcom about single mothers trying to date—but also for ease of filming Kallum's new reality show, *Kallum by the Slice*. From the fond way Bee and Sunny talked about the two of them, Teddy got the sense that no matter how unconventional Kallum and Winnie's start had been, their future was brighter than a fire in a pizza oven. Plus there was that engagement ring winking on Winnie's finger that Teddy was pretty sure was new . . .

"I didn't think the baby in question usually came to the baby shower," Teddy remarked as he sat down on a chair behind Addison, and she spun around and glared at him.

"Excuse you, this is a *sip-and-see*."

"What?"

"You sip," said Addison, gesturing at the mocktails and cocktails bar set up against the far window and clearly very irritated at having to explain something so basic. "And then you *see*. You *see* the baby. It's in the name."

"Plus we knew it would be easier to get everyone in one place in December," Bee said. "Not counting Kallum's family, who are on a Hanukkah cruise right now. So it was the best time for a shower—"

"Sip-and-see!" Addison interjected.

"—and it just so happens that we can all snuggle little Grace while we're here."

Winnie stood up, a ginger quality to her movements, which made him wonder if she'd had a C-section. She took Grace from Kallum and then threaded her way through piles of onesies and burp cloths to Teddy.

"Would you like to hold her?" Winnie asked. "We sort of see her as your movie goddaughter, you know. Because she wouldn't be here if it weren't for you and *Santa, Baby*."

Teddy's chin hurt because it was quivering so hard below his mustache, and he knew everyone could see how many times he had to swallow before he could speak. "I'd love to hold my movie goddaughter," he told Winnie gruffly and accepted the blue-swaddled baby burrito into his arms.

Grace for her part didn't seem to mind the handoff, since she was fast asleep. As Teddy settled her against his chest, she turned her head a little, as if searching for breastmilk even while unconscious, but then immediately turned back into an inert, snoozing lump again.

Teddy continued cuddling the baby while Winnie went back to opening presents and the group started chatting about going over to Kallum and Winnie's later to light Kallum's menorah. Teddy started humming low in his throat and gently patting the burrito, habits from when Angel and Astrid had been little baby burritos themselves. He missed it sometimes, the snuggly sweetness of those early days, when he'd felt permission to block out the entire world and focus only on the people who needed him the most. But of course, today's days were great too. Seeing his son in love, even if it was with—*sigh*—the extremely intense Luca. Seeing his daughter chase her eco-friendly dreams, however off the beaten track they were.

Kallum and Winnie were on the very edge of something beautiful and hard and ever-changing; and the most beautiful thing about it was that their love would deepen with every milestone, every inch ticked off on that special wall in the kitchen reserved for keeping track of growing humans. Yes, the burrito years were the ones that got *ooh*s and *aah*s and sip-and-sees, but the rest of the years were even more precious and rewarding, and the ones that made parents remember they were raising their little humans to be the most interesting and curious and kind people they could possibly be. People that they would be happy and grateful to share the world with.

Teddy was excited for them, even if he did also hope they had plenty of TV shows queued up to watch while rocking a baby, because the next few months were not going to be easy.

"So then I said *yes* to the cruise, but now I have all this stuff to figure out," Addison was telling the group. Bee and Sunny were examining Winnie's new breast pump shields from Gretchen and Pearl as Addison spoke, testing them against their own boobs.

"Like what stuff?" Gretchen asked, digging a celery stick into a glob of pimento cheese dip and then using it to point with. "How are they going to ask *you* to do an Addison Hayes cruise, and then make you figure out logistics?'

"Well, to start with, I have to bring my own security," Addison said with a sigh. "I haven't had dedicated security since my last arena tour four years ago, and I don't even know where to start."

"I think Isaac's been really happy with his team," Bee chimed in, "and he's downsizing now that he's moving to Vermont, so they'll be available."

Sunny set down a breast shield. Picked it back up. Didn't look like she knew what to do with her hands.

Teddy was abruptly reminded that despite Sunny's incredible, *ah*, performance skills, she'd never been fantastic at acting without a script.

"Isaac is moving to Vermont?" Sunny asked in a fake-casual voice that probably fooled Grace the baby and no one else. "When?"

Kallum shrugged, holding up a baby Royals onesie and giving a satisfied nod at the number on the back. "I don't know. Soon? He bought the duke mansion in Christmas Notch."

Now Teddy was interested too. "He bought what now?"

"You know, the mansion," Kallum said as he folded the onesie against his stomach with admirable expertise. "Up in the mountains? Where Bee and Nolan shot the duke movies? He said he wanted a place to hide that had less sunshine than Cali."

Nolan, whom Teddy hadn't even realized was here, wandered in from the kitchen with a plate of deviled eggs. It quickly became apparent that these were not the group's deviled eggs, but Nolan's personal plate of deviled eggs. "Isaac still owes his label an album," Nolan said through a mouthful of mustard-laden yolks. "But he's been creatively blocked since Brooklyn's death."

"Which is not really here or there," said Bee. "What does matter is that Isaac's security team will be ready for snatching up."

"Aw, man, he's even downsizing Krysta out of the picture?" Kallum asked. "She's amazing. She's like Brienne of Tarth, but maybe without the *heart of gold* part. Actually, I think her heart might be made of gunmetal and ice."

"*Hot*," Sunny and Bee said at the same time.

"Hmm," mused Addison, and years of messy adult film drama had trained Teddy to recognize that tone of voice. It was a tone of voice that said something incredibly chaotic was about to happen.

But then a crisp voice announced, "Sorry I'm late," and Teddy's heart flipped over. And then flipped over again. Because there was Steph D'Arezzo hovering awkwardly in the doorway, holding a gift card that wasn't even wrapped or tucked inside a greeting card or anything.

"Um, here," she said, shoving the gift card at Kallum, and just then, Grace started to make the tiny goat noises that preceded a Great Fuss. Wanting to give Kallum and Winnie enough time to finish opening presents, and possibly wanting to escape Steph, Teddy stood and carried Grace into the kitchen, where he deployed his proprietary sway-pat-hum combo. Within a few minutes, Grace was back asleep.

"You're good at that," Steph said from behind him.

Teddy turned, reminded himself that the pantsuited divinity in front of him had been slowly breaking his heart for the last two years. "My ex-wife used to call me the fuss-buster," he replied. "But really, it's all in the baby psychology. A uterus is a noisy and constantly moving place. You just have to make the baby feel like they're back inside their old home again."

Steph's hand came up to twirl at her pearls. Teddy would have said that she looked nervous, except he didn't know if Steph D'Arezzo had ever been nervous a day in her life. "I *was* my daughter's old home, and I was still never good at the baby stuff. Give me a soccer or volleyball schedule to manage any day." She cleared her throat, dropped her pearls. "What I really wanted to say was that I'd like to see you after this. After the sip-and-see is over. My hotel isn't far from here."

Where the courage came from, Teddy would never know. Maybe it came from being in his forties and ready for better games than *Do you even like me?* Maybe it came from Bee and Nolan and Winnie and Kallum over in the next room, all of them desperately in love.

Or maybe it came from the little lump in his arms, a gently snoring lump who reminded him that he was better at more things than making cheap movies.

But instead of saying *Yes, please*, like he would have a few months ago, Teddy lifted his chin and bravely said, "I want more than just a visit to your hotel, Steph."

Her long fingers tugged on the ends of her suit jacket. "More?" she asked faintly.

"More," affirmed Teddy. "I like you. If I'm being brutally honest, it's a lot more than liking you at this point. And if we're going to keep doing this, then I want more than sporadic moments when we're in the same town. I want moments on purpose. I want *you* on purpose."

Steph dropped her hands. She took a long breath.

"I haven't had a relationship since my divorce," she said. "And I'm going to level with you, I wasn't great at relationships *before* my divorce either. Hence the being divorced part."

"I don't care about any of that," Teddy said. "As long as you want to try."

Then he paused. "Would you like to, Steph? Try something on purpose with me?"

She ducked her head, her cheeks flushing. She looked younger and more vulnerable than Teddy could ever remember seeing her.

"Yes," she said after a moment. "Yes, I would. But it probably isn't going to work. Just so you know."

Teddy ignored the last part, focusing only on the part that made him feel like he might float right off the ground.

"Really?"

The small, sharp smile that he loved so much pulled at her mouth. "Never question a good deal when it's staring you in the face, Teddy."

He wasn't in the habit of it, fortunately enough for four of the people in the next room over.

And a few minutes later, after he'd returned Grace to her parents, made his goodbyes, and then given a final puzzled glance at the veritable fortress of diaper boxes in the foyer, Teddy took his good deal back to her hotel and showed her what *on purpose* looked like from someone who meant it. Turned out that *on purpose* looked a lot like pleasure and a lot like love.

A lot, funnily enough, like a happily ever after.

Acknowledgments

Holy bacon and pear pizza! Kallum and Winnie are really, really here, and we are pinching ourselves!

We'd first like to thank our far-too-patient agent, John Cusick, for following us to the land of pizza-tossing Santas, and for keeping all the plates spinning so we could disappear in the world of Christmas Notch once again.

We also owe our gratitude, affection, and piles of chocolate to our incredible editor, May Chen, who fearlessly plunged into Kallum's story with us and didn't blink twice when we threw bridesmaids, ancient dogs, and *Magic Mike* tributes into the mix.

We're also deeply grateful for the Avon/HarperCollins family: Jeanie Lee, Justine Gardner, Allie Roche, Brittani DiMare, DJ DeSmyter, Julie Paulauski, Kelly Rudolph, Jennifer Hart, Erika Tsang, and Liate Stehlik.

We'd also like to thank Farjana Yasmin and Jeanne Reina for another stunning cover, with Kallum, Winnie, and Christmas

Notch set off to perfection! And we'd like to thank Diahann Sturge for making the inside of the book as perfect and adorable as possible.

We're also grateful for all the members of the HarperCollins union, and honor their energy and vision in this past year as they strive to make publishing a more equitable and fair industry.

Thank you to all of our dear friends, especially everyone who's patted our hair while we've tried to hammer out the minutiae of pizza making, Claus cosmology, and lap dance choreography—Tessa Gratton, Natalie C. Parker, Kristin Trevino, Lauren Brewer, Nana Malone, Kenya Bell, and our Ashleys (both Lindemann and Meredith). We also want to thank the people who've kept us propped upright and *Weekend at Bernie's*-d us when we needed it most: Mary Kole, Len Cattan-Prugl, Serena McDonald, Melissa Gaston, and Candi Kane.

We'd also like to thank Clan Couch—Ian, Josh, Noah, and Teagan (along with Margo, Opie, Rufus, Max, and Bear)—and our families: Gail and Bob; Bob and Liz; Emma and Roger, along with Vivienne and Aurelia; Doug, Dana, Lizzie, Kathie, and Milt.

And finally, we'd like to thank you, the reader, most of all! Thank you so much for joining us on this chaotic sleigh ride of a book; thank you to everyone who asked for Pizza Daddy Kallum to get his own book; thank you for coming with us to a little town where everyone gets to have their own happy, horny holiday adventure.

We promise no actual pizza daddies were injured in the making of this book.

About the Authors

Julie Murphy is the #1 *New York Times* bestselling author of young adult, middle grade, and picture books, such as *Chubby Bunny*; *Camp Sylvania*; *Dear Sweet Pea*; *Pumpkin*; *Puddin'*; *Ramona Blue*; *Side Effects May Vary*; *Faith: Taking Flight*; *Faith: Greater Heights*; and *Dumplin'* (now a Netflix original film starring Jennifer Aniston). She is also the author of Disney's reimagining of Cinderella: *If the Shoe Fits*. Her books have been translated into more than fifteen languages.

When she's not writing, she can be found watching made-for-TV movies, hunting for the perfect slice of cheese pizza, reliving her glory days as a librarian, or planning her next great travel adventure. Julie lives in North Texas with her husband, who loves her, and her cats, who tolerate her.

Sierra Simone is the *USA Today* and *Wall Street Journal* bestselling author of contemporary and historical romance, including *Priest*, *American Queen*, and the *Misadventures of a Curvy Girl*.

Her work has been featured in BuzzFeed, *Cosmopolitan* magazine, *Entertainment Weekly*, and *Marie Claire*.

Her preromance jobs have included firing ceramics, teaching living history in a one-room schoolhouse in full 1904-approved schoolmarm attire, and working as a librarian for several years—not in that order. She lives in the Kansas City area with her husband, two children, and two giant dogs.

This is Julie and Sierra's second book together. You can find out more at julieandsierra.com.